PRAISE FOR DAM

"Meticulous local color matches sensitive characterizations, including of brave Mumbai police who try to overcome the deadly hazards of the corrupt system they have to work in. This searing portrait of marginalized people struggling for survival is unforgettable."

—*Publishers Weekly* (starred review)

"*The Blue Bar* is a meticulously crafted police procedural set in Mumbai, where the setting—both the Bollywood glitz and the city's seedy underworld—comes to life with such intensity you can almost smell the air."

—*The Big Thrill*

"With *The Blue Bar*, Damyanti Biswas has staked her claim on Mumbai as a setting for gripping crime fiction."

—BOLO Books

"*The Blue Bar* will assault your senses as the setting comes alive in this intricately woven mystery. It examines the gritty, corrupt politics of Mumbai as an inspector tries to solve cases of dismembered women when he doesn't know who to trust within his own ranks. A tale of loyalty, love, and revenge, this sophomore novel by Biswas is not to be missed."

—Jaime Lynn Hendricks, author of *Finding Tessa* and *It Could Be Anyone*

"Immersive, propulsive, and beautifully written. In this gaspingly authentic police procedural about a missing dancer and the inspector who cannot forget her, Biswas transports us to India—not only to investigate a grisly and sinister series of murders but to explore the dark and disturbing life of Mumbai's bar girls. With its heartbreaking love story and Biswas's revealing social commentary, *The Blue Bar* will change you, haunt you, and have you understanding the world in a different way."

—Hank Phillippi Ryan, *USA Today* bestselling author of
Her Perfect Life

"*The Blue Bar* is one of those books that tattoos itself onto your bones—the luscious language, the glorious sense of place, a mystery that draws you in deep, so deep that you forget there's a world around you. Best of all is Inspector Arnav Singh Rajput, the tender, lionhearted man at the story's center who will stop at nothing to see that justice is done. I'll be thinking about this one for a long time."

—Jess Lourey, Edgar-nominated author of *Unspeakable Things*

"An intense, visceral thriller that . . . will leave you breathless!"

—Lisa Gardner, #1 *New York Times* bestselling author

"In the mangrove swamps of Mumbai, dismembered bodies keep turning up. Damyanti Biswas lets us smell the spices and feel the sultry air in the city's criminal underbelly as we root for Detective Arnav and Tara to unmask the killer before he finds them first. Your pulse will race."

—Kristin Wright, author of *The Darkest Flower* and *The Darkest Web*

"Dive into Mumbai's seedy underworld in this absorbing and fast-paced crime thriller. Damyanti Biswas never fails to impress with *The Blue Bar*. Filled with characters who will enchant you and others who'll repulse you, action and mystery are weaved through corrupt police, Bollywood, and sultry dance bars. Don't miss this gripping thriller!"

—Rob Samborn, author of *The Prisoner of Paradise* and
Painter of the Damned

"A hard-hitting tale full of twists, drama, murder, and mystery that kept me riveted to the very last word and set in a world you think you know, but have no idea."

—Yasmin Angoe, Editor's Pick and bestselling author of
Her Name Is Knight

"It's almost unfair to describe Damyanti Biswas's *The Blue Bar* as a page-turner—which, believe me, it is. But that was my problem—at every turn of the page I wanted to go back and reread the lush descriptions of Indian culture and daily life, the marvelous character sketches, the intriguing settings at once familiar and foreign. This isn't just a great thriller—it's an immersive fictional experience by a writer at the top of her game."

—David Corbett, award-winning author of
The Long-Lost Love Letters of Doc Holliday

"This Mumbai-set story is simply gripping. It's about a detective who realizes his lover—who went missing over a decade ago wearing a blue sequined dress—might be the victim of a serial killer. I read it in one day."

—Kellye Garrett, author of *Like a Sister*

THE
BLUE
MONSOON

OTHER TITLES BY DAMYANTI BISWAS

BLUE MUMBAI THRILLERS

The Blue Bar

OTHER NOVELS

You Beneath Your Skin

THE
BLUE
MONSOON

A BLUE MUMBAI THRILLER

DAMYANTI BISWAS

THOMAS & MERCER

Text copyright © 2023 by Damyanti Biswas
All rights reserved.

Published by Thomas & Mercer, Seattle

www.apub.com

Amazon, the Amazon logo, and Thomas & Mercer are trademarks of Amazon.com, Inc., or its affiliates.

ISBN-13: 9781662503924 (paperback)
ISBN-13: 9781662503931 (digital)

Cover design by Faceout Studio, Amanda Hudson

Cover image: © Koukichi Takahashi / EyeEm, © Elena Popova, © Katsumi Murouchi / Getty Images; © A.D.S.Portrait, © railway fx / Shutterstock

Printed in the United States of America

For Ma. Thank you for encouraging me to always stand up for myself. (Also don't read this book, you don't want nightmares.)

The price of privilege is the moral duty to act when one sees another person treated unfairly.

—*Isabel Wilkerson*

CHARACTERS WHO APPEAR IN
THE BLUE MONSOON

Senior Inspector Arnav Singh Rajput: A senior inspector of Mumbai Police, posted at the Bandra Police Station.

Tara Singh Rajput (was Noyontara Mondal): Arnav's wife.

Pia Singh Rajput: Arnav's teenage daughter.

Sub-Inspector Sita Naik: Sub-inspector of Mumbai Police from Versova Police Station, on temporary assignment to the Bandra Police Station to assist Arnav on a string of cases. Friends refer to her as Sita, while at the office she's called Naik, her surname.

Priest: Priest at the Kaali temples.

Inspector Jivan Desai: An inspector at Bandra Police Station who reports to Arnav. At the office everyone refers to him as Desai, his surname.

Sujata Shinde, also called Vaeeni: Arnav's close friend and colleague's widow, works at Remy Virgin Hair Factory.

ACP Atul Bapat: Assistant police commissioner, Mumbai Police, and Arnav's boss.

Raghav Naik: Sita Naik's husband, former police officer and fundraiser at Ram Rajya Party.

Ram Chandra Dome: Also called Sri Sarvagya. Tantric practitioner.

Rasool Mohsin: Mumbai mafia don, also called *Bhai*.

Zoya: Tara's best friend and Rasool Mohsin's girlfriend.

Iqbal Asif: A goon who works for Rasool Mohsin.

Bina: Sujata Shinde's elder sister.

Ruchi: Bina's daughter.

Neeti Shinde: Pia's best friend and *Vaeeni's* daughter.

Ashok Shinde: Neeti's younger brother, aged ten.

Madhu: A *kinnar* working at Remy Virgin Hair Factory.

Paresh Khare: Tara's physiotherapist.

Amit Nimkar: Owner of Remy Virgin Hair Factory, also called Mr. Nimkar.

Vishal Nimkar: Remy Virgin Hair Factory owner's son.

Chitra Varli: Famous social media influencer.

Surat Tambe: Forensic officer.

Tarun Sathe: Controversial political leader.

Dr. Holkar: Tara's obstetrician.

Constable Mihir Kamble: Oldest constable at Bandra Station, reports to Arnav.

Govind: Tea seller near Bandra Station.

Nurse Nishita Kamble: Nurse working for Dr. Holkar.

Ali: Arnav's longtime trusted informer.

Tej: Arnav's informer.

Raju Dinkar: Sub-inspector reporting to Arnav at the Bandra Police Station, known as Dicky.

CHAPTER ONE

Let's kill them all.

His voice was a low growl, his large hands steepled together like monitor lizards standing against each other, dueling in the marshes behind his home.

I hadn't heard him say that before. His usual mood matched the placid marsh waters, but I could see he meant it this time. Someone had to make him see reason. My job.

We must wait, Bhai. *Do it right. I took a deep breath. Right time, right place.*

In that breath came the reek of perfume, the spice of frying food borne on sea-salt air, the incense burned for gods and demons alike, the lives and deaths of men and vermin, the inescapable, ever-present stench of Mumbai. I'd been here all my life, and yet the city came at me each day, taunting. I should have left. We all should have, but it's hard to leave the cloak of anonymity, even though there's a price to pay for it. A price we'd paid, and then some.

I've waited a long while, he said, his voice harsh, like everything else about him. Some might say too long.

Soft rain fell on the roof, dripped down and pattered over the large, shivering leaves of a banana plant. I held his hand, twice the size of mine, and caressed the sandpaper skin of his palm.

It will be worth the wait. We follow the plan, and it will be as you wish, Bhai. *A fate worse than death.*

He turned toward me, his chiseled face and mane of hair making him look like one of those cult leaders on TV gone mad.

Don't call me that. You never know who might be listening.

Bhai. *Brother. No matter what, he will always be my brother. He didn't speak, but sometimes his silence terrified me more than his words.*

CHAPTER TWO

ARNAV

Rain left behind straight lines of condensation on the window as Senior Inspector Arnav Singh Rajput's jeep flew through Mumbai's crowded roads at 7:00 p.m., siren wailing. Inside, the air was muggy and smelled of stale cologne and leftover tea. The driver, a new young constable on probation, sat ramrod straight, aware that Arnav held the same opinion on fools and catchy Bollywood songs. He suffered neither gladly.

Arnav's phone buzzed. Inspector Desai had already reached the crime scene. Arnav typed in a quick response: Has Forensics arrived?

Outside, yellow light spilled on the streets, catching men and women in dark umbrellas as they sloshed through puddles, like wraiths rushing home to get out of the onslaught. He was headed the other way.

The gloom had done nothing to dampen the spirit of celebration at his home. Tara had pulled out all the stops. Nothing deterred his firecracker of a wife—not the weather, not her wheelchair or her difficult pregnancy, nor Pia's bunch of loud friends. At fifteen, Pia would soon welcome a brand-new sibling.

He needed to stop in at home after a quick trip to the crime scene—it was Tara's *shaadh* party, a sort of baby shower to welcome the latest addition to their family. From a gory murder scene to the celebration of his wife's pregnancy wasn't ideal, but this was his life.

Well, if he was being honest, he thought—watching the splash of muddy water as vehicles sped past his—he sought to escape home, run to places where his efforts made a difference. In the past two years nothing had hastened Tara's recovery, put her back on her feet, no matter how hard he'd tried. And he was the one who'd failed to protect her in the first place, landing her in a coma.

Since then, she'd progressed from being bedridden without the use of her hands, to moving about in a wheelchair. Her physiotherapist called it *great improvement*, but would she ever walk again? Arnav shook his head to dislodge that thought.

Tall buildings flanked the road, and a few injured trees drooped in the rain, their branches freshly snapped from the storm that morning. Like much else in Mumbai, rains were unpredictable, and often defied forecasts. Weather news had declared the monsoons average this year.

Flooded streets and rail tracks clogged parts of this ceaseless city to a standstill each rainy season, and thirty-eight years spent in Mumbai told Arnav this July would be no different. It might even bring an unprecedented deluge.

Looming skyscrapers gave way to slums, and then the jeep raced on wide roads through empty fields leading up to his daughter Pia's school. The tall school building showed few lights, but beside it, a large white halogen lamp lit up the temple porch. Around the temple, another police jeep and a ragtag gathering of cars and bikes huddled under the assault of the monsoon.

Arnav sighed—a murder scene with a gathered crowd was bad enough. Rain made it worse. In a subdued tone, the driver announced they had arrived.

By the time the driver rushed out with an umbrella to the back door, Arnav had already zipped on his rain gear and stepped out. He put on his game face, an expression that telegraphed to everyone he was in charge. Breathing in the dank air, he waved the constable off, asked him to use the umbrella for himself and check if any of the other constables needed a hand.

He headed off into the downpour, trying to take in the surroundings before he reached the body. Swaying trees encircled the temple, and in the diffused light Arnav spotted piles of brick lying amid shrubbery. The temple committee had planned some sort of construction on the grounds.

With no boundary wall or gate, anyone could walk in. He noticed uniformed men putting up a perimeter, and curious onlookers braving the storm. He hailed Bandra station's most experienced constable, the portly Constable Mihir Kamble, and ordered him to use a flashlight to scan the grounds in case the killer had left evidence behind—traces of how the victim or the body were brought in here. The ever-smiling Kamble nodded, ambling off with an umbrella.

An officer turned at Arnav's approach, and at his word, they made way for Arnav. In an area being marked out by crime scene tape, a young male body lay spread eagle on the temple steps, amid a large swath of blood flowing down the white marble. The long porch had so far protected the crime scene from rain, but that could change with a different wind direction. As per procedure, constables had left a narrow path for approach so as to not lose any evidence to dozens of crisscrossing footprints. The face was unrecognizable.

Someone had taken a blade to it like a chef did to meat before sliding it on the grill. Only these were no shallow cuts. The nose was sliced clean away, and the ears. Bits of bloodied flesh lay around the face. He sighed. Humans could be the most kind creatures, and also the most cruel.

Forensics would have a tough time with this—Arnav instructed the constables to procure a tarpaulin to protect the body from all sides and bent to take a closer look. Desai should have done this already. Where was he?

A sharp object had gouged the victim's eyes out of their sockets. The vicious slashes extended all the way down to the throat, leaking blood. Scarlet hibiscus flowers, their stamens wilted, lay scattered on and around the body. Bloodied boot prints led away from it.

The rest of the victim's body remained intact, other than the genitals. The murderer had sliced them clean off, leaving behind a red, bloodied area between the legs. Unlike the ears and the nose which lay on the floor, the killer seemed to have removed the genitals from the scene.

Arnav felt a stab of empathetic pain for the nude, emasculated man. Arnav's father, a constable, often used to say, *A man is not a man without his balls. He is nothing.* That lament and anger was directed at himself, at his own impotence in the face of injustice, but the teenaged Arnav had heard those words too many times not to dwell on them. What had this man done to deserve his attacker's rage—who had taken his manhood, his life, and defaced him? Or maybe it wasn't rage at all, but a fanatic, cultish zeal.

Arnav switched on a tiny flashlight to examine the body better. On the man's chest, someone had used *sindoor*, vermilion powder that Hindu brides put in the parting of their hair to signify their marital status. Instead of merely smearing it on the victim's chest, the culprit had drawn two concentric circles, with a triangle within, pointed downward, its lowest point daubed with blood.

Arnav turned to the head constable on the scene. "Who reported the body?"

"Someone dialed 100, sir. A man's voice."

"Is he here?"

"No, sir. An anonymous caller."

"Get a recording of that call. It could be the killer."

CHAPTER THREE

TARA

It rained in a steady mist outside Tara's apartment building, neither quickening nor letting up.

Despite the chill from the third-floor windows, Tara sweated under her first-ever wig. With steroids for her spinal injury, Tara's hair had started falling out in clumps, and hadn't returned. Both Arnav and Pia had suggested getting it trimmed much shorter, but at the salon they said a shorter cut might reveal bare scalp in patches. Tara had considered shaving it all off, but that would also need maintenance—and she'd never be able to look into a mirror again.

She'd settled for a blunt cut and a cap at home. It would grow back soon, her stylist had assured her, as soon as she could stop her medication. Tara had spent all her life dressing up—her appearance had once allowed her to make money—and now here she was. You didn't realize you could lose your looks until you began to lose them.

That was not the best line of thought on *shaadh*, the day meant to welcome your child into the world. To distract herself, Tara watched Mrs. Shinde as she fussed with Tara's wig.

"You're so good at this," Tara said.

"This is what I do." *Vaeeni* met Tara's eyes in the mirror.

This was true. Mrs. Shinde's day job involved creating and setting toupees at the weirdly named Remy Virgin Hair Factory, and the wig was her suggestion. She was Arnav's best friend's widow, and he addressed her as *Vaeeni*, the appropriate term for an older sister-in-law, so that was what Tara called her as well.

"Still," Tara said, "it's nice of you to take the time out for me."

"It's nothing. I keep telling you to come visit the factory. You'll see so many other women, far better skilled than I am. It will do you good to get out a little."

Tara smiled. She did mean to go, but lately, everything had felt so heavy. Her body, her heart. Her inert legs that weighed on both.

She brushed away the thought. *Vaeeni* had done so much for them. Tara could make a small visit to please her friend, and maybe even herself. She hadn't been out of the apartment in weeks.

"I will, soon. Let's discuss a date once the ceremony is done."

"Yes." *Vaeeni* stroked Tara's wig in place. "Think only of the *shaadh* now."

Shaadh was held in the ninth month of pregnancy, but given her other medical conditions, Tara would be admitted in the hospital by then. *Vaeeni* had suggested holding the baby shower in the seventh month instead, and combining the *shaadh* rituals of Tara's native West Bengal and a few other local beliefs from her husband's Rajput ancestry, including a dance and a party for Pia.

Arnav had no living blood relatives, and Tara had long cut off ties with hers, so she liked to think of *Vaeeni* filling in for both. With flowers in her long, braided hair and her faded saree, the traditional Mrs. Shinde resembled the middle-aged sister-in-law in a multigenerational Indian TV soap: the mellow widow who doesn't care about her own appearance, ceaselessly cleans, cooks, and takes the blame for all the anarchy that visits a joint family.

"You're so pretty today," *Vaeeni* assured her, turning her to the mirror. For once, Tara didn't flinch at her own image. She did look good. Arnav would tell her the same when he dropped in from work— he never scrimped on compliments. She was supposed to be mad at him, for not staying home on a rare day of family celebration, but she couldn't stay upset for long. In the last two years, he'd stood by her when she most needed him. She had to let him get on with his job—catching killers.

"Yes, no prettier mother in all Mumbai"—Tara made a face—"or even our entire state of Maharashtra."

"You have a lovely smile, Tara. Smile more often."

Tara did. She had much reason to smile—her husband, her daughter's dance performance, and the baby to complete their family soon. She sprayed on a bit of the vanilla perfume her daughter had gifted her, and caught a last glimpse of herself in the mirror. The wig did make a difference. She appeared like the Tara of yesteryear, whose glances drove men wild.

Her best friend would have teased her. *Men understand the one thing, all right? We women need to make the best of our looks while they last.*

After her marriage to Arnav, Tara wasn't inclined to agree, but she did miss her tactless, warmhearted friend who'd given up her normal life to save Pia, and fled India with her mafia don two years ago. It made things difficult when your friend's man was on the run from Mumbai Police, and your husband was one of its senior inspectors.

Zoya, Tara whispered, praying her friend would remember her party today and call her.

CHAPTER FOUR

ARNAV

Over his years in Mumbai Police, Arnav had developed certain hab-its—a new one was carrying a pair of disposable gloves and a fresh face mask while rushing to a crime scene. He stocked packs in his office drawer, and in the police jeeps that ferried him.

Ignoring the distant clamor of thunder and the hubbub of his team's voices, Arnav took the gloves out of his raincoat pocket and, slipping them on, examined the dead body. Touching the shoulders, and around the stomach, he found the body still warm, not stiff. Rigor mortis had not set in. The man had died less than three hours ago.

Arnav waved down Constable Kamble. "How far is the forensic van? Is Surat Tambe on the way?"

Bandra station's resident busybody and genial cheerleader, Kamble tried to look his happy self, but failed.

"It should have arrived by now, sir, but Tambe says it is stuck in a traffic jam about fifteen minutes from here. The rains have clogged the roads."

So the flash floods had begun. Fifteen minutes could stretch longer. The elderly constable was right to be worried.

If the van was delayed much longer, the storm might wash away some of the evidence, making Tambe the forensic officer deeply unhappy.

"What's the progress on the tarpaulin?" Arnav said.

"A guard at the school next door is helping us get it, sir. Should be here any minute. They use it to cover their cricket grounds."

Even with the tarp, they needed to record the evidence—the tarp could contaminate the scene with mud, and they mightn't be able to hang it quick or close enough to prevent rain damage.

"Has someone taken pictures of the body, and the scene?"

"Desai sir asked me to, sir," Constable Kamble said.

"Pass me your phone."

Arnav grabbed the phone and clicked a few close-ups of the symbol drawn on the body. He forwarded most of the images to himself, and added them to a password-protected folder. Wouldn't do for Pia or Tara to see them. The drawing on the body meant nothing to him. He would have to ask around, do some research.

Arnav scanned the premises and located Desai standing near the temple's sanctum with his back to the crowd. A hulking man, built like a beat-up wrestler gone to seed, he was questioning a clearly terrified priest, whose sacred white thread swung over across his ample, bare belly, and the saffron-colored wrapped *dhoti* bottoms.

"I don't know, *saab*," the priest said. "I got here ten minutes back."

Since Hindu temples didn't allow shoes, Arnav took off his boots. Giving a wide berth to the dead body, he stepped in. Eight colorful, ornate pillars held up the temple's *mandapa*, a porch roughly the size of a basketball field. It stood open on all four sides, leading to the locked sanctum, the home of the deity. The sanctum doors hung low enough that no grown man could enter them without bowing at the waist.

The priest spotted Arnav and his eyes widened. Tara had prayed at this temple a few times while picking Pia up from school, and Arnav had accompanied her. As recognition dawned on the priest, he paused midsentence.

Desai turned. Noticing Arnav, he stepped back and cut a salute. In the months Arnav had worked with Inspector Desai, he'd understood that his subordinate meant the salute as an ironic gesture: the sardonic expression on Desai's face worked at odds with his respectful stance. Desai kept it subtle enough that Arnav couldn't officially warn the paunchy, unfit inspector without appearing paranoid.

Before Desai could speak, the priest cut in: "*Saab*, you are here! Look what has happened now. This temple has been here for twenty years, and I have served the goddess Ma Kaali for eight. I never imagined someone would desecrate the temple like this. Help us, please, *saab*."

Arnav hadn't asked the priest's name before. You addressed a man in the holy profession by his honorific. Arnav had never offered his own name, either, though Tara must have shared it. In order to offer worship to the Ma Kaali, you needed the devotee's name and *gotra*, his lineage. Arnav didn't like its class implications and, in any case, hadn't prayed in forever. Tara hadn't been an ardent devotee when he'd met her the first time nearly eighteen years ago, but after her surgery, she'd taken up praying. *Not for me, but for you and Pia, and now for this child. I must.*

Tara. Love could conjure your object of affection with startling clarity at inconvenient times. Arnav pushed her out of his mind, where she hovered all the time, and pivoted back to the task at hand.

"Why don't you answer Inspector Desai's questions? That's the only way to help find the culprit."

"I've been trying, *saab*."

Desai got a call and stepped back, letting Arnav take the lead. He lumbered out, holding up his phone to his ear.

"I locked up the temple after the evening *aarti*, and went home. I was alone. No one dropped by, due to the rain. I left the *prasad* outside, with one light switched on."

Aarti—the evening singsong prayers, with lamps, incense, and offerings, and *prasad*—the leftovers from the sweets offered to God, were the only part of temple rituals Arnav liked.

"What time was the *aarti*? Do you think someone came for the *prasad*?"

Arnav shifted his weight as he stood—the cold from the marble floor crept in through his socks as the rainstorm continued unabated outside the temple.

"The prayer is usually at seven, but I wrapped it up early today. I left at six p.m. I don't think anyone touched the plate of *prasad*—it is as full as when I left it. But I can't be sure."

"And you saw or heard nothing unusual? Are there any CCTVs around here?"

"No, *saab*, and there are no cameras. This is a temple. As I said, I left one small light on. It is an emergency light with backup. The temple can never go dark. That's considered a bad omen."

Arnav beckoned to a constable behind him. "Speak to all the shops and booths in this area all the way to the main roads—we need footage from any CCTV cameras."

Arnav scanned his watch: 7:30 p.m. Death had occurred sometime after 4:30 p.m.

"Check anything from three p.m. onward."

Best to add a margin to the three-hour time window since approximate time of death. The suspect might have been hanging around the area during the hours before the crime was committed, waiting to ambush the victim.

With the monsoon and the lack of bright lighting, the killer could've either lured the victim here and assaulted him, or brought the body here to make a display of it. Arnav would know more once the forensics came in—he hadn't seen any bloodied dragging stains. He addressed the priest again, who looked more upset by the minute.

"Does the goddess wear precious jewelry?"

It wasn't unusual for prosperous devotees to offer ornaments to the divinity once their prayers were answered.

The rotund priest smiled for the first time. "Gold. She's a gracious Ma Kaali who grants boons."

"Have you checked them?"

"Not yet, *saab*. I keep them locked in a heavy iron safe inside the sanctum."

"Do that now. Report to us if any of the items are missing."

After the priest left, accompanied by a constable, Arnav retired toward a temple pillar, away from the straggling crowd and policemen.

He dialed one number after another, activating his shadowy team of informers. Experience over his past years had taught him that his *khabri*—small-time criminals at the fringes of Mumbai's crime, prostitutes, and pawnshop owners—could be his eyes and ears in places his official team couldn't reach. A case like this wouldn't remain quiet for long. Half an hour later, he finished the last of brisk calls promising his *khabri* significant rewards for information. Mumbai Police kept a separate budget for informers, and sometimes Arnav topped up the rewards out of his own pocket.

Constable Kamble, his eyes bright with eagerness, approached him. "Sir, a shop nearby had CCTV, and as per your instructions, we checked it out."

"That was quick. Anything interesting?"

"I asked them to put it on my phone, sir." Kamble pressed an old smartphone into his hand.

Arnav clicked on the video and brought the screen closer. Iqbal Asif. Right-hand man to Rasool Mohsin, the mafia don who'd escaped India after one of Arnav's previous cases blew up. Asif spoke to a tall, broad man, whose back was to the camera. Video forensics would offer up a more accurate estimate, but at a glance, the man was the same height and build as the mutilated victim on the temple floor.

Arnav sent himself the CCTV footage, and smiled at the beaming constable.

"Submit this as evidence, and continue looking for more footage. Well done on identifying this suspect."

He dialed his star informer once again, on one of his several unlisted numbers.

"What do we know about Iqbal Asif's activities in the past two days?"

"He's been busy, *saab*." Ali's harsh voice floated in from the other end of the line. "*Bhai* is back in town, though he's staying underground. I haven't met him yet."

Bhai. In Mumbai, the versatile word *bhai* was a respectful term for a brother, but while it could be used to address anyone as a form of regard, including a Bollywood superstar or two, it also meant a mafia don. Ali had worked under the don Rasool before he disappeared, and now Rasool *Bhai* was back. He was underground, which meant he'd holed up in a hideout and wasn't moving around.

Having given Ali a terse brief to unearth Iqbal Asif's whereabouts, Arnav cut the call.

His phone rang the next moment. Tara. He'd promised her he would attend Pia's dance performance at their place. He'd missed one too many in the past months.

In any case, he couldn't proceed further before Forensics came in and his team finished interviewing some of the gathered people. This place was a ten-minute drive from his own apartment.

"Yes," he spoke into the phone, his back to the storm. "I'll be there."

Arnav called for his jeep, told Inspector Desai he would be back soon, and strode out into the rain.

Dropping in at home would let him celebrate with his wife and daughter. It would also allow him a chance to maybe establish contact with his wife's friend: Zoya. Rasool Mohsin's girlfriend might call to congratulate Tara on her pregnancy.

CHAPTER FIVE

TARA

Tara smiled at Pia, a nod of cheer at her daughter, who was about to start her dance performance. Pia's friends and their families had gifted Tara artfully wrapped packages, but unlike other parties held in large rented halls or restaurants, where they danced to club music, here was Pia, performing in the space cleared out between the dining table and the living room, surrounded by her school friends and neighbors.

Tara sent up a word of thanks that they could afford to buy this place in a good Mumbai locality, thanks to the sale of Arnav's old family bungalow. With the staggering real estate prices in Mumbai, most of Arnav's colleagues either resorted to hustling for bribes in order to afford a similar lifestyle or rented much smaller apartments. It all came down to money. Tara stopped herself: she couldn't afford to get distracted from cheering for Pia.

This dance was a huge deal for the teen. Her new schoolmates had bullied her without mercy when word leaked that Tara used to be a bar dancer. Pia had hated Tara for it for a spell—*How could you let me find out from strangers?*—but Arnav's explanations had calmed her.

Tara ignored the sofas and chairs weighed down by moms and dads, the carpet pawed by fidgety teens, the air heavy with a mix of perfumes. She focused on the rhythm of the recorded prayer recital and her Pia, who matched steps with Neeti, *Vaeeni's* daughter.

Dressed in loose trousers and tops instead of the traditional *kathak* attire, the two teens smiled as they danced, their anklets chiming in the routine Tara had taught them. Neeti was taller, with long hair and the shape of a woman. She looked older than the still-gangly, short-haired Pia. Thankfully, Pia seemed as yet unaware of this.

She'd been a handful the past two years, unable to keep up with the new school curriculum, traumatized by her kidnapping two years ago and the way the goons had chopped off her hair. Tara had kept putting off "the talk" with her daughter. Now it was too late. Tara had never imagined that a night celebrating the first time she'd been able to lift a glass of water would end in bed with her husband, and result in a baby sibling for her teen.

Pia had thrown a tantrum a day ever since she'd realized her mother was pregnant.

Tara glanced at the main door, expecting her husband's tall form. He looked handsome no matter what he wore, but the plain khaki uniform did wonders for his physique and complexion. She blushed at the direction her thoughts had taken—pregnancy hormones did weird things.

"Your daughter dances well for a girl so young." A smile crossed one of the mothers' over-made-up face. "They both do."

"They worked hard."

"But how do you . . . uh . . . you know . . . demonstrate?" The woman stared at Tara's saree-covered, inert legs, her nerveless feet, pedicured at *Vaeeni's* insistence, resting on the wheelchair footplates.

"I do my best." Tara smiled. She didn't let sarcasm leach into her tone.

Music and dance had played a curious part in Tara's life: a joy, before her father sold her to an agent who brought her to Mumbai at thirteen. It turned into a punishment for the next four years as a bar dancer. When she left behind the city of dreams, dance had allowed her to support herself and her daughter. The staccato beat of the *tabla* and the fluid keys of *harmonium* tugged at her inert feet. It warmed Tara to see her daughter thrive—all thanks to Arnav.

Her husband was surprisingly comfortable in his role as father for someone who'd discovered he had a teenaged daughter only after she was kidnapped. It was his senior police inspector's salary that kept them going. Tara could never have afforded it with her bar-dancing career.

Her phone buzzed, and Zoya's name flashed on the screen. The very person who reminded her of those times.

Tara left the phone on her lap, nodded to Pia, and wheeled herself to the next room. Zoya managed to call only at certain hours. Pia would understand.

"How is my darling?" Zoya's voice floated in.

"She's performing a dance for the guests. With Neeti."

"What? Was she okay with so many people?"

Tara explained. Yes, Pia had been nervous, but for once she was glad that the attention of the audience was directed toward her, not her mother's bulging midsection. *Vaeeni* had said that would help.

"Don't you give this *vaeeni* of yours too much importance?"

"She's Arnav's best friend's widow."

"And?"

"He died saving Arnav's life."

"From what you used to tell me," Zoya drawled, "he wasn't a good man."

This was true. Senior Inspector Hemant Shinde had been a lecher and a corrupt police officer. He'd tried to make up for decades of betrayal with one last, unbeatable effort by throwing himself in the path of a bullet meant for Arnav.

"Well, at least his daughter keeps my Pia company," Zoya continued, when Tara kept quiet. Tara couldn't say much for fear of *Vaeeni* overhearing her dead husband's name.

"Yes, between Neeti and Sita, Pia is never lonely. Sita takes them both out for a drive sometimes."

"Sita Naik?"

Another loaded silence followed. Tara glanced around to check whether she was alone. Neither Sita nor *Vaeeni* would be pleased to hear her speaking with Zoya.

Sita Naik's official brief was to arrest Rasool. With her promotion, Mumbai Police had transferred her to the Versova Police Station where *Vaeeni*'s husband had once led as the senior inspector, spending more time on the don's trail at dance bars and crime dens than at home. The widowed Mrs. Shinde blamed Zoya's boyfriend for the ruin of her marriage.

"Enough about us," Tara said. "How are things with you?"

"Same old," Zoya said, allowing Tara the awkward change of subject. "He doesn't get as drunk these days, though. His liver is shot."

"You're okay?"

"We're back in Mumbai." Zoya's voice dropped.

"When? Why didn't you tell me?"

"I'm not supposed to. He could have my throat slashed." She barked out a mirthless cackle. "Just joking."

Why did things have to be so fraught? Tara swallowed and reached for the one topic bound to change the conversation.

"When do we see you?" Tara said. "These are the times I wish I still had my legs."

"Stop it. You have your legs, you idiot. Give them time."

Zoya. Tara giggled. Reliably rude and insufferable, even when she was trying to cheer you up.

"Where's your policeman?" Zoya said.

"He'll be here soon."

"You're holding on to him, right?"

Tara blurted out some of her fears about being a pregnant wife in a wheelchair—what could be less attractive?

"There are many ways to please a man. Did I teach you nothing all those years?"

Tara's face heated, and she cleared her throat. Hearing a noise behind her, she turned. Her husband stood at the door.

"I've got to go."

Tara clicked off the call, wondering how long Arnav had been standing there.

CHAPTER SIX

ARNAV

He'd done well. Not given Tara an inkling, or told her he'd heard. But he'd got his confirmation. Zoya was back.

Rasool had once helped Pia and Tara at Zoya's behest. If he was making a mistake no don in Mumbai should, by getting mixed up in communal matters, Zoya's words might be the easiest way to make him stop.

Religion could easily become an explosive cocktail, and if someone had hired Rasool's Muslim men to mutilate, murder, and castrate men and leave them at Hindu temples, riots would follow. He'd have to take it slow with Tara, though—he couldn't mess up her *shaadh* by mentioning Rasool's issues.

Having changed out of his uniform, he stepped into his study to retrieve the gift he'd brought Tara. It sat in his drawer, and as he took it out to place in his pocket, his gaze dropped to the tiny box next to it. He opened it to reveal a perfect ring of dark hair.

Hours before he'd met his daughter for the first time, he'd slipped this black, shining lock from her lopped-off french braid. Arnav rubbed his neck, trying to seal off the flashes of memory. How he'd almost lost Tara, Pia. How Pia's braid, the length of a severed forearm, had laid in a shoebox, a threat from the men who'd abducted her. Arnav had tucked this bit of hair into his wallet. A promise to bring her back safe.

He took the silken strands out and held them pinched between finger and thumb in what had now become a ritual for his daughter's well-being. Once he'd made a wish for his Pia to remain as full of life and happiness as she was this evening, he slipped it into his wallet. Whenever he was on a difficult case, he kept it with him. A talisman. Having tucked it safely away, he turned his attention to locating Pia amid the music and murmurs floating in from the living room.

Through the door left ajar, Arnav watched his wife and daughter, the twin loves of his life. He smiled at their heads bent together amid the hubbub of guests, and wished for more such joy-filled evenings. His family certainly deserved them.

The rain gods didn't care, charging the air with an impending sense of doom. Behind Tara, fat drops pelted the windowpanes lighted by the streetlamp below. They left behind jeweled tracks of water that shone like Tara's necklace. His beautiful wife laughed and sent their daughter off to her classmates with a whispered word.

Tara had spared no effort this evening, from her saree to her coiffure and makeup, but most of all her smile that dazzled the same as when it had captured him many years ago. He noticed the effort it cost her, the slight tremor in her lightly clenched hands on the wheelchair, and made to rise, when his phone rang. Assistant Commissioner Bapat's name flashed on the screen.

Arnav's boss had declined the invite to today's party, so his call could mean only one thing. Arnav ignored it, slid the phone into his pocket, and walked out to check on his wife.

He dropped a kiss in her hair, making Tara look up and the brightly clad mothers of Pia's friends titter—Indian couples, especially firmly middle-class ones like them, kept their distance in public. Arnav didn't give a damn. He'd almost lost Tara more than once, and he'd be damned if he couldn't show his feelings when he felt like it.

Tara blushed, but he didn't miss the strain under her open smile. "Would you like to take a short break?" he said.

"No." Her smile wavered. "I'm fine."

Something was bothering her. "Will you give me some advice then, if you have a minute?"

To his relief, she nodded. He helped her make excuses to the neighbors and wheeled her into their bedroom, shutting the door behind them.

"What's wrong?" Tara said. Typical. Despite her own discomfort she would tend first to his.

He gave her the excuse he'd thought up for stealing her away from the party. "I'm not sure which tie to pick." He waved toward their wardrobe.

"You don't need one." She stroked the fabric of his shirtsleeve. "It's fine without."

She squirmed in the wheelchair, and when he caught her gaze, she sent him a shamefaced smile.

"I know." She shifted aside the open end of her cream saree draped over her chest, and pointed to where its folds were tucked into her petticoat. "I should loosen this. I wanted to dress up for today."

"You're stunning." He planted a soft kiss on her lips, careful not to smudge her lipstick, and took the folds of the saree from her hands. "Here, let me fix this."

He kept his head bent so Tara wouldn't see the fear in his eyes. Tara used to be a dancer—looks were important to her, but her doctor insisted her clothes should never cinch tight below the level of her spinal injury. It could send her blood pressure shooting up, endangering her life and her pregnancy.

His phone rang in his pocket. If it was his boss again, Arnav would have to pick it up sooner or later. He kneeled beside her instead, focused on getting her saree folds right.

"You're being good today, ignoring calls." Tara laid her hand on his shoulder as he tucked the folds back into her loosened petticoat.

"That can wait," Arnav said, "for a few minutes, anyway."

"It could be important." Humor laced the frustration in Tara's tone, reducing its sting. "Your phone is my co-wife. Never leaves us alone."

Still on his knees, he draped the free end of the saree back over her chest, fixing it at the shoulder, and slipping his hand in his pocket, he drew out the little box. Her gift. Her eyes lit up when he passed it to her.

"Open it," he said.

She took out the ring and smiled at its tiny footprint design. He slipped it on and fixed it.

"It is resizable." She laughed. "You thought of my swollen fingers."

He hadn't been around during her first pregnancy. It gutted him that he wasn't with her all the time during her second. His phone buzzed again. Bapat's name flashed, insistent. Tara urged him to pick it up, but Arnav kissed her and returned her to the party before finally clicking the green icon on his phone.

"I've never seen a case like this in my twenty-five years on the force." Bapat's gruff voice on the phone sounded sterner than usual. "I need results. Temples are sensitive crime scenes."

"I'm working on it, sir."

Solving this case might sort problems at work where he'd made more enemies than allies—one of his previous investigations having led to the firing of a police commissioner two years ago. No one liked a snitch, certainly not Arnav's boss.

Arnav's job paid for all that he cared about: Tara's treatment, Pia's school. To keep it, he must stay ahead—not an easy task in the city he lived in.

Mumbai's extremes—being India's financial capital yet home to its largest slums, having the busiest airport and seaport yet also some of the nation's most infamous road traffic, the nonstop, busy hum of Bollywood contrasted with the lazy elegance of colonial buildings—had earned it its moniker: the Maximum City. The denizens of this hive of orchestrated chaos, Mumbaikars worked longer and got paid less than most other city dwellers. Arnav was no exception.

His phone beeped with a text as soon as Bapat cut the call. It was the head constable, with the recording of the 100 call for emergencies. Arnav slipped on his headphones to listen to a calm male voice, no panic, reporting a dead body.

I just saw it. Hurry. There's a lot of blood. Yes, it is a man. Well, it was.

The voice was hollow, and if you listened carefully, sounded flat. Robotic. Someone had used a voice distorter. Why do that if you were actually a passerby reporting a crime?

Arnav called the head constable. "Did they trace it?"

This had the feel of organized crime. A murder called in from an untraceable number: more a statement than information.

"Not a phone call, sir. It was made on the internet. The forensics department is working on it. They'll try to locate the device it came from."

Arnav cut the call and spotted Pia among her group of teenage friends. In the last year, she'd made a remarkable recovery from the trauma of her kidnapping, and coped with changing schools and her mother's stints at the hospital. She deserved to have him around today.

He made his way toward her among the crush of guests, his nose assailed by perfumes and scented hair oil. Her face fell when she saw his expression, brightness fading from her eyes. She parted from her friends and stepped up to him. "You're going to leave." It was a statement, not an accusation, and it broke his heart.

"I should be here," Arnav said. "I've got to go, though. I'll make it up to you."

"You missed my dance."

"I'm sorry."

"Stay a few more minutes? There's going to be a *kinnar* dance. Ma said I can do a few steps with them, and they'll bless me, too."

"Let me see what I can do." He patted his daughter's shoulder.

Kinnar? Whose idea was it to invite them? The *kinnar* community consisted largely of those born male, who for one reason or another, identified as female. He'd heard Tara speak of their plight recently but hadn't realized she would invite them home. They blessed weddings and births, and those rituals usually devolved into a ruckus of negotiations for money.

Arnav scanned the living room for Tara, but found *Vaeeni* by his side instead.

"I know what you'll say, Arnav. Don't worry. I know these people. They have taken their payment in advance and won't cause trouble."

"How can you be so sure?" Arnav said.

"Sita is here," *Vaeeni* said, her expression shining with triumph.

Vaeeni thought of everything. With the *kinnar*, women, not men, were the right people to handle the situation. Besides, no one messed with Sub-Inspector Sita Naik.

"Ah, that's different, then. Where is Naik now?"

A thought occurred to Arnav. It should have struck him earlier.

"There." *Vaeeni* gestured toward the party. "She's with Tara."

Arnav spotted his short, unflappable ex-assistant chatting away with his wife, nodding and smiling. In her plain *kurta* and jeans, you could mistake her for a teenager escaped from school rather than a police officer. The two women had become friends over the past two years, ever since Naik had put her career at risk to help rescue Pia from kidnappers. If Rasool turned out to be Arnav's main suspect, Naik could play a major role. After her promotion, she'd moved to Versova station. Rasool's previous den fell within her jurisdiction.

Arnav must chat with her, but that had to wait until after the forensics visit at the crime scene. He messaged Desai and was told Surat Tambe and his van from the forensics department had still not reached the scene. Traffic police were trying to clear its path on flooded roads.

Arnav had a few more minutes before needing to rush out. It might prove tricky to extricate Naik and have a private word with her, but with Rasool Mohsin back in Mumbai, Arnav had to be quick. Best to speak with Naik under the cover of a family event instead of working through official channels.

CHAPTER SEVEN

TARA

Tara heard the hissed whispers and wanted to tell everyone it wasn't right to call them *hijras*. A *hijra* was often a word of abuse, a man who was not male enough. As a former bar dancer, she understood only too well their pain of being ostracized.

These performers wanted to be called *kinnar*, the mythical beings of the "third gender" who excelled at dance and song. Tara's gaze scanned the gathered parents, who looked like they were sitting on pincushions as Pia declared the troupe's arrival.

The guests seemed to understand they couldn't very well disperse. A *kinnar* dance was an age-old, fast-disappearing ritual in Arnav's ancestral village in North India, to bring good fortune at births. *Vaeeni* had said this was to bless Tara and her children.

"Mrs. Rajput"—a saree-clad mother floated up to Tara—"are you sure it is safe to bring them inside your home?"

Tara recalled the *kinnar* she'd seen on the streets: tall, broad, kohl eyed, their feminine hairdos and makeup, their voices male yet lilty, their manner going from teasing to glowering within moments if they felt threatened, the loud, typical claps, the unique way they hit their right palm against the left as if crushing a nut within them with each vehement rub-and-slap.

"Our *Vaeeni*"—Tara scanned the guests and found *Vaeeni* standing near the dining table—"feels the blessings of the *kinnar* would help me and the baby. It will only be for a few minutes."

The *kinnar* occasionally bothered women while begging, promising fertility and the welfare of children, but mostly targeted men. Men acted either lewd or embarrassed, or sometimes, when not too smart, abusive. Nobody got away with abusing a *kinnar*, at least not when a lone man did it.

"They'll bless Tara and leave after a quick dance," *Vaeeni* said.

Tara liked how *Vaeeni* had described them to her as a secretive community who looked after their own, bound by secrets and rituals borrowed from both Hindus and Muslims. They reminded her of Zoya, the way she and her Muslim best friend had set up a household together. In everyday life, the *kinnar* were yet to receive the equal rights to work, or even to exist, that the law allowed them. Inviting them to rituals allowed them to keep their dignity and earn a living.

"We'll wait for *Vaeeni* to set up the tray for the rituals," Tara said, "and she might need some help clearing a space to set it up."

Some of the women volunteered, and *Vaeeni* handed them cloth, incense, and flowers in order to arrange a mini-stage for the *kinnar* dance.

"As long as you're okay with it." The first woman turned to Tara, still uncertain. "*Hijras* can be unpredictable."

Tara didn't mind, especially with two police officers at the party. She glanced around, trying to spot Arnav in the packed living room thick with sweat, fragrances, and the rising aroma of freshly brewed milk tea.

Her gaze locked on him through the half-open study door—deep in conversation with someone she couldn't see. From the lack of smiles, she knew it couldn't be a neighbor. Sita, then. Arnav called her Naik, and most of their conversation was brisk, businesslike. Tara envied that ease and purposefulness. Arnav would never speak to her like that, all professional, with words like "*nakabandi*," "interrogation," "Section 379" peppered throughout.

She wasn't far from the door, but couldn't hear their words amid the racket the guests made while setting up the stage for the *kinnar* dance. Wanting to call them in for the ceremony, she wheeled herself closer to the study door and froze at the first words she heard.

"Right, sir. I'll keep an eye out and report on any movement Rasool makes."

"If he's behind this temple murder, we must raid his premises before he does more harm."

Rasool. Zoya said they were back, and now this. Tara leaned in to listen to Sita.

"He has a stake at that hair factory, sir. I'll need to get eyes and ears in there." Sita's voice had taken on a cold tone.

"Hair factory?"

"The Remy Virgin Hair Factory, sir. Rasool was born not two streets away from it. It has a different owner on paper, though."

That hair factory. Tara leaned closer to the door. That was where *Vaeeni* had invited her.

"If further evidence confirms Rasool's man as the prime suspect, we'll ask your station to get involved."

Tara would have stepped in to ask about Rasool, but she felt a hand at her shoulder.

"We're ready," *Vaeeni* said. "Should I ask the troupe in?"

Tara nodded. She called Arnav and Sita, asking them to join her. Her chat with Arnav could wait for later.

Tara heard before she saw them, a joyous murmur of heavy voices, a low-pitched giggle, the snatch of a prayer. Four of them sashayed in, shiny saree blouses, imitation jewelry, lipsticked smiles. The fragrance of flowery talcum powder. Wigs. Tara touched a hand to her own wig, hoping it was still in place.

She'd let *Vaeeni* persuade her about the *kinnar*, because despite the passing of two years since that fateful Diwali, the trauma of having her daughter snatched away still lingered. A *kinnar*'s blessings and curses were equally potent, and her unborn child needed the grace.

The tallest of the four made straight for Tara, and spoke the ritual words.

"Me and my sisters come to your home to bless the birth of your child."

Though they called themselves the third gender, they wore women's clothing and used feminine pronouns.

"You are welcome," Tara responded, and bowed her head so each could bless her in turn, their hard hands a contrast to the soft words they chanted, wishing the unborn child good fortune, excellent health, and a long life. Each placed flowers in her hair, touched vermilion to her forehead and her bangles, and gave her gifts: a tiny box of vermilion, a coconut, a betel nut, a red scarf threaded with gold.

"We must have song and dance."

The *kinnar* flicked her hand in the general direction of her companions. One stood beside her, and the other two carried a *harmonium* and a *dholak*.

The *kinnar* with the *harmonium* parked it on the dining table, and her fingers worked the keys into a folk ditty, while the other drummed the rhythm on the large *dholak* hanging from her neck, balanced at her belly left exposed by the saree.

The name of the hair factory echoing within Tara's mind, she watched Arnav and Sita Naik. They stood behind the crowd, Sita taking notes on her phone as Arnav spoke. She tore her gaze from them and focused on the performance.

The next few minutes turned into a blur of raucous voices and enthusiastic clapping from the performers and the audience as two *kinnar* drew Pia into the dance.

Pia matched their steps, tentatively at first, and then with increasing gusto as they largely left her untouched other than the characteristic gesture with their hands drawing away any evil eyes from Pia's face and banishing it behind their own ears with a loud click of finger against thumb. They marked Pia's forehead with sandalwood paste, did an *aarti* with a lamp *Vaeeni* brought in, fed her a sweet, and showered her with flower petals and blessings—a long life, a good-looking husband, never-ending happiness.

"What about my studies?" Pia said when the ritual song ended, and everyone burst into laughter.

"And blessings on your studies!" the *kinnar* said. "May you always be the top student at your school and become a doctor, an engineer, a collector, a police inspector."

Not a police inspector, Tara told herself. She'd seen life in Mumbai Police for her husband and wouldn't want it for anyone. She'd watched him step out at the end of the *kinnars'* performance. Her phone pinged with his message:

They want me at a crime scene. Don't wait up. Take your meds.
Love you. Need to talk to you when I return.

She had things to say to him as well: about Rasool, and the Remy Virgin Hair Factory.

CHAPTER EIGHT

ARNAV

Arnav should have been pissed off with the delay, but as he watched Surat Tambe rush through the mud toward the crime scene, he could only feel sorry. At nearly fifty-eight, the good doctor had every right to be curled up in a light shawl, reading one of his favorite tomes as rain pattered on his planted balcony. But just like Arnav, there he was. Everyone ran, slow as a proverbial turtle or quick like the hare, whether they liked it or not. No pausing for a breather. Not in Mumbai.

Some didn't even know they were running, but Tambe wasn't one of them. He knew where he needed to place his feet if he wanted to keep his dignity intact, and not dive headlong into mud, and how much older he was than his young assistant, who jogged along right behind him.

The grounds around the temple had begun to pool with water. Besides the swishing rain, the murmurs from the policemen, and the dispersing knot of people, the honking song of mating bullfrogs filled the air.

Arnav liked Surat Tambe, and made no secret of it. While Arnav's father had remained clean shaven throughout his career as a constable, even on holidays and weekends, Tambe made a show of his beard. It was pristine white now and hid his throat, making him appear venerable, yet strong.

"You look like shit, Rajput," Tambe said by way of greeting, and Arnav felt some of his wry sympathy evaporate. Tambe spoke his mind often, without giving a toss about his audience.

"I wish I could say the same for you," Arnav replied with a grin.

Forensic officers could make his life difficult, showing up late, dawdling on the results of a forensic examination, deferring postmortems. They were overworked, underpaid, and didn't report directly to police officers. It was important to keep them in good humor.

Tambe chuckled as he set up behind the tarp the men had erected, donning his gloves, a mask, and a plastic PPE kit that he must have bought for himself and his assistant. The budget didn't allow for those. His assistant scurried about, setting up lights and unpacking the cameras.

"I assume you have already conducted your own examination," Tambe said.

"I've tried to get the scene secured, Doctor, but not much beyond that. The rain isn't helping."

"This blue tarp was a good idea. It has protected the body from the worst of it."

The soothing patter of rain on the tarp contrasted with the grim, bloody scene before them.

"Let us know if you need any assistance," Arnav said, watching his constables speak with the knot of people who had now entered the temple *mandapa* to escape the rain.

"Aren't you a senior inspector now?" Tambe said. "Where's your inspector? Aren't you supposed to delegate inspectors to crime scenes, especially on a night like this?"

Tambe was a senior in the forensic department and as such took liberties another forensic officer might not. Arnav had instructed Desai to get a hold of Tambe if at all possible, because this fierce member of the old guard had helped put a few cases to bed. There was little Arnav could offer Tambe, because the man was close to retirement.

Recommendations meant nothing to Surat Tambe anymore. He fancied himself a detective—lived for gossip, and traded its currency. Snippets of information kept him invested in his job. Arnav couldn't afford to give Tambe any details, though.

"Inspector Desai is following up on a lead," Arnav said, "so we can interview a suspect." Once Arnav returned to the crime scene, he'd sent Desai sniffing at Iqbal Asif's known haunts.

"Your *khabris* give you something? The underworld?"

"Something like that." Arnav let the forensic officer come to his conclusions.

"Interview a suspect, you say?" Tambe chuckled as he adjusted his PPE. "Your inspector is known for taking witnesses aside and putting the fear of God into them."

"Each of us has our methods, Doctor," Arnav said. No point in commenting on a practice that was common knowledge in Mumbai Police.

"Yes, as do I. Only I coax dead bodies to speak to me and tell their stories, and your lot stops at nothing with live ones." Tambe cast a shrewd glance around. "They don't like you much at your office, do they?"

Arnav could cut the man down to size, but saw no point. He'd never been popular at work. His current situation wasn't unprecedented.

"What makes you think so?" Arnav peered into the camera, where Tambe was checking his first shots, his camera making soft clicking noises. Skin and blood and scarlet flowers.

"Rumor has it you're a straight shooter, won't take bribes, and won't stand up for your upper-caste buddies. Snitching against your best friend hasn't made you a hero."

Arnav could have shared his conflicted sentiments about Hemant Shinde and their two-decade friendship, but held back. The man was dead, and his family had suffered enough. They didn't need more trouble.

"I'm a policeman. I'm supposed to be honest."

"Not disputing that. You and I are alike. We'll do our jobs right and to hell with everything else. That's why I came when your inspector called. I know he reports to you. His upper-caste ass thinks I respect his clout."

Instead of responding to that comment, Arnav flicked on his phone, ready to take notes. "What can you tell us about the body?"

"You want me to shut up about you. Okay, let's see what we've got."

"We want a head start on this one. It could catch media attention."

"Homicide, clearly. Based on the amount of blood at the scene and the developing postmortem stains, I think the murder occurred here. Check these out." Tambe gently turned the arm and pointed to reddish-purple patches on the skin touching the ground. "This post-mortem lividity happens quickly after death, and is found only in the parts of the body touching the ground. Gravity pulls the blood down when it is no longer being pumped in the arteries."

"You're sure?"

"Let's see." Tambe cleared his throat. "Patches have developed only on the underside of the body. Had the victim died somewhere else, the patches would be in other places currently not touching the floor."

If the man was killed here, the culprit must have been a wizard to inflict such carnage and leave the scene quickly enough not to get caught in the act.

Surat Tambe opened a box and began lifting blood samples from the floor, using a gauze pad and tweezers.

"Which of these cuts is the cause of death?" Arnav said.

"This could be it. The jugular." Tambe pointed to the side of the neck at the same level as the man's Adam's apple. "The wound looks deep, so they might also have accidentally hit the carotid artery, which is about two finger widths beneath the skin. The victim would have died within a minute. I'll be able to tell during the postmortem."

"Wonder why the man wouldn't fight for his life when someone slashed at his throat," Arnav said.

"He might've been unconscious. An examination of the stomach contents and blood will show if he'd been drugged or otherwise incapacitated."

"So you think the culprit knew what he or she was doing?"

Arnav considered the victim—nearly five feet ten inches tall, and broad at the shoulders. His arms were muscular. If there was only one killer, chances it was a woman were slim to none.

"Maybe. Maybe not." Tambe's voice broke into Arnav's thoughts. Impossible to tell the cause of death for certain until I've washed off all the blood and done a proper examination on the table."

Tambe was one of a few forensic technicians who actually dissected the bodies instead of trusting it to attendants. Indian law required that the autopsy be carried out by a medical person, and most doctors who stood by at autopsies let a morgue attendant make the incision, scoop out the organs, and report his observations.

Meticulous in his actions, Tambe dusted surfaces with a black powder, and took close-ups of the body, as well as the blood flow and spatter.

"Do you think we'll find the killer's blood here?"

"I don't see any defensive wounds on the victim." Tambe lifted one of the inert hands. "I'm not sure he inflicted any injuries on his attacker."

The victim's hands were bloody, but after a closer look, Arnav noticed they weren't injured. The blood was from other wounds.

"So no blood from the killer on the scene?"

"I didn't say that," Tambe said. "The weapon they used might have grown slippery with blood. If it slipped and happened to cut the assailant, we're likely to find traces. Those will be hard to distinguish from the victim's blood. That's why I took all these different samples."

"How much time would it have taken for someone to inflict all these wounds?" Arnav said.

"Based on the way they flayed the face and worked on the throat, not more than a few minutes. I can't tell how clean the castration cuts are because of the blood, but all told, I would say about seven to eight minutes."

Constable Kamble had reported no wheel marks on the grounds. Whoever came in did so on foot. Or maybe a two-wheeler—a motorbike or a bicycle that they rode right up to the steps. Rain might have washed away the tracks. The killer had taken some risk, bringing the victim here: taking his life, disfiguring him, castrating him.

Even if it all took less than ten minutes, anyone could have interrupted the attacker. Unless he had help. If Iqbal Asif was doing this to fulfill a contract for the don Rasool, he would easily have that hand.

After waving goodbye to Tambe, who left with the body loaded in his van, Arnav asked for the head constable. There had been no updates from the priest about the jewelry.

Most of the constables and many of the onlookers had left, so the head constable's footsteps echoed in the near-empty *mandapa*.

"The priest cannot find the key to the safe, sir," the head constable reported, his khaki uniform damp in patches.

A castrated dead body at the temple premises was terrible enough, but if the gold jewelry went missing, the temple management board would show up at his police station and never leave. A lost key was bad news.

CHAPTER NINE

· TARA ·

The party broke up soon after the *kinnar* left. Some of Pia's friends had turned up without their parents and felt at a loss when the festivities ended early. They had asked to be picked up later.

Sita offered to take them home on her way out.

"Please come back after you drop them?" Tara said to her. "You barely ate anything, nor did *Vaeeni*, and I never got to chat with you. We'll wait."

Sita gave a quiet nod as she followed the children out.

Tara smiled as *Vaeeni* brought out tea for Tara and herself. The aroma of cardamom in the *masala* tea filled the air. From her bed, Tara could watch Pia and Neeti at the dining table, their heads bent together, sorting through the gifts.

"Should I help you take the wig off?" *Vaeeni* said.

"Are you sure it looked all right this evening?"

Tara regretted that whispered question as soon as she'd voiced it, but she couldn't ask her daughter. Her husband wasn't at home.

"Yes, of course. I'd added clips, but no one could see them." *Vaeeni* kept her voice pitched low.

"I forget you're an expert at this," Tara said.

"Normal to feel this way—this was the first time you wore it in public," *Vaeeni* said, her expression soft. Unlike Zoya, who didn't have a clue when she hurt you, you could count on *Vaeeni* to make you feel better. "Did everyone like the party?"

"Of course they did," Tara said, her voice now raised back to normal. "All thanks to you, but I wish you wouldn't tuck yourself away. I hardly saw you all evening."

"I feel more at home in the kitchen." *Vaeeni* smiled. "Neeti laughs at me because I can't rest unless my hands have something to do."

Neeti glanced up at the mention of her name and snorted. "She can't even sleep without counting prayer beads."

Tara reached out and patted *Vaeeni's* hand, from one mother of a teen to another. *Vaeeni* returned the smile, and worked on taking off Tara's wig, her fingers nimble. She placed the clips in Tara's open palm.

Teens tossed out thoughtless remarks and forgot about them, but *Vaeeni* had enough on her plate already, having lost her husband and not received the official compensation for her husband's death.

"Thank you so much." Tara held *Vaeeni's* hand once she was done.

"You're welcome," *Vaeeni* said. She looked exhausted. She'd been asked to vacate the police quarters and now lived in her old neighborhood, the crumbling *chawl* surrounding the Remy Virgin Hair Factory.

Tara could invite herself for the factory visit and find out more about Zoya's boyfriend. She could ask *Vaeeni* now, but she felt awkward in her saree, without the wig. She fixed on her cap, and spotting the housekeeper at the door, beckoned the woman in to help her back into her regular clothes.

By the time she wheeled herself out to the dining room in a top and skirt, she found *Vaeeni* gathering her things, ready to leave.

"What's wrong?"

"Bina called." *Vaeeni's* voice shook. "They asked her to come in for a night shift, so Ashok can't stay with her."

Tara bit back her frustration—she should have spoken to *Vaeeni* already.

Vaeeni's boy, Ashok, was nine. He often remained with her elder sister, Bina, in the same *chawl*. This evening he was in bed, recovering from a bout of fever.

"It is nine p.m., though," Tara said. "Shouldn't they let her know in advance?"

"At the factory they have few jobs and many people keen on them. We can't afford to say no."

Interesting. If Rasool was the real factory owner, he ran the place via his men with an iron fist. Tara was about to ask *Vaeeni* to have her dinner before she left when Neeti interrupted them.

"Can I stay back tonight, Ma?"

"Ashok isn't well. We'll take the bus home."

Arnav and Tara had asked *Vaeeni* and her family more than once to stay with them, but she'd refused. Now she'd have to take a long ride home in one of Mumbai's red buses, with passengers packed in like sardines.

"He only needs you, right? I have a test tomorrow morning, and I can study with Pia. I even have my old spare uniform here from last month."

Pia gave Tara a pleading glance, but Tara knew better. *Vaeeni* would decide what was best for her daughter.

"Neeti." There was no mistaking the steel in *Vaeeni's* voice.

"It will be hard for me to focus with you wandering around, and that brat coughing away."

"Get your—" *Vaeeni* didn't get to finish, because Sita called Tara from the living room, and entered the dining area.

A glance at all their faces, and Sita said, "Everything okay? Sorry it took a while—one of the girls couldn't find her way home."

"I'll leave, Tara," *Vaeeni* said. "See you again soon, Sita."

"Let me pack your dinner for you and the children."

"I'm so late."

"I can drop you home," Sita cut in. "Quicker than taking the bus. You can finish dinner."

"Thank you, but you've returned . . ." *Vaeeni* trailed off, nonplussed.

"Where's your place?"

"Near Andheri West."

"It's on the way to my station in Versova. It will take fifteen minutes."

Vaeeni, defeated, put her bag down. "All right. That would be nice—I guess."

Over dinner, Tara marveled at the casual way Sita had turned the topic to where *Vaeeni* worked.

"Your factory makes all the wigs?" Sita probed.

"Our factory is not all that big. The best wigs are made in China, not India. We just wash, comb, and export hair. Sometimes we make hair extensions. All the pop stars that you love—every one of them with long hair wears hair extensions."

"No," Pia cut in. "Really? Even Rhianna, Beyoncé?"

"Yes," *Vaeeni* said.

"This is an interesting line of work"—Sita spooned another helping of lentils on her rice—"but I guess these owners aren't different from those in other factories."

"Rich people are all the same," *Vaeeni* agreed. "We have a good nonprofit that supports us, though."

"What sort of assistance?"

"Childcare, education. They provide classes to young girls where they can learn skills useful at a hair factory. They make some hair product samples."

"That's good," Tara said. "Someone's taking an initiative."

"Yes, Bina helps run it. She works extra hours. You can meet her when you visit."

"Sounds like a great idea, Ma," Pia piped up, her eyes bright. "You should go out more often, like Papa says. And with Shinde Aunty and her friends around you'll feel comfortable."

"Let me check with the physiotherapist," Tara said, not wanting to sound too eager. She hadn't yet spoken to Arnav. He might object to a trip to a factory owned by Rasool.

"You tell me a date and I'll let Bina know to expect you," *Vaeeni* said. "You can bring Pia, too, if you like, and check out some of the new hair-extension samples the girls have created."

Tara glanced at Pia, whose gaze remained on her plate. Strange. She'd sounded keen on the factory moments ago. She would worry about that later—she needed to accept the invite and make the visit happen.

"Sure," Tara said. "I'll call you this week."

"Take your time," *Vaeeni* said. "Eat some more. You can't be careless with your diet."

"I ate one of your *laddoos* earlier this evening. They are so filling."

"*Laddoos* are good, but they are sugar and nuts. You must eat vegetables," *Vaeeni* said, spooning some onto Tara's plate. Turning to Neeti, she gestured toward their bag. "Gather your things. We'll leave soon."

"This is what you always do." Neeti clattered her spoon on her plate. "It is *you*. Ever since Daddy died, *you've* made our lives miserable. You are why Ashok is sick. That place stinks. Grown men sing songs at me, and those filthy catcalls. I hate you."

Neeti rushed off, and they heard a door bang somewhere in the apartment. Pia ran after her.

"That girl . . ." *Vaeeni's* voice trembled.

Tara didn't know what to say. If Neeti was being harassed, it was natural for her to act up. It sounded like goons visited the locality.

Another reason she must check the factory—if things were bad, Zoya should know so Rasool could rein in his men.

Vaeeni patted Tara's hand and dashed inside to find Neeti. Sita sat at the table, an island of calm. Tara turned to her.

"I'll call *Vaeeni* a cab."

"I don't mind," Sita said. "It's five minutes from my station, and I must go in anyway."

Sita Naik was so thoughtful. For a moment it made Tara feel sorry about being best friends with Zoya, a don's girlfriend. It meant she could never be close to Sita.

At the crash of footsteps, Tara turned around to find *Vaeeni* returning, her face ashen.

"Neeti won't open the door. I'm so sorry."

"She can stay here for tonight." Tara measured each word she spoke, worried she might hurt *Vaeeni*. "Call me if you need help with Ashok."

"You've already done so much."

"It is you who ran the show this evening," Tara said, letting her eyes show her gratitude.

Vaeeni left with Sita. Wheeling herself toward Pia's room, Tara found the door locked from the inside, and heard peals of high-pitched girlish laughter.

Neeti sounded happy at the moment, but someone must check on her accusation of catcalls, make sure she was safe. Arnav would burst a blood vessel, so Tara must approach someone else. Sita. Sita was a woman and a sub-inspector. She would know what to do. Besides, she might like a good excuse to sniff around the Remy Virgin Hair Factory.

CHAPTER TEN

ARNAV

Arnav had to raise his voice above the roar of the storm while he spoke on the phone to Bapat, updating him on the progress with Forensics, and the 100 call sent in for tracing. The buffeting wind brought a fine spray of rain into the temple. Arnav zipped his waterproof jacket closed.

Desai loomed up from behind the temple sanctum, and spoke before Arnav could ask him the obvious question.

"No sign of Asif, sir. I've left men on watch at some of his haunts. We'll know if he's seen near any of them."

Further bad news. Arnav hoped Naik, and his own informer, Ali, would produce better results.

"Where's the priest?" Arnav said.

"He's on another search of the temple along with a constable, sir, in case he dropped the key on the premises."

"Does anyone have a spare key?"

"It's with the trustees. I've sent a constable for it, sir."

"Is the priest a flight risk?"

"His family and children are here, sir. And he's on dialysis."

"Best to have him followed, then. Get someone on it. Track this priest's movements for the next week."

Arnav debated interrogating the priest in front of Desai, a vehement Hindu, the kind who wore smears of sandalwood on his forehead on festival days. Under Desai's police cap, a *shendi* sat at the back of his head: a tuft of hair traditionally kept by the priests and upper-caste Brahmins.

Arnav could order Desai away to make sure he didn't intimidate the priest, but maybe scare tactics weren't such a bad idea.

"Bring the priest here."

"They're locking up the sanctum, sir. The head constable will escort him."

Desai drew close to Arnav. "I think the priest is mixed up in all this, sir. He's from one of those lower-caste families, no knowing what they are capable of."

Before Arnav could respond, the priest waddled up, head bowed.

He looked the worse for wear, as if he'd walked a mile in a storm.

"So, *panditji*"—Desai used the polite honorific—"explain to Rajput *saab* here where the key went?"

"I promise you, I don't know. It was on me when I came here, and now it isn't. It seems like magic."

"Of course there's black magic in your temple, from what we have seen of the body."

Arnav raised his hand to stop Desai, and held up his phone. "What do you think of this symbol?"

The drawing on the body was a tantric symbol, Arnav had discovered after an internet search on the way back to the crime scene. From his cursory research, it appeared that the tantric cult had a centuries-old history in both Buddhism and Hinduism. Over time, the Hindu rituals of the *tantra* had been misinterpreted, and many believed that tantrics engaged in black magic. Desai's accusation might have been strong, but he wasn't far off the mark as far as common perception went.

"This mark is on the body?" the priest said.

"You didn't see it?"

"I have tried to stay away from the body. I worship Ma Kaali, and she is a fierce goddess, but I did not want any images of dead bodies in my head. I devote myself to her benevolent aspect."

"Someone has drawn it using vermilion powder."

"Well, *saab*, it is a tantric symbol. It means, uh, the *yoni*, the gateway to a woman's womb."

Typical of a priest to indicate "vagina" in a roundabout way. The bare-chested priest sweated despite the chill in the rain-laden air.

"Why would someone draw this on a naked man's chest?" Arnav said. "After having chopped off his genitals?"

"Who knows, *saab*? You police know more than anyone else that people do not need a reason to be evil. Please remove the body as soon as possible, and find out who did it. If the temple gets a bad name, devotees will avoid it."

Arnav sighed. No matter what religion, the number of devotees mattered.

"Did anyone hold a grudge against the temple?" Arnav said.

"Not that I can remember right now, sir." The priest's voice quaked.

"Could it be," Desai addressed the priest, voice loaded with derision, "that the killer wanted to turn the man into a woman? Is it part of some old tantric ritual by some of those lower-caste people?"

Tantric rituals had turned melodramatic thanks to Indian TV soaps. The shows had given tantrics a bad name: they apparently worshipped the mother goddess but often lost their way to greed or lust.

"*Saab*," the priest said, "I follow regular Hindu rituals—prayers with flowers, sweets, light, and incense."

"There are hibiscus blooms strewn around the body," Desai said. "Those are supposed to be Ma Kaali's favorite flowers, aren't they? The goddess wears a garland of human skulls, and another made of red hibiscus."

Tara worshipped the goddess Kaali. The word *Kaali* simply meant black or dark feminine, but Kaali inspired fear as well as devotion. In one hand, she carried a demon's severed head by the hair, and a deadly scimitar in another.

"Yes, we venerate her with red hibiscus. Each morning, I adorn her with a fresh garland."

"Isn't she also a goddess with a taste for human blood?" Desai's brows rose. "There used to be human sacrifices in tantric rituals for her, right? Your *tantra* believes lower-caste shudras and women can be spiritual gurus."

Like many others in his circle, Arnav understood little of the *tantra* or the caste system. Women and men could be whatever they wanted, as far as he was concerned.

"You'll have to ask a *tantra* expert, *saab*. I'm a simple priest."

A man had been murdered and castrated, and the key to the safe had gone missing from the temple where this "simple priest" ran the show. He could have deeper connections. Desai's men might not suffice to watch this portly messenger of god.

On his phone Arnav began writing his case notes.

Iqbal Asif, Rasool Mohsin's man, was seen on CCTV with possible victim.

Victim was killed on the spot, with a knife. Weapon missing. Body will be analyzed for drugs and exact cause of death.

The 100 call was made on the internet, using a voice changer.

Priest has lost keys to temple safe.

The symbols on the body belong to a tantra cult, and the symbol means the sacred vagina.

The keys arrived right then, in the hands of a messenger from the trustees escorted into the temple by a constable.

"Watch him as he checks the safe," Arnav said to Desai. "Let's make sure all the jewelry is secure."

CHAPTER ELEVEN

—

TARA

Tara's clothes prickled against her skin; her pillow scratched her cheek. Rain beat an unsteady tattoo on her windowpanes, taunting her. From below her bedroom window came the harsh call of a hawker. Who wanted vegetables at five in the morning? Not Tara. She wanted Arnav home, but he hadn't returned last night. The pillow beside hers was fluffed up. It smelled of laundry, not her husband's shampoo.

Her brain craved sleep—she hadn't found a restful position all night, and reclining on her side with her large tummy hadn't helped, not even after she'd set up pillows. Her back hurt worse than ever, but she was trying to cut down on medication. She had to get up before her housekeeper, Pia, or Neeti came in to remind her about the physiotherapy session. Neeti's name reminded her that she wanted to talk to Sita Naik.

She must place a call to Sita and request to speak face-to-face.

She'd tried to call Zoya back on the number her friend had called from, with no luck. Zoya called when she could, but remained unreachable—that was how it had been ever since she began life on the run with Rasool two years ago. Now, when Tara wanted to send her friend a message, she didn't know how. Had she been up and about, like everyone else, she could have gone out, asked around in Rasool's former neighborhood.

Instead, she was on her bed, immobile. On her TV screen, a fast yet deceptively low tsunami flooded into riverbeds. Waves smashed boats and trees, taking people unaware. Smoke columns rose from volcanoes. Tornadoes rampaged in dark funnels that picked up jeeps, carts, and signboards, tossing them across fields, while puffing out a few flowers, scattering them on the puny adjoining shed.

Over the months, all she'd stared at was an endless, self-feeding loop of doom: the glare of the TV and the faraway cries of shock and terror lulled her into a remote-clicking, frenzied trance that kept her daily life at bay.

A child's cry from the screen startled her.

She found herself stroking her belly, running her fingers in circles. Gratitude swept her—she could move her hands now, even though she couldn't feel her fingers on her skin. Her hands hadn't cooperated with her up until a year ago. She crooned to her baby, making it a promise of protection. All mothers struggled. She'd be no different.

The sight of her fingers soothing her belly pacified her gnawing anxiety about Arnav being out all night. Where was he? Had Rasool been involved in a murder at a temple? Would Mumbai break out into Hindu–Muslim riots with her Arnav caught up in the vortex? The good people of Mumbai often put knives, fires, and guns to devastating use. And why not? All stories hurtled toward one logical end.

No. Tara collected herself. Resisted the havoc that called to her from the screen, and hauled herself up with the help of the braces Arnav had installed on the wall beside the bed.

She heard the front door unlock, and his deep voice greeting Pia and Neeti as they prepared for school. She wanted to both fling herself at her husband and yell at him in relief, so she settled for a cursory hello when he stepped in and began to put away his things. Cap, badge, wallet, belt. All the items that witnessed blood, killing, and rotting flesh—the ugly savagery of this city.

It was the worst moment for the catheter alarm on her phone to buzz in silence. She had to go to the toilet. She tried to calm herself: *We're all slaves to our bodies, confined by its limitations.* It didn't work. The humiliation of having someone else assist her with her catheter was a thing of the past, but like many spinal cord injury survivors, she still had to self-catheterize every five hours. Her body couldn't tell her when she had to go. With growing alarm she watched Arnav turn and head toward her for the habitual kiss at her temple.

She'd either have to call out for the housekeeper who was busy getting Pia's things for school, or ask him to aid her to the toilet. Couldn't she even be upset with her husband without her body's whipping demands for her attention?

"What's wrong?" Arnav said, his voice soft with concern. "Does your back hurt?"

For answer, Tara snatched up the earthen lamp beside the bed and sent it sailing toward the wall. Having heard it go with a satisfying crash, she straightened herself as best she could.

"I need the toilet." Her gaze remained fixed on the TV screen, her voice not quavering.

Arnav lifted her, and took her to the toilet without a word.

When she was settled, he said, "I'll go check on Pia and send the housekeeper in to assist you." He pulled the door to, leaving it slightly ajar.

Could the girls hear the crash from where they sat in the dining area? She hoped not. Too late now.

The piled-up anxiety of the night before leached out of her. Her phone would ring, she assured herself, and she would speak to Zoya.

Then, she would drag herself up. She would find the words to tell Arnav about her planned visit, accept *Vaeeni*'s invitation to the hair factory, and dig up the dirt on Rasool's schemes.

CHAPTER TWELVE

MUMBAI DRISHTIKON NEWS

Bollywood Bytes

Chitra Varli makes fun of Hindu festival, faces criticism

7:00 AM IST 16 July, Mumbai.

Maharashtra is in the national conversation again.

A Hindu Rashtra Party opposition MLA, Tarun Sathe, has said that Hindus should not tolerate disrespect to their religion.

This came in the wake of a social media storm following a tweet by social media influencer, activist, and Bollywood actress Chitra Varli questioning the relevance of Hindu festivals like *Teej*, a celebration primarily for married women during the monsoons.

In her post, Chitra Varli said, "Why should women be the ones fasting and dressing up during these festivals? These are obsolete Brahminical practices, imposed by the high-caste *savarna* majority. Let men fast and cook for the entire family for a change. Let them dress up and wait for the women to feed them their first morsel of the day."

Tarun Sathe asserted the importance of the Hindu religious practices and their influence on the cultural rubric of India.

"Women should follow traditions. *Teej* is not just about the fasting, it is a celebration of the reunion of the gods Shiva and Parvati, and their union leads to abundance both in nature and human households. Let us not forget our rituals and festivals. We don't need to bring casteism into each and every festival, and women should keep quiet in important matters like religion and tradition."

These statements are likely to prove inflammatory, and already, there have been calls for his resignation from other members of the Maharashtra Assembly. Other MLAs have defended him, saying he had only spoken about the sanctity of the majority religion in the country.

The Chief Minister of Maharashtra has called for calm discussions, and a lowering of the rhetoric ahead of the elections.

"Hindus from all castes have lived side by side for centuries in this country. We respect our women and their judgment. Harmony and tolerance are the bedrock of Hinduism, and those are the values we must all uphold."

CHAPTER THIRTEEN

SITA

Sita Naik woke with a start from a dream of the goddess Ma Kaali chasing an unknown assailant out of her temple, her hair a funereal cloak darker than the night.

In the morning gloom, Sita's husband, Raghav, lay on top of her, snoring. She braced at the weight of him, trying to gather the energy to move him off. Their one-bedroom *kholi* in one of Mumbai's better *chawls*—the low-cost housing the Maharashtra government called "middle-class housing" but were in fact tenements originally built by the British for mill workers—was barely enough for the two of them.

Mumbai came grumbling into her *kholi* with its city-traffic noise and fumes, the clatter of her neighbor's kitchen, weak monsoon sunlight. Sita tried not to think of her mother-in-law, who lay in the living room that doubled as Raghav Naik's runty real estate office and Sita's pantry, possibly dreaming of a grandson. Lord Hanuman knew where they'd put such a son if he were to arrive.

Lord Hanuman. The monkey god. The one with a vow of an eternal celibacy. The god of loyalty, integrity, strength so immense he carried a mountain on his shoulders and flew to the rescue of those fallen in battle.

Her mother-in-law said only men might worship him, but Sita fasted each Tuesday in his honor, in secret, because at work she needed all the strength she could get. Being a policewoman in a man's world was hard enough—she was a policewoman with no women's toilet at her workplace. She was also one of the few who refused the *hafta*, the weekly bribe to let things slide in her precinct.

Sita shoved her husband aside and tried to stretch her cramped arms. She'd considered leaving her husband ever since their first night together. Sub-Inspector Raghav Naik had been her grandma's favorite, not hers. This marriage was Grandma's condition for Sita to enter the Mumbai Police Service.

She earned enough now as a sub-inspector that she could leave him if she wanted and still get by. Raghav and his mother wouldn't survive, since Sita's salary ran the household.

If she did that, her grandma and mother-in-law, fast friends, would label her disloyal at home, and her colleagues would do the same at work. The thought of her colleagues brought back the image of one man—fair, square jawed, tall. Kind eyes that gazed only at his wife, anticipating her needs before she voiced them—passing her food or a napkin, pinning her saree, arranging her feet on the wheelchair footplate.

When he'd mentioned Rasool, she'd hoped he would ask her to work with him again. Maybe it was the don who had ordered the victim at the temple castrated. She could help him, be needed at work—she didn't expect more.

As he'd detailed his plans, she'd worn her expression clean and starched, just like her khakis, the color of the uniform the only thing she had in common with him, cloth that made men and women unremarkable beings, like the *teetar* from her childhood village. Speckled and gorgeous on its own, but set against the brown soil and others of its kind, each gray partridge looked the same as any other.

Raghav was one of their number till he lost an arm in the line of duty—shot, infected, amputated at the elbow. He milked it, with his mother, with Sita, friends, his previous coworkers. Sita had never fallen for it, but she'd stood by him at his hospital appointments for his artificial arm, and the lobbying for compensation that the bosses hadn't approved in all those years.

Raghav slid his good arm over her waist again, heavy like a dead animal. The phone buzzed beside her head. She slid out from under her husband's arm and into the alcove that worked as the kitchen. They wanted her at the office. She must run. She responded, asking them to send someone to pick her up, and shrugged on her khaki uniform, shoving her unwashed hair under her cap.

She freshened up in the tiny toilet, using as little water as possible. The others might forget to fill the buckets when the water supply switched on for the two usual morning hours. On the way out, as she picked up her umbrella, Sita wanted to bend down and whisper in her husband's ear, tell him he'd never succeed in his nightly efforts. She had an IUD and took pills for good measure.

Rushing down the stairs, she picked up her buzzing phone to tell her pickup she was on her way, but froze. It wasn't her office.

Tara Singh Rajput. The one person on earth she didn't want to talk to this early in the morning. She wanted not to hate the very pregnant, *laddoo*-eating Tara.

Sita had never been in the picture with the one man at whom she'd ever cast a second glance. She was married, for one. She was also the most traditional, her colleagues said. More conservative even than *Vaeeni*. No one saw the woman underneath the khaki uniform and the *mangalsutra* and *sindoor* Sita was obliged to wear as marital flags.

By the time she reached the street, the phone rang off, but started again. Sita looked up at the gloom of rain clouds and answered.

"Hello?" She cleared her throat and straightened her umbrella against the drizzle.

She tried never to call Tara by her name, or Tara *Vaeeni*, as would have been natural.

"Sita, did I wake you?" Tara's voice was soft. "I'm sorry."

"No, please tell me. Everything okay?" Sita hated the eager note her voice took on when speaking to Tara, overcompensating for her illogical, stored-up guilt.

"It is about Neeti . . ."

"*Vaeeni*'s daughter? Is she okay?"

"Yes, I'd rather not talk on the phone. I was hoping you could come by when you have a few minutes. I would visit you, but . . ."

"I'll call you and come in this evening."

Raghav would be out at one of his local Hindu community meetings, so Sita didn't have to worry about his dinner, and her mother-in-law could get her own.

"Thank you, Sita. Please dine with us if you have time."

Dinner at the Rajputs'. Part of her hoped he would be there; the other wished the opposite. She cut the call and raced onto the road to wait for her jeep. Despite the rain, traffic had picked up on the narrow highway, the morning calm shattered by honking buses and trucks. The humid air was heavy with the fragrance of breakfast frying in the colorful stalls.

Sita loved the spice of the curried potatoes in *poori-bhaji*, the way the spiced *bhaji* contrasted with the round, bland *poori*. The two together became a harmony—the melty potatoes and the crisp-fried bread. She could pack herself and her constables some breakfast.

It was a Saturday, though. Ma Kaali blessed offerings on Saturdays—the dark goddess of doomsday and death.

Sita twisted the sacred red thread of Hanuman tied to her wrist. Maybe she should follow the goddess Kaali instead. Hanuman did not provide the kind of strength she needed these days. In any case, the lord had so many devotees—he wouldn't miss her.

She would fast today for Ma Kaali then. Raghav's friend worshipped her.

He spoke with love of Kaali's large eyes that held rage and tenderness, her tongue that hung long and fearsome, blood dripping;

impossible to tell whether it was from accidentally stepping on her husband's chest in her bloodlust or from slaying a wicked demon. Strange man, Raghav's friend, but like most of his friends, devoted to Raghav, making her wish she had such friends, too. Sita snorted. Enough of letting her mind wander.

She headed toward the food stall, letting the raindrops patter a greeting on her umbrella. She couldn't eat, but it wouldn't hurt to stop by the stall to pack breakfast for her colleagues. This early, the stall owner's assistant would have his hands full, but no one to talk to. Maybe she could ask some questions, ferret out the whereabouts of a few people, those who would know where she could find Rasool's man, Iqbal Asif.

CHAPTER FOURTEEN

TARA

One hour after her fight with Arnav, Tara wheeled herself into the living room to find her physiotherapist Paresh waiting for her: a small face and a brawny marionette body in search of a personality—as if he'd pumped iron an hour ago, and worn clothes borrowed from a cousin two sizes smaller than him.

She was late, once again. As usual, he didn't comment on it. He was never late, not by a minute, not once.

"*Namaste*, madam." Paresh wore his usual patronizing smile. "Here you are."

She returned the greeting, apologized for being late, and readied herself for the torture that would be the next two hours of her life. She couldn't do much, given the advanced state of her pregnancy, but even the stretches felt like an insult to her weary body.

"Let's start with exercising your legs."

If she continued with her therapy and got some more flexibility into her lower back, they could do the operation to remove scar tissue that had formed near her spine. It would happen sometime after the delivery, once her body recovered from giving birth, but it could restore mobility in her legs. She must keep pushing through the agony.

"Pain is a good thing, madam, remember that," Paresh said, as if he could read her mind. "When you experience pain, it means you've got your feeling back."

Tara could have laughed at that. Whether in the body or mind, better to feel anguish than nothing at all.

"Yes," she said, trying to lift her inert legs with all her will, while they sat there like they belonged to someone else.

"I'm going to hold you here, madam"—he gripped her ankle—"and lift your leg to this height." He pointed to his knee. "All right? Let's go."

His eyes remained downcast, and he was a thorough professional, but she sensed his resentment—as if working for a woman tested his patience. It didn't matter. At the end of the day, his combination of hidden annoyance and overt encouragement worked for her—it made her want to slap him and shake his hand at the same time.

"You must try to step out, madam," he said after a while. "Fresh air is important."

For once, she had a different answer. She wanted to visit that factory. Over the clatter from the kitchen, where her housekeeper seemed to be putting dishes away, she said, "My friend wants me to go with her."

"That's good! You have nice friends, madam. Where will you go?"

"To the place where she works, the Remy Virgin Hair Factory."

"Ah, really? She works there?" His face was bent over her feet so she couldn't read his expression, but she heard the shock in his voice.

"Yes. Do you know the place?" Tara said.

"It is a few minutes' walk from my *kholi*."

"You are *Vaeeni*'s neighbor?"

She described *Vaeeni* to him, but he didn't recognize her.

"I'll introduce you if she stops by one morning," Tara said.

"Sure, madam. There are so many other places to go—visit someplace in the open air, near the beach? Why go to a factory?"

His brows rose, in surprise and annoyance—silly woman, who doesn't know beaches offered more fresh air than factories.

Beaches. Arnav used to take her and Pia up until a few months ago, but Tara didn't go anymore, not since her pregnancy had advanced. She hated going out. Now, though, she'd found one thing she'd missed: a purpose other than overcoming her disability. Locate Rasool Mohsin.

"Madam, I'll lift your arm and try to stretch it toward your toes now. You can ask me to stop anytime. All right?"

Tara tried to focus, but her thoughts wandered back to her husband, who had eaten a breakfast she hadn't cooked. The housekeeper had made the usual Marathi fare, *poha*. The spice of mustard and curry leaves and the tang of chili wafted in from the kitchen. Come to think of it, she hadn't cooked him breakfast since she'd stayed with him at his *dojo* nearly two years ago.

That must change. She could cook if they adjusted the kitchen to her wheelchair. She would make that *poha* for herself and her family, toss the softened rice flakes with potatoes and peanuts in a hot pan. Having made up her mind to take more charge of her life from now on, she followed Paresh's instructions, considering ways to broach the factory visit with Arnav.

CHAPTER FIFTEEN

ARNAV

Arnav took his time gathering the pieces of the lamp Tara had shattered. Behind him, raindrops gathered and slid like tears down the frosted panes of the living room.

He ignored his wife as she entered the bedroom after her physiotherapy session—sometimes her anger found a misplaced target. She wheeled herself straight to him, and he felt her soft hand on his shoulder.

"I'm sorry," she said. "You have few things left from your mother's home."

This was Tara. She lost her temper, but felt sorry right after.

Arnav picked up a piece of blue ceramic. "Ma had bought this the year before Asha died. Asha wanted something nice for Diwali, but Ma didn't have the money for the TV Asha wanted. She got this instead."

Asha. Not a day passed without him thinking of his sister, who would have turned fifty this year had she not taken her own life. He was a boy then, a mere thirteen, but the memory of her red-saree-clad body hanging from the roof haunted him still.

Tara kissed his head, stroking his hair. He turned, and once their eyes met, he rose to take her into his arms, and into bed. She nuzzled him at his neck, right beneath his ear. He lay down, and she peppered his face with tiny kisses.

"I'm sorry I'm such a harpy these days." She leaned over him, her sweat, talcum, and flowery perfume overpowering his senses. "And I'm stinky after all the workout."

"You're not," Arnav said, and then conceded after a peek at her laughing face. "Okay, well, you have a lot going on."

"So do you."

"It's just work. Speaking of which, I have a question for you."

Having grown up in a village, Tara knew more about tantrics and caste dynamics than he did. Mumbai was a metropolis, and he'd grown up isolated from his extended family. The school textbooks talked about caste, but as history, not part of lived reality. She might know things he didn't.

"I'm all yours," she said, the temptress, her face inches from his.

"That you are." Arnav reached up and nipped at her earlobe, his hand easing over her pregnant belly. "No one doubts that. But quit distracting me and listen."

As he spoke about *savarna* men, he noticed Tara growing still. Maybe he should have taken his caste questions to someone else.

"Tara?" Arnav gazed up at her.

"Well," she said, after a long minute, "I don't know all that much about *tantra*. There used to be a tantric back in my village, an old man, but I was a child then. My Ma said he dug up dead bodies, and worshipped over them, but those were rumors."

This was intriguing. He'd never met a tantric before.

"How do you know?" Arnav said.

"I spoke to him—he was the only man in the whole village who was kind to me. He worshipped the dark goddess Ma Kaali, and yes, he did sacrifice roosters and goats during the Kaali Puja Festival. He used the blood for rituals."

Arnav marveled at his pregnant wife chatting about blood sacrifice without gagging, and prompted her when she paused.

"But?"

"In the end he was just a kind old man," Tara said, her gaze trained far away outside the window, "who believed that women should have power. More of a father to me than my own was. He would give me and my friends food to eat when we didn't have enough at home. Once, he bandaged my leg after my father broke it during one of his drunken brawls."

Arnav leaned across and held her hand, but he didn't interrupt.

"He was from the lowest caste, a Dome," Tara continued. "He helped at the cremation *ghaat* at the river near our village. In his Ma Kaali's eyes, all men and women were equal. He said the goddess accepts the worship of all castes, making no discrimination between the upper-caste Brahmins, or the lower-caste Shudras, and even the Achoot—the untouchables."

"What's the difference? I know only the basics."

"Well, you're high caste yourself, so you never needed to find out more. I know a little, but not all of it."

She was growing angry. Dr. Holkar had insisted that he keep Tara calm. Arnav drew her to him, stroking her arm. "Well, tell me what you know."

"The highest caste is the Brahmins. Well, like your Inspector Desai. They make all the rules. Most priests are Brahmins."

This much he knew, but something didn't make sense.

"The Kaali temple priest isn't a Brahmin, according to Desai."

"Exactly—that's because the goddess Kaali doesn't discriminate between castes the way society does. After the Brahmins come Kshatriyas, the warriors. All rulers used to belong to that caste. Your Rajput clan are Kshatriyas. Then come the Vaishyas, the traders and farmers."

A memory slid into place. "My mother used to say we come from a family of soldiers," Arnav said.

"She's right. My parents were Mondal—Shudras. In the old times, the people in professions like weaving or pottery or medicine were given

63

the name of a caste as per their skill. All those castes were Shudras. Not high caste, but also not without caste."

Tara sighed, then continued. "Those without caste are the *avarnas*. They're also called Achoot: the untouchables."

She grew animated, so Arnav made her sit back, leaning against the headboard. The doctor said excitement wasn't good for her.

"I see," he said, trying to process it all. "Thank you."

He placed a pillow to support her back, and peppered a kiss or two on her shoulder.

"Why do you want to know about tantrics?" Tara looked curious, intent.

"It's for work."

"If you need more, you can speak with Ram Chandra Dome."

"Dome, so a lower caste, you said? Who is that?"

"Yes. Without caste. An Achoot. He's a tantric. I met him at the Kaali temple near Pia's school."

Arnav sat up. "The Kaali temple?" In all his visits to pick Tara up from the temple he'd never met any tantric.

"Yes. He's not there all the time, so you haven't seen him. He asked me to wear this locket." She picked up the heavy silver locket from where it lay beneath her collarbones. "Why?"

Arnav reached for it. "A locket? He gave this to you?"

"No, it's Zoya's. It was empty—Ram Chandra had me put in strands of your hair, mine, and Pia's. I'll put in the baby's hair after the birth. He prayed over it and blessed it. It's for the health of our family."

Arnav held the delicately carved, hinged locket, and examined it up close.

"What sort of a person is this Ram Chandra Dome?" he said.

"Well. He's not so old. He's angry most of the time, but he does know his tantric rituals. Ma Kaali is a fierce goddess, but she offers strong protection to her devotees."

A tantric whose temper flared often. A frequent visitor to the Kaali temple. A dead body, castrated, at its steps. Arnav kept his tone as casual as he could.

"Was he ever violent?"

"Well, this once, when someone called him a *neechi jaat*, an Achoot. An educated man with an expensive gold watch, Mr. Banerjee, one of those stuck-up Brahmins, you know. Ram Chandra snatched up a fruit knife, and pointed it at that Brahmin, daring him to call him that name again. His voice was low and harsh, but it echoed in the temple. That man didn't dare. He turned and ran down the steps."

Arnav fought for calm, terror clogging his throat. "You never told me before? Someone flicked out a knife."

"The priest stopped him. He's the priest's nephew."

The priest hadn't told them about Ram Chandra Dome. Arnav grabbed his phone and fired off a couple of messages to Desai.

Watch the priest closely, he's not telling us the whole story. Ask around for a man called Ram Chandra Dome.

Bring Dome in for a chat. He seems to be a tantric.

Messages sent and confirmation received, he turned to Tara.

"This man was volatile. Someone called him names, and he pulled out a knife in response? How long have you seen him there?"

"Last few months. And those were not just any names, Arnav. You won't understand."

"What do you mean?"

"You're a Rajput, a Kshatriya. You don't know what life is like for an Achoot."

She made no sense. He'd never seen anyone suffer for their caste in Mumbai. Mumbai was a large melting pot, where only two things counted: your initiative and your street smarts.

"All of that ended years ago," he said. "No one believes in it anymore."

"That's what you think." Tara flushed, her nostrils flaring. "You think calling all the untouchables so-called technical words like 'Scheduled Caste' and giving them some reserved seats make it all go away. You've never had to suffer because of it."

He shouldn't give in to anger, not when it could harm Tara, but it was so unfair. Yes, the term "Scheduled Caste" was the official way of denoting a caste low in a pecking order that went back many generations, based on birth, not actions.

But Arnav recalled the many times he'd seen that Scheduled Castes had seats reserved for them, in the police force, in professional colleges, at universities, in the state assemblies, and in the Indian Parliament. *They need to score fewer marks for the same placements,* Arnav wanted to protest, *they win elections with no qualifications other than their low caste.* He couldn't say that, but he couldn't stay silent, either.

"I don't think we should reserve seats for them," Arnav burst out, "not in government, not in schools and colleges. All of it should be based on merit."

"Easy for you to say." Tara turned away. "You've never spent a day as a Scheduled Caste."

"You and I are not the same caste, and we got married without problems. Shinde and I were friends, and he was a Scheduled Caste. None of that made a difference except he got quicker promotions."

"I'm not a Scheduled Caste"—Tara hissed the words—"so no one from your community had a problem. Your colleagues' wives have asked me what caste I am—they don't feel good that I'm a Shudra, not a Kshatriya like you. Do you know what it feels like to be an untouchable? Their ancestral profession is to clean out the mud toilets, to carry out people's shit and carry it on their heads, in containers. In some villages they do it even now. Do you know how their children are treated? They are called scavengers."

"Tara—I'm sorry—" Arnav raised his hands in a gesture of surrender. "I didn't know it still occurs—"

"You asked, so I'm telling you why the name Achoot hurts. We had them in the village, the untouchables. They weren't allowed to draw water from the well that belonged to the Brahmins. Not even during drought. They weren't allowed inside temples, or weddings. Only the end of funerals, where they helped burn the dead. That's the caste of a Dome in West Bengal. A Dome puts bodies on pyres. Makes sure the bodies burn. Roots in the hot ashes for the bones, hands over the remains. And is then told he can't step inside a temple. No amount of quick promotions or reservations can make up for that." Tara clenched her hands when Arnav tried to hold them. "And have you ever wondered why, despite all your trying, you can't get your Scheduled Caste friend's compensation for his widow?"

"Tara." Arnav took a deep breath, and laid a hand on her shoulder. "Don't 'Tara' me."

"I'm sorry, I'm going to find out more." Arnav reached for her. "I didn't know. And you're not one of them, so why are you so upset?"

"This." Tara poked a finger at his chest. "This is why. My father, who nearly killed me in a drunken fit, was called a better man than that tantric who fed me when I was starving. My father was not 'one of them,' you see. So he was the better man."

"I'm sorry."

"And do you know what they did to the tantric when they found out he fed hungry children belonging to Shudras and Brahmins? They lynched him. He bled out, right there at the village Kaali temple."

Tara sighed as Arnav touched his forehead to hers. She sagged against him, and they sat there for a few moments, not moving. She backed away after a while.

"I want to go to the Remy Virgin Hair Factory. With *Vaeeni*. She said she'd take me."

A change of subject, but not one he'd expected. That factory. *Vaeeni*. *Vaeeni* worked there, but Tara didn't need to go within miles of that place. Not when Rasool might own it.

"Why would you want to visit a factory all of a sudden?"

"She said they have a nonprofit."

"A nonprofit at the factory?" Arnav schooled his expression into casual curiosity.

"It's nearby."

"I know of slums and a *chawl* or two in that locality. It isn't safe. And not wheelchair friendly."

"Nowhere is safe, Avi. And most places are not wheelchair friendly."

There was no arguing with her when she was like this. The only course was to distract her.

"Let's talk about it later." He kissed her, slow and soft, and the air between them grew charged.

"Take a bath first," he murmured into her ear. "Let's get you undressed."

Over the last two years, the words *Let's get you undressed* had turned mundane, medical. Today, though, with the wind singing through the panes, his lack of sleep and worry for her, and the way she kissed him back, the words turned into something else, and the longing of years past came over Arnav as he kissed her. How young they'd been, how clueless. He loved the way she mapped his shoulders and back with searching hands as he carried her to the shower, mouth glued to his. Sometimes, making love was not about feeding your body but your soul.

Arnav's phone rang in the bedroom. He let it ring out, but it started squealing again the next moment, and then again. "Give me a minute," he said, lowering her gently on the chair she used in the shower.

He smiled at her reflection. This was his Tara, bright eyes, lips a bee-stung, darker shade, a blush on her cheek. Arnav cleared his throat and rushed out to the phone.

"Yes, Desai."

He paused at Desai's words. Would he never receive any good update from this man?

"Why did it take so long to figure out two necklaces were missing from the safe?"

"He didn't notice, sir. And I missed them on the list from the trustees. The priest was tired, sir. He's not well."

"That's no excuse. We're all tired."

"Should we put him under arrest, sir?"

"No. We'll get more out of him by setting a watch. He can't run when he's on dialysis, can he?"

Arnav snatched a fresh uniform from the closet, and began slipping into it as he heard Desai out. He tried to think of the best way to keep things smooth till they found the sacred jewelry. His boss, Assistant Commissioner of Police, would know how to reassure the wealthy, easily offended temple trustees.

His phone flashed his boss's name as he clipped on his belt and badge. It appeared ACP Bapat wanted to talk to him, as well.

CHAPTER SIXTEEN

MUMBAI DRISHTIKON NEWS

Crime Beat

Gruesome murder footage: Chitra Varli alleges hacking of her social media

1:23 PM IST 16 July, Mumbai.

Purported details of a grisly murder have surfaced on the Instagram account of Bollywood actress and social media influencer Chitra Varli. The video was taken down minutes after it was published, but it has since been downloaded and put up on various sites.

Chitra Varli denies all involvement and has offered to cooperate with Mumbai Police, who will be interviewing her today.

The video was of poor quality, but it shows the body lying within temple premises. Based on the statues seen on the pillars, many have speculated that it could be the Kaali temple on Saint Theresa Road. The spine-chilling murder footage shows a man in his prime, castrated and lying spread out on temple steps amid a pool of blood and what look like red flowers and *sindoor*.

Social media has boiled into furor over this incident. The heinous and unspeakable act of violence has been met with widespread condemnation from all corners of civil society. As more details of the murder emerge, several celebrities and ministers have taken to social media platforms to express their outrage.

Hindu Rashtra Party opposition MLA, Tarun Sathe, said the incident needed to be investigated by the Central Bureau of Investigation and the culprit brought to justice immediately.

"I have a feeling this is the work of a certain 'peaceful community' whose depraved acts have been tolerated by Hindus for a long time. No more. If other communities and religions want to exist in India, they must stop desecrating Hindu places of worship," he said, while addressing journalists at his party office.

This is not the first brush with controversy for Chitra Varli. She has expressed her opinions on everything from the itinerary of the Prime Minister to the lack of national fervor in certain communities. Her fans are already on social media defending her innocence, but only a detailed investigation can verify if she was hacked as she claims, or the truth lies somewhere else.

CHAPTER SEVENTEEN

ARNAV

Arnav's uniform felt damp from catching spatters of rain despite the raincoat. The curtains were drawn in his boss's office, but from the outside, where it poured, came distant crashes of thunder like cymbals of doom.

Stocky Assistant Commissioner Bapat, with his flourishing mustache and thinning hair, spoke on the phone, having waved him into the room. He kept saying *yes, sir* at regular intervals, making Arnav guess it was the commissioner of police on the line. The top police boss of Mumbai.

Arnav took his time glancing around the room that smelled faintly of cleaning fluids and stale flowers. Bapat had garlanded a picture of Maharashtra's saffron-clad, dark-glasses-wearing maverick leader, but the marigold blooms had dried up. The picture hung at a prominent place on the wall—right above the shelf that showed off ACP Bapat's medals and pictures with various politicians, well-known businesspeople, and movie stars. Arnav might have exposed the nexus between all three and Mumbai's underworld, which had cost the previous commissioner of police his job—but police officers still prided themselves on their connections. That was where their power, and some of their money, came from.

In Mumbai Police, the number of years you spent on the job determined your position. Not the cases you'd solved, or the crimes you'd prevented. The force rewarded those successes with medals, but Arnav's rise to the position of senior inspector after a mere three years of working as an inspector was an anomaly. Arnav had made too much noise about a case that had hit the headlines, and the culprit had taken advantage of the deeply rooted corruption in Mumbai Police to have him transferred, with a promotion, expecting Arnav to stop investigating the case.

That hadn't worked then. Not much would keep Arnav quiet now.

Going by the way Bapat spoke on the phone and drummed his fingers on the table, the call wasn't going well. A part of Arnav wanted to excuse himself, but if the ACP had desired privacy, he wouldn't have waved Arnav in.

Arnav checked his phone: no messages from Desai. Ram Chandra Dome. What a terrifying coincidence: the man they'd connected with a gruesome murder had given Tara a locket for the well-being of their family.

"Good morning, sir," Arnav said once Bapat had finished his call.

"Morning, Rajput." Bapat cleared his throat. "That was the commissioner on the line. The temple trustees have been talking to him. Those two necklaces were the most expensive of the lot. About fifteen lakh each. That, on top of the murder."

"We have the pictures of the necklaces from the trustees, sir. Whoever has them won't be able to sell them in Mumbai. We've also done *nakabandi* of the roads heading out of the temple, and out of the city."

Mumbai Police usually set up checkpoints to detect contraband items—but inspecting vehicles via *nakabandi* wouldn't help if the murderer had taken the necklaces and hidden them someplace. The only way to locate them was to find the culprit. Arnav waited for his boss to point that out.

"Have you seen Chitra Varli's news this morning?" Bapat said.

This was strange—what did the stolen necklaces have to do with Chitra Varli?

"Chitra Varli, sir?"

Arnav's family had absorbed him this morning, and he hadn't performed his usual ritual checking of the Mumbai papers. Chitra must have hit the headlines again.

Chitra Varli was a faded Bollywood star who had reinvented herself as a top influencer with nearly a hundred million followers on her social media. She made it her business to show up in white or saffron clothes at religious events, ranted about the religious and political events of the day, and was seen as a contender in the upcoming state elections.

Arnav checked out her profile—social media provided better information than news portals these days. Clicking on her avatar brought up a notice.

"Her account is suspended."

"You need to keep up, Senior Inspector Rajput." Bapat's tone was a mixture of humor and jaded resignation as Arnav continued his internet search.

Chitra Varli's outraged face popped up on the front page of Arnav's favorite news portal. He read the bites about her posting a video of the body of a man castrated and murdered at a Kaali temple. The same temple Arnav had been at last night.

It had gone viral on other platforms, with countless tags for Mumbai Police. The footage had been removed, but with a few clicks Arnav ferreted out the link to an obscure site.

Through the shaky camerawork, he could make out the male body posed on the white marble temple steps. The river of blood at the juncture between the legs. The filleted throat and face. The hibiscus flowers. The bloodied floor.

"You were at the scene," Bapat said.

"Yes, sir."

"How did this footage leak? Did we not follow protocol?"

The crime scene came back to Arnav. The tearing rain, the knot of people gathered around the temple. The constables struggling with the flapping tarp. The ringtones on the constables' phones. The flashes from Surat Tambe's camera. Arnav replayed the video—did one of those men standing in a group near the temple, who had later crept into the pillared *mandapa* for shelter, capture the video? A constable? The new recruit who'd driven Arnav's jeep? Arnav replayed the video again. Something wasn't right.

"The regional TV channels have picked up the story. I don't think Mumbai Police can afford to be on national news one more time. And once again, all thanks to you. Speak to this Chitra Varli—find out if she's involved."

It wasn't a good look for Mumbai Police the last time, but the fault on that occasion had lain with the force. Now it could be down to Arnav's misstep. He needed a quiet moment to come up with an answer for his boss. Something caught at the edge of his consciousness.

"I'll speak with Chitra right away. Give me a minute, sir. I think I've got something."

His irate boss responded with a long-winded comment of his own, but Arnav paid him no mind and replayed the video one more time.

The phone camera hovered close to the body. The footage came from a cheaper model—it was unable to zoom in as much as some of the more expensive brands on the market. Whoever took the video had moved within the crime scene, crossed the yellow tape. That wasn't possible, or at least not easy, because Arnav had seen Desai post two constables to guard the scene. The cameraman had either entered the scene before the tape was put in place, or sneaked in after Arnav left.

Arnav clicked off the video and examined the crime scene photos on his own phone. Quick-scrolling through, he found what had snagged his attention. The bloodied boot prints in the photos, but not in the video. Mr. Tambe had taken close-ups and measurements of those prints.

"Sir, this video was taken before we reached the scene." Arnav interrupted whatever ACP Bapat had been saying, and passed his phone with the pictures to his boss, pointing to the prints.

"Whose boot prints are these?"

"We haven't matched them yet, sir, but the body had no shoes on, and this doesn't match any police boot prints. Forensics are examining them now. They could belong to the killer if he wasn't being careful."

"You're saying the suspect took this video?"

"It's possible, sir."

"What would they have to gain from it?" Bapat said. "They must know that the video could point us to them. And why would Chitra Varli post it on her account?"

The motive was a big question. Most regular killers tried to hide dead bodies. This one had made a display of it, made sure that it was not merely found, but also talked about. Chitra Varli's involvement made it even more puzzling, because the victim's physique ruled out a lone woman committing the assault.

"I'll request video forensics support right away, sir."

"The cybercrime division will collaborate on this. I'll call them."

"I appreciate that, sir. We'll need all the support."

"Have you been able to identify the body?"

The constables on his team had combed through the missing person files, trying to find a match.

"Not so far, sir."

"If Chitra Varli is involved, I want you to handle it with kid gloves. Don't make any decisions without asking me first."

"Right, sir."

"With her millions of followers, she's bad news and we don't want more of that. Make this case the priority at your station, Rajput. Pull men from other teams if you have to. I want the killer nabbed and the necklaces found within the week."

On the way out, Arnav called one of his head constables and asked him to keep a watch on Chitra Varli's building on Saint Cyril Road, and speak to the security guards. A Mumbai Police identity badge worked wonders in these cases, Arnav found. Use intelligence, but if fear works, don't hesitate to use that as well.

Next, he called his Crime Branch computer forensics contact. Whoever had uploaded the video wanted the body found and the case discussed, but they had also given him ammunition: a possible geo-location of the video. Thanks to its experience tracking terrorists, Mumbai Police had a few tricks up its sleeve.

CHAPTER EIGHTEEN

ARNAV

About to enter the Bandra Police Station, Arnav leaned back in his car, plagued by thoughts of his wife. He hadn't even had the time to say a proper goodbye after their first heated kiss in months.

He'd tried to get Tara to go out and take in the air for so long, but now, of all places, she wanted to go visit that hair factory. He hadn't said no outright. The easiest way to make her do something was to tell her she couldn't.

On his car dashboard, his phone buzzed with a message from one of his inspectors, asking his permission for a raid, snapping him back to office mode. He glanced through it, tapped out a reply, and considered the best way to get a handle on the Kaali temple case.

Almost sixteen hours since he'd spoken to Ali. Time for an update. Ali picked up his call on the first ring.

"*Ji, saab*, I was about to call you."

The standard Ali greeting. The man was good at his job, but he couldn't forever be on the verge of calling when Arnav dialed him. Arnav grimaced, and barked out a simple command.

"Tell me."

"I've not seen Iqbal Asif, *saab*, but I saw *Bhai*."

"You met him?" Ali's *Bhai* was Rasool Mohsin.

"No, *saab*, I can't meet him unless he specially asks to see me. I was on a watch when I spotted him this morning with Tarun Sathe."

Tarun Sathe. Used to be something of a goon himself before he joined politics. He'd risen to power as a member of State Assembly purely by dint of inflaming the Hindu community. Why would he meet a Muslim don?

"Are you sure?"

"*Ji, saab. Bhai* was wearing glasses, and he has a beard now. No one recognized him, but I did. I've known him for years."

This was interesting.

"How long did they stay?"

"About ten minutes, but they shook hands at the end."

This could bode no good, even though it made Arnav smile in wry recognition of Mumbai's spirit—it didn't matter that one man was a Muslim don, and the other a Hindu politician. They must have shaken hands on something that was a win for them both. Mumbai was driven by one thing alone—ambition.

"Did any of them spot you?"

"No, *saab*. But I'll keep an eye."

"And Iqbal Asif?"

"No sign of him, sir."

In a few brisk words, Arnav made it clear to Ali that the reward for any info on Iqbal would be not insignificant, and cut the call. His phone pinged with a message from Desai. They were bringing in the tantric, Ram Chandra Dome.

From his vantage point, Arnav watched as a pair of Desai's sub-inspectors escorted the tantric into the Bandra Police Station. He'd formed an image of tantrics based on glimpses in old Indian horror movies his mother used to watch long ago. Far from the flowing robes, the eyes lined with kohl, a large smear of ash on the forehead, bare arms wrapped in beads, Ram Chandra Dome sported a faded blue shirt and gray pants.

In his thick glasses and scuffed shoes, he resembled an overworked accountant who might volunteer polite answers to financial queries in a drab monotone. Perhaps modern tantrics were different. Ram Chandra walked in, head held high. They had called him in for a chat, but chats with Mumbai Police, famously, could go sideways fast. The tantric's calm impressed Arnav.

For once, Inspector Desai seemed fired up—he marched with intent as he led his team into the stone-and-wood police station that was once an old bungalow, like he was late for an appointment. Different from his familiar stance: let his subordinates do the work, take all the credit if they were successful, none of the blame if they failed.

Arnav lost sight of the procession as they entered the corridor, but he noticed policemen about their business pause on the stairs leading up to his second-floor office. They gawked at the scene below: Desai's team must have escorted the tantric into the interrogation rooms on the ground floor.

This was too important to let Desai handle on his own. Arnav scanned the other messages Desai had sent him.

He calls himself Sri Sarvagya—his professional name.

Sri Sarvagya. Literally, the respected all-knower. Arnav smiled. God-men from all religions tended to give themselves fancy catchphrase names. He scrolled down to the next message from Desai.

Low-caste crook, sir. CCTV footage shows him near the crossing, at time of murder, on a bicycle.

Arnav was about to exit his vehicle when his phone rang again. It was the constable sent to Chitra Varli's building. The security guards had told him that the influencer had organized a video shoot at her apartment.

Arnav tuned out the traffic noises around him and weighed his options. Saint Cyril Road was near his station. Had it not been pouring buckets, he could have walked there. In his car it would take him less than ten minutes. It was best to confront Chitra Varli with people at her place. She would be wary of creating a scene, and unable to avoid questions.

The Bandra Police Station was the first port of call to most celebrities, simply because a majority of Bollywood stars and their families lived in the prime sea-facing locations in Bandra. They stepped in to make complaints, but none liked to be summoned for a case—if Chitra Varli objected to him showing up at her apartment, he would invite her over to the station. He doubted she'd like that.

Arnav fired off a message to Desai. Talk to Ram Chandra, but take it easy. I'll be there soon.

CHAPTER NINETEEN

It's not been easy to change the way I see the world. For so long, I've been used to accepting things as they are, and being grateful I get to have what I do.

The last few months, I've had to make changes. I watch Bhai. *I think of my child. And I feel a certain satisfaction. Thrill, almost. They will pay, each one of those people.*

I watch as he sharpens the knife, and tell him he shouldn't. A blunt knife for maximum pain. They deserve it.

We must choose, Bhai *says. Pain or success? You want to hurt the man, or you want to kill him and get away with it?*

The latter, I say. Definitely.

We must get away with it. We have to. Bhai *can't afford one more mistake, nor can I.*

CHAPTER TWENTY

ARNAV

The lift deposited Arnav on the sixth floor of Chitra Varli's apartment building with a soft plink. Her social media clearly didn't make her enough to afford the top floor in one of Mumbai's most exorbitant rentals.

Once Arnav rang the doorbell, Chitra Varli's lanky, bald secretary invited him in after verifying his ID, and showed him into a tasteful, sparsely furnished living room. As soon as the secretary left him alone, Arnav used his phone to take quick snapshots of all the framed pictures along one wall and a high mantelpiece. Long years of dealing with criminals had taught him habits like these—they wouldn't pass a sniff test, but they helped him dig deeper into the lives of those he visited during an investigation. Photos clicked, he moved to the window, which showed a tree in the parking lot. Rain streaking down the windowpane blurred its outlines.

Arnav's phone beeped with an update from the team of paid informers watching the Kaali temple priest. The priest had stayed home, other than to take care of his work at the temple, and hadn't stirred about. He must know his nephew had been taken to the police station.

As Arnav typed a response, Chitra sauntered in, straight backed, dolled up, ponytail swinging, ready to do battle. Tall and broad in a pair of faded jeans and T-shirt, she looked every inch the actress who had recently snagged a supporting role as an aging boxer.

"I knew one of you would show up again." She shook his hand when he introduced himself, and sank into a chair, waving him into another. Her citrus perfume hung heavy in the air. He refused her offer of tea and dived right in. His research on her told him she thrived on controversy and unpredictability and had revived a flailing Bollywood career by participating in a reality show. He couldn't bring himself to like this woman, but he admired her grit.

"How did the video land in your account? It went out to about a hundred million followers."

"Like I said in my interview this morning, I have no idea. You saw my secretary just now—he works with a social media manager, my team of stylists, and makeup artists. That's how we keep that account going."

"So we can interview all your staff?"

"Be my guest. They'll say the same thing. We reported the breach before they suspended my account."

He could verify this with the social media company. The staff interviews could help trace the video's origins. So far, she'd cooperated with the investigation.

"What security measures do you take? Who has access to the account?"

"I have it here on my phone, of course, as does my social media manager."

"Have you spoken to your manager?"

"She swears she didn't post it. She had to go throw up after she watched it the first time, poor thing. She's been protected all her life—doesn't know what it takes for a woman to survive in a man's world."

"You've been vocal about stronger punishments for crimes against women."

A good cause, but Chitra thrived on sound bites, overlooking the fact that the strictest of punishments meant nothing unless enforced.

"I'm sure you agree." Chitra leaned forward.

"You've often recommended chemical castration as a punishment for rapists."

Arnav recalled some of her videos saying those words, her fists clinched, gaze feral.

"And you don't see that they deserve it?" Her eyes flared in anger, and she paused. "Wait, you don't think I castrated this man, and posted the footage? If a man deserved it, yes, I'd have loved to. I'm not squeamish, let me tell you that right away."

"Where were you yesterday afternoon?"

"Here, in my apartment."

"Your secretary or the staff can verify that?"

"I was home alone, but sure, ask them." She stood up. "Listen, I'm the victim here. Losing that account could cause me losses you can't even imagine."

"Isn't your account insured?" Arnav said. His research said that huge influencers had begun to get their "digital assets" insured. She would not only recover her account but also get a decent daily payout till it was.

"That's private financial information. Unless you're arresting me, I would let you get on with your day."

"Irrespective of who that victim was and what he'd done, he didn't deserve to be mutilated and killed."

"How would you know who deserves what, Senior Inspector Rajput?" She raised her penciled eyebrows. "Maybe he deserved it."

At the door that led toward the inner rooms, she turned. "Most men do, in my opinion."

A swish of her ponytail and she was gone, leaving only traces of her perfume behind. The secretary materialized at Arnav's elbow, and followed him to the main door.

Once outside, Arnav stared at the two water-filled brass bowls flanking the door. He hadn't seen them on the way in. Dozens of scarlet hibiscuses floated in the water, their long, delicate stamens waving in the breeze. Each bowl sat on a drawing in red and white, using chalk and vermilion: two concentric circles, with a triangle within, pointed downward.

CHAPTER TWENTY-ONE

MUMBAI DRISHTIKON NEWS

Crime Beat

Mumbai Police raids vice dens for escaped don Rasool Mohsin

5:45 PM IST 16 July, TMD.

A police team conducted raids at "several target venues" to track down Rasool Mohsin, who is reported to have returned to Mumbai after police in Thailand made it difficult for him to stay in the country, sources said. Mumbai police suspect his involvement in various cases of extortion, money laundering, and smuggling of drugs.

For those who haven't been following this don's journey, he was involved in several shoot-outs two years ago, and ran away from Indian shores to escape jail time. He had taken along his girlfriend, who used to be a bar girl at the Blue Bar.

"His possible location is in South Mumbai and police teams are actively searching for him. We will arrest the accused at the earliest," a police source said, not revealing further details.

CHAPTER TWENTY-TWO

ARNAV

Rain poured in torrents, rendering Arnav's gear and umbrella ineffective while he got into and out of his car from Chitra Varli's apartment. By the time he entered his office, Arnav was soaked through.

Once he'd changed into a dry pair of jeans, and a dark T-shirt, Arnav picked up his phone, ready to rush to the interrogation of Ram Chandra Dome. Before he could leave, Kamble knocked and entered.

"I thought I heard you come in, sir." The heavyset Kamble placed a tray bearing a steaming cup of *cutting chai* and a heap of fluffy *bun muska* laced with cream and butter on a plate, his round face wreathed in smiles. "With this weather, black tea just wouldn't do."

Cutting chai, literally, half a cup of strong milk tea, that came in its customary small glass, half-full, its spicy fragrance filling the air, was Mumbai's favorite street beverage.

"Very tempting, Kamble, but I need to go out right away."

The elderly constable appeared crestfallen. "Right, sir, sorry. I thought you should eat something first."

It was way past lunchtime, and Arnav had forgotten about meals.

He might be unpopular for his history of reporting on fellow officers, but the constables at his station lived to make his life easier. Besides, Kamble's offers of tea usually came with a reliable report on the activities around his office. Arnav didn't want to upset this man who meant well and often came in handy during investigations.

"Thank you, Kamble." He picked a soft bread to please the elderly constable.

"You're heading to the tantric, sir?"

"Why do you ask?"

"I don't think it's going well, sir. The man was on the CCTV, but his clothes and nails are clean. He could have hidden his bloodied clothes somewhere, so there is that, of course."

A sip of the hot, spiced tea revived Arnav. "What's your feeling about the man?"

"So normal, and polite. That is scary for a tantric, sir. You hear all kinds of stories—the hexes they can put on people, and their mad disciples."

"He has an alibi?"

"Not a good one, sir. He rode his bicycle back home, where he ate dinner alone."

"Did he speak about the victim?"

"The victim is cut up bad enough that not his mother nor wife would recognize him, sir. This Sri Sarvagya didn't even flinch at the photographs. Tough little tantric he is."

Arnav needed to get back to work now. He said his thanks to Kamble for the excellent *cutting chai*.

"I'll tell the tea seller, sir. He'll be happy to hear that. I'll get him to collect his glasses."

Kamble opened the door and beckoned, and a young man with hair styled and gelled up in a high quiff came in and picked up the tray.

"This is Govind, sir."

"Big fan of your work, *saab*," Govind said as Arnav walked around his table, ready to step out. "You look like you can be in the movies."

"That's not going to earn you any concessions if your tea stall sits on the pavement without a permit." Arnav held back a smile. It was impossible not to grin at Govind's expression.

"Don't worry about it." Kamble patted the man on the back. "*Saab* likes your *cutting chai*, and your father has renewed the permit for your stall."

While Govind cleared the tea things, Desai entered after a knock, and approached Arnav's table.

"Good afternoon, sir."

Arnav returned the greeting and acknowledged another of the man's ironic salutes with a nod. Desai's smug grin didn't bode well for the tantric. Arnav asked for a status update.

Govind left, but Constable Kamble lingered in the room, arranging files in the sideboard. His gossip traveled both ways, and he knew Arnav would ask him to leave if required.

"I think he did it, sir. He has no alibi, and his phone's internet search history shows he's researched items required in sacrifices to the goddess Kaali. He was caught on CCTV not far from the crime scene. He has an average build, but could easily have overpowered the victim in an unexpected attack."

"What about Iqbal Asif? We haven't spoken to him yet, nor do we know if he has an alibi. Besides, we need to wait for forensic evidence. We don't have anything specific that ties Ram Chandra Dome to the scene. Did you check his shoes?"

"We haven't searched his home, sir, but we can do that now that we have probable cause. He's involved in all kinds of nefarious cult activities, I'm sure. These Achoot people, they don't change because they're wearing Western clothes. He shouldn't have been inside the temple in the first place. He may have hidden those boots. We'll find them."

Arnav watched the ashen look on Kamble's face as he lowered his head and crept out of the room, shutting the door quietly behind him. Kamble belonged to a Scheduled Caste. *Neechi jaat.* An Achoot, according to Desai.

Arnav recalled his chat with Tara, and her outrage at how the lower castes were treated. Kamble's caste was obvious from his surname, now that Arnav thought about it. He hadn't made the connection earlier. He raised his voice above the drumming of the rain outside the window.

"Let's not speak about caste here, Desai. Mumbai Police is a secular organization."

Desai's smug expression disappeared.

"I'm sorry, sir, but I wish that were true. These Scheduled Caste fellows have reservations in the entrance exams, and once in the force, they get quicker promotions than those in the open category. You treat them equal, let Kamble bring you tea, but they will only take advantage of your generosity."

Tara was right about privilege protecting Arnav from questions of caste. It had taken him all this while to understand that someone like Desai wouldn't drink tea if it were touched by Constable Kamble.

"We won't make an arrest unless we have forensic evidence linking Ram Chandra Dome to the murder. Any updates on the priest?"

"He hasn't tried anything funny. He takes care of the worship at three other temples. Nothing has gone missing from any of those."

"He didn't admit that Ram Chandra Dome was his nephew?"

"He has, but the tantric doesn't admit to a connection."

"What have you learned so far from him?"

"He hasn't said anything useful so far, sir, but I've got him on remand for the next seventy-two hours. If I can't find evidence linking him within that time period, we can let him go. We've picked up samples from his hairbrush and sent it to Forensics."

Arnav could reverse the remand, but Desai had followed procedure, and it was a matter of opinion now, not protocol.

"You should have consulted me before getting him on remand, Desai. Make sure you do that next time. Consider this a warning."

CHAPTER TWENTY-THREE

—

Sita

Sita bit back a smile at Inspector Desai's attempts to enter the muddy premises of Ram Chandra Dome's rooms on stealth mode. Given the width of his shoulders and his caveman-like steps, he caused a racket by stumbling on the old utensils, brooms, and tattered shoes piled in the courtyard of the ground-floor rooms the tantric occupied. Rain fell in sheets, blurring out the shabby apartments all around.

Her boss had called her this morning, and asked her to partner with Desai on the search for a suspect. The suspect's name had given her pause.

"Ram Chandra Dome, sir?"

Ram Chandra was a familiar name, from her husband's circles. He had visited their home a few times. He was an accountant with the political party where Raghav worked as a fundraiser. The two men used to joke about having the same name. Both Raghav and Ram Chandra were names of the same Hindu avatar, Lord Ram.

"Yes, do you know him?"

"Could you send me a picture of the suspect, sir?"

Her phone beeped with a message, and she saw the man's picture. "Yes, that's him, sir."

Why was Raghav's friend involved in a murder investigation? Was his political party mixed up in illegal activities?

"How do you know him?" Her boss's deep voice had sounded curious over the phone.

She told him.

"He's a political leader?"

"Of a sort, sir. He leads the meetings for the Ram Rajya Party. All about the power and protection of lower castes. Raghav jokes that the party is theirs—well—because of their names, sir."

Ram rajya, literally, the kingdom of Lord Ram, a mythical time and place that saw no injustice or suffering thanks to their ruler.

"They will be contesting in the upcoming elections?"

"They do have followers, sir. He represents the feelings of many from the Scheduled Caste, but I doubt they have the funds to contest an election. From what I know, Ram Chandra doesn't come from money."

That lack of money was evident where she stood, an old *chawl* about to collapse, no better than the one where Neeti lived with her family. Inspector Desai looked uncomfortable, and totally out of place. The sort who did better with giving orders than following them—he didn't get that they should comb the area beginning at one end and move to the other side in careful steps.

He lumbered on till she stopped his beefy forearm with a gesture, and asked his permission to finish the search.

"I'm smaller, sir," she said. "It will be easier for me to navigate the corners."

It was the only way at the workplace: to get a man to listen, a woman must shrink herself to fit his idea of her. He said yes, of course, and let her get on with it. This bullnecked man outranked her because of the number of his years in the force and little else.

Sita unlocked the main door and stepped in.

Must and gloom greeted her, like a solid presence. Ram Chandra Dome didn't seem to need light. The night lamp contained the only bulb in the room. Its blue light quailed in the darkness.

Sita felt strange, riffling through his things. She had no clue what Ram Chandra and Raghav did together. With his disability, Raghav had a hard time holding down a proper job, and flared in anger when asked any questions. Besides, she never felt curious—content to have him out of her way as she focused on her office. The reason she was here in the first place: to do a job.

Sita flicked on her flashlight, slipped her gloves on, and shoved aside the sheets on the bed. Stained mattress and pillow. Beside the bed, unwashed dishes with leftover food that had gathered fungus. Sita held her breath against the reek of spoiled food.

In the lone cupboard, shabby clothes. Sita's flashlight shone on framed pictures of Ma Kaali. Different sizes of boxes. She opened them to find various powders: ashes, vermilion, sandalwood. Incense. Dried flowers: hibiscus and cape jasmine. A bottle of water, which Sita assumed must be the holy water of the river Ganges. Another with a yellowish liquid—cow piss, possibly. The urine of sacred cows was considered purifying. Metal bowls and glasses. All the items he used for worship. A knife, with dried blood.

That blood could be human. They might find the victim's missing genitals somewhere on the premises. Sita turned toward the door when the beam of her light caught a pair of boots. She picked them up with her gloved hands. Dried blood at the bottom.

She'd seen the crime scene photos. The tantric could be the suspect they were looking for.

CHAPTER TWENTY-FOUR
SITA

The morning's assignment in Versova to visit the hair factory pleased Sita Naik. Maybe Ma Kaali was the right deity to worship—within a day of praying to this goddess, Sita was back working for Arnav Singh Rajput, her previous boss. Ram Chandra the tantric was right about the deity's prowess, but what else was he right about? Inspector Desai had interrogated him, and he'd been retained on remand, pending further evidence.

Sita had considered talking to her husband about it, ask him about his friend, but her boss had cautioned her against it: *This is a murder investigation, Naik. Don't speak to Raghav for now.*

Visiting the Rajput household wasn't her favorite activity, and she was now doing it three times in three days. Yesterday, she'd popped by for a few minutes, refusing to stay for dinner.

She'd known that Tara would want to speak about Neeti.

She'd heard the girl lose it with her mother, complain about being harassed by men in the neighborhood. Sita had experience with that from when she was a teen, less than ten years ago.

"I'll check on her, don't worry," she'd assured Tara.

"Arnav shouldn't know. Not unless he has to. Neeti is like his daughter, especially after her father died."

Sita had nodded, keeping her face expressionless.

Tara's husband had asked Sita to accompany his wife, but to actually nose around the hair factory under that pretext. If Rasool was a silent partner at the Remy Virgin Hair Factory, he or his men would show up there, sooner or later. She was to pick Tara up from home, and hang out at the factory, watching, and take pictures whenever possible.

Sita hummed to herself as she sat in the rear seat of the jeep. Soon, Tara Rajput would join her there. Sita tamped down the thought before it surfaced—yes, Tara had the life Sita would have liked for herself, but Tara also faced challenges. More challenges than most.

The jeep dropped her at the lobby of the Bandra apartment complex, and she took the lift to the Rajputs' door. She knocked, waited, and receiving no answer, entered to find Pia crying at the dining table. She flounced out the minute Sita entered.

Sita heard anxious voices from inside. Her boss and his wife.

"Let's postpone this visit to another day, Tara."

"I promised *Vaeeni* I'd be there today. The children at the nonprofit will be waiting."

"Your daughter is upset."

"I know she is. I'm upset, too." Tara lowered her voice, but there was no softening of her resolve. "But she won't give up. Not on my watch. She's scared of anything to do with hair. That has to stop."

"You can't just make her stop being afraid. And I'm her parent, too."

"Where were you when she was born? Through all her illnesses? When they took her?"

Sita was about to leave when her boss stormed out of his bedroom. An awkward pause later, she wished him good morning.

"Good morning, Naik. The driver will bring Tara and Pia. You can meet them there."

"Sure, sir," she said. "I'll wait nearby."

She could use the time to take the temperature of the neighborhood, find out what she could about the reason behind Neeti's complaints. If Rasool's men ran the hair factory from behind the scenes, that would embolden the louts in its neighborhood.

CHAPTER TWENTY-FIVE

ARNAV

Arnav paced the lobby of the government hospital, waiting for Desai, calling upon his reserves of calm. After a night of ceaseless downpour, rainwater flowed high in the gutters, which couldn't drain the road fast enough. Soon cars would stall in the driveway, coughing and spluttering as they tried to start again.

He'd skipped breakfast and driven to the hospital as soon as he got the call from Tambe about Desai. He turned at the sound of rushed footsteps, expecting Desai, but it was the forensic officer striding along, almost at a run, his white hair in disarray.

"I managed to stop the mortuary van," he huffed.

"We haven't identified the victim yet," Arnav said, "and it's been less than two days."

"It was strange. Desai asked the morgue attendant to arrange a handover of the body for disposal. All without asking me. That, too, with a case that's already in the papers."

It wasn't just in the papers. The video of the dead body had gone viral in the worst possible way, as Arnav's boss Bapat had feared. Some were calling it Hinduism gone mad. Men pointed at women's rights activists, challenging them to deny that violence against men was a reality in India. Twenty-four-hour TV channels featured panels with shouting matches between hurriedly rustled-up "experts" and the usual suspects, analyzing the publicly available facts of the case, some conjectures, and several downright lies. The dead body was the result of gang vendetta, caste politics, or personal vengeance, depending on who you asked.

"What time did Desai come in?" Arnav said.

"Early. Before I reported for work. He claimed that the culprit was under arrest, so he would take the body off our hands."

"Why would he do that?"

Mumbai had struggled with a shortage of morgues for years, it was true. Less than a dozen morgues at government hospitals coped with an intake of twenty bodies each or more per day. The storage facilities could barely cope. The morgues often stored bodies at a higher temperature than that required for complete preservation. Despite this, police officers tried not to get involved with unclaimed bodies, because the funeral arrangements fell to them, and sometimes they had to pay out of their own pockets. Desai's actions were puzzling—no police officer would release a body for its final rites so soon.

"Maybe because he didn't want me to challenge him? I sent both of you my conclusions from the case after a call from your boss."

"Bapat sir called you?" Arnav said.

This wasn't great news. The assistant commissioner had spoken to the Forensics in-charge, but not to Arnav, the senior inspector. Arnav headed the police station. The buck ought to stop with him.

"Come on, don't act all innocent now. You asked him to rush me."

"I did not," Arnav said. "You sent me your conclusions?" Arnav whipped out his phone. "On my email?"

"I don't believe in that new age claptrap. I sent printouts. Two copies in one envelope: one for you, and another for Desai's records. It was handed over to Desai's office."

Arnav hadn't seen it. Two possible explanations—Desai received it and didn't bother to send Arnav his copy. Or he sent it and it was misplaced. Arnav suspected it was the former.

"Could you share the conclusions now?" Arnav said.

"I took some pictures—they are in my office, if you'd like to follow me."

Morgues were seldom pleasant places to visit, but this particular one was worse than most. Dead bodies from fourteen police stations ended up here, most of them unidentified, and some visually unidentifiable. The unrelenting rain of the past week had encouraged rot and fungus everywhere, and this place filled with corpses was no exception.

The first thing that hit you was the smell. The entire corridor was thick with the miasma of rotting cabbages. Arnav followed Tambe down the corridor and into his office, a bare room cut off from the autopsy area with a flimsy partition. Its only furnishings were a shaky table, three plastic chairs, and a steel cabinet with chipped paint. Cobwebs hung from the corners.

"We all know how it is." Tambe swept his hand about his office. "I barely have enough cotton or gloves, or disinfectant, and I buy my own equipment most of the time. I must be a ghoul to be able to take it."

Arnav disagreed. Tambe and his white beard looked too pristine for this place.

"I appreciate your efforts. You're one of our best."

Praise was the only currency Arnav had to offer for Tambe to hurry up the investigation, and in this case it wasn't undeserved.

Tambe slapped a few snapshots on the table: the pubic bone surfaces.

"Based on the condition of his bones"—Tambe pointed to one of the photos—"this man was between twenty-five and thirty years old. He's had no operations from what I could tell."

Arnav nodded, indicating he'd understood.

"I've taken the victim's fingerprints and dental impressions. The results are yet to come in—in case they match fingerprints from our database, we can then check his dental records, if any. I also took footprints, just to be sure."

Arnav nodded. Dental records were not universally available in India. Many people visited unlicensed dentists, and many dentists didn't follow any record maintenance protocols.

"You've already sent the prints for analysis?"

"Yes. To the Kalina forensics lab. I wanted them in the system given how high profile the case is, with the suspect in remand."

Kalina was the main lab, but they took a while to release results.

"The blood samples from the crime scene?"

"There *were* two different types of blood. One was not the victim's, so it could be the attacker. I had enough for a DNA profile, so I've sent that to Kalina, along with the viscera. Desai told me there was no need, but you know me. I don't listen."

"What about the time of death?"

"You were right. It was not long before we were on the scene. Between four p.m. and six p.m."

"The 100 call came in at five forty-five p.m. And you're sure the prints can be matched to the boots in question? And the blood on the knife found at Dome's place?"

The evening before, Sita had discovered the bloodied boots in the suspect's home.

"I've sent the knife to Kalina as well. Desai's men brought in the boots last night. We don't have enough daylight yet, but I can get you my conclusions in a while."

"Daylight? What about indoor lighting?"

"I try to work during the day because the lights are not strong enough. There are no funds, they tell me. I pooled in cash the other day so the morgue workers and attendants could buy a geyser, and take baths in hot water before leaving the premises. They complain that stray dogs follow them because their skin and clothes reek of this place. I live nearby, so it's easier for me."

Arnav didn't have a response to this. He was saved from commenting by a message from Desai, who'd arrived at the hospital gate. Arnav took his leave, his heart heavy with the burden of people like Tambe and his staff, forced to take health risks and suffer avoidable mental anguish in a government hospital.

Sheltering from the rain, Desai leaned against a pillar in the lobby, checking his phone. He straightened when he saw Arnav, and cut another of his salutes. "Good morning, sir."

"Why was the body taken over for cremation?" Arnav saw no point in beating about the bush.

"Sir . . ." Desai didn't meet his eyes. Arnav allowed the silence to linger between them, a dry island amid the hubbub of the deafening rain, a thousand footfalls where they stood, patients limping in, sobbing women being led out on the arms of their relatives, the anxiety and grief of relatives milling in and out of the dilapidated government hospital.

"I don't see a single reason," Arnav said, "why the investigator of a high-profile case that began two days ago would release an unidentified victim's body for cremation."

"We've already made the arrest, sir."

"No, you have him on remand. We increased its duration to get a search warrant for his place of residence."

"Yes, sir"—Desai stood straighter—"and we recovered evidence. The bloodied boots. There was vermilion at his place, and also stale hibiscus."

"We're yet to confirm that the boots are a match to the prints found at the crime scene—I spoke to Tambe just now. And half the Bengali households in India use vermilion and hibiscus flowers. My wife has them in her *puja* room."

"I didn't mean to . . ."

"Do you have a point that makes sense, or is pertinent to the case?"

"Sir, I thought it was best to release the body after we found the killer."

"I see. Did you instruct them to retain the relevant evidence? The viscera and blood samples?"

"Mr. Tambe is too obsessed with procedure." Desai made a face, his nose curling up in disdain.

"He should be, as should you. Protocols and procedures serve a purpose. If you don't get hold of supportive evidence, how long will you be able to detain the suspect? When the victim's identity is discovered, isn't it a priority to hand over the body to his relatives? As per procedure, it should have been kept for at least seventy-two hours."

Desai lowered his eyes. Arnav let the man stew till he blurted out, "Sir, you don't understand. We must stand beside the brothers of our own caste."

"What? Has the victim been identified? How did you learn his caste?"

"Sir, I meant a Kshatriya and a Brahmin may not . . ."

Desai meant him and Arnav. This was getting ridiculous.

"You tried to get the body destroyed. You want to arrest the suspect based on flimsy evidence. The postmortem report that went to your desk contained a copy for me that never reached my office. What's going on?"

"Sir, I received only one copy of the report." Desai met his eyes squarely for the first time.

"So is Mr. Tambe lying, or am I?"

"I received the postmortem report in a large brown envelope— you know how Tambe is about printouts instead of emails. Since I'm the lead on the case, I came here to verify details and then let the body go. The morgue is crowded enough as it is. I wanted to make Tambe's job easier."

A bald-faced lie. Desai the upper-caste Brahmin could not stand Tambe. Arnav had overheard this said many times: Tambe belonged to a lower caste, and he dealt with dead bodies for a living. Nothing could be lower than that, in Desai's opinion. Some other factor lay at the root of this. Arnav needed to sniff it out.

"Did you ask Ram Chandra Dome again about his uncle?"

"He still maintains that he's not related to the priest, sir. I think we should arrest the priest as well. The two of them might have sold those missing necklaces, and conspired to kill the victim. The attention in the news will increase the traffic of devotees. We should get them to confess."

"We have no concrete forensic evidence yet."

"Sir, there's no concrete evidence against Iqbal Asif, either. He's a Muslim. How would he have known about tantric symbols and rituals?"

"We've not arrested Iqbal Asif yet. Sub-Inspector Sita Naik is following that line of enquiry."

"She will do everything she can to save that low-caste tantric, sir."

"Naik went on the raid with you to Ram Chandra Dome's place. She found the boots."

"That could be for show, sir."

"You're making caste-based aspersions on a colleague, and sabotaging the investigation you're supposed to lead. I've got no choice but to take you off the case for now."

"Sir, that tantric has been seen at midnight in cremation grounds, following ugly occult rituals. I have witnesses who have made statements where he said child sacrifice for Ma Kaali was a common practice a few decades ago. He is involved, sir, I'm telling you."

"The court rules based on evidence, not hearsay."

"We're sure to dig up more evidence as we interrogate him."

"Yes, but you won't be doing it. That's an order. Take some time off. If work stress has proven too much for you, I suggest you see a doctor. When you return, I need you to be at your best, or I'll make this an official warning."

"This is not fair, sir."

"You can protest as you like, Desai. Make a written complaint. I'd enjoy watching you explain yourself to ACP Bapat."

"The boot prints will match, sir. As will the blood samples."

"My order stands. I haven't yet suspended you or ordered an enquiry. Don't tempt me. Go rest up and return once you've got your head screwed on right."

Arnav watched Desai leave, his shoulders defiant. Oddly enough, it reminded him of another pair of shoulders. His daughter this morning, upset before the hair factory visit.

Tara had got her way, after all. He dialed her number.

CHAPTER TWENTY-SIX

SITA

Once in Versova next to the Remy Virgin Hair Factory, Sita zeroed in on the nearby bus stop, and pretended to wait for a ride while she noted the comings and goings into the *chawl* directly opposite.

A steady drizzle kept everyone moving. Men hurried under black, drab umbrellas, while a few women and children carried more colorful parasols.

If Sita were a man, no one would've spared her a second glance no matter what she wore and where she stood. As a woman, though, hanging about anywhere other than a bus stop in this neighborhood would attract attention. This, even though she wore a bland *salwar-kameez*, and had wrapped the *dupatta* like a scarf about her face, like a traditional, modest woman from North India.

Unlike the well-to-do homes on the other side of the road behind her, clothes hung on the long railings of the triple-storied *chawl*, like prayer flags of desperation. Each door stood open, because the residents would otherwise suffocate. A unit, or *kholi*, was made for two people but often crammed in ten or more. The railings hung frail, the wall paint eaten away by decades of damp and moss, the only cheery aspect the noise of children playing in the mud. The stink of the three common toilets, which served hundreds of people, wafted up.

Sita had dropped *Vaeeni* here late at night, but daylight showed the true plight of the residents. She herself lived in a *chawl*, but her *kholi* featured a private bathroom that she shared only with her husband and mother-in-law. It was palatial in comparison to this building.

A tall, fair man strolled by and called out a lewd suggestion at her. At any other place, this would have earned the man a sound thrashing and a night at the Versova station lockup, but Sita was here to watch, not act. She let him pass, but made a note of his vehicle registration number when he got into a car parked nearby. If he was ever reported to her station, she would know who to believe.

"Sita Naik?" A male voice made her turn, her hackles raised, but she took a breath when she saw it was Constable Kamble in an ill-fitting shirt and trousers. He looked shabbier than when in uniform. They had worked together at some point at a different station, and he was not as annoying about her being an ex-policeman's wife as most of her colleagues, but he was the last person she wanted to see. A gossip. Within minutes, everyone at Bandra station would know where he had met her.

"How are you?" she said.

"You're here—are you on the job?"

Just like that, because he was an older man, he thought he could ask questions of her even though she outranked him.

"Why are you here?" She stood tall, changing her posture to Sub-Inspector Sita Naik. "Are you on a break?"

Constable Kamble shrank. "I'm on night duty today. Running an errand for the wife. She wanted something picked up from a shop around here."

"I see. I don't want to keep you then." Sita checked her phone. "Your wife must expect you at home soon, sending you out in such gloomy weather."

Kamble nodded and scurried across the road. As she followed his progress, she noticed something curious at the end of the alleyway opposite.

A battered black Hyundai Santro came to a stop at the back gate of the Remy Virgin Hair Factory. Two men slid out of the back seat and hurried in, while the car screeched off. They wore the rough clothes of the streets. Not laborers, because those wouldn't show up in a car, and clearly not management. Ruffians. Sita noticed a shop near the factory's back entrance. She headed that way, crossing the busy road, and from her small handbag, produced a folded shopping bag. She needed to get a closer look at the men when they came out.

CHAPTER TWENTY-SEVEN

TARA

Seated in her wheelchair beside Pia, Tara stared at the luxuriant wig on the mannequin, its tresses shiny, defiant, a sharp contrast to the figure's vacant expression.

The waiting room at the Remy Virgin Hair Factory smelled of incense and kerosene, a single window showing the bricked boundary wall. If Arnav and Sita were to be believed, this was where Rasool possibly hid his men and some of his less-than-savory activities.

Pia and Tara had navigated a narrow alley, and without the benefit of ramp access to the factory, been forced to use the dozen or so steps. The security guards, factory hands, and the driver of her car had hoisted Tara's wheelchair up to the lobby. This had left her embarrassed, furious with herself, and worried for her grim-faced daughter.

Tara saw in Pia's eyes a mixture of frustration and shame—for a mother who was not just wheelchair ridden, but with child when none of her friends' moms were. Also, terror. Pia was scared. Ever since her kidnapping, when her abductors had forcibly lopped off her long braid in order to send it to her parents as a warning, Pia had worn her hair short.

She reached out for Pia's hand, but her daughter flinched and jerked it away.

"You got your way, Ma. Must you hold my hand, too, now?"

"It's not like that. I want you to know I'm here for you. There's nothing to worry about."

"I'm not worried, okay?" Pia's lips trembled. "Nor am I scared. I'm not afraid of some stupid hair."

Tara wanted to check the factory for Rasool's doings, but she also wanted this to be the first of many visits for Pia, especially at the non-profit they would see later.

"If you come with me to the nonprofit, you'll see . . ."

"Yes, I know. Poor children who don't have enough. We used to be that way, though not anymore, and we mustn't take it for granted. Be grateful. Got it. Whatever."

"Pia."

Pia was about to mouth off again, but the door opened, and a woman of middle years ambled in. Tara adjusted her expression into a smile. The woman's hair was streaked with gray, her lips chapped, and her saree faded and wrinkled, but her smile, the exact replica of *Vaeeni's*, bore a huge welcome.

"I am Bina," the woman said, "Sujata's sister."

Sujata? Tara's moment of confusion cleared when she recalled *Vaeeni's* name. Sujata Shinde. She introduced herself, and Pia.

"Sujata said you might like to visit." Bina folded her hands, responding to their *namaste*. "Glad you came on a Sunday. We have less people at work, so I can give you the tour."

"Thank you for taking the time," Tara said, watching Bina smile at Pia.

"We usually receive client visits, foreigners who want to make sure we are all aboveboard. Hardly any local visitors. It is good to have you."

Bina beamed at Pia, who carefully arranged Tara's saree so it wouldn't get caught in the wheels. Bina held the door open, and Tara nodded her thanks as Pia pushed Tara's wheelchair into a long, poorly lit corridor.

She'd once led Pia into her kindergarten, then her school. Now Tara couldn't see her daughter's face, and her eye level was reduced to adult waists. Like a child. She wasn't yet used to this aspect of being out and about in a wheelchair, this automatic change of equation with strangers.

She placed a protective hand on her midsection. She'd merely stepped out of her home with her children. All in a day's work. She was among friends.

"I'll take you through the entire process." Bina cast a glance at Pia, who pushed the wheelchair. *Vaeeni* might have told her about Pia and her trauma with hair.

"Yes, please, it will be interesting, especially because we'll visit your nonprofit later," Tara said.

"Sure. Once you see the factory, you'll have a better idea of what we do at the nonprofit."

The corridor opened to a hall in the distance, but Bina opened the door to a room right next to them.

"This is where all the stock is received."

Inside the gloomy room, a portly man sat on a chair near the door, an open register on the table in front of him, where he made notes. He rose when they walked in. The room smelled of cheap shampoo and naphthalene. Gray-colored metal racks stood in neat rows, and on each shelf, packages of hair, some wrapped in paper, others in plastic, some simply bundled together, the hanks secured by rubber bands.

Tara felt a shiver crawl through her. So much hair. Each roll of hair was once a part of someone's body, their identity. Pia stiffened behind her. Tara reached over her shoulder to hold her daughter's cold hand. This time, Pia didn't resist.

"There's so much of it," Tara said to break the hush.

"Ours isn't a big operation. You should see some of the supply warehouses."

"Where does all this come from?" She waved toward the shelves.

"Mostly from temples—temple hair."

"Tirupati?"

Vaeeni's sister smiled. "Yes. People donate their hair to temples like the one at Tirupati, and the temples sell them to finance their budgets."

"Is it legal, to make people give their hair?" Pia said, a slight tremor to her voice.

"It is a tradition—no one forces them. People see it as their holy duty, the one thing they can give to their god. The temples collect them and hold open auctions. Mr. Amit Nimkar, our CEO, bids, too. You might see him on the way out."

"Who cuts the hair?" Pia said, her tone skeptical. "Don't the donors hate it when someone shaves off all their long hair?"

"People make wishes, Pia." Bina smiled as she closed the door and led them down the corridor toward the hall. "They promise God their hair, praying their wishes are fulfilled, and visit the temple to make good on that promise. There are temple barbers who have done this work for generations."

"So the hair in wigs is real?" Pia asked Bina.

Tara felt a glimmer of pride. This time, Pia's voice didn't shake. She glowed under Bina's attention.

"That depends on the price. The most expensive ones are made of real hair."

"How expensive?"

"Well, some of the hair we buy for Indian rupees we sell in dollars. Lots of US dollars. Some wigs and hair extensions cost thousands of US dollars."

"And the women give away their hair for free? Do they know how much it sells for?"

"Yes, for free. No, I don't think most of them do."

Tara let Pia ask more questions as they went from one table to another in the hall—each large Formica table a station—starting with women sorting through hair, and later, a courtyard where they soaked the hair in giant metal tubs overnight to wash away the impurities.

Two women washed by hand each hank of hair that slithered like dark, threatening snakes amid soap bubbles.

"I'll show you the drying of the hair at the end," Bina said. "That's upstairs."

She took them through the cycle of hair being sorted by hand using a hackle, an enormous wire brush fixed to a work bench like rows of shark teeth. Short hair fell to the ground as the woman held a bunch of long hair, combing it like it was still attached to a head, tying it together with red rubber bands, trimming off the ends to make it even. Someone came and swept up the short hair. *For a witch's brew.* Tara's mind flashed with a memory of her grandmother's tales. Her imagination ran riot as she watched Pia observe the process, loosening up even further under Bina's beaming regard.

As Pia chatted with a few of the women, Tara turned to Bina.

"Does Mr. Nimkar allow paid holidays?" Tara said. "This is hard work."

"Not all of it is Mr. Nimkar's decision. He has a partner who mostly stays away but has a big say in how things are run."

Was she speaking of Rasool Mohsin?

"Who is this partner?" Tara said.

"He lives outside the country, I've heard," Bina said. "His men come and go, supervise things."

"The women are all safe, though?"

This was important to Tara—in her previous life at the bar, safety was a common concern.

"Mostly, yes. But the men who come in—well, some are goons. You know, the *bhai* log. As with everywhere in this city."

Tara would have probed further, but Pia returned to them, a smile on her lips.

Pleading a need for rest, Tara asked Pia to go ahead with Bina, parking her wheelchair in a corner, and soon the women forgot about her and began gossiping and laughing among themselves, reminding Tara of her erstwhile friends when she worked as a bar dancer. Tara let her gaze wander, in search of the goons Bina had mentioned. If she spotted any men in the premises, she might try to talk to them. She wanted a message sent to Zoya, to tell her about the storm of allegations against her boyfriend—but how would she convince any of Rasool's men she was on their side?

Tara checked her watch. The factory might not have a wheelchair-friendly restroom. Pregnancy involved needing to pee often, an annoyance for a woman who could use a toilet. To Tara, it felt like an injustice. She must wrap up quickly and return home before her catheter alarm rang.

"Do you want me to call your daughter?" a male voice said, and when she turned, Tara was disoriented to find a woman in a saree walking up to her.

"Thank you, yes," Tara said as a memory clicked in place. "You came to our place to bless me."

This was a *kinnar* from the *shaadh* ceremony, her hair oiled and combed, delicate bangles twinkling on hard, manly, but perfectly hairless forearms.

"Yes," the *kinnar* agreed. "I can take you to them if you want. They have gone up to the roof."

Tara smiled back, not sure she wanted to be pushed into a lift by a stranger. People standing behind her where she couldn't see them made her nervous, bringing back thoughts of the jackal who had nearly obliterated her and her family two years ago.

Like Zoya said, though, she couldn't remain a timid little soul.

The *kinnar* noted her hesitation, and her smile faded. "I could ask one of them to take you instead?" She gestured toward the women. Most people shunned the *kinnar*, and this one had misunderstood her hesitation.

"No," Tara said, "no, that's fine. I can go with you." She decided to speak the truth. "I haven't been outside my home for a while, so I'm slow to respond. I'm Tara. What's your name?"

"I'm Madhu," the tall, strapping *kinnar* said, and gripped the handles of her wheelchair. "All right, then, let's take you to your daughter." Madhu's name meant honey, and could be a boy's name or a girl's. Tara wanted to ask Madhu who had named her, but held herself back.

Tara's phone pinged, and she smiled. Sita was here, and on her way through the gate. Tara huffed in relief. She wouldn't have to depend on a stranger, or share space with them within the confines of a lift.

"One second," she said, "could we wait for my friend? She's visiting the factory, too."

"Sure," Madhu said. "I'll get myself some water. Should I bring you a glass?"

The cooler at the end of the hall didn't look clean, smudges on its steel body. Besides, Tara had other issues.

"I can't drink too much water," she said, her hand over her middle.

"Okay, wait here." Madhu parked the wheelchair.

Tara sent off a text to Sita, asking her to head to the lift, and watched Madhu stroll to the watercooler, adjusting her maroon-and-blue saree, blue streaks in her hair. Tara noted how well matched Madhu's outfit was: blue earrings, dainty blue sandals on her hard feet, and a tiny bag with a thin blue strap looped over her wide shoulders and resting on her straight hip.

Tara had seen *kinnar* often enough in her life, but never at close quarters. That evening of the *shaadh*, she hadn't been able to indulge her curiosity, but now she scrutinized Madhu as the *kinnar* tucked her saree and bent forward to cup her hand under the cooler tap to drink. Her gestures and clothes were so feminine, her body hard and masculine. Her Adam's apple bobbed as she drank from the tap.

Tara wondered what it was like for Madhu to refer to herself as a woman, and dress as the feminine gender, while her body insisted on behaving like the exact opposite. In Western countries, some of the videos she watched told her that the *kinnar* and others who didn't subscribe to either the male or the female gender insisted on a pronoun that was theirs alone. They, them.

As a bar girl, and now a woman in a wheelchair, she felt estranged, not part of normal society, but her very identity had never been in question. She was a woman, a wife. A mother twice over. A surge of gratitude for herself and compassion for Madhu overcame her, and contrary to her usual surface nonchalance, she felt herself break into tears.

"What's wrong, Tara? Are you okay?" A woman's voice. Sita bent over her, wearing a faded *salwar-kameez* like a conservative student on a budget—the *sindoor* at the parting of her hair near invisible.

"It's nothing. Pregnancy makes you unstable." She smiled through her tears, drying her eyes with the end of her saree.

"Anything I can do? Water?"

"No, Pia has been away with *Vaeeni*'s sister. I wanted to find her. Madhu here was trying to help."

Tara turned, but saw no sign of Madhu.

"How strange," Tara said.

"Who is Madhu? Is she a supervisor here?"

"I'll explain on the way. Let's go to the roof. Bina has taken Pia upstairs."

Once the lift doors had closed with a slow clank, Tara explained.

"I'm not surprised," Sita said. "She knows I'm a policewoman, from the other evening at your place. *Hijras* don't like the police, and I must say sometimes the feeling is mutual. They're often mixed up in gang business, or commit petty thefts."

Tara considered sharing her own thoughts on the *kinnar*, but Sita was present when Tara had corrected others on the evening of her *shaadh* ceremony. Giving up, Tara watched as the slow-climbing numbers on the lift crawled up to the fourth floor.

"Did you talk to anyone around *Vaeeni*'s place? About Neeti?" Tara said.

"Yes, her *chawl* isn't far from here."

The lift clanked open, and Sita wheeled her out into a small corridor. The metal door to the roof, painted a bright sky blue, stood ajar. They moved toward it.

"Did you hear anything about any guys who pester women?"

"I hung out at the local bus stop," Sita said, "where they exchange gossip, but haven't heard anything so far."

Maybe Neeti was making it up, then—she had a tendency to exaggerate her misery in order to gain Pia's sympathy. Had it been true, *Vaeeni* would have asked Arnav for help.

Pia's voice, alarmed and trembling, pierced through the silence. Tara strained forward, toward Pia.

"Will you be okay if . . . ?" Sita stood beside her now.

"Of course!"

Sita made for the door, and Tara wheeled herself forward, breathing hard.

A few moments later, as Tara neared the door, Pia stormed past, her face crumpled, wiping her tears as she sobbed.

"Pia? Pia. I'm here. Pia, wait!"

Pia didn't stop. She clattered down the stairs that opened not far from the lift.

Sita rushed back through the door.

"Pia ran down." Tara pointed to the stairs.

"I'm going after her, okay?"

"What happened?" Tara called out.

"Bina says she got scared of all the hair," Sita yelled as she ran down. "Wait on the roof."

"I'll take the lift."

"Stay there. That's an old lift." Sita's breathless voice echoed as she ran down the stairwell. "You don't want to be stuck inside alone."

CHAPTER TWENTY-EIGHT

MUMBAI DRISHTIKON NEWS

Maharashtra Politics

Tarun Sathe given election ticket again from Bandra East

6:16 PM IST 17 July, TMD.

Even as the current opposition party in Maharashtra State Assembly claimed a moral high ground while announcing the withdrawal of one of its candidates from the assembly bypoll because he had a history of charge sheets in criminal cases, they have proposed a familiar name: Tarun Sathe, whose term will end by the end of this month.

While giving the election ticket to Tarun Sathe, the leader of the opposition party, Mr. Gokhale said, "We have every faith that Mr. Sathe will continue to champion the rights of the common man. He's likely to win the seat at Bandra East this time, and perhaps take a seat in the ministry someday soon."

Observers maintain that the Muslim vote will determine success at the Bandra East constituency, and giving the ticket to a Hindu radical figure like Tarun Sathe with his violent rhetoric is likely to inflame tensions in what is already set to be a fraught assembly election.

CHAPTER TWENTY-NINE

TARA

This was what made Tara most furious—her inability to keep up with her daughter as she used to. Two years ago, she would've sprinted down the stairs faster than Sita, anxiety and adrenaline fueling her. Those remained at the same levels, but now they simply raised her blood pressure. Given her pregnancy, she couldn't afford that. She took a fortifying breath.

Sita was right. Tara shouldn't risk taking the lift alone. If she got stuck, she'd add to the trouble, not lessen it. She required assistance. She hated asking for it, but she must. The nearest person was Bina, somewhere on that roof beyond that bright blue door.

Tara wheeled herself toward it, but froze once she was able to see outside.

Hair. So much hair hanging from long ropes strung across the open roof, like witches slung up in some medieval ritual against a gloomy sky, threatening rain. Even in broad daylight, though, the thick clusters of dripping hair made her think of watching eyes, of dark, fetid places. Her skin crawled at the sight of all that shiny black, swaying gently in the wind, sinister, assessing, as if ready to rise in the air and surround her.

She wanted to call out Bina's name, but a strange apprehension smothered her. No wonder Pia had been frightened—Tara couldn't deny or tamp down her own terror. The scent of shampoo and wet dog mingled together when Tara took another long breath to calm herself.

All of this was a mistake. Tara should have come alone first, seen the place for herself before inflicting it on her daughter. She hadn't thought this through.

Where was Bina? Should she not have followed Pia out? Tara's thought found an echo, and she caught the flicker of Bina's saree as *Vaeeni*'s portly sister emerged from behind the uneven, dark curtain of hair.

"I'm so sorry," Bina said. "I left Pia alone for a moment while I took care of some work, and she panicked. She dashed off before I could catch up."

"Can we go downstairs?" Tara said. "I'm worried about Pia. Let's hurry."

"Yes," Bina said. "Give me one second? I was on my way to come find you. Don't worry, your friend is very capable, and Pia can't go outside the factory—there are high boundary walls and a gate. I've informed security to watch out."

Bina trekked off even as she spoke, without giving Tara a chance to respond.

Whispers came to Tara—a smothered giggle that echoed against the walls of the surrounding brick buildings.

Women worked in distant corners of the roof, some of them untangling the bundles of wet hair, others hanging out towels and cloths to dry. They stilled at Bina's approach, nodded and went back to their work, while Bina took one of them aside. Tara chafed at the delay. She needed to be with Pia, now.

"Sorry," Bina said when she returned, "but I suspected Pia might have dropped her phone, and a woman picked it up. I wanted to get it before it disappeared."

It wasn't Pia's phone, but Tara's. Pia had forgotten hers at home today.

"I think it slipped from your daughter's hand before she ran. I heard a clack and came running and glimpsed one of them picking it up. I should have caught the woman then, but I was trying to stop Pia."

"Thank you. Let's hurry now." Tara began to dial Sita's number, but the phone rang, and Sita's name flashed on the screen.

"I've got her," Sita said. "She's fine. We're at the car."

Tara sagged with relief. Pia was not the only one carrying trauma from her kidnapping.

"I'm coming down with Bina. Hold on for five minutes. Is she crying?"

"She's quiet, just staring out the other window. I'm outside your car." Sita paused, and continued in a lower voice. "I think Pia could do with a little space. If you're okay with it, I can take her home in my car, and you can come back in a while? Only if you think that's okay."

She didn't want to be parted from Pia. Two years ago, when kidnappers had snatched her from the road in the middle of a school day, terror and despair had clouded her mind. That storm had returned in the last few minutes. Pia needed her, sure, but maybe it was she who needed to touch Pia now, hold her to make it real. That she was safe.

"No, that's okay." Tara's hands shook. "Thanks for finding her. I'll come now."

They headed down the corridor to the lift. Tara focused her thoughts on Pia—and shuddered at the memory of that roof, the bundles of dark, ghostly hair parted from human scalps, swinging in the breeze.

Bina's voice jolted her.

"Tara, I wondered if you wouldn't mind stopping by the nonprofit for a bit? I'd spoken to the teachers and the girls, and they prepared a small performance for you."

"My daughter . . ."

"Of course," Bina said quickly. "I get it."

Bina's face showed she didn't. Tara wanted to tell her about her problem with her catheter, but it was easier to just finish what she'd come for. On her doctor's advice, she'd worn an adult diaper.

Pia was safe. The children had prepared for her visit, and would be disappointed. It wasn't as if Tara could run down to her daughter, either. They would have to find men to lift her wheelchair before she could leave, and Pia would witness the process another time.

"How far is your nonprofit?" she found herself asking as Bina wheeled her out of the lift.

"Right next to the factory if we take the back exit."

Tara's phone buzzed again. A text from Sita. I'll send the driver to you now?

She was about to say no and explain, when the phone flashed Arnav's name. She gazed up at Bina, her gaze requesting privacy. They'd arrived at the end of the corridor that led to the hall with the workstations.

"I'll check a few things with the supervisor. Will you be okay here for a minute?"

Tara nodded, picking up Arnav's call once Bina had left.

"I was beginning to get worried," her husband's voice floated in from the other end of the line.

"I'm all right," Tara said, her breath shaky. "Pia is not."

"What's wrong?"

"She was terrified."

"I did tell you."

Yes, he had. Several times. He'd been gentle, spoken in the most reasonable words, but all she'd heard was him trying to tell her what to do about their daughter she'd raised by herself for more than a decade.

"*Vaeeni's* sister took her to the roof ahead of me where they dry all the hair."

"Are you sure that was all it was?" Arnav said. "Do you know if anybody spoke to her?"

Ever the policeman. Arnav's words brought her back to the present. Pia was upset with her mother, so it stood to reason that her father's ear might make her feel better. She took a breath, and launched into the only sort of apology she felt capable of.

"Yes, I'm sure. All that drying hair scared me, too. This was stupid. I should never have brought her here. She hates me now." She regretted the last words the moment she said them.

"I'm sure she doesn't. I've got work, but I can make a quick pit stop to pick her up if you like. She relaxes on long drives. All she needs is a little time to zone out."

Arnav's voice was kind, and Tara lost her desire to punch him for being right.

"Sita can drop Pia home, if you have time to have lunch with her," she said. "I'll stay here and give you some time to talk?"

"Don't stay too long. Is *Vaeeni* there?"

"No, but her sister is. She'll take me to the nonprofit now."

Tara messaged Sita, telling her to go ahead. She would join them later.

Half an hour later, rain sprayed the asbestos roof of the nonprofit premises, its tinny patter adding to the music. Tara sat transfixed by the performance the nonprofit had put up.

Little girls, some as young as six, danced to a popular comedic Bollywood tune, their faces beaming with wide smiles. They didn't stick to the beat, and the teacher in Tara itched to correct them, but when she thought of the circumstances some of these girls came from, her heart softened.

A bunch of them were cancer patients, Bina had told her, some cured, some between treatments. They wore wigs to make up for hair loss. Others who wore wigs suffered from problems like alopecia, their baldness leaving them vulnerable to bullying. Almost all the girls lived in the nearby *chawl* and surrounding slums. Their parents couldn't afford good day care. This nonprofit stepped in wherever possible.

The song on the speaker changed as the younger girls trotted off and a few teens took the makeshift stage: an area cleared up in the hall strewn with mats, bundles of fiber, and hanks of hair.

These older girls wore frayed *salwar-kameezes*, and wore less joy on their faces than the smaller kids had displayed. Life had got to them.

"They have survived trafficking and child abuse," Bina whispered in her ear. "We're teaching them some basic math and languages, training them to make wigs, and teaching hairdressing skills so they can work at factories and hair salons."

Tara nodded. This is where she should've brought Pia, not the factory. She would apologize to her daughter, and coax her to come again, but only to the nonprofit this time.

Performances done and Tara's gifts of pencils, notebooks, and erasers received, the girls clamored for the main event: the distribution of snacks and drinks. They forgot about her, focusing on the laden table. Several of the smallest children sneaked a few extra fried items into their pockets. Some didn't eat at all—saving all of it to take home.

Tara sighed. This was the poverty and want she'd known once.

"We were hoping you could visit a few times." Bina brought her a paper plate of snacks. "Maybe teach them to dance? Some of the girls would like to audition for reality shows they watch on TV."

Behind them, the children laughed and played, their voices high and gleeful, and Tara found herself wanting to be the reason for some of that joy. "Who teaches the girls now?"

"Some of the *kinnar* who visit here and work part-time at the factory. They use our wigs, too."

"Ah, so Madhu works here?"

"Yes, Sujata asked Madhu to take along some friends for your *shaadh* ceremony. The child is due soon?"

"Yes, but I'd like to come and help. Let me talk about this at home."

As she thought about it, the idea grew on her. She hadn't found Rasool or his men—she'd need another trip. Even after she'd sorted that out, teaching these little girls would be a huge improvement on lying in bed all day, watching doomsday on loop. Here was a way to give thanks, and teach Pia that her lifestyle was a privilege, not a right.

She texted Arnav to ask after Pia. They were at home, eating lunch, and it was time she joined them.

In the car, she checked her phone. A message from Sita.

Talk to Pia when things calm down. I don't think it was just the hair.

CHAPTER THIRTY

ARNAV

Having spent time with Pia and calmed her, Arnav rushed back to the station. He had his work cut out for him, because the Kaali temple trustees had threatened to go to the media about the missing gold necklaces.

Time to speak to the priest's nephew.

He dialed one of his constables, and ordered Ram Chandra Dome placed in an interrogation room. They had shoved the suspect into a separate holding cell because none of the other detainees wanted to share the lockup area with a "holy man," fearing misfortune. The constables hadn't bothered with the complaints on the first day, but when the others started yelling to be separated on day two, they'd given in. The detainees had reported strange sightings at night, long-haired women peeping through the bars, red eyed and menacing, whispers echoing through the corridors.

Arnav had questioned the constables, and they'd shifted on their feet, neither confirming nor denying the rumors. In the end, Arnav had sent them off with stern warnings about treating all detainees the same.

He opened his case notes, and began typing out his ideas, and the suspect list so far.

Iqbal Asif, Rasool Mohsin's man, was seen on CCTV with possible victim. Has since gone underground. Rasool Mohsin has been seen meeting controversial Hindu MLA, but can't be found despite raids.

Naik reported suspicious men outside the Remy factory.

Victim was killed on the spot, with a knife. Weapon missing. Body will be analyzed for drugs and exact cause of death. Desai tried to cremate body without identification. Victim yet to be identified. Push Tambe on this.

The 100 call was made on the internet, using a voice changer. The video upload not yet geo-located. Follow up.

Priest has lost keys to temple safe. Trustees sent keys. Two necklaces missing. Priest is uncle to the tantric Ram Chandra under remand, but Ram Chandra has refused to accept the connection. Ram Chandra has political connections and is friend to Raghav, Sita Naik's husband. Priest on watch. To be interrogated next as he's not moving anywhere other than temple.

The symbols on the body belong to a tantra cult, and the symbol means the sacred vagina.

Similar symbols found at Chitra Varli's home. Chitra Varli has controversial history. Video of scene released from her account. This video included no boot prints. Bloodied boots and knife found at Ram Chandra's home. Blood yet to be matched to victim's.

The tantric looked like he hadn't slept since his arrest, which was very close to the truth. Desai's men hadn't spared him—dark circles under his eyes, a half-healed bruise at his jaw, dry lips. He sat with his head bowed, hands on his lap, in the same clothes he'd worn when he came in. The reek of sweat and urine that rose from him told its own story.

"What's your name?" Arnav said. It was an opener meant to infuriate the man. By the time someone asks you your name for the forty-seventh time, you begin to lose your cool.

"Sri Sarvagya," he said, his voice reedy with exhaustion.

"Say, 'sir.'" The constable shoved the tantric.

"Stop that." Arnav raised his hand. "Let the man talk."

The constable assumed that Arnav's bid to stop suspects being hit was the standard good cop, bad cop routine, but with his years of training at the *dojo*, all he wanted was for men to not be hit unless they hit first.

"Is that your real name? No surnames?"

"My official name is Ram Chandra Dome, sir."

The tantric was a Scheduled Caste and had changed his name to conceal his lower-caste surname. This was part of Desai's argument.

"You know why you're here?"

"No." The tantric flinched when the constable swooped forward, menacing. "Sir."

Arnav didn't object to the theatrics of interrogation. It was expected by all parties, and effective.

"Did my men not tell you what crime they'll charge you with?"

"They did, sir, but I have nothing to do with it. I hadn't even gone to the temple that evening. They never want to listen to my side of the story."

"Try me."

"Sir, that day I was coming back from an aimless bicycle ride."

He had no alibi. So far, Desai's story bore out.

"Why?"

"I'd been fired."

"Fired? Why?"

"I told Mr. Amit Nimkar that his son had withdrawn unauthorized funds. Then his son came, slapped me around, and fired me."

This was new. The interrogation notes for this man didn't show any other employment other than as a tantric. Naik had mentioned his political connections, but possibly didn't know about his job.

"Mr. Nimkar. What company was this?"

"The Remy Virgin Hair Factory."

That factory, again. Everything led back there.

Arnav kept his expression neutral. "What was your job?"

"I was the head accountant, sir. I'd simply asked for a note or a message from Mr. Nimkar before I gave money to his son."

"Why have you never spoken of this in your previous interviews?"

Desai should have made a note of this.

"I tried to, sir, but the inspector won't let me talk. All he wanted was for me to confess. I'm an accountant by day, a tantric only by night. My devotion is my legacy from my father."

Ram Chandra Dome's voice took on a note of strength and pride. He was either a good actor, or he was telling the truth.

"I can't understand why they keep saying they saw me on camera. They say I've walked with boots in the temple. No tantric will wear shoes inside a temple. I don't own any boots, sir. I like wearing comfortable shoes."

"They found the boots at your home."

"Those cannot be mine. I don't own boots."

"But you have no one to vouch for where you were at the time of the murder."

"I was feeling a bit lost, sir. They wouldn't give me a recommendation. Without one, it won't be easy to get another job. I tried to meet Mr. Nimkar, but he won't see me."

"When was this?"

"The day after I was fired. Same day you found the body. I missed lunch. I was upset, so I started drinking on an empty stomach. By evening, when I was returning home, I was drunk."

"What did you do?"

"I went straight home and crashed. Your men woke me late the next morning, trying to break down my door."

"So your uncle didn't help you, either?"

"I don't have an uncle, sir."

"What about the priest? He's related to you."

Ram Chandra worked hard not to react, but his jaws clenched at the mention of the temple priest.

"He's no uncle of mine." Ram Chandra's shuttered expression spoke otherwise.

"What about this symbol?" Arnav showed him the picture on the phone.

"This is a *yoni*. They kept showing this to me and saying I drew it, simply because I have vermilion at home and I'm a tantric. Why would I do such a sacrilegious thing? We draw this symbol to invoke the goddess. They say I killed and castrated a man. Why would I do that? I need a job. How will it help for me to murder someone?"

"You don't know the victim?"

"No one knows who he is, sir, not even you. They showed me pictures. It is a naked man with his face slashed up. I am in jail for two days now. It's ruined my reputation, sir."

"If you haven't done it, there's nothing to worry about."

"Who will give me a job? Please let me go now at least, sir."

"They're analyzing all the evidence to check if any of that matches you."

"If you torture an innocent man any further, my Ma Kaali will curse you all. Your wife comes often to the temple, does she not? You have much to fear from ill omens these days, sir."

Fury rose white hot within Arnav at the thought of Tara coming to harm, but decades at the *dojo* had taught him to stay focused.

"A tantric is a holy man, Ram Chandra. I'm sure the goddess you worship doesn't like you cursing innocent women, either."

CHAPTER THIRTY-ONE

This is the kind of game I like.

We know everything, we are watching, and they don't have a clue.

It is all a power game, Bhai *says, and we're right. For so long, the police have had all the power. They think they will get us, but they have no clue we've got them.*

When they gave such a blow to him, taking away his home and his hearth, and they thought all of us weak, small. Who is small now?

Bhai listens to her all the time, and not me—goes to her for advice, because she has the best eyes and ears, knows what goes on, and that's all right.

It is me who keeps it together when they all have temper tantrums, when they need a place to meet, when he has to summon the others.

We'll be on the hunt again soon, but for now we rest, and bide our time.

CHAPTER THIRTY-TWO

ARNAV

At the *dojo*, it was all about flow. Some days you found it, not so on others.

The next morning both Arnav and Pia struggled, sparring, blocking, hitting, but in a mechanical fashion, without the poetry and power that usually marked their movements. Against the backdrop of the faint, soothing *dojo* music, silence hung between the two as they hit and parried—Arnav's mind far away. Neeti watched as usual, but said nothing.

No matter what tactic Arnav tried, his daughter refused to tell him what had happened on the roof.

The *dojo* itself brought back mixed emotions on difficult days—memories of *Vaeeni*'s husband crowded Arnav. Hemant Shinde had brought Arnav to this place, at thirteen, after Arnav had lost his father. He'd practiced here for more than two decades. At first with just Shinde, and then with his daughter watching. Neeti cheered them, but had never wanted to step on the sparring mat, unlike Pia, who'd begun training soon after she came to Mumbai. She'd practiced for less than two years, but had already made marked progress.

He parried as she tried to land a punch in his midsection, spinning away.

"So you won't tell me what happened at the factory," he huffed as he returned within the range of his daughter's kicks.

"It was nothing."

Pia's words came to him, breathless, as she rushed him with a high kick. He couldn't shake the fear she was lying. Teenagers made excellent liars.

"Why did you run, then? And you're not going to school today." He blocked the hit with his arm, stepped away.

"All that hair." Pia's eyes looked haunted. She attacked with a flurry of punches punctuating her words. "I'm. Not. Going there. Again. Not Ma. Neither."

She'd answered his first question, but not the second. He wouldn't push it, just for today. Pia's footwork had improved. Her traditional dance lessons with Tara had helped with the footwork and breathing.

Pia's Ma. Tara. Did she have to be that stubborn? Despite last evening's fiasco, she wouldn't give up her mad idea to volunteer, seven months pregnant, at a nonprofit that lacked a ramp for her wheelchair. From what Sita had told him, you could only access the factory via stairs. The nonprofit sat near the factory's back entrance, and didn't have proper wheelchair access.

"What if they drop you while carrying the chair up?" he'd asked her last night, trying to keep his voice low.

"They won't. And Bina said they'll arrange a ramp within the week."

"A makeshift ramp that could collapse. Why can't you see the danger in this?"

He couldn't point out that she was endangering the baby—she would immediately point out yet again that he hadn't been around for their first child.

"Don't make a coward out of me. Like I keep telling everyone, I'm pregnant, not ill. Besides, Zoya . . ."

She'd clammed up after that. She did that whenever her best friend's name came up.

Arnav released his breath on a whoosh as one of Pia's kicks smashed into his midsection, her very first kick to land over the months they'd sparred.

She whooped, her pale and shaken demeanor gone. Now she was the picture of triumph, war-dancing across the hall they practiced in, drawing cheers from Neeti, who echoed Pia's yells. It warmed him to see these two teens he adored find sisterhood in each other.

"I finally got you, Papa!" Pia yelled, punching the air, sweaty and tousled in her white karate gi and yellow belt.

"Yes, you did." Arnav grinned. "Dignified poise, remember?"

That was what their sensei said: win or lose, maintain dignified poise. A glance at the wall clock startled Arnav. He must leave for office from the *dojo*—no time to return home. He called a halt when Pia returned from her high-fives and leaps with Neeti.

"There's nothing you want to tell me?" Arnav said.

"I . . . it is a hair factory, Papa. And you know after what they did—" She touched her short, wavy hair.

He hated his daughter's crestfallen expression, and pulled her into a quick hug.

"You're safe now. No one can get to you—I'll make sure of that. Let's go now, I'm late."

Outside, the rain shrouded the city in gloom—relieved only by the shine of pale-blue tarpaulins brought in to cover shops and slums in the vicinity. Once in the car, Arnav opened the dashboard to pull out the usual packets of cookies he'd kept for Neeti for all the years he'd known her.

"Thank you, Uncle," she said, and immediately passed some to Pia.

"He always brings these for you, not me," Pia grumbled. "I hate you." But her grin said otherwise.

"I was here first," Neeti said. "And I hate you, too."

Pia made a face, and the two burst into giggles.

"Oh, I forgot." Arnav reached in and drew out another packet. "For you both."

"What's in it?"

"A surprise. You said you missed having me around."

Remote locators—one for Pia, and two for Neeti, so she could pass one along to her brother Ashok. Rasool had helped save Pia once, but things could have changed in the last two years.

Pia had asked for these a while ago so she could find things for Tara, while also playing cops and robbers, her favorite game since she discovered her father worked for Mumbai Police. Unknown to her, these locators also contained GPS trackers. Along with Pia, he wanted to keep an eye on Neeti and Ashok. If history repeated itself and someone nabbed one of them, he'd know where they were. Phones would be confiscated, but these looked like tiny game remotes with buttons.

Pia and Neeti squealed at a pitch reserved for teenaged girls, and Arnav shushed them when his phone rang.

He needed to drop the girls back to his place, and head to the station. His informer had called, saying Desai had stepped out of the Remy Virgin Hair Factory a few minutes ago.

CHAPTER THIRTY-THREE

SITA

Sita didn't believe a word Pia had said. That girl was terrified. She'd seen marks on Pia's forearm before the girl pulled down her sleeve. She'd considered telling Tara about it, but Tara was pregnant, still recovering from the trauma of her accident, and didn't need the stress. She'd merely asked Tara to watch Pia.

She had to ensure Pia came to no harm. It wouldn't prove all that difficult given that Sita was back in the neighborhood of the Remy Virgin Hair Factory in search of Rasool.

That was the only place not raided yet, due to Mr. Nimkar's close ties with Mumbai Police. Rasool had chosen his partner well—and those were probably his men she'd seen entering the premises the day before.

Did one of those men assault Pia—imagining her a threat as a policeman's daughter, not knowing or not caring about the Tara-Zoya connection? Any of the women at the factory could be reporting to Rasool Mohsin and his gang as well.

For her watch, Sita had picked a time that fell within work hours for Mrs. Shinde and her sister, Bina. She didn't want them to recognize her and start asking questions while she was hoping to fly under the radar.

Mrs. Shinde and her two children had lived in an apartment before, as the family of a senior police inspector. How did they manage in the *chawl*?

Sita was back at her vantage point at the bus stop, wearing a cleaner's uniform in order to blend in better than last time. Scanning her periphery, she spotted louts at the entrance of a lower-floor *kholi* in the *chawl*, catcalling passing women. They didn't look like local residents. Their puffed-up chests, the spread-eagle postures, screamed challenge.

Sita chafed to turn into an avatar of the goddess Kaali and send the men scurrying, but she was here to take notes. They started with calling names at passersby, and then burst into raucous songs that rose faintly over the din of the traffic.

"They're at it again," a woman beside her grumbled under her breath.

Sita turned, and found a young girl standing next to her. Her backpack an obvious fake of a famous brand, faded-jeans-old-long-shirt attire, and scuffed shoes—the outfit of a college student trying to break out from the locality.

"I'm taking a job there." Sita waved toward the area behind her, on the other side of the main road, opposite the *chawl*. "Is it usually this unsafe around here?"

The location Sita had asked about was less than ten minutes' drive from Versova Police Station.

"Oh no, no, that side is okay. You mean over there, right?" The girl pointed to the tall apartments on tree-lined avenues.

"Yes, I got a housekeeping job at a penthouse."

"No issues in that neighborhood. They wouldn't dare. It's only in this *chawl* area, and the slums alongside it. You don't have to worry unless you're going this way."

The road where they stood ran between the *chawl* area and the posh apartments.

"You stay nearby?"

"Yes, I'm waiting for those loafers to leave before I walk down—they have made life hell for us."

"No one complains to the police?"

She must take the beat constable in this area to task.

"The police? They support these louts. Some of them are *savarnas*. Upper-caste people. On our side most of the homes belong to the Scheduled Caste."

"You mean the police won't help?"

"You're new to these parts. The police will laugh at you, tell you that you deserve it for stepping outside the house. We *neechi jaat* people need to stay in our lanes."

Sita's face flamed at the girl's words about the police, and the girl paused.

"Sorry," she said. "I didn't mean to offend you. I didn't know you weren't Scheduled Caste. From your uniform, I thought . . ."

It was true that most cleaners came from the lower castes.

"You're not wrong, and I'm not offended. I'm angry with the police." Sita let rage as well as sadness underline her words.

She'd overheard remarks about how she had received her promotions because of the reservations, and different advancement rules, for her caste.

"I understand," the girl said. "I feel the same."

"If the police took action, would the women of that area come forward to testify?"

"Ha. The police. They take *haftas*, all of them, bribes from the rich people who own the factories around there, so no one will harm their businesses. Some of those louts work at the factory, too. Supervisors."

"Is it easy to get a job at the factory?" Sita asked, making a note of this *hafta* business. If this was true, her constables would answer for it. She couldn't take pictures of the men without spooking the girl. She was too far to properly identify them, but she tried to make a good mental note of their appearance.

"Why?" The girl's eyes turned curious. "Do you want a job at the factory?"

"I work a housekeeping job with a company. I won't mind better pay."

"You might get better pay, especially at the hair factory, where my mother works. The Remy Virgin Hair Factory. This area is not safe for women, though. We would move if we could afford it, but you know how it is with *chawls*. Very difficult to rent a *kholi* at good rates."

"Have they hurt any women?" Sita asked.

"Those men? I don't know if they were the ones responsible, but women have been raped around here. If it gets late, I call my brother to pick me up. I should go," she said.

The men had all risen and were wearing their helmets. They paired up and drove off, riding pillion. Sita straightened her fake housekeeping uniform. She must ask her constables about the cases of rape and molestation in their area.

Neeti might easily have been harassed by these men. And if Tara ever brought Pia along for volunteering stints, the girl would be in danger. It must have been someone scary the other day—Pia hadn't tried to use her martial arts training to defend herself.

Sita needed to set a twenty-four-hour watch on the factory, and tell Pia's father. She scolded herself—why could she not pronounce her boss's first name even in her mind?

As if someone were watching her guilt-ridden thoughts, her phone rang, and a name flashed on the screen. Senior Inspector Arnav Singh Rajput.

CHAPTER THIRTY-FOUR

ARNAV

Arnav waited for Naik to answer his call. He would soon have to grit his teeth through a question-and-answer session with the media about the case at the Ma Kaali temple, but he wanted to catch Naik during her lunch hour, because this was not office business.

"Good afternoon, sir," Naik said, her voice shaky. He heard traffic noises around her—she must be staking out one of Rasool's hideouts.

"Good afternoon. Is this a bad time to call?"

"No, sir. I'm outside, but I can talk."

"I wanted to ask you about Pia. Yesterday at the hair factory, you were the one who found her and drove her home. Did she speak with you?"

"No, sir," Naik said. "She sounded terrified. I don't blame her, sir. It resembles a horror movie set, with all that hair hanging, without heads, as it were."

"See if you can have a chat with her. Unofficially."

"I will, sir. And . . ." Naik paused.

"Yes, Naik?"

"I don't think that area is safe for Tara or Pia to visit, sir. I don't know if it is for me to say, but it might be best if they stay away."

The next time Tara brought up the topic, he would share Naik's opinion with her.

"Desai has been spotted walking out of the Remy Virgin hair factory. Keep an eye out for him. We need to know why he was there."

After a pause, Naik said, "Yes, sir."

He said goodbye to Naik, and asked for Constable Kamble to bring in tea.

Then he dialed Tambe for forensic updates, but was told to meet in person. He waited till Govind, the cheerful tea seller, served him another glass of *cutting chai* before dialing his contact at the Crime Branch who was helping him trace the call to the 100 emergency number.

"The call came from the vicinity of Bandra station," Arnav's contact said. "Somewhere in Saint Cyril Road, but I can't be sure."

"How accurate is the location?"

"Not sure, but the general area. They're masking the exact IP address."

Saint Cyril. Chitra Varli's apartment building sat on that road. Arnav cut the call and added this to his notes, marking her on his list of suspects.

"What about the crime scene video?"

"Give me time. My team is working on an urgent Crime Branch case. I'll call you."

Arnav cut the call and pored over his case notes and the list of suspects.

Iqbal Asif was still elusive.

The tantric was not strong enough to overpower the victim on his own.

His mind spun with possibilities. Did Asif bring an assistant? Maybe a Hindu assistant—did the tantric and Rasool know each other? Hindus and Muslims would conspire together if it suited their ends. From mafia dons to politicos and priests, money was Mumbai's love language, its most sacred religion.

The steady drumming of rain on his office window did nothing to calm his senses. He longed for his days as a rookie constable when all he had to do was follow instructions and focus on the job at hand.

He needed all his fabled calm for his upcoming encounter with the media. The local journalists reminded Arnav of hyenas. Hunting in packs, scavenging food no matter how stale or vile as long as it was free, and cackling in voices not unlike that of the animal. ACP Bapat had made it clear that Arnav would face the cameras till they made progress on the Ma Kaali temple case. Arnav sighed. Bapat would step up the moment they arrested the accused—it was Arnav's music to face until then.

One hour later, exhausted by all the pointed and some downright rude media queries, Arnav sat in his car across the road from the Bandra railway station, scanning the milling crowd.

Arnav opened the passenger door to his car after he spotted Tambe in the rearview mirror, his trademark brisk gait and white beard marking him out among the river of people exiting the station.

"Let's go, please," Tambe said as he got into the car and shut the door, bringing with him an unmistakable chemical odor from the labs. He had come in from work.

After they had driven for a while, Tambe relaxed in his seat. "I'm not sure what is going on, so I thought it best to talk straight to you."

"Tell me."

"Don't ask me how I know, but I can confirm that the forensic report I sent in to Desai the last time went missing from your office."

Tambe had his own grapevine, but this was too much—accusing Arnav's office of losing documents meant for him.

Arnav sat up straighter, and let a touch of steel creep into his voice. "You do know what you're saying."

"Yes. This was why I wanted to give you these new reports in person."

Arnav turned the car into a lane off the main road, and parked his car under a *neem* tree weeping with rain.

Tambe handed over a large brown envelope. "Here they are."

As Arnav shook the papers out, Tambe continued, "The boot print is a match for the shoes found in the suspect Ram Chandra's home."

That would bear out Desai's theory. The tantric had some explaining to do.

"What about the other samples you took from the crime scene, the various spatters? And the blood on the knife?"

"The blood at the crime scene came from two people. One was the victim. The report from Kalina says the other doesn't match the suspect's DNA. The results for the knife will take a while. I sent them in this morning."

The lack of a match didn't rule out Ram Chandra entirely, but opened up the possibility that he wasn't the killer. Or there were two, and the other had bled on the scene, not Ram Chandra.

"The victim's viscera, and fingerprints?"

"Thanks to calls from your boss, they put a rush on this. The viscera show that the man had been drugged. Ketamine. They also ran the fingerprints as a preliminary procedure, and found a match."

Tambe had already suspected the drugging, given the victim's lack of defensive wounds.

"Who is the victim?" Arnav said.

"His name is Vishal Nimkar. He was arrested on molestation charges last year, and was let out on bail."

Nimkar. Arnav knew that surname. Could this Vishal Nimkar be a relation to the owner of the Remy Virgin Hair Factory, the Mr. Nimkar the tantric had mentioned? Was the gruesome crime Ram Chandra's vengeance—castrating the man who had gotten him fired and made him less of a man?

Arnav's informer had spotted Desai at Nimkar's factory. How was the inspector involved in all of this?

"I'm afraid of your inspector." Tambe's voice cut into Arnav's thoughts.

"Desai?"

"Yes, that's why we're here. I know he's not in the office at the moment, and you might've taken him off the case. I received a call yesterday, warning me not to share the conclusions of this Nimkar case with you. Not someone high enough up the ladder that they can meddle with the forensic lab in Kalina, clearly. So they tried to scare me."

"Did you record it?"

"No."

"Arrange to do that the next time."

"Okay, but the threat has worked. I'm about to retire after forty years of service. I plan to spend my retirement gardening, reading, and writing the papers I want. Not slashed up in some temple."

"Thank you, Tambe. I'll take it from here."

"I'll go home now. I don't think I was followed."

Arnav watched as Tambe shuffled out of the car and onto the main road, where he hailed a black-and-yellow auto-rickshaw. Tambe clearly thought Desai's behavior suspicious. Arnav had worked with Tambe on many cases over the years, far longer than the twenty-one months Desai had reported to him.

Corruption was not new to Mumbai Police. Desai could easily have accepted bribes to hide the facts of the case.

If he was taking bribes, did he know the killer, or the person who had ordered the hit? Was that how the bloodied boots showed up at Ram Chandra's residence? And if the boot prints were not in the footage leaked on Chitra Varli's account, who had worn them and walked the scene?

Most instances of police corruption served a nexus of land sharks, the mafia, and politics, all of whom depended on the mafia for their own agendas. Was Rasool Mohsin trying to cook up some mischief along religious lines a few weeks ahead of the assembly elections? He had recently met Tarun Sathe.

If this Vishal Nimkar was indeed the son of the hair factory owner, one way to dig up leads on the case was to speak with Mr. Nimkar and inform him of his son's death. Another was to investigate Desai.

His head in a whirl, Arnav drove to the hospital—trying to push his turmoil to the back of his mind for a while. Tara's appointment with her doctor was in half an hour. His phone rang, and the news didn't please him.

Another body had been found, a man, castrated, not far from a Kaali temple. Arnav asked one of his sub-inspectors to take charge of the scene, and as he turned into the street leading to his apartment, he tried to make himself relax.

For the next hour or more, Tara's welfare needed his entire attention, but a part of him took a mental count of the number of things that could go wrong at the crime scene in his absence.

CHAPTER THIRTY-FIVE

TARA

Tara smiled to herself as Arnav wheeled her into the hospital corridor. In another lifetime, when she'd fallen pregnant with Pia, she'd dreamed of this. Holding hands with Arnav as they walked into exactly this sort of hospital that could pass for an expensive hotel, with paintings on its walls, plush sofas in waiting rooms, a coffee shop, a gift shop.

Her smile faded as memory gave way to reality. Rain flowed like tears against the huge glass windows in the hospital lobby.

She was seventeen when pregnant for the first time, terrified to abort the baby and unsure she wanted to keep it. In the end, she'd run like a thief in the night, left Mumbai behind. Arnav hadn't known she wasn't nineteen at the time, nor that she'd been pregnant. Now that they were finally together after all these years, she sat in a wheelchair. How was that fair? She couldn't suppress a sob.

Arnav stopped the wheelchair. She didn't look up as another muffled sob escaped her. Ma Kaali, not now. This wasn't the place to create a scene. What was with her and breaking into tears? She'd never been like this, not even when bedridden at the hospital. She could sense people staring: at her in the wheelchair, and at Arnav's khaki uniform. Her face warmed with embarrassment.

"Tara?" Arnav kneeled before her, his voice filled with concern. "Are you all right?"

She kept her gaze lowered on her clasped hands, trying to cope with her swinging moods.

Arnav had his hands full with a high-profile case, but he hadn't missed the prenatal appointment, getting the driver to bring her into the hospital. He was trying. She may not be able to stand up, but she had a husband who cared for her and their family. You couldn't rewrite history, only revisit it. Your only choice lay in the present moment. The now.

"Yes, all good," Tara said.

"You scared me." He rose. "All of this is a first for me . . ." Arnav paused, midsentence, his hand on her shoulder.

The history between them came crashing in. Zoya had held her hand during Pia's birth instead of him.

"Let's go. We'll be late." She patted his hand. "You know how busy Dr. Holkar is."

Dr. Holkar's clinic was a wood-and-glass affair at the end of the corridor. Women in various stages of pregnancy reclined on the sofas, some chatting with their partners, others scrolling down their phones, all immaculately turned out. They gazed up, and Tara caught the fleeting pity in their eyes before their gazes slid away. One or two of the women she'd met on previous visits smiled.

The women cast covert glances at Arnav and his uniform. Why did he have to look so dashing in his khakis? Arnav parked her wheelchair beside the sofa and offered her his hand. She took it. Soon he was scrolling on his phone with the other. He placed a call, to question some hapless man trying and failing to find someone called Nimkar.

Tara felt sorry for the man at the other end of the line, and let her mind wander. She wished Zoya could have come along for these checkups. Zoya had no children. Nor did she want any, she said. Your children belong to a police officer, mine would come from a don. But Tara caught the wistfulness in her friend's voice. Why had

Zoya not contacted her? Did her friend know they were hunting Rasool?

When it was their turn to go in, Dr. Holkar smiled her usual maternal smile, her gray hair pinned back, her spotless white coat over her beige saree a little crumpled from the entire day's work.

"Come in, Mr. and Mrs. Rajput," she said. "How are you feeling, Tara?"

While a nurse helped Tara prep for the examination, she heard the doctor ask Arnav questions about her meals, her sleeping habits, and so on. It was a relief to visit a clinic with wheelchair-accessible weighing scales, and exam tables that lowered for easier transfers.

After the scan, the swabs, the weight measurement, and the samples for blood tests, Dr. Holkar asked her about her physiotherapy sessions.

"Paresh hasn't come in," she said. "I only missed one class."

"You didn't tell me?" Arnav said.

Tara glared at Arnav, and thankfully, he shut his mouth. Yes, she hadn't told him, because it wasn't such a big problem and she'd enjoyed her break.

An enquiry with the nurse revealed that Paresh Khare hadn't reported at the clinic, either, and no one had been able to get in touch with him.

"We'll send you a replacement," Dr. Holkar said, the very picture of calm, but Tara saw the doctor's tight knuckles.

"I can wait this week out, Doctor," Tara said. "I tire quite easily these days."

"Being tired is natural, Tara—you're carrying a baby, at twenty-eight weeks. I don't want to unduly concern either of you, but given your injuries and other medications, we must be very careful."

"She's planning to volunteer at a nonprofit," Arnav said, "with no wheelchair access. It's also located in an unsafe neighborhood."

Tara gritted her teeth. If only she could throw something at his arrogant head.

"These restrictions will only last for two months, Tara. Once you've recovered from the birth, you can resume all normal activities."

Tara nodded.

As soon as they had exited the clinic into an empty corridor, Tara said, "What was all of that about? Why did you have to tell Dr. Holkar about my volunteering?"

"She's your doctor, Tara. She should know. I had to tell her the truth."

He spoke from behind and above her. They'd ordered a power wheelchair. Tara couldn't wait for it to arrive.

"You can't . . . ," Tara began, but stopped when she heard Arnav answer a call with a quick, *Sorry, I have to take this.*

"Yes, sir," he said, "I'll be headed there soon."

Tara heard his voice change register, becoming deeper.

"No, sir," he continued as they reached the lobby, "I gave him some time off to gather his wits. I'll be there soon. Right, sir. I'll send an update when I've examined the scene myself."

He pushed her wheelchair out of the lobby and down the ramp, while she texted the driver to wait at the front entrance. Rain lashed the palms that flanked the porch, humidity weighing the air.

By the time Arnav cut the call and stood in front of her, she knew what he'd say.

"I've got to rush. I'll try to come in by dinnertime."

She forced herself to conjure a smile. A look at his face, and it turned real. He wasn't having an easy time of it, either.

"Take care out there," she said. "We'll see you tonight."

Once Arnav had seen her into the car, he jogged up the stairs toward the parking lot, avoiding the rain where he could. As her car turned into the driveway, Tara spotted a man in shabby clothes shamble out from behind a pillar and follow her husband. He must have stood there for a while, getting drenched. A chill ran through Tara.

About to send a message, she stopped herself. Was she overthinking this? In the last year, she'd told Arnav several times that he, or Pia, or she herself was being followed, but it had all come to nothing. Maybe that man had entered the parking lot on his own business and hadn't stood there long. Tara scrolled through her contacts, wishing she had a number to reach Zoya.

Her heart remained heavy. Life was so fragile. It changed in moments. She sent up a prayer to Ma Kaali for the safety of her husband.

CHAPTER THIRTY-SIX

She is close to the one in the wheelchair, Bhai *says. Almost like a sister.*

I smile. Best friends forever, huh. Sometimes I feel sad for that wheelchair girl. She hasn't done a thing, but she must suffer. And then I remember. Neither Bhai *nor me have done a thing, either, and yet here we are.*

The good thing is, we've got wheelchair girl where we wanted her—she'll give us all we need, by confessing everything to her best friend. They have known each other for years now. Trust takes time to build, especially when you intend to break it.

CHAPTER THIRTY-SEVEN

ARNAV

Many things plagued India's Maximum City, but the worst of them on this day was the monsoon. Arnav hoped it wouldn't result in flood warnings. It poured in sheets around the industrial area where Arnav headed toward the crime scene. The buildings loomed in robot-like silhouettes. The roads had turned into streams. Arnav let the new-recruit constable navigate the flood with the police jeep and focused on his calls.

He tried Mr. Nimkar's phone over and over, but it kept ringing. Mr. Nimkar was indeed Vishal Nimkar's father, as it turned out, his next of kin. Since they couldn't locate the father, Arnav dialed the Nimkar residence.

"Hello?" A woman's voice on the line. Elderly, given the fragile tone.

Arnav introduced himself. She immediately handed the phone to a man.

"Hello, Inspector. This is Nimkar speaking."

"Mr. Amit Nimkar?"

"No, I'm his brother, but you can leave a message with me. What is this regarding?"

"Vishal Nimkar, your nephew."

"Vishal is out of town. Amit sent him on some official business."

This was strange. If Vishal was supposed to be away on work, how had he ended up castrated and murdered at the Kaali temple near Bandra?

"I'm afraid we found Vishal's dead body," Arnav said. "We would like to hand over the remains to the family. I'm so sorry for your loss."

Arnav explained the situation to the stunned man on the other end of the line, and asked him to reach out to the Bandra Police Station.

Next, Arnav called Ali.

"You know about your *bhai's* girlfriend?"

"Ji, saab."

"You can get her a message from me?"

"*Bhai* doesn't let her out of his eyesight for very long."

"Find a way. Tell her I need to speak with her."

The don had proved elusive. Zoya would call Tara again, sooner or later, but he couldn't risk his marriage by tapping Tara's phone. He must talk to Zoya—reach Rasool through her.

Fearing the jeep would stall, they parked it at higher ground to try to access the crime scene on foot. Rain trickled down Arnav's cap, and soaked him through despite his gear as he waded through knee-deep water. The constable followed him. If there was an open manhole someplace ahead, Arnav didn't want his constable to be the one to fall in feetfirst.

He made slow progress, and his mind zinged from the doctor's concerns about Tara's pregnancy to the matter of Mr. Nimkar. Arnav had sent constables off in search of Mr. Nimkar at his office and his usual haunts but they hadn't located him yet. The rain had slowed it all down. Every few minutes, Arnav received alerts on people stranded in flooded areas of Mumbai.

Arnav's careful steps took him to this new Kaali temple. Carvings of animals and plants flowed into one another on the pillars of the shrine wedged between two buildings in a narrow alleyway. A *peepal* tree with its heart-shaped leaves had grown behind the small temple, and its canopy formed a whispering, dripping green umbrella over the pointed gable.

In the storm, a long red flag on top of the spire flapped like a tongue, reminiscent of the deity within. He checked his notes—his informers had tailed Tara's priest to this very temple.

Arnav squared his shoulders. He'd not been able to protect his sibling or parents, had goofed up while protecting Tara and Pia. Would someone related to this victim wonder if they could have protected him? Arnav tamped down the twinge of sympathy he felt for all victims, and stepped into the temple premises.

Despite the rain, he spotted the yellow crime scene tape, the red cones holding it in place, and Tambe's scurrying figure.

"Here we are again," Tambe said by way of greeting as his assistant organized the samples already collected. "I told you not to involve me after the last time."

"Have you received any more threatening calls?"

"Not yet, but thanks to you, I might soon. I want a steady, peaceful retirement, Rajput."

"I'll do my best."

Tambe grunted and kept at his work.

Unknown to Tambe, Arnav had set two of his informants to tail the forensic officer. This would help keep Tambe safe, and maybe find out the entity behind the threats. Or the murders.

"Same suspect?"

"Why don't you take a look around first?" Tambe said, inviting Arnav into the temple as if it were his own living room. Sarcasm galore, but Arnav didn't react.

The scene reminded Arnav of the previous victim at the other Kaali temple, the body posed the same way, spread eagle, castrated, blood everywhere from the wound between the legs, the cuts on the face, and the slashes across the throat. Whoever had done this couldn't have escaped unmarked by blood.

The violence had escalated, the rage more intense. The suspect had torn up the hibiscus flowers before scattering them, and smeared the vermilion powder in a circle on the stomach, like an open wound. It wasn't a neat circle. A fine layer of the red powder covered a large section of the cement floor.

In all that red, a jagged scribble stood out. Based on the presence of the *aum* in Sanskrit, it seemed like a prayer—most prayers began with that syllable. While Tambe clicked away, Arnav took a few snapshots of his own, adding them into his password-protected app. The pictures gushed red: blood, vermilion, scarlet hibiscus.

"Preliminary conclusions?" Arnav dived right in.

"The victim was in his prime."

Arnav couldn't disagree. The man was muscled: his thighs like columns, wide shoulders, narrow waist, chiseled midsection and chest. He could have been a professional bodybuilder.

"I would guess not older than forty, but maybe not younger than twenty-five. I must perform other examinations to confirm. Has been dead a few hours, at this site. The murder might have taken place very early in the morning, between five a.m. and seven a.m., but not earlier."

Amid the rain and the dark, the suspect must have caught the victim unaware, and made the most of the time available. Since this was a slightly less isolated place than the Kaali temple near Pia's school, they had to be very careful the victim made no noise.

The man was either dead or deeply unconscious when he was mutilated, like in the previous case. How had the killer lured the victim here? Was he brought in for some kind of ritual? The previous murder had received a fair amount of coverage on local TV channels—why would the victim visit a Kaali temple during a dark, stormy dawn?

Arnav spoke to the sub-inspectors on the scene: the CCTV footage from a lighted warehouse near the temple showed only a few pedestrians, but since they all carried black umbrellas, it was hard to make any identification. There might have been one couple, a man and a woman, but they couldn't be sure. They all wore pants. The lights next to the shrine didn't work. Darkness shrouded the area.

"The light bulbs have been missing for a day or two, sir," one of the sub-inspectors said. "We made enquiries with the security guards in the surrounding area."

"Check if they heard or saw anything unusual in the early morning, between four and eight a.m."

"Right, sir."

"Has the priest been summoned?"

"Two constables have gone to pick him up," the sub-inspector said.

Same priest, the same deity, similar murder. All of it pointed to the same culprit.

Arnav returned to the body where Tambe was wrapping up.

"Now that you've finished your examination—is the killer the same as in the previous case?"

"Impossible to say for certain, but the slashes on the face are similar. The knife is held in the right hand, and is pulled left to right, from low to high, in both cases. The gouges in this one are deeper. Same flowers and vermilion, but this time the vermilion wasn't used to draw a figure."

"Could you lift prints anywhere?"

"The killer was meticulous—contrary to the reckless savagery of the mutilation. With fine vermilion dust I'd hoped to find more than a few, but I think the killer wore gloves. And that scrawl there"—Tambe pointed to the writing on the floor—"they've used a piece of cloth to draw it, and wiped away any footprints as they left the scene."

Arnav made a note of that. The killer knew that prints could incriminate them, so he couldn't be an uneducated crook. This one understood the basics of a police investigation—avoiding leaving evidence behind, and being seen on CCTV.

"Do you think we'll find the killer's blood again this time?" Arnav said.

"I've taken samples. What you should find are witnesses. The blood spatter from these slashes are significant, and can't be hidden with ease."

"The constables are already canvassing the area."

"Well, we can safely say that the part-time tantric in your custody hasn't committed this particular crime."

Arnav considered that. The part-time tantric and full-time accountant was not directly responsible for this crime, but did that mean he should be released? He was a Kaali worshipper, and the second murder had occurred in the premises of a Kaali temple. Was there a way Ram Chandra Dome could have instructed the killer? He might not have held the knife in the previous case, but he could have been standing by, conducting a ritual.

Arnav glanced at the body now ready to be bagged and transported to the morgue. Tambe was right: the injuries were more consistent with rage than ritual. Had he killed before and gone undetected? Why was he making such a display of the bodies? And who had called in the previous murder?

"You're deep in thought," Tambe remarked, ready to leave.

"We must determine if the same suspect was responsible for both killings. If yes, that rules Ram Chandra Dome out for both murders."

"I'll check if the killer drugged this man," Tambe said.

"Yes. Also, get the Kalina center to test all the blood samples against the previous case."

"And if the samples don't match?"

"Possible," Arnav admitted. "What if Ram Chandra Dome was the first killer, but this second is the work of a copycat? We need to comb all the evidence once again, after the forensic results of this case come through."

"You mean someone who's read about the first murder in the news decided to stage a similar killing? Why would they do that?" Tambe stroked his white beard lovingly, as if it were a cat. On anyone else, it would have looked amusing.

"Any number of reasons," Arnav said. "They might want to pin this one on a rumored 'serial killer.' Or they want the thrill of getting away with it."

Arnav intended to change that. Three days after the first murder, here was another one.

His phone buzzed, and he stepped aside under the porch of a neighboring warehouse to answer Bapat's call. After he'd updated his boss on his findings, he waited for the hard questions. Bapat didn't disappoint.

"So we have a serial killer castrating men in temples now?"

"Technically, no, sir. It has to be three or more instances, with significant intervals in between."

"That's all mumbo jumbo. The same killer for both, right?"

"Tambe says that's a possibility, sir."

"Any other leads?" Bapat snapped.

Arnav detailed the steps they were taking, and that the previous victim had been identified.

"And the suspect in custody? He couldn't have been behind this second case."

"He could still be involved in the previous case, sir, or have a connection with the killer. He had motive to kill Nimkar's son."

"Have you spoken to Mr. Nimkar?"

"He's still unreachable, sir."

"Who's the lead on the case, now that you have given Desai a time-out?"

"I've retained it myself, sir, given the sensitive locations of the crimes."

"If we don't sort this out soon, either the Crime Branch or the Central Bureau will begin sniffing around. The media isn't making it easy."

"I'll update you on developments, sir."

Arnav left the sub-inspectors in charge of the canvassing with instructions to be very thorough. The rains had let up, but waterlogged roads would still take a while to negotiate. He considered the buildings in the vicinity, trying to zero in on one that might provide a view of the temple. The sky threatened doom.

Out there, somewhere in the city, a killer was either pissed off enough to want men dead and neutered, or a fanatic who wanted to sacrifice them to a deity. Arnav's phone buzzed again. This time it was his office. One of his sub-inspectors was on the line, with a panicked garble.

"Speak slower this time. What did you say?"

"The tantric has gone, sir. We don't know how. His cell is locked, but he isn't there."

CHAPTER THIRTY-EIGHT

SITA

The wiper ticked back and forth, slicking away rain from the windshield of the unmarked car Sita had borrowed for police business, but was using to run an errand of her own.

Parked at a red light on the way to Neeti's school, Sita frowned as she watched laborers carrying piles of bricks on their heads, up the uneven steps of a construction site beside the road. The biggest lie Sita's grandmother had told her was that hard work led to success. If that were true, all those laborers would be billionaires.

Hard work on its own was as effective as a bullet outside a gun. It meant nothing, a heavy, dull thing—valued, but inert. A bullet came into its own only when you slotted it in the chamber.

To succeed, you needed to find a slot in good fortune. The way Tara had. She had lost her legs, true, and that was tough, but she had also married a man who doted on her. She'd moved away from a life of penury and disrespect as a bar girl–cum–cheap choreographer. Same with Pia. Pia had gone from shabby quarters in Lucknow to a fancy apartment in a prime location for upper-middle-class Mumbai. She attended an international school.

Pia's friend Neeti, on the other hand, had descended from a decent apartment to a *chawl*. They were friends because Pia, as the ex–bar girl's daughter, had few at her own school.

Neeti's school was not far from Pia's, but it was one of those hope-
less government affairs where you shone only if you received outside aid,
or wanted to study badly enough. Sita had the latter. Neeti was hoping
to get by with the former.

On the few occasions Sita had spent time with Neeti and Pia, she'd
studied them. Pia would protect Neeti to the death. The other half of
the equation was less clear.

A long chat with Neeti might help. Pia might have confided in
her. Teens and their parents formed a family, but they might as well be
different species when it came to communication. Teenagers told each
other things they wouldn't confess to their parents at gunpoint.

Sita turned into the road toward the dilapidated government school
for girls, its small driveway waterlogged, its walls dark and spotty, and
parked her car near a deserted bus stop. Sita had timed her visit to coin-
cide with the hour classes ended at Neeti's school. The rain had petered
into a faint drizzle, so Sita rolled down her window as she waited. A
hum of children's shrieks and laughter floated up, and soon the girls,
clad in blue-and-white *salwar kameezes* poured out into the grounds.

Sita spotted Neeti from a distance. A tall and curvy sixteen-year-
old with a long ponytail, her sky-blue *kameez* neat but her white *salwar*
bottoms spattered with mud from the grounds, she walked out alone
while other girls trooped out in groups of threes and fours, or pairs. She
didn't seem any more popular at her school than Pia was at hers—still
the new girl despite nearly two years. Since this wasn't the kind of place
where parents could afford to pick up and drop their children, the girls
took their time loitering before they dispersed.

When Neeti passed by Sita's car, Sita said hello.

"Naik Aunty?" Neeti gaped. All women were either *Didi*, *Bhabhi*,
or Aunty. A sister, or sister-in-law, or aunt. Though she never spoke
about it, it bothered Sita that Neeti and Pia called her Aunty. She was
only ten years older than Neeti.

"How are you, Neeti?"

"Okay, Aunty. How come you're here?"

"I came to pick you up and take you to jail." Sita pulled a serious face.

Neeti gasped, her eyes wide, her arched eyebrows rising. She clutched the fabric of her blue *kameez* in her fist.

Sita hadn't figured Neeti wouldn't get the joke. "My car ran into trouble with all the waterlogging," she added quickly. "I saw you passing by."

"Will it run?" Neeti's smile bloomed with relief. "Do you need a mechanic?"

"I think the engine needed a break. Let me take you home."

"No, no, Aunty. I'll take the bus."

"Why? You're not going to Pia's school?"

That was usual between the girls. Neeti walked to Pia's school, and then either the driver for the Rajputs, or Pia's father, picked them up.

"She's not gone to school. She's not well."

Sita feigned surprise, though of course she knew. Tara had called.

"I see. Hop in. I'll drop you."

"How do you like your school?" Sita said once they were both buckled in, and Sita set the car into gear.

"How do you think I like it?" Neeti turned away toward the window. "Two years ago I used to study at Saint Thomas." She took a lip gloss out of her bag, and turning the rearview mirror, applied the pink shine over her full lips. A gift from Pia, no doubt.

Saint Thomas was a good private institution, and the change must have been nothing short of a catastrophe for a young girl. For anyone, really. Private schools meant group trips all over the country, gardens on the premises, well-stocked libraries and canteens, and friends from rich families.

"I studied in a government school," Sita said. "I know what it's like."

"You did?" Neeti turned toward Sita.

"Yes. Then I cleared the police exams. My grandmother said I had to get married before I joined the police, so I did that, too. I live in a *chawl* with my husband and my mother-in-law."

"But you're a sub-inspector. You could move out if you chose!"

"You're growing up. You know the choices women can make and those they can't."

"We are where we are because of my mother. She took us out of Saint Thomas and into that hellhole where Bina Aunty lives. Arnav Uncle offered to pay for our education, and to let us stay at his home. They don't have a lot of room, but it would have been so much better than our rathole of a *kholi*. They have a real TV, running water. They can shower in their own clean bathroom. They need not queue up to go to the toilet. They drink filtered water, and they have their own car."

Sita let the girl vent.

"Why did your mother say no?" she said, when Neeti fell silent, and turned away again.

"She doesn't want to take favors from anyone, even though Arnav Uncle and Tara Aunty are so nice. I hate it in the *chawl*, and I can't stand being called names on the street."

"Who calls you names?" Sita kept her tone neutral.

"Well, my mother sure knows. She won't do a thing about it. She can put a stop to it with a word. But she won't, and wouldn't let me ask, either." Neeti sighed, and wavered. "And why am I telling you this . . . you are the police."

"Your father was a police officer."

"I've heard what they said about him at our police quarters."

"We won't speak about him." Sita paused, letting the silence lengthen.

"My mother tried to register a police complaint, but they won't listen. These men from the upper caste, they think they can do what they want, because the police only support them."

This had the ring of truth. Sita's upper-caste colleagues lost no opportunity to band against her.

"The other day a man grabbed my hand and tried to drag me onto his bike."

This was more than catcalling.

"What happened then?"

"My mother happened to pass by, and saw what was going on. She threatened to tell Tara Aunty."

"Why Tara?"

"Her physiotherapist, that Paresh Khare, was one of the louts egging the man on."

Okay. This would be a tricky one.

"Why didn't you tell her? He should be charged, and not be allowed into their home."

"My mother won't let me. Paresh Khare also works the night shift. He's Bina Aunty's boss."

"How do you mean? He's a physiotherapist. Your aunt works in the factory."

"He's the night shift manager. It's lighter work because there's less staff at the time. Bina Aunty says he mostly sleeps on the job."

"They haven't tried to report him to the bosses at the factory?"

"Who'll listen?"

Sita gripped the steering wheel hard, her gaze on the road that was beginning to clog with rush hour traffic. This wasn't easy to hear.

"I shouldn't have told you." Neeti's voice was barely a whisper.

"You should've told me earlier. The *chawl* is under my station's jurisdiction."

"Will you tell Tara Aunty I told you?" Neeti's voice shook. "My mother will kill me."

"I won't need to. I've already seen what's going on for myself, and will take action on this gang in any case."

She must check the files from this area and pull up the constable on beat patrol.

Now that she'd put Neeti at ease, she asked the one question she sought an answer to.

"Did Pia talk to you about her factory visit?"

"Only that she hated it." Neeti looked out the window.

"Nothing else?" Sita probed. "Are you sure?"

"Not the details," Neeti turned to Sita, but didn't meet her eyes. "But someone grabbed her on that roof. A man."

Just as Sita had suspected. Someone had attacked Pia on that afternoon. One of Rasool's men, maybe. She wished she could search the factory, turn it upside down, but they had no warrant, and no solid grounds. Yet.

"What did he say? Did he hurt her?"

"She won't tell me. All she says is she won't let her mother go anywhere near that factory." Neeti paused and met Sita's eyes. They were now parked by the roadside. "Will you tell Aunty about her physiotherapist?"

"Once he's arrested, Tara will know. Not from me, and not about you."

"My mother will be very upset if she knows I'm talking to you," Neeti said. "She wants me to be like Ruchi."

"Ruchi?"

"My cousin, Bina Aunty's daughter. She helps at the nonprofit. She's deaf, and speaks only in sign language, but she's very smart. Updates all the papers at the nonprofit."

Sita wished to ask about Pia, but let Neeti lead the chat instead. In Neeti's place, she'd have wanted to talk, get things off her chest. She wanted the girl relaxed when she dropped her. Neeti would prove an asset if Sita wanted to keep track of events at the *chawl* and the factory.

"You don't want to be like Ruchi?"

"I'd like to, but I don't like math or science. I like the languages. I can sing. My mother says all that is useless. You're sure you won't tell?"

"Not if you don't. Here's my number." Sita scrawled her number on an old receipt.

"Drop me at the next bus stop."

"Okay, but I'll watch to make sure you reach home safe."

Neeti was about to step out when she changed her mind. "Pia said it was a big man, wearing black clothes, but he had a cloth tied over his face. Paresh Khare wears black. Do you think it was him? I should have told her about him, right?"

"We can't be sure. I'll deal with Paresh Khare. Sit tight. Call me if you hear or see anything I should know."

"All right."

"Did Pia tell you what the man said?"

"No." Neeti met Sita's eyes. "I'm not lying to you. It was something horrible, she said, words she could not repeat."

CHAPTER THIRTY-NINE

ARNAV

In a childhood game of hide-and-seek, Arnav had once been terrified out of his wits when his elder sister had disappeared into thin air in front of his very eyes. Their neighbor's home featured a hidden door in their attic he knew nothing about, and she was right there all the time. In the end, her half-smothered giggles had given her away.

At the police station, it was an entirely different sort of hide-and-seek. The constables stood around in knots, but straightened up as Arnav walked in. Arnav had already called ahead asking his other inspectors and sub-inspectors to assemble at the conference room at 7:00 p.m. He would have to call in Sita Naik to ask her about her husband's friend, but first he needed the picture from his team at the station.

Arnav entered his office at 6:55 p.m., his clothes damp despite the protection of the heavy rain gear he'd left dripping on the frayed carpet outside. Picking up his notebook and pen, he headed to the conference room, where the officers had begun to gather.

He asked the inspector in charge of the lockup area to make a report.

"Sir, we don't know exactly when and how the tantric escaped."

"This moment onward, we'll stop calling him the tantric or Sri Sarvagya and refer to him by his documented name: Ram Chandra Dome. We won't entertain any rumors about how he used his 'powers,' so please stick to facts as we know them so far. We're a police station, not a cult. We'll find logical explanations and solutions. Clear?"

"Yes, sir," the inspector continued, chastened. "Ram Chandra didn't rise in the morning when they left tea for him, but the constable didn't wake him because we had no interrogation planned. He was unwell, and as per your instructions, we tried to make sure there was no custodial incident."

"Custodial incident" was a soft term for deaths while in custody, a phenomenon not unknown in Mumbai Police.

"Okay, so he was in his lockup cell this morning?"

"We can't be sure, sir. The constable saw his shape on the floor and assumed it was him. The light in his lockup wasn't working. At afternoon teatime when he still didn't rise, the constable went in to check, only to find him gone."

"His clothes?"

"His clothes are all there, sir."

"You mean he left the station unclothed?"

"We're not sure, sir. We've combed through the CCTV footage but don't see him leaving the cell."

"Let's watch it."

The inspector inserted a thumb drive into his laptop and switched on the projector. A hush descended on the room as the CCTV footage flooded the screen. It showed the locked gate of Ram Chandra's cell.

Constables flitted back and forth in front of it on fast-forward, like marionettes in a silent film. A constable did indeed leave biscuits and a cup of tea in the morning, and then again a plate at lunchtime. Throughout, the door didn't open or close as the inspector scrolled through the footage at a brisk pace.

"He is human, not a ghost. He was unwell, and he had no clothes. Hand me the footage—I'll deal with it."

The inspector extracted the thumb drive and passed it to Arnav.

"I've called Forensics. We'll get the cell swept for fingerprints."

"Right, sir."

"Have you set a watch on his home and workplace? And the temple?"

"Yes, sir."

"He had help, that was for sure. He couldn't have escaped alone."

"Sir? Are you saying someone at the station was involved?"

"We can't rule anything out at this stage. Until the suspect is arrested, everyone at the station during those hours will be held to account. It's unacceptable that a suspect escapes our lockup, in the presence of the entire staff on duty. As far as I'm concerned, all of us are responsible, so salaries will be docked for all, including me, the other officers, and all constables."

The room went silent for a moment, and then murmurs rose.

"If you're discussing how to catch the suspect, please continue. If it's about anything else, I'll take questions now."

The elderly Constable Kamble spoke up. "Can we have a *shanti-pooja* done, sir? It's been raining nearly nonstop for more than a week now—we should do something to appease the gods."

Arnav doubted the existence of gods, or, at the very least, their propensity to be appeased.

"A prayer for peace is a good thing. Sure, we can organize one. After the escaped suspect is arrested."

Arnav walked out. For now, he couldn't trust anyone at his station. He called the forensics lab and personally handed over a copy of the thumb drive.

This was not the kind of senior inspector he'd expected he'd become. His own inspector trying to sabotage an investigation. A suspect escaped from his lockup. Rumors of paranormal activities that called for a peace prayer. Once Naik was back from her assignment trying to locate Rasool Mohsin, he would put her to work.

Having taken care of sending the CCTV footage for analysis, Arnav stepped into his office, and Constable Kamble came in with *cutting chai*.

"Is the interrogation room ready?" Arnav said.

"Yes, sir."

"Make sure there's a bottle of water and a glass. I'll be speaking to a victim's father, not a suspect."

"Right, sir," Kamble said.

One of his inspectors had finally located the owner of the Remy Virgin Hair Factory.

"Sir, the Kaali temple priest has also been brought in."

"Are they taking down his details?"

"Yes, sir."

"Make him wait. No one should talk to him."

Arnav stepped into the interrogation room to find a bald man of middle years sitting with his elbows on the table, his face in his hands. He peered up at the sound of Arnav's approach, his eyes red, his expression blank. Rain hammered on a tin shed outside, its rising noise like distant, muted gunfire.

"I'm very sorry for your loss, Mr. Nimkar."

"What are you talking about?"

"I'm very sorry for the loss of Vishal Nimkar, your son."

"He's out of town." Mr. Nimkar tried an impassive expression, pursing his lips. "I don't understand the harassment you're putting me and my family through."

"I get your wanting to deny your son's death—denial is the first reaction to a catastrophe. But you must face the truth at some point."

Arnav let the silence fester. He didn't know Vishal, nor why he had turned out the way he had, but the father in him felt sorry for this man who'd lost his son in such a horrific fashion.

"My boy is traveling." Mr. Nimkar blurted out the words, and reached for the glass of water.

"We've matched a sample of his DNA. He was taken into custody last year on charges of molestation. His details are in the system."

Nimkar blanched at that, and his shoulders sagged, as if someone had pulled the air out of him. The interrogation room smelled of damp. Maybe it was the man's clothes. Or Arnav's own. Rain permeated the air, clothes, broken hearts, papers on file, wooden doors. Arnav sighed. Nothing in Mumbai would ever be dry again.

"Why would that be my son? He's never gone near a temple on his own."

"Which is what we need to find out—why would your son go to a temple, and who bore him a grudge big enough to injure him?"

"Vishal had his flaws—the young generation, you know, they watch all these videos and movie stars and think all of it is real—but he was not the devout sort and would never go to a temple without the family."

"We have no doubt it is him. If you want justice for your son, you should tell us more about him. We'll hand over his body to you in the next week or so."

"He had a fight with our accountant, and fired him. Ram Chandra Dome. You have him in custody now; I saw that on TV."

Arnav couldn't tell Nimkar about the absconding suspect. "Talk about Ram Chandra."

"I thought he was a good man. Kept himself to himself, did his job. I didn't know about his side hustle as a tantric for a very long time. When I found out, I asked him to stop. I employed him, a lower-caste man, because he was educated and capable. I didn't want any silly rumors influencing his work performance."

"Did he stop?"

"He told me he did."

"Why didn't you file a missing person report for Vishal?"

"He often disappears for days at a time. And in any case he'd spoken to us two days before . . . before the temple."

"So you thought he would reappear, as usual."

"I'd asked Inspector Desai to keep an eye out for him. He's from the same caste as I, and we have a common prayer circle. He'd asked for identifying marks, and I told him about this patch on Vishal's thigh. He called me the other day . . . and when I saw pictures of the body taken for postmortem, I had to do something."

"You knew it was your son, and disowned his body?" Arnav couldn't hide his disbelief.

"My son"—Nimkar put his face in his hands again, dulling his words—"was unmanned. Our family's name will be ruined—I've got daughters to wed. No one will marry into a dishonored family."

Arnav's disbelief turned to shock. Here was a man so terrified of societal pressure that he was willing to let his murdered son go without justice, cremated as an unidentified body, with no mourning or even the traditional rituals.

"So Inspector Desai has known this was Vishal?"

"Yes"—Nimkar raised his eyes to meet Arnav's gaze—"and I paid good money to make sure he was the only one who knew. He promised the body would be cremated without identification. We've known each other all our lives."

So this was what Desai was up to. In the end, all of it boiled down to one thing. Money.

"You can be charged with obstructing a murder investigation," Arnav said.

"I didn't want my family's name dragged in the mud."

"I must speak to my superiors about further course of action, Mr. Nimkar."

"Please make sure my boy's name doesn't get leaked in the media." Mr. Nimkar rose. "My daughters, my family—we would be ruined."

"It pains me to say this, but your family's reputation was not enhanced when your son was arrested for molesting women."

Mr. Nimkar sank back into his chair. Arnav poured a glass of water, and handed it to the devastated patriarch.

"At this time, he's a murder victim," Arnav said, "and it's my job to discover the culprit. What time did the argument between Ram Chandra and Vishal occur?"

"In the evening, a few days ago."

"Did your son hold a position at the factory?"

"He's on the governing board. I was trying to get him to take on responsibility."

"What were the grounds for Ram Chandra's dismissal?"

"It wasn't on solid grounds. I let it stand because I wanted my son to feel respected at the factory."

"Do you think Ram Chandra could've committed the murder?"

"He's a Dome by caste, after all. Domes in West Bengal cremate bodies, and help at morgues. Foolish of me to employ him—his baser instincts took over, I think. He is a tantric: he lured my boy to the temple, overcame him, and then . . ." Mr. Nimkar was unable to continue.

"Had Ram Chandra made any statements threatening your son?"

"Yes, he came back drunk the next day and shouted threats and abuses from outside the factory gates."

"I'll send you to a sub-inspector now, who'll record your statements, Mr. Nimkar."

"I don't want word to get out. I gave so much money to Desai."

"That can't be helped. If you wish, you can file a complaint against Inspector Desai, and we'll investigate."

"No, that's fine. I don't need more publicity."

"Your son was murdered, and the main suspect is an accountant who worked at your factory. We would like to examine the premises."

"You don't understand. I'm a businessman. I have a foreign client on a visit now. There can't be any police poking around. I've lost Vishal, but if I lose the factory, the rest of my family will be on the streets."

Mr. Nimkar stumbled out of the interrogation room.

The saffron-clad Kaali temple priest rose and hailed the factory owner. Mr. Nimkar made as if to avoid him, but relented in the end, and paid his respects.

"I was here on an official errand. I'll see you soon," was all Nimkar said before shuffling away, leaving the priest wearing a puzzled frown.

A constable escorted the priest into the interrogation room with deference in his posture for the "holy man." A priest commanded a show of respect even at a police station.

"Your men picked me up and brought me here, sir. I've been telling them I know nothing."

"We need your help to answer a few questions."

"I already answered so many."

"We have more." Arnav gestured the portly priest into a plastic chair. "How do you know Mr. Nimkar?"

"He's a big donor to the Kaali temples. His wife is a devotee of Ma Kaali."

"Has his son been to either of the two temples?"

"His son? Seldom. He brought his mother when his father was not in town. Why do you ask?"

"It is interesting that similar murders happened at both Kaali temples you take care of."

"There aren't many Kaali temples. Kaali worship requires difficult rituals, so people like to employ me. I worship at two more temples."

"Was there any jewelry at this second Kaali temple?"

"No, it's a small place. The jewelry is gold-plated, not gold."

"And you haven't found the gold necklaces that went missing from the other temple?"

"Not so far." The priest's face betrayed his unease with this.

Arnav flicked open his pictures from the second crime scene, and showed the priest the scrawl left in the vermilion powder spilled on the floor.

"This is a tantric mantra," the priest said. "Basic, but considered very powerful. It is written in a different script, but it is *Aim Aum Hreem Kreem Hoom Phat.*"

"What does it mean?"

"It is invoking the goddess Kaali. I've heard it before."

"Where?"

"This was the main mantra Ram Chandra used to chant."

"Why didn't you tell us Ram Chandra is your nephew?"

"We've had our differences."

"He says you're not related."

"He would say that, wouldn't he? He's my sister's son. His mother's dead. His father died in jail. I brought him up till he became a teenager. Then he ran away from home with some tantric monks who passed through our neighborhood. He returned with all these rituals."

Arnav imagined Ashok living on the streets, and couldn't imagine not stepping in. He continued with his questions.

"Do you think he's the killer?"

"He's still in custody."

"Why is he angry with you?"

"I'm the one who should be angry with him. I'm on dialysis. I've asked him to take care of my family later if needed, but he went and lost his job instead."

"When was the last time you met Ram Chandra?"

"Two days before the incident at the first temple."

"Did he act normal?"

"He's weird, but yes, as normal as he can be. He mentioned fighting the upper-caste people, making plans, but I didn't ask questions. He likes to talk."

Arnav's phone buzzed, and he picked it up. It was his source, the technician from computer forensics.

"Your lockup footage was doctored."

"How do you mean?"

"There's a period of five minutes at 4:32 a.m. when the footage from both the cameras, in the corridor with the lockup cell as well as the main gate, was tampered with. Someone took footage from another time period, when all activity was normal, and looped it for those five minutes."

CHAPTER FORTY

S ITA

The next day, Sita sat at her desk, steadily working through the bloated pending files from her Versova Police Station jurisdiction.

After her chat with Neeti, it felt like the right thing to do, so she'd decided to stop by her permanent desk and examine the cases filed from the surroundings of the *chawl* Neeti lived in.

Her mind wandered as she considered Neeti's words. How much could she tell Tara without risking stressing her out? She had to tell Tara's husband now, or put two teenagers at increased risk. Guilt stabbed Sita at her betrayal of Tara—but she had no choice.

Most of the complaints in her area rose from the vicinity of the Remy Virgin Hair Factory. Water or electricity supply turned off. Women harassed. Men beaten up. Families forcibly evicted from properties they had rented for years, without adequate notice. The accused were invariably the same: one or the other in a gang of men who hung out together. *Savarna*, upper-caste men, harassing an entire colony of Scheduled Caste families.

Sita clenched her fists to keep from slamming the table as she riffled through the cases she'd argued over with her colleagues. The ones she'd flagged up to the seniors only to be told she should follow orders and stay in her lane. She wanted to shortlist cases that she could resolve with the cooperation of witnesses from the community. Whether they would work with Sita or be coerced into silence by the goons was a discussion for later.

She must identify possible witnesses first.

While flipping through the pages of yet another file, a recent case caught her eye: a man reported missing by his wife. She paused when she checked the name. Paresh Khare. Tara had said he hadn't come in to work.

Sita typed Paresh's details into the system, searching for a match of his parameters. A constable had reported no matches found, but she hit pay dirt almost right away. A dead body. Same height, age, and build. Bandra Police Station. Investigating officer: Arnav Singh Rajput. Forensic pathologist: Surat Tambe. She picked up her phone and dialed Tambe.

Half an hour later, she was convinced the victim in Tambe's morgue was Paresh Khare. His wife had stated that the middle toe on Paresh's right foot was as long as the big toe. And there was a circular bald patch behind his head from an old injury, hidden underneath his otherwise thick hair. Both details matched. Tambe was now hoping to confirm this with DNA evidence.

She took stock of the things she'd have to tell her boss.

About Neeti being harassed. About Paresh being one of the harassers. She closed her files, separated the shortlist, and called her constables for a quick meeting.

Before leaving, she checked her face in her phone camera. When at the police station, she wore the barest smidgen of vermilion, and kept her *mangalsutra* well hidden. These were the signifiers of her marriage. All her colleagues knew her as Raghav's wife, even though he hadn't worn a uniform in nearly a decade. Once a wife, always a wife.

Soon she'd be handing Senior Inspector Rajput a break in his case. He'd made no secret of the fact that he liked her work as an officer and was grateful for her help in saving his family two years ago. That was enough. She didn't crave more. Did not. She straightened her shoulders and, snapping open the umbrella, marched out into the rain, careful to avoid puddles. A passing car splashed muddy water pooled beside the road, but with a nimble jump she saved her uniform, and got into the cab she'd called.

Her phone beeped with a text from her boss.

Stop by the office for briefing. We need all hands on deck.

Sita gazed at the screen, her smile ironic. She was heading to a work meeting. A tricky one, but that was all it was.

CHAPTER FORTY-ONE

TARA

It rained outside the window, a nonstop, unvaried pouring from the heavens, and it rained within Tara's heart. Decades ago, her mother's chief complaint with Tara was that she wouldn't cry. If you cried harder, her mother said, your father wouldn't beat you as much.

Tara didn't care. At ten years old, she took it, teeth clamped, dry eyes, gaze unlowered. Her father used shoes, thin sticks from the ragtag garden outside, his fists. Feet, when he was tired or drunk. She refused to give him the satisfaction of a job well done, and ended up with large bruises—on her legs, her arms, her neck. Her face. He didn't care who saw them. Everyone in the village knew when he was raining blows on his family, and did nothing to interfere. It was a man's right.

Tara had prided herself on this hard-earned skill of never giving in to tears, even when her father sold her into the bar scene in Mumbai. She remained dry eyed through her dance-bar life of being groped and dancing for dangerous private assignments.

It all changed as her pregnancy with Pia advanced. Tara had cried for days at a time. A good thing, Zoya said. It made her an authentic bereaved widow—the story they'd given out in their new neighborhood.

Zoya, Zoya, Zoya. Where was she, and why hadn't she called? By now, Rasool knew, and so did Zoya, that the police had found out about his return. Did Zoya think Tara had tattled? Was that why she'd stayed away?

Tara hauled herself up in bed. Her damned eyes wouldn't stop leaking. She called Arnav, but the call went to voice mail. He hadn't returned home again last night—damage control over an escaped suspect, and extra hours on other pending cases.

Hormones, Dr. Holkar said when she called the clinic. We can recommend a good therapist. Keep your mind engaged in an activity.

Tara's housekeeper ran the house like an efficient matron, and might have made Tara feel redundant even had she not been in a wheelchair. Years ago, when she was hustling to earn her keep and raise Pia, she would have killed for this sort of help with the household.

Tara stared at the TV screen, the unvaried loop of floods and landslides, and remembered the doctor's words. She must thrive, not just live, for Pia's sake and Arnav's, and also for the little life she carried within her. That baby wouldn't know a Tara who could walk. Tara wished there were more such people in her life, unaware of her history, uncaring of it. Arnav wasn't one of them—he'd known her when she possessed not only a pair of sound legs, but also the lithe body of a seventeen-year-old.

The one time she could remember having fun in the last few weeks was at the nonprofit. Those little girls dancing. They didn't know a Tara outside of a wheelchair. They might need her the way her husband and daughter didn't. And at the factory, Tara could find a way to reach Zoya.

Each time Tara had tried to speak with Pia, Pia had remained aloof, feigning too much homework or a headache. Zoya might have gotten a word or two out of the girl.

Tara dialed Bina's number.

That afternoon, Tara found herself at the gates of the Remy Virgin Hair Factory once more, but this time the security guards guided her car to the rear entrance. Tara touched her wig, clipped on and secure. She'd dressed in a modest top, a flared skirt, and a dull cap. She'd debated with herself against the wig, but she liked how it made her appear. Normal, healthy, and confident. Time for her to take charge of what little of her life she could.

Bina waited under a large black umbrella to protect herself from the soft-falling rain, wearing another of her faded sarees, and a very bright smile.

"You came," Bina said.

"I missed the children." Tara tried to keep her voice level as the driver and a woman from the nonprofit helped her into the wheelchair.

"Pia didn't join you?"

"She has school. I wanted to come and see what needs to be done first."

She didn't tell Bina that no one other than the driver knew she was here, and she'd bribed him enough he wouldn't report back to Arnav, or Pia. She would go back before either of them returned home.

"Be careful," Bina said to the driver, "the ramp isn't very strong. It's slippery due to rain."

Tara glanced around while the driver wheeled her in, and her gaze caught the large board with the factory's name.

"I didn't ask before, but do you know why the factory is called Remy Virgin Hair?"

"It sounds a little funny outside of the industry, doesn't it?" Bina laughed. "Remy hair is human hair with its cuticles intact. We collect the hair so the root and tip travel in the same direction, to ensure the cuticle doesn't tangle or mat. It fetches a higher price. We also make synthetic wigs, but that's mostly for the local market."

"And virgin hair?"

"That's because it's untreated—no coloring, heat treatment, curling, or straightening."

"So the name indicates that the factory supplies the best kind of hair?"

"We can only hope. If you ask me, some of the best hair is what we work with right here at the nonprofit. The girls' families donate them."

They'd entered the main hall, where girls sat in small circles on colorful mats, sorting through bunches of hair. The hair still gave Tara a turn. Remy hair. Hair with cuticles—would Pia ever agree to volunteer here? And without her, what could Tara teach? Certainly not dance.

"You said you wanted me to train the girls?"

"Yes. We don't have good teachers—we need help with singing, dancing, and English."

"My English is basic, and I can't instruct them on dance unless someone can demonstrate the steps for me. We could maybe work on a little singing today?"

Tara smiled back at the eager faces surrounding her. The children repeated the phrases she sang to them with more passion than skill, but she didn't mind. She stroked little five-year-old Uma's frock, praising her when she got the tune right. Uma had lost all her hair to chemo treatments. Meena, smaller and thinner than Uma, but older, clung to Tara's skirt, her voice no louder than a whisper. Most of the girls had it much worse than her Pia—with painful cancer treatments, the hair loss, and the circumstances they lived in.

Tara could hear Meena's voice by the time the session ended. Hope bloomed within her. She could do this. The smaller girls touched her arm, asking her to return soon. She said yes, and distributed the sweets she'd brought along.

Bina left to work her shift at the factory, so Tara surveyed the rooms at the nonprofit as best she could. She'd underestimated the challenges of wheeling herself on the uneven floors.

Tired out, she took a break and messaged her driver. He could take her to the factory, and if anyone stopped her, she'd say she wanted to say bye to Bina.

Tara had failed the last time, but she could send a message to Zoya if she spotted someone likely to be one of the don's men.

Sitting alone at one end of the hall, she couldn't shake the feeling of being watched. She turned around, letting her eyes wander across the hall, the heads of the girls and the two other volunteers bent upon their work. She detected nothing out of the ordinary. She sighed her relief when she spotted her driver hurrying toward her.

They had left the hall behind and reached the ramp when Uma darted to her, left a small piece of folded paper in her hands, and whirled off.

Expecting a note thanking her, Tara unfolded the paper.

You will lose your family very soon.

The world went silent for a few seconds, and then Tara heard a harsh gasp. Her own. The paper slipped from her fingers, but she managed to snatch it in her grip and turned quickly to find the girl. That unexpected motion swiveled the wheelchair on the unstable ramp. It tilted forward.

Tara felt herself slide out of the wheelchair, tried to grab the armrests, failed, her hands unable to hold on, her thought molasses slow and lightning fast at the same time—*I must not fall, cannot fall, will not fall, let me not fall, must save her, Ma Kaali save her*—as she tipped over, landed on her palms, and felt pain ricochet through her wrists, arms, shoulders, clenching her body in blind panic, waiting for her limbs to spasm, something that would tell her how the fall had impacted the lower part of her body.

Amid the clang of the tumbling wheelchair and the terrified cries of her driver, who rushed to pick her up, Tara waited, breathing through the pain in her arms. She was fine. The baby would be fine. Her body would cushion the fall, take upon itself all the pain. As the driver gripped her hand, Tara hardened her resolve and let her gaze drop toward her top and then her skirt, her pregnant belly. She couldn't feel its warmth, but there was no mistaking the splash of red on her skirt, staining outward from between her legs.

CHAPTER FORTY-TWO

SITA

Her boss looked haggard. His promotion hadn't changed a thing—Senior Inspector Arnav Singh Rajput still stayed overnight when on a high-profile case.

"Good afternoon, sir," Sita said, her tone professional.

"Afternoon, Naik," he answered, his eyes bright despite the shadows on his face, unevenly shaven cheeks, and messy hair. "We need a plan, and you might be the best placed to work it."

He didn't wear a mustache like the rest of the men in Mumbai Police—he had shaven it off ever since he married Tara. To Sita, this showed a vulnerable, sensitive side to him. She ignored it. It helped that he had tasks for her—she preferred the adrenaline of working together.

"I'm here, sir."

She sat through his curt, rapid-fire description of what had gone down at the station. Ram Chandra Dome, disappeared. The doctored footage. Inspector Desai and his deal with Nimkar. The priest's interrogation.

His question at the end brought her up short. "Has Raghav Naik spoken about Ram Chandra in the last day or two?"

"No, sir. I've been doing stakeouts. Haven't been home for more than a few hours."

"He'll be watched. I need to know where you stand on this."

She'd signed up for the police force to do the right thing. All her life she'd seen women being silenced, lower-caste men being harassed and dominated by those from the upper caste. Criminals bribing police. She'd wanted to right those wrongs—she gathered her breath, collecting a faint scent of air freshener, let it out, and squared her shoulders before giving her answer.

"I'll do whatever it takes to nail the suspect, sir."

"Would you remain objective? We'll have to question him officially. If I think the case might be compromised, I must remove you from the assignment."

"Yes, understood, sir."

If Raghav was involved in shady activities, the court would question his wife being part of the investigation.

"Raghav Naik has been an upstanding policeman on record—I've checked through his files. It might be a case of him being friends with the wrong person."

"Right, sir."

"Good." He leaned back in his seat. "I want someone I can trust, Naik. There's a mole at our station."

"Do we have any suspects, sir?"

"The entire staff on duty at the time Ram Chandra ran." He slid a paper across the table.

"He escaped at four thirty a.m." He continued, "According to forensics, the second victim was murdered sometime between five a.m. and seven a.m. Ram Chandra had help while escaping, and if he were to get a vehicle, he could be our killer. He had motive against Vishal Nimkar. If we can identify the second body, that might tell us if he had a motive there, too."

Sita's heart lifted. She had the right answer.

"I was at Versova this morning, sir. A missing person report may be connected to the Kaali temple murder case."

"Tell me." He leaned forward.

She launched into the facts as she knew them. It brought her a sense of rightness, reporting to him, explaining her process and conclusions in quick, clear words, watching him listen, keen and professional. Quite like the old times, the countless conversations over three years before he transferred out.

"Tambe is sure Paresh Khare is the victim?" he said.

"He's ninety percent convinced, sir. He'll call you with results after he's able to confirm them."

"Give me a minute." He dialed an extension to call a constable working under him, asking him to visit Tambe and collect the report in person.

"Paresh Khare lives in the Versova area," he said. "Tara told me his place is close to the factory."

"He works there. As the night shift manager."

"I see." He lapsed into thought, his lips pressed together in a grim line. "I must call Tara. She'll be very upset to hear about Paresh Khare, but it's best she learns as soon as possible."

"I'm sorry, sir. I hope she finds a good replacement physiotherapist."

"That incident at the factory has stressed Tara out. Did you speak with Pia?"

This was her cue to tell him all she knew. She hesitated. Tara wouldn't be pleased, nor would he.

"Naik?"

She hated it whenever someone referred to her by Raghav's surname, which was all the time, the way it reduced her to being his wife. But that was protocol.

"Yes, sir."

"Is there something you'd like to tell me?"

Sita remained silent for a beat longer, then spoke about the marks on Pia's forearm, mentioning her suspicion that it could be one of Rasool's men, trying to scare Pia and Tara away. Next, Sita summarized her chat with Neeti, sticking to the facts, making it sound like an official report. His face remained bland, but she'd watched him too closely over the years to miss the slight clenching of his jaw, the brief flare of anger.

"Why do you think that Rasool's men might have touched Pia?"

"I've spotted suspicious men around the premises. Rasool owns a stake in that factory. His men wouldn't want a policeman's family there. Maybe they wanted to do this without involving Zoya."

Her boss paused in thought. Outside the office, the business of the station continued, its din trickling in.

"Neeti has been facing this for how long?" he said.

She saw the effort it cost him. Tara had gone to Sita. Neeti and Mrs. Shinde, his *Vaeeni*, had told him nothing. The physiotherapist, a lecherous goon, had been darkening his door.

"A few months." Sita didn't know how to phrase it. Neeti had bloomed into a woman recently, losing the awkwardness of her teen years.

"And when did Tara tell you about this?"

"Two days ago."

"I see," Arnav said, a frown marring his high forehead. "You're saying that Paresh Khare and his friends were to blame for the disturbance in the area?"

"Khare belongs to the upper caste, sir. And I saw many of them catcalling women—I didn't intervene because I was on a plainclothes trip to watch the neighborhood. We also have Neeti's statement—and Mrs. Shinde was a witness to him harassing her daughter."

With Senior Inspector Rajput, you could be sure of two things: his relentless drive to solve the case, and rejection of any sort of discrimination. She'd never worried about her caste in the time she'd worked with him—but the entire world wasn't like that. Caste reared its ugly head and led to deaths more often than not. His privilege didn't let him see it.

"And yet I get to hear all of this today." His low, deep voice grated with temper. "After Paresh Khare's death."

Her first instinct was to apologize, but she bit down on it. His wife had asked her to keep her mouth shut. Women explained and said sorry altogether too much, even when it wasn't their fault.

Before she could say her next words, a phone on the table rang, and her boss snatched it up.

"Tara?"

It gutted Sita, that husky concern which would never be directed at her, not from this man, nor from her own husband.

"Bina? I don't understand. How do you have my wife's phone?"

Sita heard his voice change timbre, turn lower, firmer. This didn't bode well.

"Which hospital?" He rose. "I'm on my way."

"Tara's had an accident," he told Sita, rushing out. "I must get someone to pick Pia up from school so she—"

"I'll do it, sir."

"I can ask someone here—"

"Spending time with her might help me talk to her about the other afternoon."

He ran, forgetting his cap in his haste. Sita itched to pick it up and run after him. She stepped out the other door instead, intent on reaching Pia.

The downpour continued. It was days since she'd seen sunlight. The fearsome clouds promised days, weeks, months of rain. As if the heavens, tired of human antics, had resolved to wash all of Mumbai away in a flood.

Tara's accident at the factory. Could Rasool's men have gone too far? Would they dare touch a police officer's wife, though? The answer was yes, if they'd already tried to molest the daughter.

Was Rasool simply trying to keep danger off his property, or did he have a role in the murders?

Two *savarna* men dead, butchered and emasculated at a Kaali temple. One who lived there and was a known troublemaker, Paresh

Khare. The other, the son of the factory owner, Vishal Nimkar. Neither man had a great reputation with women. And Ram Chandra was a suspect—a Scheduled Caste, just like her and her husband.

Given what the *savarnas* had been doing in the neighborhood, he had enough motive, and now he'd escaped custody. Between Ram Chandra and Iqbal Asif, the former was the likelier suspect. But even if the killer proved to be Ram Chandra, how had he gained access to Chitra Varli's social media? And who was the mole? How did Iqbal Asif fit into all of this?

Sita's phone buzzed with a strange number as she sank into her seat. A text.

Be careful what you wish for.

CHAPTER FORTY-THREE

ARNAV

Many years ago, when Tara left him and disappeared without a word, Arnav had longed for a glimpse of her. After she returned to Mumbai and his life, he'd resolved to never let her out of his sight again, only to have her land in the hospital and remain there for months.

On that occasion it had been squarely his fault. He'd tried his best, but got things wrong. Tara had been shot trying to save Pia.

Now, as he saw her, her belly swollen with his child, lying sedated in yet another hospital bed—he wasn't sure he was to blame. For some of it, yes.

He was the reason she was in a wheelchair in the first place, no matter who said what about her getting caught in the crossfire two years ago.

Their unplanned baby was an accident with failed protection.

His job didn't spare him enough time to spend with her.

All of this was true.

She was depressed, and desperate to carve out her own space—which was why she'd rushed to this nonprofit to volunteer even though it wasn't safe. He understood her frustration at being homebound, but didn't she realize she couldn't be this irresponsible? Pia would be lost without her, and she was endangering the child in her womb.

Despite himself, anger rose within like fire in a home doused with petrol. How could she be so reckless? Why go there despite him asking her not to? What would he do without her?

A light clearing of the throat interrupted his brooding. Dr. Holkar strode into the room, followed by a nurse. She nodded at him in greeting.

"I'll speak to you once I've checked her again. We've stabilized her now, so there's no immediate reason to worry."

Dr. Holkar drew the curtain around Tara's bed, and Arnav stepped out. His phone buzzed with texts, but he ignored them all. *No immediate reason to worry* meant there *was* reason to worry. Of course there was. Falling from a wheelchair when heavily pregnant couldn't be good—even he knew that. Once he was done with Dr. Holkar, he would ask his boss for leave.

A suicidal move for his career. How would he support his family without a job?

Unsettled by the direction his thoughts had taken, he checked the latest messages on his phone.

A confirmation from Tambe that the body was indeed Paresh Khare, and there was ketamine in his system.

An enquiry from Bapat, about the escaped tantric.

Two missed calls, one from an informer, the other from Naik.

He dialed Naik first. "Is Pia all right?"

"She'd like to come to the hospital," Naik said.

"Where are you at the moment?"

"At your place, sir. I thought she should eat before I told her anything, so I had lunch at your place. I also picked Neeti up, so Pia won't be alone."

"Thank you, Naik. That was very thoughtful. Let me speak to her—Tara isn't awake yet."

Naik was reliable, but she had a demanding job, and a husband. The only person who could help would be *Vaeeni*—she'd refused before, during Tara's earlier stint in the hospital, but knowing what he knew about Neeti now, it was the best solution for them all. He'd insist, and make her agree.

Vaeeni and the children would be safe till they received the compensation and gratuities from Shinde's death, and could afford better accommodation. In the meanwhile, Pia wouldn't be alone.

Pia came on the line, sounding distraught, and Arnav reassured her in calm, measured tones, not believing a word he told her about her mother. His police training came in handy during family situations.

He would know the truth from Dr. Holkar soon. Having calmed Pia down, he dialed his informer, Ali.

"*Ji, saab*," Ali said, "I had called you about the tantric you asked me about."

"Yes."

"Word is he was in a big ruckus involving the man you mentioned. He fought with the factory owner's son and threatened to set fire to the place if he was let go."

Ali went on to describe the entire argument. None of it sounded like Ram Chandra Dome's account. It had apparently come to an exchange of ugly words, and that had led to him being fired.

"On the streets, they're saying this man had deep political connections as well as his reputation as a tantric," Ali continued.

Arnav recalled Sita's description of Ram Chandra Dome, his political aspirations.

"How deep?"

"He can draw a crowd. All the Scheduled Caste. Not top-line yet."

"What sort of company did he keep?"

Ali spoke of the priest, Ram Chandra's upbringing, the running away with traveling monks during his teenage years.

"He got into drugs, along with tantric rituals," Ali continued.

"Drugs?" Arnav said. The ketamine in the first victim's system came to mind.

"Yes, but that was a while ago. He cleaned up his act in his twenties, got a degree, and was working as an accountant."

"And his tantric worship?"

"I don't understand all of that very well, *saab*. I got a Hindu boy to ask around at Dome's uncle's place."

Ali was a Muslim, so that made sense.

"And?"

"The priest's neighbors say Ram Chandra did that only on the side"—Ali cleared his throat—"and gave advice to those who came to the Kaali temple to pray, if they asked. He made some extra money that way."

That was Ali's way of politely saying that someone had seen Tara seeking such advice.

"That thug has been gone for at least twelve hours now," Arnav said. "Any information leading to his arrest will carry a reward on top of our usual agreement."

Arnav didn't need to tell Ali that Ram Chandra had inside help. Ali worked in the shadowy world of Mumbai's mafia, and knew how things worked.

Arnav didn't know who to trust, and if the tantric was devolving and had been the one to murder Khare, time was ticking away toward another horrific death.

"I get it, *saab*."

"The reward won't be small."

"I've watched the news on TV, *saab*."

"Also find out what you can about Paresh Khare."

"Khare, *saab*? He's from the same area near Versova."

"How do you know him?" Arnav said.

"He is tall, big built, muscles?"

That was Khare, all right.

"He is a manager at the factory," Ali said. "Is he in trouble? Nasty sort, this Khare. Used to beat his wife."

"How do you know about him?"

"He's Iqbal Asif's brother-in-law."

"Iqbal Asif's sister is married to Paresh Khare?"

Hindus and Muslims didn't marry without consequences, not unless they were Bollywood stars.

"The sister is Hindu, *saab*. Stepsister to Asif. He loves her very much. Recently found out Khare is beating her. Next time he does it, Khare will be history. I know Asif. Man of his word. Besides, *Bhai* will be happy with Khare gone."

"Why does your *bhai* not care for Khare?"

That would be motive for Paresh Khare's murder.

"Khare used to live in one of *Bhai's kholis*, paid rent. When *Bhai* had to leave India in a hurry, Khare grabbed the *kholi*. He's staying there now, but pays no rent. *Bhai* will want him gone. What is the matter, *saab*?"

"Did you manage to pass a message to Zoya for me?"

"No, *saab*, but I know where she'll be. I'll call you."

"Right."

"This will be very difficult, *saab*. If I get caught . . ."

"I'll make sure you don't regret it."

Arnav cut the call. He might have to pay out of his own pocket, but a chat with Zoya would be worth it. He could have asked her for a call, but a call was proof, and very dangerous. To her, and to him.

Dr. Holkar stepped out of Tara's hospital room, her usual serene self in her saree and white coat. Arnav hurried up to the doctor, trying to read her face for clues.

"Let's talk in my office," Dr. Holkar said, giving nothing away.

CHAPTER FORTY-FOUR

Our fearless leader is full of glee, chanting all the time—We've got this. Watch how they'll suffer.

Bhai doesn't know, but we might have gone a little cuckoo. Mad, raving, greedy. Especially one person, the bane of my existence for as long as I can remember.

When we were children, I was always the slowest. The one who suffered the most. Who kept suffering, even when no longer a child. Now those around me suffer, too.

We're going too fast. We need to slow down, I tell our leader, but when has anyone ever listened to me?

We're not slowing down, are we?

I feel it, this terrible, hurtling speed of everything we're up to, all the moving pieces on the board, and no matter what our leader says, I foresee a crash. That policeman may not know what he's doing, not yet, and we may draw him away from where his eyes should be, but like I keep telling Bhai, I don't have a good feeling about this.

Too much this is, too soon.

CHAPTER FORTY-FIVE

ARNAV

Arnav settled down in Dr. Holkar's office, trying to keep his breathing slow and even. The blown-up pictures of smiling babies and pregnant women in gardens made him choke up. Outside, rain pelted the window and poured down the glass, unceasing like a new widow's tears. He refused the good doctor's offers of tea and begged her to get straight to the point.

"Pregnancies with spinal injuries come with their own set of challenges, which is why we recommend extreme care, but in this case—"

"Is Tara fine? And the baby?"

"The baby is fine, but after checking Tara and her test results, I'm afraid she has to remain in the hospital."

"Is her life in danger?"

"She has what we call a placental abruption. The placenta has begun to separate from the lining of her uterus. It is marginal, but it is there—any more severe and it could affect the baby's nutrient and oxygen supply. We think it happened due to the trauma of her fall. She needs to stay in bed from now on, and given her bleeding, we'd prefer to keep her here."

Arnav's terror burned into anger. On the phone, the driver had been beside himself with guilt, saying it was all his fault for not being able to control the wheelchair, but the accident wouldn't have occurred if Tara had stayed put, or at least waited for someone else to go with her.

Now she was at peril not just from the injuries. A hospital was a hotbed of infections. Years ago, Arnav's mother had caught one during a chemo trip, and never returned home.

"You'd recommended hospitalization at the end of the eighth month," he said.

"Yes, but this has changed things. There are various factors to consider. Any stress could lead to premature labor, and with Tara's spinal injuries, she won't feel the contractions. We might have to do an emergency cesarean operation at any time."

"Why not do it right away?"

"The baby should stay in the uterus for as long as possible for the best chance at optimal health. We must prevent any situation where Tara gets mentally and physically stressed and goes into autonomic dysreflexia—"

"Is that the one about blood pressure?"

Given her spinal injury, Tara had been told to stay careful of any added pressure on her bladder, tight clothes, or devices that might send her blood pressure dangerously high.

"Yes, that's one of the symptoms, and it could be dangerous for both mother and fetus. We can monitor her for physical stresses, but you must ensure she has no mental stress from this point onward. I recommend counseling for her mental health."

"She's obsessed with doomsday videos, and she had to go—"

"Mr. Rajput, she's been through a lot. From what she's told me, she used to lead a very independent life, and chafes at being confined to a wheelchair. A majority of patients with spinal injuries struggle with depression. We must be extra careful." She opened a desk drawer. "I thought I should hand this over to you."

Dr. Holkar passed him an envelope. Inside was a scrap of paper.

Arnav read the words scrawled in capital letters and clenched his fists.

"You are in a high-stress job, Senior Inspector Rajput. We found the paper crumpled up in her hand. I think this might have had something to do with her accident."

Arnav examined the words again:

YOU WILL LOSE YOUR FAMILY VERY SOON.

A handwritten scrawl. Who would have sent this? Experience told him that the mafia usually sent notes like this one—and if Rasool had connections at the hair factory, he could have sent it.

If Arnav wanted a forensic analysis of the note, he'd have to state which case it was for. With a mole in his office, things might grow trickier. He pocketed it—hoping for a spell to sit down and work out all the implications. He'd failed to protect his wife once again, but dwelling on that wouldn't help.

Once he left the doctor's office, he dialed *Vaeeni*—the situation was more serious than he'd anticipated, and he needed someone he could trust staying with Pia when he was caught up with work and the hospital. He would hire additional security for Tara as well. He listened to the call ring out and checked his watch. *Vaeeni* was still at work.

He used his burner phone to dial Naik's other number. He'd last dialed it when asking for her help two years ago.

Naik picked up on the first ring.

"I was about to call you, sir."

"Pia?"

"She's fine, sir. I couldn't talk to you earlier on my office number, given that we may have a leak."

When she told him about the warning she'd received via text message, he paused for a moment. This was the second instance of a warning. And there was the incident with Pia. Sita had received the message on the way to Bandra from the vicinity of the hair factory. These could be connected.

"Do you want to step away from all of this, Naik? You're still the one your family depends on."

"No, sir. I can't let anyone sending me silly warnings get away with it. I've set up a round-the-clock watch at the factory. If there's any suspicious movement, we'll hear about it."

"I'll try to push for a warrant to search the place," Arnav said. "But we need evidence to base it on."

"I'll do my best, sir. I'll be here till we get some additional security at your place."

"I'm setting it up. Thank you, Naik. I appreciate it."

Naik did a most un-Naik thing, and laughed. Arnav was about to ask her why, when she said, "You're welcome, sir."

His office phone rang. The sub-inspector he'd left in charge of canvassing the second crime scene, the neighborhood of Paresh Khare's murder, wanted to make a report.

"Tell me."

"Sir, we have interviewed witnesses. A guard from a nearby warehouse says he saw three people entering the neighborhood and going toward the temple at dawn, but only two of them leaving."

"He can identify them?"

"No, sir. He saw only their shoes and their clothes. The top half was covered by large black umbrellas. They shared two umbrellas between them. They were all wearing long pants and shoes. One wore a raincoat."

"CCTV footage?"

"We are combing through the CCTV footage, but so far we can only find that one shot of three men, and others of men in ones and twos. Five in total. One sounds like the people the witnesses describe. Three men, two umbrellas."

"Register it as evidence and send me a copy. You have recorded the statements?"

"Yes, sir."

The minute he cut the call, his phone started ringing yet again. Bapat. In all the chaos, he'd forgotten to call his boss. He braced himself to make a report and face the inevitable reprimands that would follow. To make progress, he must get that warrant for the Remy Virgin Hair Factory. Something lay in wait at that place. Or someone.

CHAPTER FORTY-SIX

TARA

No no no. No. This was not where she wanted to be, back in a hospital bed so soon. She thought they had time yet.

Tara peered through half-open eyes, taking in the private room, its large windows gloomy in the rain—she couldn't see the door. It was a suite. This must cost a ton. She needed to call Arnav, ask him why she was here and to take her back home right away.

She tried to reach for the bedside table, but her arm wouldn't cooperate. Cold terror seized her. Had the paralysis returned? In a panic, Tara tried to rise and thrashed about. She sank back in relief—no paralysis. A loud groan escaped her. She felt for her locket, and found it nestled on the bed, near her neck. She clutched its comforting weight, willing it to warm up in her hand.

"Tara?"

Arnav came rushing in, and with him returned the details of the events that had landed her here. No, it couldn't have been—she hadn't fallen out of the wheelchair. The pain in her hands and arms, the blood on her skirt.

"Is the baby okay? What did Dr. Holkar say?"

"Yes." Arnav stroked her hair. "So are you."

"Why am I here then?"

"Tara."

Tara detested that long-suffering expression on her husband's face. That glance was fine for Pia. He had good reason to be upset, but she would push what advantages remained with her.

"I want to go home."

If he was going to treat her like a teenager, she'd behave like one. She raised her hand to her head as Arnav turned to find the bell to call the nurse. They had taken away her wig and her cap. She kept her bedroom dark so Arnav wouldn't notice the bald spots between thinning hair, but the hospital light was white, and harsh.

"Dr. Holkar has kept you under observation for now," Arnav said. "The pregnancy needs monitoring."

Guilt flooded her. Her unborn child had paid the price for her quest for some agency in her own life. She could've waited till she recovered from the birth. She placed her hand on her belly and stroked it. She had access to half the touch: her hand sensed the texture of her skin, but the skin on her midsection didn't register it. Maybe her baby could. She kept her hand going in circles.

Her husband's stubble had begun to darken, and his collar was askew. His day at work hadn't been good to begin with, and now she'd gone and made it worse.

"She's fine," Tara said. "Here, you can check for yourself."

Arnav smiled, but she watched it falter. Behind him, the window grew dark with gathering clouds.

"There you go calling the baby a she again," he said. "What if it's a boy?"

Tara tried to read his expression. Arnav was trying hard to lighten the air. What had Dr. Holkar said to him?

"I'd never give birth to a male." She brushed off the thread of fear. "Bad enough I'm married to one."

He wanted a girl, too, but kept up the banter and laughed—their usual exchange about their baby. His laugh had lost its spark, though.

In that moment, life had beaten down her husband, and that didn't suit Tara.

"Aren't you going to ask me why I went to the nonprofit?" Tara goaded him. "How dare I fall? Don't I get a lecture?"

"Just stay put. For our baby."

A nurse came in, followed by Dr. Holkar. Arnav stepped out to the en suite room.

The usual checkup. No, Tara felt no pain in her midsection. Yes, she'd fallen, but on her hands and her side. She kept her breathing even as the doctor applied cold gel on her belly and handled the ultrasound as if Tara were a soap bubble, not a woman made of flesh and blood.

Tara breathed deep and tuned in to Arnav's voice floating in from the other room.

"Are you sure, Tambe? Okay, then . . . what about your conclusions from the lockup where the man was held? . . . Check against the police database, we need to know who entered the place. I'll pass you the names of the men on duty at the time . . . No, I've had it checked against the CCTV. Yes, I know fingerprints can be from earlier or later . . . we're clutching at straws here, Tambe—we need that man in custody."

His voice echoed in the quiet hospital suite. Arnav never saw a day without stress at work, but this sounded out of the ordinary. He needed a break, but her incident had made it unlikely. Once the baby came, it would be harder still. She wished she had Zoya to rant to, but that woman had disappeared, along with her boyfriend. They might have skipped town.

"The baby is fine, Mrs. Rajput." Dr. Holkar interrupted the drowsy torpor Tara had sunk into. The white-coated doctor put away the ultrasound machine, and the nurse helped Tara cover up again.

The doctor's calming assurance didn't do its job. She asked the question weighing on her.

"How long will you keep me for observation?"

She heard the doctor out, panic and anger rising within her.

"But that's impossible. Till after birth? That would be two months at least. We couldn't afford two weeks at this hospital."

"I'll take it from here, Doctor." Arnav appeared beside Dr. Holkar as if he hadn't been on the phone all this while.

"Remember that there should be no stressful situations around the patient."

"I'm not a patient," Tara protested, "just pregnant."

"You've had an injury, Tara. Till you recover, you're absolutely a patient. I'll request that you make your baby's health a priority."

Dr. Holkar left, mumbling polite asides to Arnav about leaving the two of them to chat.

Arnav walked over to her bedside. It broke her heart, how handsome her husband was, even when ruffled up by a terrible day with work and family. And how loving. In the sixteen years they'd known each other, he'd doted on her when they were together, and in the years apart, he'd longed for her. Now he was adjusting her blanket, and hovering over her bed like a nurse. She didn't deserve him.

"I'll stay for now," Tara said, her voice teary, perversely angry with herself, him, the entire goddamned situation. The hospital bills would send them into further debt. They were still paying the lease on the car. The money from the sale of Arnav's ancestral bungalow had bought them the apartment, but all the remaining cash had gone toward her treatment, because Arnav's insurance didn't cover it all. They had to think of Pia's school fees and higher education.

Arnav said nothing for a while, kissing her cheek.

"You rest, okay? I need to get back to work, but I'll bring Pia in the evening if I can."

"That's all very well, but we've got to talk about it sometime. We can't afford a private hospital. I don't need all this fancy paint and cushions."

"This place is much more than that, and Dr. Holkar has taken care of you since the beginning."

"She can do that at the time of birth. I could rest at home. I have the housekeeper, and Pia can keep tabs on me."

"Listen to me, please."

"We'll talk again, all right? If I'm better in the next few days, I'm going back home."

Her tone mutinous, she expected Arnav to give in, and placate her with a few soft words. His tone was soft, but the words were not.

"You will lie down here in this bed for as long as the doctor thinks you must. Enough already, Tara."

He stroked her sparse hair like she was a used-up woman with sagging breasts, wrinkled face, and missing teeth who deserved all his pity, and that was what it took for Tara to lose all sense of perspective and start tossing sharp-edged, poison-tipped words at him, and then the papers and board and pen and glass within her reach.

Her father used to tell her what to do, as did her boss at the bar. And then Arnav, *Watch this on TV, not that, don't lift this, don't go there.* She was tired, so tired of it all. And furious. Done with this pestilence of men who wouldn't let her talk, would not respect her as a human with an independent will of her own.

Her head throbbed, her skin felt warm, her breath came in harsh gulps, and her heartbeat turned to a loud thunder in her ears, echoing the one that crashed outside, the flash of lightning turning the room bright as day for a few seconds.

A nurse rushed in, and then Dr. Holkar, shoving Arnav aside. It all happened fast: the shushing sounds and words from Dr. Holkar, the rapid prick of the injection, and then descending darkness.

"I tried, Doctor," she heard Arnav say before she blacked out, "but she doesn't—"

Darkness loomed, and Tara struggled to hear the rest of the words, but couldn't.

CHAPTER FORTY-SEVEN

ARNAV

Working steadily through the files he had to sign, Arnav mulled over ways to sort out the mess he was in.

He could start with visiting *Vaeeni* and find out why her phone was switched off.

Or head to his boss's office and demand that no matter how much his boss liked Nimkar, they must raid that hair factory.

Or take Pia to the *dojo* to give her some semblance of normalcy.

After Tara's outburst the evening before, he'd retreated from the room, tempted to withdraw from life for a while. He didn't have that luxury.

The heavens had opened up yet again this morning, and outside Arnav's window the world was frayed out and white, same as inside his mind.

Had Hemant Shinde been alive, Arnav would have called him, and set up a round of chess and tea. He corrected himself. No, he wouldn't. Had Shinde been alive, Arnav might not have spoken to him.

Last evening, the woman he loved had called him names that didn't bear repeating. Dr. Holkar had explained that Tara had gone catatonic with stress and still not overcome the effects of sedation, but there was no mistaking his wife's fury.

Some of it was justified, and he loved that girl inside Tara, the one who never gave up. Maybe she was running low on that firebrand spirit, and needed him. He would remain by her side no matter what—but he didn't know how to show her. She'd flinched when he'd touched her hair.

Strands of hair crisscrossed her pillow, and gathered in the drains after he bathed her, but that was just the medicines. Whenever he washed her hair, tenderness overcame him at the pale bald spots as he worked in the lather, and he wanted to hold her. Kiss each bit of her soft, vulnerable skin. Keep her safe. If only she could see herself the way he saw her.

Her hair would return, and what did it matter if it didn't? If the lesion on her spine could be excised through surgery as her condition improved, she would walk again—he had to believe that.

A soft knock on his office door. Arnav looked up. The friendly face of Constable Kamble peeked in.

"Tea, sir?"

The world could end, and Constable Kamble would still be serving tea.

"Sure," Arnav said, to please the old man. He had no real desire for refreshments. The genial constable nodded and left.

Arnav picked up his phone, and opened the encrypted folder where he kept all his pictures related to his cases. He clicked on the photos of the Kaali temple case.

The mutilation. The hibiscus flowers. The red vermilion. He'd seen the flowers and the red powder in one other place. The home of Chitra Varli, who had still not regained access to her social media account. Scrolling through the snapshots, Arnav came to the pictures he'd taken at her home. He hadn't found a moment to browse them. Not the most urgent task at his desk, but a good place to start consolidating his thoughts on the case.

His suspect list so far consisted of Ram Chandra, who had escaped custody, and perhaps the gangster Iqbal Asif, Khare's brother-in-law. He'd need more from his informer, Ali, before he could connect Asif to the first murder, of Vishal Nimkar. If he considered for a moment that Chitra hadn't been hacked like she claimed, she could have posted the video of Nimkar's dead body, and perhaps knew the killer. He opened his notes and considered what he had thus far:

Iqbal Asif, Rasool Mohsin's man, was seen on CCTV with possible victim. Has since gone underground. Rasool Mohsin has been seen meeting controversial Hindu MLA, but can't be found despite raids. Iqbal Asif: brother-in-law of Paresh Khare, the second victim. Possible access to ketamine, found in both victims. Could overcome Paresh with help.

As his mind pinged from one suspect to another, Arnav enlarged the photos of Chitra Varli's living room.

The windows, the corridor, and the sofa, but most importantly the pictures on a wall and the high mantelpiece. Pictures of Chitra as a child, alone, and with her family. Of her screen debut as a teen and her short-lived career as a movie star. Her life as a yoga enthusiast and an influencer. Her spiritual retreats.

Arnav paused: in one picture, Chitra Varli bowed to a known face. Ram Chandra Dome. The tantric himself.

The ring of his burner phone startled him. Naik. Arnav snatched up the call, hoping for updates.

"My husband might know where he is, sir," Naik said.

She didn't use names, but she meant Ram Chandra Dome. Her husband's friend.

"You're sure?"

"I'm sending you the location, sir. Please hurry."

Arnav stood, got his gun, and ran full tilt into Govind the tea seller with his tray. Hot tea splashed on his hands and all over the floor. Pain seared through his skin, but that had to wait. He assisted the hapless young man, ignored his apologies, and rushed to wash his hands. He left as quickly as he could, following the location signal Naik had sent him. It came from a tracker.

At a traffic light, Arnav checked his gun, wishing he had help—someone to drive, and act as backup. Naik's husband was an ex–police officer. He wouldn't be easy to follow, or take by surprise if the situation called for it.

Arnav's reddened, burning hands annoyed him as he drove through the rain and soon turned painful. He ignored them and dialed Naik.

"How are we receiving the live location?"

"I suspected his involvement because I had set a *khabri* on him after we spoke. He bought food, clothes, and medicines, and headed somewhere last night. This morning I woke early, cooked his favorite dishes, and packed him a lunch box. He doesn't like spending extra money, so he took it with him. The tracker is stitched into the bag."

"The location shows the Colaba area. What can you tell me about the place?"

"I haven't been there, sir. The *khabri* didn't have a good phone, so he sent no pictures. He says it's an old building. I checked the records. The place used to store petrochemicals."

"Should I expect armed men?"

"My source said he's seen two people go in. Raghav, and a large man he didn't recognize."

"Has your informer identified the suspect?"

Rain pelted the windshield as he hit yet another traffic light.

"No, sir, but I think it's Ram Chandra. It might be important to call for some backup, sir."

Of course, but Arnav couldn't trust anyone at his station. Once arrested, Ram Chandra would go to a proper jail, not the station lockup. Arnav watched the wiper work hard to clear the windshield glass, but the rain kept on coming. The presence of an unidentified large man worried him. It would be three against one. Not ideal, but not Naik's problem.

"I should be fine on my own," Arnav said. "Someone at the station helped him escape, and I don't know who yet."

His network of *khabri* hadn't picked up any gossip about a mole at his station. Once he got Ram Chandra in custody, he must deal with that. Set a trap in his office, and use all methods, official and unofficial, to nail whoever aided in the escape.

"I'm coming in, sir."

That would be a step too far. He couldn't ask her to risk her marriage.

"We don't know much about the situation," he said, injecting bored authority into his tone. "You'll be a liability if identified."

"I'll make sure that doesn't happen, sir."

"How's that possible?"

Sub-Inspector Sita Naik had clearly lost her mind. Her husband would recognize her in an instant. No way would Arnav have missed Tara in a crowd, even before her accident. Tara's posture, her voice, her outline were imprinted in his mind.

"I'm not far from the area, sir. I won't show up unless necessary. I'll be careful."

"This has to be a legal arrest." His hands burned. He lowered his window to put his right hand in the rain to cool it down.

"I'm sorry, sir, but given the situation, isn't all that matters is that there is an arrest?"

Arnav was tempted to say yes. He couldn't afford to lose Ram Chandra. He opened the dashboard and checked on the handcuffs before he answered. He had two pairs.

"No, Naik. We must do it right for the case to stand."

"Okay, sir. I'll try to call Raghav and get him to come out. If he doesn't, there's no help for it. I'll be there."

"He's your husband—and maybe just rescuing a friend he believes in. Do you really want to do this?"

"He used to be a police officer, sir. He should have thought twice before aiding a suspect and a potential murderer."

Arnav considered ordering Naik to stay away, but she wasn't wrong.

"Wait for my word before you step in," Arnav said.

"Yes, sir."

Arnav thought he heard a smothered chuckle right before he cut the call. He was known for his propensity to jump into escalating situations without backup, but as a junior reporting to him, Naik had never pointed this out. His erstwhile assistant had changed since the time they worked together, and Arnav didn't know what to make of it.

About to turn into the neighborhood in Colaba, he watched his phone buzz again.

He picked up the call from his informer trailing the priest at the Kaali temple.

"The priest is in Colaba, *saab*. He has entered an abandoned warehouse."

CHAPTER FORTY-EIGHT

MUMBAI DRISHTIKON NEWS

Maharashtra Politics

Parties snipe over arrest of Dalit leader Ram Chandra Dome

4:31 PM IST 20 July, Mumbai.

The state of Maharashtra is no stranger to pre-poll violence, but this time the assembly elections might take a difficult turn. Amid threats and counterthreats of violence from both sides of the divide flying thick and fast, observers feel that the police might need to tighten security measures in various parts of Mumbai.

It has emerged that the leader of the Ram Rajya Party, Ram Chandra Dome, is in custody for murder in the sensational murders involving castrated men in Kaali temples across Mumbai. Mumbai Police have been exceptionally tight-lipped on the matter.

ACP Bapat of the Bandra division said, "The cases are under investigation. I can tell you that we're working closely with Versova station, as per instructions from the DCP of Zone 9. We will solve the case and maintain communal peace at all costs."

This might prove difficult with rising rhetoric from the opposition MLA from Hindu Rashtra Party, Tarun Sathe, who has said that accused like Ram Chandra Dome should be removed from any possibility to stand in the elections, irrespective of whether they were from high caste or low.

On the other hand, the leader of the Muslim front, Jalaluddin Memon, has spoken to eminent members of the community, asserting that they must fight for their constitutional rights, because this election could be a fight for their very existence.

CHAPTER FORTY-NINE

ARNAV

Rain battered down like scattershot bullets as Arnav stepped out of the car and into a deep puddle. He'd worn a raincoat and boots this morning, but both would soon prove useless in this deluge. He sent up a prayer to whoever was listening. With Tara in the hospital, he didn't need a Mumbai in flood.

Pushing away that strand of anxiety, Arnav took stock of his surroundings. The deserted, rain-drenched buildings had not seen a lick of paint in years. Ahead of him stood a warehouse that looked more gray than white—his destination. Not far from the gate, a bare flagpole stood lonely yet strong against the onslaught.

Ram Chandra, Raghav Naik, and the Kaali temple priest lurked inside. Arnav thanked his stars that the large individual had turned out to be the priest. With his burned hands, Arnav himself stood very little chance if it came to fists.

Naik was already here, and had taken position behind the building, on the other side of a shed. Arnav checked his gun one last time before heading in. He stuck to the wall, near the swollen drain that carried the stench of refuse, and flowed like a swift canal.

Naik's voice over his Bluetooth was faint. "He should leave soon and will pass your way, so please take cover."

Naik meant her husband. Arnav cut the call and entered an old guard-room next to the gates. The gates themselves were long gone, but the structure of the small guardroom remained, despite the broken windows and absent doors. He crouched low, and heard footsteps pass by. Raghav Naik.

Unable to peer out without risking discovery, he remained frozen in position, counting off the seconds before he could peek. He didn't want to fire his gun unless he had to.

About to step out, he heard another set of heavy steps splashing through the water of the broken, grassy driveway. The steps paused close to the guardroom.

Arnav uncurled himself and peered out to find the old priest under a black umbrella. The man startled at the sight of Arnav, a cry escaping him, thankfully covered by the peal of thunder above. Arnav had worn his cap low, so the priest hadn't recognized him right away amid the downpour. Without missing a beat, Arnav snaked out, pulled the large man aside, twisted his arm, and cuffed him to the flagpole. The priest offered less resistance than a sack of potatoes.

"If you yell, that will be the last thing you do," Arnav growled. He couldn't afford to let the priest identify him or alert the suspect. The potbellied priest whimpered and gathered his breath for a scream. Arnav silenced him with a karate strike to the neck, and let the man collapse, still cuffed to the pole. He checked all around, but he seemed to be alone.

Got the priest. Arnav tapped on his phone. What about suspect? Live location shows tracker still in the building.

Bag left in the room, came Sita's response. Have barred the back exit—locked from outside.

What about earlier visitor? Arnav typed in. If Raghav Naik returned, that would complicate matters.

Near the main road now. I can see him from here, Sita's text pinged.

Any movement inside?

The windows all dark, sir. Will provide covering fire if needed, and follow you in.

The warehouse appeared long abandoned, but muddy shoe prints led in and out of the entrance. He tried various doors in the corridor ahead of him, anticipating an ambush at any moment. The burn in his hand had now become a throbbing ache.

Arnav tried a door, and a black cat streaked out, its feral yellow eyes shining in the half gloom. He turned at a noise, and pointed his gun at a squat young man who'd walked in.

"It's me, sir," the young man said. Naik's voice. Arnav would've laughed, but they had a job to do. Signaling to Naik that he was going in, he pried the door a crack, to hear low droning chants in Sanskrit ending in loud claps at the end of certain phrases.

He crept in to find a gloomy room, which led to another, the noises coming from within. He smelled incense and camphor, like in a temple.

With Naik right behind him, he pushed the door, and it opened to reveal one of the weirdest sights he'd set his eyes on in his entire policing career.

Ram Chandra Dome, wearing not a stitch of clothing, was reciting in Sanskrit in the dark room, facing a small fire. In that instant before he shouted his standard police warning, Arnav spotted the vermilion drawings on the floor surrounding a brass pot with scarlet hibiscus flowers, a bowl filled with milk, and the body of a black rooster, its head snapped off, blood dripping into a metal bowl.

CHAPTER FIFTY

SITA

Sita was glad she'd worn the *mufti*—her padded disguise made her a squat man.

At the shouted warning, the totally naked Ram Chandra turned and crashed a plate he'd been holding. Vermilion flew into the air in a red cloud, and milk spattered on the uneven floor. He cursed, and bending over, picked up the knife he'd used to chop off the rooster's head and brandished it at them. When Senior Inspector Rajput warned him to drop it, training the gun on him, Ram Chandra placed the blade at his own throat, a manic gleam in his eyes.

"I swear by Ma Kaali, I'll kill myself if you come any closer."

"You can try," her boss said, his voice low and calm. "It will only lead to more pain. For you."

"How will you explain a dead body here?"

"I won't."

"You'll regret this," the tantric said, his smile unhinged, as if his rage had driven him mad.

His hand rose to slash at his neck, and Sita had to freeze herself and not fire her own gun as the room filled with the explosion of a gunshot. The knife clattered to the floor, and from the tantric came a yell of agony. The shot from her boss had gone through Dome's right palm, making a bloody mess of it.

Senior Inspector Rajput was a blur of movement while he cuffed the tantric's left hand and wrapped him with the cotton floor mat. Sita cleared all the other rooms, one by one. The black cat startled her when she entered a room toward the rear where it had hidden after escaping earlier, but there was no one else. By the time she returned, the room was empty. She checked the room and found a phone in a corner. Ram Chandra had a phone—someone had clearly been providing for him. Her husband, or the priest. Pocketing it, she ran out to find her boss dragging a yelling Ram Chandra toward the car.

Between them, they shoved Ram Chandra into the back, hand-cuffed him to the front seat, and bandaged his ruined hand so he wouldn't bleed out. They hauled the blabbering priest across, and fitted him right beside his nephew.

The priest complained, his reedy, high voice a contrast to his giant body. Ram Chandra Dome groaned but didn't say a word, despite the priest's pleas to speak up and swear their innocence. She offered to drive, because her boss's hands showed burns—large blisters on both. He watched the suspects in the rearview mirror, making no mention of the state of his hands or her strange clothing.

Later, she went and changed into uniform while the men were processed. They retained the Kaali temple priest on remand at Bandra Police Station while placing Ram Chandra Dome at Arthur Road Jail. The tantric needed heightened security after his escape from the station lockup, but his uncle might not weather the overcrowded jail infamous for housing Mumbai's most dreaded gangsters.

In the car headed back toward Bandra Police Station, her boss remained deep in thought. Sita led with the question uppermost in her mind—shame and fear warring within her. "Shouldn't we be interro-gating Raghav, sir?"

"We've yet to find out the true extent of his involvement—watching him might be more productive. Right now, I'm concerned that when he reaches home, he'll figure out that your call was a ruse."

"No, sir. His mother was unwell, and wanted me to go home. I asked him to go instead, saying I'm assigned to a murder investigation."

Her boss seemed to consider his words before he spoke.

"So I've done a clean sweep of my office, Naik. I'm going to lock my room and do a search each morning till we find the mole at the station."

"Sorry, sir?"

"Whoever helped Ram Chandra escape had other support, and understands technology. They were able to loop the CCTV, switch it off, and add in the footage. They must have filmed the crime scene video to upload on Chitra Varli's social media account."

"She's an activist, sir. Yes, she has religious leanings and speaks on political issues, but she wouldn't do such a thing."

For an answer, Senior Inspector Rajput scrolled down his phone, and showed her a picture. "Chitra and the tantric knew each other."

Chitra Varli bowing to Ram Chandra Dome, offering flowers at his feet.

"She's behind this?"

"We have no evidence, but her team has the know-how to do all the electronic handiwork we've seen so far. It wouldn't be a stretch to imagine they put a device in my office."

That was terrifying. If it was Chitra Varli, she had dared take on a Mumbai Police station: Bandra was one of the biggest in the metropolis.

"Why Bandra, though?" Sita said. "She could pick any other. Isn't it too convenient?"

"We'll only figure that out once we've interrogated her. She didn't tell me she knew Ram Chandra. Ram Chandra has political aspirations, and so does she—both could be united in a Scheduled Caste campaign. Vishal Nimkar and Paresh Khare were upper-caste men."

A part of her exulted at the punishment meted out to upper-caste men, but Sita stopped short. Violence and othering were the tools the *savarna* had used for centuries. If she adopted or supported these, even when the victims might have deserved punishment, how was she any better than them?

"How can I help, sir?" she said.

"With interrogation," Senior Inspector Rajput said. "We must question Ram Chandra, the priest, and Chitra Varli. Ram Chandra should be much more cooperative after a night in Arthur Road Jail."

That was true. Suicides and murders were not unheard of in that prison. There, the money you paid jail officials could determine your fate.

"I can't trust my men to interrogate Chitra Varli," he continued. "As a woman, you might get better results than me. We need to find out what went down—how she knows Ram Chandra, whether the two could have collaborated in some way. If Ram Chandra took the video and sent it to Chitra."

"Right, sir."

His phone pinged with a call, and as she heard him speak to a contact, her mind wandered to her own household.

What was Raghav up to—why aid a murderer? On some days, she wished all men in her life would disappear.

Her phone rang, and flashed with her husband's number. She let it ring out.

The next call her boss took startled her into paying attention.

"Yes, Desai." Her boss's tone was casual.

Desai had been taking bribes. Why was he calling Senior Inspector Rajput while on suspension?

"I can see you have eyes and ears at the station." Her boss moved his hands about—those burns must hurt.

When he cut the call, she confronted him.

"I couldn't help hearing, sir. Inspector Desai called?"

"To wish me well for the burns. He's ready to return."

"How did he find out this fast?"

"That's for him to know, and us to figure out," her boss said, his lips set in a grim straight line. "We have our work cut out for us."

CHAPTER FIFTY-ONE

ARNAV

The next day, Arnav admired his handiwork. No one stepping into his office would know they were being watched. His Crime Branch stint had taught him a few tricks. He'd done some of this last night while working through a mountain of paperwork.

Just because the Kaali temple case was taking up all the media oxygen didn't mean crimes had stopped within his jurisdiction. Last night, a vice raid had revealed a prostitution ring not far from Bandra's poshest localities. Arnav had met with the inspectors in charge of that raid. He had to finish examining all the reports they'd filed.

He raised his head, his neck a mass of aches, and considered the office. He'd swept his room for any video and audio recording devices, and finding it clear, added some of his own. A camera fit into one of the wood and metal plaques. Another on a pen stand. Listening devices that could be mistaken for screws, on his table.

If someone messed with this room, he'd know. He'd taken great care to fit a camera on Naik's desk, facing away from her and into the corridor that led to the lockup. Another that faced his office door. She knew where they were, and would rip them out should she need to do that to prevent discovery.

The mole, whoever he or she was, might have been watching, so each time he fitted a device, he got Naik to stand guard or gave a constable or two an assignment that would distract others—cleaning a fan, or hanging garlands on the pictures of former prime ministers and chief ministers.

A risky move, wiring his own station, but Arnav saw no choice. Until he found the mole, his investigation into the temple murders would remain hamstrung. If the only officer he could trust was Naik, he simply wouldn't have the resources and the mole would continue with their sabotage.

Desai's call had been the final straw—had he got Ram Chandra whisked away to subvert the investigation? Or prove that Desai himself was indispensable?

Arnav glanced through the list of constables and officers present during the tantric's escape. Pia had gifted him a pen out of her pocket money, and he gripped its cold metal as he whittled the number of top suspects down to three, based on motive, the various CCTV footages, and the ability to get into the CCTV room and his room without attracting notice.

He would pass this on to Naik. Of the three, two were constables. One was the chatterbox Kamble. Arnav was tempted to take him off the list, but process was process. The other was a shifty character who'd been known to sneak away office stationery. The third was a sub-inspector, and Arnav assigned him temporary duty at another station, arranging documentation.

His eyes on the rain pattering against the window, Arnav placed a call to his source in computer forensics at the Crime Branch.

"Any updates?"

"I've finally managed to geo-locate your crime scene video—the coordinates match the location you sent me. It was taken at about five thirty p.m., on a phone. I'm sending you the phone model, but not sure of the exact serial number."

So the time of death for the first victim, Vishal Nimkar, was now established. He'd died before 5:30 p.m.

"No idea where it was sent from?"

"An internet café in Bandra. Not too far from your police station. They did use a VPN to mask the source, but I was able to get around it."

"Send me the location of the café," Arnav said. "Any progress on the 100 calls?"

If they could identify the person who called in the first murder, or was calling Tambe, that could lead to the killer.

"I gave you the approximate address near Saint Cyril Road. Some of the calls made on the internet might prove very difficult to trace, but note that both the video and the 100 calls originated near that same Bandra location."

"Let me know the minute you find new info. This is top priority."

"Sure. What about the items you wanted for your office? All set?"

"Yes. Now we wait."

After a quick visit to check on his sleepy and still-grumpy wife, Arnav headed to meet Ram Chandra at Arthur Road Jail. Surrounded by high-rise buildings, this stone-and-concrete holding facility built in 1926 housed some of Mumbai's most infamous denizens. Here, rival gangs often took fatal swipes at each other.

Waiting in the reception area to be let inside the jail, Arnav felt his phone buzz against his thigh.

A number he didn't recognize, and a message that simply said, Saab I know where she is. Will send location.

Ali. With Zoya's whereabouts. If he hadn't called and was using a different burner, Ali was close to her. Arnav made a mental note to keep checking his phone—he might have to run at a moment's notice.

He tapped out an *ok*, and was guided to a gloomy interrogation room that stank faintly of vomit and urine. Ram Chandra jumped up at the sight of him.

"I can't stay here, sir. Please, sir."

Ram Chandra wore a regulation white jail uniform, short-sleeved *kurta*, and a pair of shorts, because he'd arrived wrapped up in a cotton mat. Smears of vermilion still clung to his skin; his hair hadn't seen a comb in days. The bandage on his shattered right hand looked filthy.

"You only have to tell me the truth."

"I told you already, sir," Ram Chandra said. "I didn't kill anyone."

"You ran away from custody."

"I escaped, it is true, but I didn't recognize the man who helped me run, sir. He wore a cap, a cloth about his face, and a jacket. I ran because I was afraid."

"Let's begin with how you left, and reached that warehouse."

"I was sleeping, sir. It was still dark, when someone woke me and told me to follow him. I was scared, sir, I thought it was a constable. When I didn't get up, he dragged me up. He asked me to take off my clothes if I wanted to live. He had a knife. He gave me clothes and hurried me out. I was out the back door before I knew it."

Ram Chandra's voice trembled, but Arnav had seen excellent acting capabilities among hardened criminals. This man could easily be the killer.

"Was he tall or short? Broad or thin?"

"Average height, sir. I can't be sure of his build under his jacket, but he wasn't fat. Young, by the way he moved. Very quick."

"He took you to the warehouse?"

"He poked me with a needle, and I was dizzy. He put me in an auto-rickshaw, and I fell asleep. He shook me awake, and once we entered the warehouse, he handed me a phone. Before I could ask him a question, he left."

"A phone?"

"Not my phone, but when I opened it, it was unlocked, and it had all the numbers, exactly as I'd saved them."

"Who did you call?"

"A friend."

"Not your uncle? How did he know you were there?"

"My uncle came on his own, claiming someone told him where to find me."

"So he *is* your uncle?"

"We don't get on very well, okay?"

"And Chitra Varli, did you call her?"

"I don't know anyone like that, sir."

"You agreed not to lie." Arnav scrolled down to the image of the famous influencer bowing to him.

"I'm sorry, sir," he said, eyes wide. "Yes, I know her—we've spoken a few times, but that is all."

"Well, you can stay here, then. We know what you've done. We just need the evidence to prove it—and you know us. We'll find it."

This was a shot in the dark, but Ram Chandra looked terrified enough. Fear made you spill secrets.

"Wasn't my idea, sir. I swear. I'll tell you all. I just need a doctor."

It had worked. Arnav feigned boredom, and turned away.

"I'm waiting. Give me good information and you'll get taken to the hospital. If it's not worthwhile, you can spend a few nights here. Your hand will develop an infection. They might have to amputate it."

"This time you can trust me, sir. None of those videos were my idea."

CHAPTER FIFTY-TWO

SITA

Sita made her way to Chitra Varli's home in Bandra, where the influencer was reportedly starring in a rainy video shoot. A social media maven like Chitra was bigger than many movie stars in some ways—her rabid online following had created India-wide trending hashtags demanding that her account be reinstated.

In the last few days this had splashed the Kaali temple cases all over the media, and brought Mumbai Police the wrong sort of limelight. Sita wanted no part of it.

Her anxiety raced faster than the police jeep. Ram Chandra was Raghav's friend, and Raghav had lied to her to deliver food to Ram Chandra. As if in answer to her thoughts, her phone rang. Her husband again. She'd avoided his calls, headed home very late last night, and left early this morning. But that couldn't go on forever.

"Hello," she said, and suppressed a sigh at the angry grunt from Raghav at the other end of the line.

"You left without speaking with me. Mother isn't well."

"I've been assigned on a murder investigation," Sita said, her gaze on the waterlogged road. "You've done those before."

He would let that pass. Her salary ran the household.

"Have you seen Ram Chandra?" His tone turned curious. "I heard he was arrested in the Kaali temple case."

Her husband had been lying to her about this, was lying by omission even now.

"Have you spoken to him since?" she shot back.

"That man is innocent, Sita. You've met him. He only has the occasional flare of temper, a weakness for women, and gets drunk. He's not a killer."

Sita wanted to challenge Raghav's lie, ask him why he'd aided a murder suspect, but she'd almost reached Chitra Varli's place.

"I've just reached my meeting."

And then a question occurred to her. "Do you know Chitra Varli?"

"Everyone knows her." Raghav's gruff voice floated across the line, steady as ever. "What about her?"

"Have you met her?"

"She invited Ram Chandra and me to an event once. What time will you be back tonight?"

"Is she supporting your party?"

"It does not hurt to have an influencer on your side. She supports equal rights for the Scheduled Castes."

There it was. Her husband, Chitra Varli, and Ram Chandra.

"Do you think she released the video herself?" she pushed further. "Someone sent it to her?"

"Why ask me? Ask her. I would, in her place."

"You would?"

"Why not? Look at the coverage she's got. She may have lost followers on one social media platform, but has multiplied it on all the others. She won't lose sleep over this."

As Sita watched Chitra Varli at work, she understood the truth of what Raghav had said about the influencer. Amid her reported crisis of losing her social media account, Chitra posed under the spotlight against a glass window, wrapped in a transparent, embroidered saree, an off-camera assistant spraying water on her face as she pouted and closed her eyes in ecstasy. She moved to the beats of a tinny Bollywood number about getting wet in the rain, a remixed version of an old hit.

Three cameras took in the sight from various angles. Sita made a show of walking about the living room, and strolled up to the wall plastered with pictures. You had to be truly obsessed with yourself to plaster an entire wall with your own pictures and face it every single day. Chitra's snapshot with Ram Chandra Dome was small, and not easy to find, but it was there. As was another picture, equally small, with Sita's husband in the frame. Chitra Varli and Raghav Naik, with matching grins, posing like best friends.

So much for Raghav saying he'd met Chitra just the once. Sita checked the other photos, but they were all family shots, pictures with other actors, a politician or two. Sita looked around and the surrounding chaos captured her attention: the crisscrossing wires, the clothes racks, bottles of lotions and other beauty products.

After scant minutes of Chitra's seductive writhing, a male voice called, "Cut." Chitra straightened, and a tall, bald man handed her a towel, and her phone. Her secretary. He must also have whispered a few words about Sita, because Chitra Varli gazed up at her and nodded to him. He walked over to Sita.

"Madam will see you now."

Sita followed Chitra to a sofa that someone had covered with plastic sheets. It crackled under Chitra's weight as she sat down in her wet saree.

"I spoke to someone from the Bandra station. Arnav Singh Rajput," she said.

"New information has come to light."

"Yes? Did your team figure out who could have hacked my account? I need to prove to customer service that I didn't post that video."

"I've spoken to their representatives, and they say there's no evidence of hacking. Someone used your username and password, on one of your approved devices, to put up the post."

"How is that even possible? The police have interviewed all my staff. All of my devices are logged out now."

The secretary came with a tray bearing two paper cups of coffee—Sita refused, but Chitra took hers, visibly shivering in her thin, damp saree.

"Where did you meet Ram Chandra Dome?" Sita said.

The question gave Chitra Varli pause.

"You mean Sri Sarvagya?" Chitra said, and when Sita nodded, continued, "My mother visited a Kaali temple, and met him. She brought him home one day, and I was impressed by his beliefs on social equality. He wants to go into politics, and I think he should."

"You know that he's a suspect in the murder investigation?"

"No. He is idiosyncratic, but he's a Kaali worshipper, a huge believer in the feminine energy. He respects women, and believes they can do whatever they set their mind to."

With all the news and hashtags on social media, there was no way Chitra didn't know about Ram Chandra's arrest.

"You placed flowers at his feet."

"You've been looking at those pictures. My mother likes them on the wall. That one was taken at a family worship, my mother's doing. She's a devotee of Ma Kaali."

"Has Ram Chandra met any of your staff?" Sita consulted the notes Senior Inspector Rajput had passed her. The staff had alibis for the time of the murder. Chitra Varli didn't. The staff also spoke of the tantric taking a shine to the female assistants. Not many lasted very long under Chitra.

"My secretary here, for sure. He's been with me for more than ten years."

"Who else?"

Chitra rattled off the names, and Sita noted them down. She would have to cross-check this list with the staff who'd already been interviewed.

As Sita scribbled, Varli's secretary came to stand by her side. The next shot was ready. Chitra Varli stood up.

"Will you enter politics soon?" Sita said.

"In public, the answer so far is no. I can tell you, though, that politics has become a dirty word, when it shouldn't be. If you can give voice to the voiceless by joining a political party, you must."

Sita's phone rang. One of her informers, who was tailing her husband. She cut the call, but Chitra had risen, ready to take her leave. Sita lost the opportunity to ask the influencer further questions as Chitra Varli said her goodbyes before walking off to the camera.

Sita's phone pinged. Her boss.

Urgent. Ram Chandra says Chitra Varli has been shooting underage porn videos. Use during interview. Staff might be involved. Check for evidence.

Sita tried to contain her shock and her frustration. If only he'd sent it a minute ago. Chitra Varli had ended the meeting. If Sita tried to speak to her again, she risked spooking the social media queen. If Chitra swept away all clues of porn shoots, they'd have no case, despite testimony from any coerced participants.

To find hard evidence, they'd need a raid, but given Chitra's profile, ACP Bapat would insist on proof of wrongdoing before he got a warrant signed. Sita could see why her boss had called it urgent. No way she could enter this apartment again without a warrant.

She glanced around. The entire crew seemed focused on the shoot, where Chitra berated the cameraman, asking him to get the angle right.

Unseen, Sita slipped through a door that led off the living room. She could say she needed to use the toilet if someone challenged her. It wasn't a washroom, though, but a tiny office. She paused, considering. She wanted this case solved: for the sake of her career, and to help the one man who had showed her kindness without fail. Would the result justify the risk?

The words *underage porn* came back to her. If a policewoman turning a thief could help exploited children, so be it. She shut the door behind her.

CHAPTER FIFTY-THREE

ARNAV

Arnav had rushed out of Arthur Road Jail the minute his phone pinged with the much-awaited message from Ali, giving Zoya's location. Strange to return to the same place he'd visited Tara this morning—this time in order to intercept Zoya—Dr. Holkar's hospital.

Turned out Zoya was going to see the same doctor. Arnav had mulled over the weird coincidence, but it occurred to him that Dr. Holkar specialized in difficult pregnancies. If Zoya was about to give birth for the first time, she'd qualify because she'd be in her mid-forties by now. It could also be a regular checkup.

Arnav tried to recall Zoya's face from all those years ago, when he'd seen her dancing with Tara on that stage at the Blue Bar. He found he didn't remember all that much. A woman of average height, thick about the middle, long hair.

At the waiting area, he scanned the mothers-to-be, and soon found a black-burka-clad woman sitting in a corner, scrolling on her phone. The best cover—and Tara had told him Zoya used to wear black burkas. Tara often borrowed them from her.

Arnav risked a slap or two in case the woman turned out to be someone else, but the faint start when she saw him gave Zoya away. Her eyes widened behind the net in her burka veil.

"You've not been to see your friend." To everyone else spread out around them, he spoke into his phone.

Zoya took the cue, and pretended to receive a call.

"Leave," she whispered into her phone. "Now."

"Your friend fell off her wheelchair and is in the hospital."

"What? When?" Zoya's hand holding her phone shook.

"I need you to talk some sense into him. Or at least pass on a message."

"He has me watched." Zoya's voice trembled. "By now, he knows you're here."

"Doesn't he trust you?"

"No one. Please. Go."

There was a note of real terror in her voice. Arnav paused. Was she in danger? Tara wouldn't forgive him if Zoya came to harm. He wouldn't be able to forgive himself.

"He's meddling in Hindu–Muslim business. You know what happened the last time a don did that."

No one could forget the Mumbai communal riots of 1993, and the bombings. Thousands died. Zoya spoke in a long, breathless whisper as if she knew time was running out.

"I don't know if he is, I know you'll arrest him if you get a chance, and I also know he came back to India because I couldn't take it anymore. And yet he could kill me"—here she laid a hand on her midsection—"us, tomorrow. It's hard to explain."

"Zoya—"

"Just go. You love Tara and Pia. I deserve a chance, too, don't you think, after all I've done?"

Before Arnav could respond, a nurse called Abida Begum inside, and Zoya rose.

"Please, Arnav," she said. "Hug Pia for me."

So Zoya was here for a checkup, under a false name. She was pregnant.

His phone rang. An unknown number. Expecting Ali, Arnav picked up the call and said hello.

"You can't trace this, so don't try," a high, thin voice said. He'd heard recordings of it before. Rasool Mohsin. "Don't ever talk to her again."

Even as he listened to Rasool, Arnav typed on his other phone to contact his office, and glanced around for signs of who was watching him. Given her pregnancy, Rasool wouldn't take chances with leaving Zoya alone for too long.

"Stop meddling in communal situations, Rasool. I know you met Tarun Sathe. These temple murders won't help you."

"I'll kill who I like when I like, and stop telling me who I should meet. You get a lot of slack because of your wife. Quit hiding behind her."

Arnav's message to his office got a response. They were trying to trace the call. He just had to keep Rasool talking a little bit longer.

"You're the one hiding," Arnav said. "Now that you might have a shot at a family, don't ruin it."

"You like people suffering and dying around you, don't you? Tell your zero dial his days are numbered. And if you have a conscience, you won't touch her." The call cut off.

Zero dial. That was what the mafia called informers, the ones who dialed zero to squeal to police. Arnav took a deep breath.

Rasool may not know yet who had given Zoya's location away. Arnav must ask Ali to lie low, and be very, very careful.

Arnav called two of his informers, and asked them to tail Zoya at a distance once she emerged from the hospital.

CHAPTER FIFTY-FOUR

SITA

Sita slipped out the thumb drive she'd swiped from Chitra Varli's apartment and, having scanned it for viruses, inserted it into a spare laptop.

She lowered the volume, and after a few seconds was glad she'd done so. She'd have to hand this over to her boss, and let him deal with getting ACP Bapat to agree to Chitra Varli's interrogation. She had to finish her other task for the day: chatting with the temple priest after his overnight stay in the lockup.

Sita closed the interrogation room and barred entry to the staff at the Bandra Police Station. It sent out a message: she might be a temporary transfer from her station in Versova, but she had the ear of the station's big boss, Senior Inspector Rajput.

She ignored the rumbles of dissatisfaction from the rest of the team and focused instead on the giant of a man slumped on the plastic chair.

"Let me go, madam," the priest said in a high voice. "You know I'm on dialysis. I've got children."

"Didn't that occur to you before you ran to Ram Chandra?"

"What to do, madam. He's the biggest mistake of my life. My wife was right all along."

"Why did you help him?"

"He's my nephew after all." The priest shifted in his seat.

He was lying through his teeth, but she couldn't get a constable involved. This man's flabby body couldn't take punishment.

Sita slammed the wooden table against the wall. "Tell me the truth if you want to get out of here. I can charge you with aiding a suspect."

The priest burst into sobs. Sita watched him shudder, and took her time handing him a glass of water. The lockup stint had softened the priest. All she had to do was wait.

"He's a thief, madam. That's what he is."

There it was. A new confession. Sita loomed over the priest, in the space where the cries of a hundred suspects echoed, and traces of blood and urine, sweat and vomit, lingered in the air. She kept quiet, letting the priest work up the steam to continue.

"He was an orphan, my sister's son. I raised him. But he turned bad—mixed with the wrong crowd."

Sita heard the priest out while he repeated all that he'd said to her boss, before he reached his point. "I raised my nephew so he'd take the responsibility for my family. He refused. Worse still, I think he stole the necklaces."

Sita let the silence linger.

"I don't know for sure, but my son said two days ago that he has seen duplicate keys with Ram Chandra. Keys to the safe. I keep the keys at home, and he used to visit. It is possible."

"Why didn't you tell us before?"

"Because he scares me. You should see him when he gets angry. I wouldn't be surprised if he actually killed those men. He said one day he would avenge himself—all the men who did him wrong."

"Despite being afraid of him, you went to see him at an isolated place all by yourself."

"I lost my key on the way to the temple, and the temple has been robbed. If I lose my job now, the trustees will not give one rupee to support my family. I thought Ram Chandra was running from police—if I helped him, he could help me, and tell me about the necklaces."

"Why the *tantra* ceremony?"

"He called me. He was alone and scared. Someone had kidnapped him from the lockup and left him there. I got him clothes, and told him to pray to Ma Kaali—I took along all the ingredients he asked for the ceremony."

"Prayers? Hadn't you gone there for the stolen necklaces?"

"I wanted him to trust me first, the way he does with Raghav. That man led him astray."

Sita asked the question despite knowing the answer. "Who is Raghav?"

"Ram Chandra's friend. Raghav Naik visited the temple. They were always talking, making big plans about their political party. They fell silent when I walked in."

Her husband. She'd have to tell her boss.

A message pinged Sita's phone. A constable she was working with at the Bandra station.

New body found. Not at a temple, but the same injury. Victim a white man.

CHAPTER FIFTY-FIVE

TARA

Arnav came in, and Tara's heart broke at the sight of her husband. The lack of sleep and anxiety showed in the dullness of his skin, the droop of his eyelids, and the shadow on his cheek.

He made an attempt at a bright smile. It faded. Wasn't a good sign when her husband felt too tired to pretend.

She spotted his bandaged hands and tried to sit up.

"How did you hurt yourself?"

"Nothing to worry about. Hot tea."

"Tea, on both hands? Why were you in the kitchen?"

Tara wanted to call her housekeeper and demand an explanation. Why was her bone-weary husband making tea?

"This happened at the office. I ran into the tea seller, on my way out to an urgent arrest."

She didn't even know when and how he got hurt these days. That thought drove her mad, but she bit back the helpless fury. When fate stepped on you, all you could do was persist, and wait for its attention to turn elsewhere. She reached out, and caught a whiff of antiseptic.

"How badly are they burned?"

He didn't present them to her.

"There wasn't enough time for first aid, so it looks a little worse than it should. The doctor has treated the blisters now."

"It must hurt." Tara eyeballed the bandages, wondering at the extent of her husband's discomfort.

"I spoke to Dr. Holkar," he broke into her thoughts.

Tara wanted to say she was sorry. That it was entirely her mistake. She shouldn't have gone to the nonprofit on her own. But in the moment he took to respond, her husband said exactly the wrong thing. "I hope you'll mind her, if not me."

"Why would I listen to anyone? Look where that's got me." She glared at her inert, hospital-sheet-covered legs. She didn't mean those words, and a part of her hated herself for saying them, but she ached to speak her mind, even if she was in the wrong.

"This has got to stop—" Arnav broke off midsentence as Pia barreled into the room. At fifteen, this happened less and less often, but it gave Tara a jolt of emotion to see a wide smile on her daughter's face.

"Ma!"

Tara opened her arms, and Pia dived into them, while Arnav said, "Be careful."

"I'm fine," Tara said. "How's my little girl?"

There was silence from Pia. Tara felt her daughter stiffen, then relax. When Pia raised her face, it was composed and the smile was back. Children grew up when you were not looking. Tara held back a sigh.

"Your phone broke, so Papa said I should bring you another from home." Pia handed her an old phone with buttons.

Tara hugged her daughter and thanked her.

"Papa says Neeti, Sujata Aunty, and Ashok will stay with us from now on," Pia said.

Tara glanced at Arnav. They'd tried time and again to persuade *Vaeeni*, but she'd refused. What had changed?

"I haven't asked *Vaeeni* yet." Arnav answered the question in her gaze. "Her phone is switched off. I'll stop by their place later."

"It will be great, Ma. Neeti won't ever have to go away."

"That will be lovely."

"Also, Sita Aunty will drop by often, too."

"She will?"

"She's helping Papa solve a big case."

"That's wonderful," Tara said, trying to mean it, a heaviness settling on her at the thought of Sita and Arnav working together. This was strange, and entirely without reason. It felt wrong, but Tara brushed it off.

Sita was a fine officer, and a good friend to the family. Her words returned to Tara: *Talk to Pia when things calm down. I don't think it was just the hair.*

"I can hang out with her when she visits," Pia chimed in. "She might let me hold her gun. One day I'll be a police officer like her and you, Papa."

"She'll lose her job if she lets you near a gun." Arnav laughed.

"Between your karate lessons and chats with Sita, you can be my bodyguard next time," Tara said. "I'll be volunteering with those girls at the nonprofit."

She wanted to get it out there, make it a positive thing, not a place of fear. Her daughter froze, and then held her hand in an iron grip.

"You're not going there again, Ma. None of us are."

"Why?" Tara said.

"No, Ma!" Pia's eyes blazed. The note of fear under that anger sent a cold shiver through Tara. What had happened on the roof that afternoon?

"Pia, *bete*, listen to me for a second." A term of endearment Tara rarely used now that Pia had grown up.

"Promise you won't go there again, Ma." Her daughter was shaking. "Just promise me, okay?"

"What's wrong? Tell us."

"Nothing happened," Pia flared. "It is *you*. Why are you so selfish, Ma? Why do you get to do exactly as you please, but we must listen to you? You knew you shouldn't have visited the factory, and yet you did. What if it had been worse?"

Pia would have rushed out, but Arnav caught her in his arms and held her. Pia sobbed, quietly, defeated.

"I won't. I promise," Tara said. "Come here."

She couldn't afford to lose this piece of her heart. She'd taken a bullet for Pia, and would do it again. Tara waited. In her haste to have a say in her own life and in her daughter's, she'd blundered into the factory without thinking it through. Arnav's gaze met hers over the top of their daughter's head. He nudged Pia toward her.

Pia didn't meet her eyes, but she walked to the bed. Tara reached for her daughter's hand. If Pia wanted her to stay away from the nonprofit, she would, until they got to the bottom of Pia's fear.

"You'll stay in the hospital like the doctor wants you to?" Pia asked.

Tara had survived by never doing another's bidding. She didn't let go of Pia's hand, though she wanted to. She turned to her husband, who sat typing on his phone.

"Don't look at him, Ma. This is between you and me."

Tara didn't answer. Pia needed reassurance, but Tara took a beat too long before she answered. Pia exploded.

"Why is it that I'm told I must grow up each time you don't like what I do? I'm fifteen. But you'll go against the doctor's advice and that's fine."

Pia was crying now, flicking off her tears with the back of her hand.

"Enough now," Arnav said. "Come." He drew their daughter toward the door, kissing her on the top of her head. "Why don't you go wash your face and get yourself a snack while I talk to your mother. Go on."

Pia left without a word, and her husband returned to her, his gaze filled with concern.

"Will she be okay? Maybe you should—"

"She needs some space. She'll be fine."

His phone rang, and Arnav's expression changed. Alert, tense.

"Naik?"

He paused, listening, his eyes narrowed.

"Are you sure? How is that possible? We have the man in custody."

His hand fisted, he gathered himself and stood straighter.

"I'll be there in half an hour. Yes, stop the interrogation and head to the new crime scene. Take charge until I get there."

He cut the call and turned to Tara, his expression clouded. "There's been a new development in the case. Naik needs me there."

Tara nodded, and her hands went to the locket at her chest for reassurance. She could speak to the tantric about her fall and ask for prayers. She picked up her replacement phone, but it didn't contain all the contacts in her list.

When she asked Arnav, he paused. "The replacement phone Pia got you isn't working?"

"It is. I need my contacts."

"I'll check if I can get someone to retrieve the numbers from your device and feed it into a new one. Maybe Naik."

She wasn't sure why, but she didn't want Sita to have her phone. "There's no rush."

"Okay then."

"I'll be back soon as I can, okay?" He stroked his knuckles over her cheek. "I'll get the driver to take Pia home. Be good."

After dropping a quick kiss on her forehead, he strode off. Tara missed that, the ability to leave a room on her own feet.

Too late she remembered the note the little girl had handed her at the nonprofit: *You will lose your family very soon.*

Was she already losing her family? She tried to call Arnav, pass him the note, but her voice caught. Tara checked under her pillow and every part of the bed her hands could reach. Had Dr. Holkar found the note? Was that why Arnav was so bossy—did he see the note, and assume she'd deliberately kept it from him?

Tara considered his words again. *Naik needs me.* Distressed, she held on to her locket, and ran her other hand through her hair, only to end up with a clump of it in her hand. Maybe she should begin saving them to sell. *Vaeeni* said there was a market for them, that people went door to door to buy hair.

Family could be a pain, but it was also the balm. She couldn't lose hers. She needed someone to keep an eye on Pia. Wiping away her tears, she crossed her fingers, hoping *Vaeeni* would agree.

CHAPTER FIFTY-SIX

SITA

Sita considered the news. A white man this time. Not young, not old. Similarly castrated as in the other crimes, and left in an alleyway behind yet another Kaali temple.

The priest had spilled an entirely different can of beans during her interrogation—the tantric was not as innocent as he claimed. But he was still in custody, and couldn't have committed this particular murder.

The last two cases bore many similarities. Both were young men, in good physical condition, and from the upper caste. A white man didn't sound like the same profile.

What was this victim doing in an alleyway at night, in the nonstop rain that had plagued Mumbai this week? What had the murderer used in order to lure him there?

The rain had slowed to a drizzle, so she opened the window a crack to let in the air wet with dreams and longing. She laughed at the notion. The only way to deal with your attraction to a much married, hopelessly-in-love-with-his-wife man and a devoted father was to make fun of it. She had taken on this investigation for herself. As her boss at Versova Police Station kept reminding her, each solved case added up to the promotion once she'd slogged the requisite years.

She reached the scene and got a constable to call Surat Tambe. Other constables milled about. She instructed them to mark the scene, pointing out the areas to be set apart with yellow tape, one route leading toward the head so any latent boot prints could be preserved for forensics.

She'd seen pictures of the other bodies, but this one seemed different.

The body lay on its stomach, for one, the slashed-up ghastly mess of the face turned to one side. They'd found it not on the Kaali temple premises nearby, but in a narrow alleyway outside, on a heap of stinking refuse. The thick moss on the brick-and-mortar shack to the right showed a fine spatter of dark blood. Expletives in black and green screamed from the corrugated tin wall on the left, but those looked old. Fresh, rusty stains evoked blood, but she must wait for Tambe to confirm. The roof of the tin shack had protected the body from the rain, but Tambe wouldn't be happy—any prints might already have been washed out.

Sita turned her attention to the body itself. The wrinkled skin of the back and neck, the manic slashing. The nose chopped off, lying in the refuse. Cuts across the neck, extending to the shoulders. Rage—no other way to describe it. No vermilion around the body like in the other cases, but shredded hibiscus flowers lay scattered about, a few stray petals scarlet against the man's pale buttocks, on which a tattoo stood out. Two triangles, pointing upward, with a tiny overlap. One blank, and the other pink.

Sita checked the photos from the earlier cases. In the first case, the killer had used vermilion to draw an inverted triangle within a circle, and daubed its tip with blood. The second featured no drawings. But the case notes said that the priest had identified the script scrawled through the vermilion on the temple floor: a basic tantric mantra in praise of the goddess Kaali.

Sita made a note of the tattoo and turned away from the river of blood between the spread-eagle man's legs. That part of the carnage had not changed. With slight variations, the method of killing was the same.

Was this one of the tantric's followers? A follower like Raghav, who had rushed to his rescue? Sita flinched at the thought, but caught herself. Her husband would be questioned soon.

A slight flurry among the constables told her that her boss had arrived. It was stupid not to refer to him in her head by his surname. She would think of him as *Rajput sir* from now on, keep it totally professional inside her mind and out, and that would be that.

She turned and cut a salute, like the rest of them, and he nodded, his expression guarded. After he'd examined the dead body and she'd recited her update, he led her out of the drizzle to stand under the privacy of the porch of a building nearby. A romantic setting, but the discussion was anything but.

"Chitra Varli?" he began.

Sita told him what she'd learned, and ended with the thumb drive she'd sneaked out of Chitra Varli's apartment, and its ugly, incriminating contents.

"We can't use it, but we can test it to confirm it came from her devices," Rajput sir said. "It might be enough to convince Bapat for a warrant to search her premises."

"Right, sir." She handed him the drive.

"Tambe—why isn't he here yet?"

"On his way, sir."

"This murder occurred sometime at night," Rajput sir said. "Rigor mortis has set in. You said this was an anonymous tip-off?"

"Yes, sir, same as before. Someone dialed 100. But tracing the call shows it was again made via the internet."

"The culprit is tech-savvy, and wants us to find the bodies."

"Chitra Varli fits the profile better than Ram Chandra, and he was in custody during this murder."

She brought him up to date on the priest's confession, about Ram Chandra and the necklaces. The fact that the tantric could have stolen them.

"We're missing clues here. Ram Chandra and Chitra Varli are connected, and now we suspect he may have stolen the necklaces. We need to interview the entire staff, and get them watched where necessary."

"Right, sir."

"And Naik, about Raghav."

She gave him the priest's testimony: that Ram Chandra and Raghav might be collaborating on some plans, and the priest's belief that Raghav wasn't innocent.

"I'm sorry it has come to this, Naik. I'll have a chat with him before we bring him in. Give him a chance to come clean."

"Yes, sir."

"You can't be involved."

"I know, sir. He took his mother to the doctor and attended a political meeting in the evening. My *khabri* says he visited an internet café on the way, but made no attempt to go back to the warehouse where we made the arrest."

"He should have visited Ram Chandra this morning. Someone has told him about the recapture. We haven't made it public—neither the escape, nor the arrest."

Who did Raghav know at the station? Sita wished she'd kept better tabs on her husband.

"So we have two lines of investigation," Arnav said. "Chitra Varli, Raghav, and Ram Chandra on one hand; Rasool Mohsin and Iqbal Asif on the other."

He briefed her about his meeting with Zoya, and Rasool's call on his phone. She focused on his words, trying to make sense of it all.

"Neither profile fits the murder of a *gora*," Sita said.

A *gora*, or a white man, was not the usual murder victim in Mumbai.

Ram Chandra was under arrest. Raghav knew of his rearrest. The spotlight on Chitra pinned her in place. Rasool Mohsin would think twice before ordering a hit on a white man.

"Search through the missing person records," her boss said. "A white man would be reported missing, sooner than later. Besides, he's not a poor man."

"How do you reckon, sir?"

"The hands are manicured, and I noticed a tan line from a thick ring. Either the victim took it off earlier, or the murderer did."

"That makes sense, sir. We'll know more when Tambe comes in."

"Follow up with him—he won't be happy. Like you and Tara, he's received threats."

"Right, sir." The senior forensic officer would be grumpier than usual.

"We don't have much time. Bapat managed to keep the escape of a suspect under wraps last time, but a white man won't stay out of the papers for long."

Rajput sir's boss, ACP Bapat, wouldn't let him breathe. Sita gave thanks she wasn't the one answerable yet.

As they fixed their plans and parted, Sita tried to get a handle on her anger at her husband, giving her temporary boss a polite smile and a nod as he left. With Raghav's antics, she could forget about a promotion. They would likely fire her.

Her mood blackened to wrath not only at her husband but also at the male suspect, for it had to be a man to warn her not to poke her nose where it didn't belong. Well, she'd show him that her nose was not to be trifled with. She would sniff him out—her face broke into a fierce grin at the pun—and once she had, he'd rue the day he'd sent her that threatening text.

Her phone rang. An unknown number.

"Sita Aunty?" The girl at the other end let out a sob and a hiccup.

"Hello, Neeti, what's wrong? Whose number are you calling from?"

"Another friend's. Didn't want to worry Pia."

"What's wrong?"

"You said to call you if I needed help."

"Yes. Of course."

"Someone trashed our *kholi*."

"Trashed it? Why? Do you know who it was? Where's your mother? Let me speak to her."

"She won't report this. Not to police. Won't tell Arnav Uncle, either. She doesn't care if we're safe."

"I'll come down for a visit."

"She'll know I called you."

"Okay. I'll make sure she doesn't know anything about this call. Wait for help."

She calmed the sobbing Neeti. The minute she cut the call, she dialed Rajput sir.

CHAPTER FIFTY-SEVEN

ARNAV

Your Vaeeni *is the most stubborn woman in Mumbai.*

Hemant Shinde's words about his wife echoed in Arnav's ears as he queued up at the petrol station. The incessant rains had caused cars to back up. A lone attendant worked the pumps, taking his time about it.

Arnav could have stepped out of his car—one look at his uniform and the attendant would drop all other customers and guide Arnav's car to a pump.

He and Shinde had once sat surrounded by petrol fumes at this very station.

"My wife won't cook anything else this week."

"You mean you'll eat cabbage every day?"

"Well, Ashok didn't want to eat fried cabbage. That's Sujata's way of making sure he never says no again."

"He's only six, though."

"She doesn't care. All of us will eat cabbage until he eats it, too. Nothing melts her. We've tried."

Shinde might have been a cheating husband, but he knew his wife.

Vaeeni's home had been trashed, but it was Neeti who had called Sita. *Vaeeni* hadn't reached out to him. In her pride and her dignity as a traditional widow, she was indeed like a stone. If not for Naik, he might never have known about the incident.

He'd promised Naik not to let on that Neeti had called.

At a knock on his window, Arnav peered up to find the petrol pump attendant.

"Sorry, *saab*, you had to wait."

"I can queue up just like everyone else." Arnav moved his car forward and switched open the fuel inlet. In another country, he would fill up the tank himself.

His phone rang. Naik.

"We have a match for the white man's body, sir. Tambe is here. He says that though the tattoo can't be considered conclusive, he can bet the victim is Gary Scott Williams. The US embassy reported him missing, sir."

"Well done, Naik. This was fast."

"He vanished less than twenty-four hours ago. His daughter is some kind of a diplomat, sir. She called the embassy when he didn't show up for an important family video call."

"Interesting. What do we know about him?"

"He's an expert in hair weaves and wigs, and owns a business in the United States, selling them to various salons."

This victim, too, had connections to the hair industry. Was it to Remy Virgin Hair? Rasool's factory.

"Find out the victim's schedule, whether he was in India on a work trip or vacation, his last known whereabouts. He's related to a diplomat. Media sharks will churn the waters, Naik. We've got to stay ahead."

"He had put up at the Kanthavan Hotel, sir."

A five-star hotel in Mumbai.

"I'll meet you there after I speak with *Vaeeni*. I'm on the way to her place now."

"Right, sir."

"Wear plain clothes. Hotels don't like the khaki on their premises. Bad for business."

Petrol filled, Arnav made a hurried pit stop at the attached convenience store and picked up chocolates for Ashok and Neeti, his usual "visit ritual" for years now.

Arnav was turning the car out of the station when his phone rang again, the burner. It was the informer tailing Zoya.

"She entered a building in Versova, *saab*."

Arnav was in Andheri West, less than ten minutes away.

"Watch her, and let me know who else goes into the building."

"No one else went in, *saab*, but my friend here says you have a big reward for information on Iqbal Asif."

"And?"

"I think we spotted him just now, leaving that same building. My friend is following him."

"You can confirm this?"

"Yes, *saab*."

"Where is he now?"

"He's headed toward Andheri West. My friend has sent me his live location."

"Send it to me."

Arnav considered his options. With his burn injuries, it was already hard to drive with his bandaged hands. He could hold a gun, but he wasn't sure of his aim. He could call for backup, but he didn't trust anyone at his station. That left Naik, but she was investigating the latest murder.

He checked the location. Iqbal Asif was headed in his direction, and had entered a *chawl* not far from *Vaeeni's* neighborhood.

A five-minute drive showed him nearing the suspect's location.

The smell of the *chawl* hit him before he made the turn to see it: the stink of piled-up humanity battered by rain, an overripe dampness, and different kinds of cooking. He'd never lived in a *chawl*, but had visited them often enough during the course of his career to know they didn't feature lifts. This one was a flat building with stairs on one side.

The informer's location dot showed him heading to the top floor. Asif must have gone upstairs.

Arnav found a place under the awning of a shop down the road. He considered going in alone, without backup—but he was no rookie, and he couldn't afford to fail.

He dialed Naik, and returned her greeting with a brisk one of his own.

"Do you have any sub-inspectors you can trust at the Versova station?"

"Yes, sir."

"Ask them to report at the *chawl* location I'm sending you now. Iqbal Asif is holed up here."

"Sure, sir. Should I bring a few constables as well?"

"No, stay back and find out more about the white man—we need to solve that."

He clicked off the call, sent Naik the location, and contacted the informer on Asif's tail.

"He's gone into the *kholi* on the top floor, *saab*. I can't stay here for long."

"Keep an eye out. I'll be there in a few minutes."

He couldn't enter the building in his uniform without alerting any gang members, so he changed clothes in his back seat, thanking his stars for the heavy rain that concealed his movements.

Clad in a shirt under his rain jacket and a shabby pair of jeans, he crossed the busy road, his ear ringing with car honks. Vehicles zoomed past, splashing his legs with rainwater. He cursed and hurried across. Cold and damp were his default state these days.

Rain pelted his cap, and coated all the buildings around him in mist. He turned to make sure he remembered where his car was parked and caught the skyscrapers in the distance: some of the most expensive real estate in the world right across the road from the *chawl*.

He let his body go slack and bowed his shoulders, a technique learned a long time ago. It allowed him to melt into the surroundings, make himself small.

As he climbed the stairs of the century-old building, which used to be a prison during the colonial era in the 1920s, his gaze dwelled on the peeling paint, the unswept floor, the clothes hanging from all corners, damp, or dripping, the wind making them look like a slow dance of departed souls. Twenty rooms stood along a long, roofed balcony corridor that ran the length of the building. On each floor, two bathrooms at one end served all residents of that floor. The miasma of damp, urine, and human waste lay heavy in the trapped, humid air.

There was only one escape route: the way down the stairs he'd taken. A ping on his phone told him constables would cover the exit downstairs in five minutes. Two sub-inspectors from the Versova Police Station would take the stairs as backup.

Arnav walked up those stairs now, broken, dimly lit, with walls a collage of moss, scribbled words of abuse, and tobacco spit. The air in his lungs congealed with stink, but Arnav ignored it, keeping an eye on his phone as messages pinged from Naik's colleagues, and the *khabri*.

He'd never met this informer in person before.

"He's in there, *saab*, the last *kholi*," a short, skinny man with unkempt hair mumbled as Arnav passed him by.

Arnav paused. He could be walking into an ambush. His *khabri* were not the police, nor his brothers. He barely recognized this man, a small-time criminal, and for all he knew, it could be a trap set by Rasool. Damp washing hung on rods and lines, giving off a steam of mold and detergent. Arnav stepped around the discarded cartons and piles of paper lining one side of the corridor.

Not losing sight of the informer, he checked his phone. The sub-inspectors stood in the alley next to the *chawl*. He had to make the call now. Go in himself or send someone else. There was a very real chance Asif was armed and would shoot first and talk later. Tara's pale face in the hospital bed flashed before Arnav, but he girded himself.

It was his job. You sign up for a task, you see it through.

The minute a sub-inspector came up the stairs, Arnav ordered the officer to take position.

"I'm going in. Don't let Asif escape."

"I'll knock at his door, *saab*," the skinny *khabri* beside him said. "You nab him when he opens the door."

"It's not safe," Arnav said. "Take cover."

The little man dashed ahead before Arnav could grab him. "You saved my son's life, *saab*," he said. "Last year, when he was caught in a drug bust. I owe you."

"Come back," Arnav said, not daring to raise his voice. If any of the residents came out, they'd get caught in the crossfire.

The man didn't pay attention, so Arnav followed him, determined to haul him back.

"My name is Tej, *saab*," the man said when Arnav caught him by the elbow. "Be ready."

Arnav would never forget Tej's steely eyes, the quivering lips as he slipped away from Arnav's grip, reached the door, and, having made sure Arnav was in position right beside him, knocked. Arnav's mind slowed down, picturing the towering Asif inside, willing Tej to get out of the way in time, while his own body went into autopilot from dozens of such situations over his career, muscles coiled and handcuffs in one bandaged hand, the other ready to draw his gun. He hoped he'd get to use the former. Not the latter.

At the knock, Asif opened the door after a pause, and Arnav paid little attention to Tej's words while he himself pounced with his handcuffs, managing to click one on but losing his grip on the handcuff due to his bandages. Asif whipped out a gun and shot, the report deafening, sprinted off as Arnav shot at his retreating form, catching him on the leg. The gangster staggered, turned, and was about to shoot again, when he crashed to the ground. One of the sub-inspectors had shot Asif down. A coughing sound broke the silence after the gunshot, and Arnav turned to find Tej bleeding on the floor. Asif's first bullet had found him.

CHAPTER FIFTY-EIGHT

TARA

A shadow crept into the room and closed the door. Was it night already? Hadn't Pia left a few minutes ago? Arnav had asked her to be careful. Now they had found her.

She wouldn't go down quietly, but when she stretched for the call button, it was just out of her reach. Her heartbeat felt loud enough to rouse the entire hospital—maybe it would set off the sensor they had put across her pregnant belly. If it didn't, maybe she could help it along. The intruder may not notice the fluttering of her fingers as she tried to disengage the sensor. Dry mouthed, she swallowed a gasp of panic. Arnav said he had a security guy here. He would come rushing in—wouldn't he?

The shadow drew nearer. In a fit of desperation, Tara had raised her hand to yank at the sensor when a familiar voice said, "Don't, Tara."

"Zoya?" Tara's voice came out in a croak.

"Shh."

This had to be a dream. Tara closed her eyes, opened them again, and this time the shadow was nearer, and the scent she'd missed, the rosewater Zoya splashed herself with, assailed her senses.

"It really is you. What time is it? How are you here?"

"Three p.m."

"It's so dark," Tara said.

"Yes, this storm means business. Outside it looks like evening already. Plus your blinds are drawn."

Tara gripped her friend's hand, and drew her close. "You're wearing a nurse's uniform. What are you—"

"That's not important."

"I would've tugged the sensor they put on me in case of contractions."

"Ever the feisty one, weren't you?" Zoya patted Tara's shoulder.

Tara had missed this woman whose face she couldn't see very well in the gloom. She wanted to get up and hug her friend. Zoya was not a hugger, but she got Tara like no one else, even in the semidark. She helped raise the bed so Tara could sit up, and let herself be held a second. Tara breathed in the rosewater scent that had kept her anchored when she first stepped on the stage as a bar girl, at thirteen.

"I can't even see you properly," Tara said.

"Nor I you, but we can do that over a video call."

"I've tried to reach you the past few days. Why didn't you call?"

"That can wait. I met Arnav a while ago—he told me how ill you were, but we didn't have much time to talk."

"He met you? Where?"

"Downstairs, if you must know. At Dr. Holkar's clinic."

"You came there to meet me? And Arnav found you—"

"No. I was there for a checkup. I had my suspicions. Dr. Holkar confirmed I'm pregnant. Very early days."

Tara wanted to jump out of her skin with happiness and reached for her friend. "Zoya!"

Zoya hugged her back for a brief moment. "I know. After all my dialogues about not wanting a don's offspring. I haven't told him yet, run away for a bit to see you. He'll know I've sneaked off and will be mad, but he'll forgive me. Always does."

"I'm so happy for you." Tara didn't want to let go of her friend.

"We only have ten minutes." Zoya ruffled Tara's hair. "Tell your husband Rasool might be many things, but he doesn't want a riot in Mumbai. It will kill as many Muslims as Hindus."

"There's no reasoning with Avi."

"Look, Rasool isn't a good man, but he won't lie to me. Not about this."

Tara told Zoya about the threatening note. About Pia's escape from the factory terrace, and her refusal to talk about it. About the man who'd followed Arnav.

"I'll talk to Pia. And get Rasool to find out all he can. He often says, if not for Pia, I wouldn't be with him—but he's angry right now, at Arnav. After all he's done . . ."

There was a sound at the door. Both of them froze, but no one came in.

"My guard. Time's up. That was the signal." Zoya lowered the bed.

She held Tara's hand for one last time, giving it a squeeze, and crept out like the shadow she was now.

Tara brushed away her misgivings about Rasool and Arnav, and smiled to herself, feeling lighter than she had in months. Zoya was pregnant, too.

Her phone beeped, and she strived to reach it. A text. She checked the time: 3:07 p.m.

You think you're very smart? You will lose your friends and your family. Watch.

CHAPTER FIFTY-NINE

ARNAV

Arnav returned to his car, his heart heavy as the storm clouds that punished Mumbai. They couldn't save Tej. Arnav had left the scene in the hands of the Versova Police Station sub-inspectors. This was their jurisdiction, and he didn't want his name associated with the shoot-out, at least for now. Iqbal Asif was a gangster, but he deserved to be tried in the courts for his crimes. There would be an enquiry into the action, and Asif's death. Rightly so.

For now, he'd sent out messages. To Ali—to go underground—hide away as far from Mumbai as possible. To his other informer, to find out more about Tej's family, so he could inform and support Tej's next of kin.

Arnav checked his watch. Less than an hour since he'd entered the building, but it had seemed like an endless day. His mind felt like his hands: fragile, with blisters that could break at any moment. He should have waited for more backup. Not let Tej knock on the door. Removed the informer bodily from the scene before the action began.

He took off his rain gear, checked his gun, and started the car. He still had to visit *Vaeeni* and then rush to the Kanthavan Hotel. His father used to say that death was a part of life. But no matter how many times Arnav saw it up close and personal, he couldn't inure himself.

Rain battered his car as he drove up to *Vaeeni's* chawl, not very different from the one he'd just left. *Vaeeni* lived on the second floor of this one. Not bothering with his raincoat, he grabbed an umbrella from the back seat.

Some *chawls* in Mumbai housed middle-class denizens, who managed to pack in all modern amenities in their 180-square-feet *kholis*, but this wasn't one of them. When he knocked on the open doorway of *Vaeeni's* home, it was plain to see from the bare, shabby furniture that the Shindes struggled. Despite the noise of the children running in the corridor, the pattering of rain on tin roofs, and the distant traffic noise, the silence inside the *kholi* seemed suspended, dense.

The sofa cover lay in tatters. The structure doubled as a bed. *Vaeeni* must have brought it in from her earlier apartment. The *kholi* didn't allow space for both sofa and bed. The kitchen utensils lay scattered about the floor, and the shower curtain that separated the tiny bathing area from the rest of the room hung in tatters. A small old fridge thrummed in a corner, but someone had torn apart the old lace curtain *Vaeeni* had used to cover it.

He called out *Vaeeni's* name and heard footsteps nearing in the long corridor.

"Arnav?" *Vaeeni's* eyes widened into saucers for a second before she dropped a curtain on her expression, falling back into the sedate, resigned, almost morose air that had settled upon her ever since her husband's death.

"*Namaste, Vaeeni*. I didn't hear from you the past few days so I came to check."

"My phone broke. I should have told you."

Vaeeni never said sorry. Not that she ever had reason to.

"That's all right. I'm here now. Haven't seen Ashok in a while—he's been having temper tantrums?" Arnav stared pointedly at the disarray in the room. Assigning the blame might rile her up enough to talk.

"No, no, he's actually been a good boy. Sickly, but very well behaved."

"How did this happen, then? Neeti?" Arnav righted the chair and began picking up the spoons scattered on the floor.

"Nothing much. The storm." Her gaze hovered toward the door, as if expecting someone to come in and interrupt them.

"I'm a police officer, *Vaeeni*. Tell me the truth."

"I had taken Ashok to the doctor. When I returned, the *kholi* was like this. Neighbors tell me some goons came in, broke the lock, and trashed the place. They did the same with Bina's *kholi*. Thank god none of us were at home."

"Your sister?"

"Yes."

"She lives in this *chawl*, too, right?"

"Yes. That's why I moved here, so her daughter can be around for Ashok and Neeti when I'm not at home."

"Can we see the damage at her place?"

"Why?" There was challenge mixed with fear in *Vaeeni*'s expression.

"Because nobody gets away with attacking Neeti and Ashok's home. After you and Shinde, I was the first to take them in my arms when they were born."

Vaeeni's expression softened at that.

Arnav didn't let her build her defenses again. "You'll live with us, you and the children. Or I can ask Pia to stay here. Your choice."

"I cannot impose . . ."

"Don't do it for me. Do it for the children, yours as well as Tara's. Tara's hospitalized—your sister may have told you?"

Vaeeni looked stunned. "In the hospital? How did Bina know?"

"Tara had an accident at the nonprofit, which led to complications in her pregnancy. I've been trying to reach you ever since."

"Oh no," *Vaeeni* said. "I had problems at the factory, then lost my phone, then this." She gestured around her *kholi*.

"You're staying with us." Arnav waited. He hadn't been able to save Shinde, had landed Tara in a wheelchair, and had left the entire Shinde family in shambles. He'd be damned if he let them put let their lives in peril.

Vaeeni paused, squared her jaw. "I can't leave my sister and her daughter alone."

"They should come as well."

"That will be five of us. Where will you put us all?"

"It's only me and Pia at home now. The housekeeper leaves at night because Tara's in the hospital. I'm away most of the day. I'll make sure you're all comfortable."

"I must ask Bina *Didi*."

Didi. Vaeeni's elder sister. Arnav hadn't met her before.

"Sure," Arnav said. "Can you take me to Bina's place now? I need to check the damage."

"What is the point in taking this further?"

"I understand." He couldn't force her to file a report. "I can see Bina's place, though?"

"Let's go," she said, and finally glanced at his hands.

"What happened?" She pointed to the bandages.

"A slight burn." Arnav stepped out and waited for her to follow him. "You left the door open."

"Nothing here for anyone."

"Who do you suspect?"

"It happens during elections. They know that Paresh Khare was murdered, and I had argued with him. All upper-caste men stick together, and we are an easy target."

This tracked with what Naik had told him, but Arnav couldn't ask *Vaeeni* about Neeti. Fury raged within. *Only because you choose to remain a target,* Arnav wanted to say. As they walked, *Vaeeni* leading him down the corridor and up the stairs to the third floor, he considered the situation.

In one way, being obligated to him, another *savarna* man, might feel offensive to her. Tara was right. He had no clue. When you are born in a palace, you don't know the plight of those living in the basement. You may not even know that a basement exists.

No one would dare trash his home due to his caste, or harass his wife or daughter. He followed *Vaeeni's* saree-clad figure, the stance of her shoulders like a crossbow ready to fire. None of this was easy for her.

As he walked into the corridor, he'd expected a replica of *Vaeeni's* floor, but a dark mass hung from the ceiling. Swaying, it looked like a dozen robes of incensed witches. Arnav hid his groan of surprise under a cough.

Hair. Lengths of it thick as arms hung on a metal structure with prongs, like a perverse chandelier from a horror show. It stank of a large furry beast that had been wet for a while, an animal stench, dire and menacing. Arnav struggled not to cover his nose. Pia had seen an entire roof filled with these.

"From the nonprofit." *Vaeeni* turned to him, and gestured to the hanks of hair. "The place has been waterlogged, so Bina had to get some of this home."

Vaeeni walked into the *kholi* without knocking, and a striking young woman, possibly in her very early twenties, sprang up from a stool where she sat stirring a curry. The smell reminded Arnav of his mother's kitchen. *Kadhi-chawal,* the sour tang of the yogurt-filled *kadhi* gravy, the melt-in-your-mouth dumplings made of gram flour.

The girl smiled and signed to *Vaeeni—Did you leave your stuff behind?*—before freezing when she saw Arnav standing behind her. Arnav couldn't see the signs *Vaeeni* made, but the girl used sign language: *Who is that and what does he want?*

It had been a while since Arnav had used ISL for one of his cases, but he signed back, clumsy due to his bandaged hands: *My name is Arnav, and I'm a friend of your uncle. Pia's father.*

The girl startled and glanced at *Vaeeni*, who turned to Arnav. She caught the last part of his communication and smiled.

"Ruchi here is not used to people outside the family being able to talk to her."

Ruchi folded her hands in a *namaste* and offered to serve lunch. Her eager yet shy expression brought Pia to mind.

Thank you, I've eaten, Arnav lied. *I'm visiting because of the goons.*

A shadow passed over Ruchi's face as she gazed around the windowless *kholi* at his words. She'd made an effort to put things right, but the floral curtains were torn in shreds and she'd piled broken glasses in one corner, along with torn-up books. On the brown paper cover of one of the books, Arnav recognized Pia's handwriting. She'd gifted some of her books to Ashok the last time he visited their place.

Do you know if any of the neighbors can identify the men who came here? Arnav said.

No, she responded. *And they won't do it even if they could. They're too afraid.*

She stopped at a gesture from *Vaeeni*.

Where do you study? Arnav asked Ruchi instead, figuring the signs as clearly as he could with his blistered hands.

I don't anymore. I work at the internet center nearby. It is closed due to the rains.

Where are Neeti and Ashok? Vaeeni cut in.

Ruchi turned to her. *Ashok went to play with his friends downstairs, and Neeti didn't want to leave him alone, so she went along. She's in* kholi *326.*

That seemed to reassure *Vaeeni*.

"They're fine?" Arnav said. He fished out his phone and clicked the app that would beep the tracking toys he'd given Pia and Neeti. If they had the beepers on them, they'd know he was here.

"That's the only good thing about a *chawl*. People look out for each other."

He followed *Vaeeni* out as she stood on the balcony and, holding a pillar, put her face out in the drizzle and yelled for Neeti. Neeti yelled back—she was on her way up the stairs.

Vaeeni smiled at that.

"Is Arnav Uncle here?" Ashok's reedy voice called up.

"Here," Arnav yelled down into the rain, enjoying this shouted, joyous communication.

"Coming up!" Ashok yelled, and a long cheer floated up from the stairs.

"You're going to work?" Arnav asked *Vaeeni*.

Of course she was. She couldn't lose the day's earnings. Arnav knew that.

"I'll return and sort it all out," *Vaeeni* said.

At Arnav's look, she continued, "I'll talk to Bina. If she agrees, I'll ask Ruchi to send you a message, and we will move to your place by tomorrow at the latest."

Ashok and Neeti hurtled down the long corridor, evading the drying clothes that would slap them otherwise, sprinting over the cartons and passing by the monstrous chandelier of hair as if it were no more than a heap of old clothes, and Arnav sat on his haunches to catch the laughing Ashok in his arms, lifting up the frail nine-year-old with shadows under his eyes. This boy still acted like a five-year-old when he was delighted. It charmed Arnav.

"The toy beeped!" Ashok whispered in his ears. "Neeti *Didi* says it is our secret!"

It was a secret, but the boy didn't need to know how important. Rasool would hear of Iqbal Asif's death soon, and he knew of Arnav's weakness for Ashok and Neeti.

Arnav smiled and said yes as he put the boy down.

Neeti was shy, so he patted her shoulder and handed over his usual offering of chocolates. Neeti's hand trembled, possibly afraid her mother might find out that she'd called Naik.

"I'll wait for your message," Arnav said to *Vaeeni*. "I'll be worried till you're safe."

Vaeeni nodded, her smile somber as she gazed at her children.

Arnav's phone buzzed in his pocket, but he didn't check it till he was out of *Vaeeni's* sight.

Seventeen missed calls, some from Bapat, two from a journalist, a few from Naik. He replied to messages as he took the stairs down, and snapped open the umbrella upon stepping out.

Busy on his phone, and his view blocked by the umbrella, the ambush by a bunch of saree-clad women took him by surprise. They spoke all at once. Their hoarse voices, and their rough-skinned, but heavily made-up, faces gave them away.

Hijras. Or *kinnar*, as Tara insisted he call them.

"*Hai*, he smiles." One of them clad in a traffic-green saree made an attempt to stroke Arnav's face. "Look how *chikna* he is."

A few years ago, Arnav would have scared them away. But his time with Tara and Pia had softened him. He raised his hands as if in surrender. "My wife has friends among you. She's pregnant. Of course we need your blessings. So be kind"—he reached into his pocket—"and bless her."

"What's her name?" another *kinnar* said, blue bangles clinking as she adjusted her saree.

"Tara." Arnav resisted the temptation to give a made-up name instead. The minute they realized he was a policeman, they would scram as fast as they could, but Tara believed in blessings. Why be rude to these *kinnar* who braved the rain to make a measly amount at the end of the day?

"Tara? Now I remember! We went to your place. For her *shaadh* ceremony."

So they had. Arnav remembered sneaking out while they were in the middle of it, making Tara furious.

His new acquaintances nudged another, tall, broad *kinnar*, the best dressed of the lot, who was scrolling on a battered secondhand smartphone. "Madhu, you went with us, too."

Madhu glanced up. "I'm sorry she's not well," she said. "We all bless her."

"Yes, we all bless her," the others took up the chorus, "she'll give birth to a healthy baby, her baby will be a doctor-collector-inspector, will never lack for love or money, so we say, and so shall it be."

For a moment, the chant grabbed Arnav's attention. He sent up a wish. He then passed them the money, thanked them for their blessings, and entered his car in one smooth movement before they could stop him or bargain.

Driving off, Arnav checked his phone again. No alerts from his cameras—he would have to watch the footage later to verify—but Naik had sent a message.

Inspector Desai is here, sir. At the Kanthavan Hotel. ACP Bapat has assigned him back to the temple murder cases.

CHAPTER SIXTY

They're blind. Can't see us, in plain sight. Look closer, *I want to tell them.* Bhai *laughs at me, his harsh laughter that scares the birds.* Whose team are you on? You're going all soft, *he says, and he's right.*

We've got the rumor mills going, haven't we? They're focused on everyone but us. Wheelchair girl is in the hospital now. Bhai *says she'll receive a visit soon.*

I spoke to him, *he says.* He won't be so happy, and he won't dare touch what's ours. He thinks he can hurt us and get away with it.

It's always been us against the world, only this time we're stronger. They've taken so much from us.

I think of the lives we could have led. The money we could have made. Our children, their lives that could have been, and I don't feel guilty. No, not one bit.

Now it's time for their punishment. They will pay. A cock is a small price, right? Bhai *says, and I laugh.*

CHAPTER SIXTY-ONE

SITA

Standing at the atrium lobby of the Kanthavan Hotel, Sita resisted gaping at the twelve floors of suites and rooms that surrounded it. Like stairways to heaven. With muted lounge music playing in the background, she imagined thousands of eyes watching her from the greenery-laced, lighted, covered walks—so different from the dingy balcony corridors she trudged through every day at her *chawl*. They didn't belong in the same city.

Sita came to a stop beside a proud grand piano. Cobalt, it shone in the liquid glow from the tall skylight and the floor-to-ceiling windows bathed in rain. Curtained by the stormy downpour, the distant sea hung from the horizon like an ominous, dark mass, the snapshots of Mumbai coast a blur, the hotel gardens pretty yet bedraggled. None of that chaos trickled into the hotel, unruffled and confident in its luxury. Sita didn't belong here, either, with her damp everyday jeans and *kurta* and her scruffy shoes on the creamy-white marble floor.

The staff sensed this and tried to remove her and the bull-like Desai in his khakis away from sight. Desai rumbled at a cheerful, soft-spoken but determined receptionist who held her own in a crisp long-sleeved blouse and pale saree.

Sita had offered to talk to the hotel staff, but Desai outranked her, and had shot her down. Unlike Rajput sir, who would have held back if that meant they got the job done. She wished she could remind Desai that he should be in jail for taking bribes, but that would help neither her nor the investigation.

They didn't have a search warrant yet. The hotel staff wouldn't let them go up to the Ocean View rooms occupied by Gary Scott Williams unless their manager said so, and the manager had been "on his way" for half an hour.

Sita bit back a smile. Rajput sir had texted to say he was less than fifteen minutes away. Desai had now folded. He'd said yes to the receptionist's very polite offer of a glass of orange juice and refreshments while he waited.

"I'll sort them out soon enough." Desai walked past her and sank into a cushy chair.

She paced up and down while Desai bit into brownies, destroyed tarts and tiny cucumber sandwiches, his uniform sprinkled with crumbs. Long minutes later, Rajput sir strode in. He nodded to her and headed to the reception. He could have been one of the actors who frequented this lobby on their way to fancy Bollywood parties, not because he was personable, which he was, nor because he was well dressed—he wore a simple pair of muddied jeans and a black shirt. He had that air of self-assurance, which made her stare after him. And she was not alone. Heads turned around the lobby.

By the time she'd reached him, Rajput sir was bent over his phone screen, along with a member of hotel staff, a man this time. Sita had sent him pictures from the Gary Scott crime scene.

The manager materialized soon after, and with a minimum of fuss, guided them to the lift. Desai caught up with them, and said, "Bapat sir has reassigned me to these cases, sir."

"Sure. Good thing you're here getting work done, then." Rajput sir shot a pointed glance at the crumbs on Desai's uniform. "We'll inspect the victim's hotel room."

Desai brushed his uniform, littering the floor with crumbs, earning a brief look of pain from the manager. The rest of the journey in the lift continued in silence other than the faint background music.

The manager used his key card to unlock the door that displayed an electronic Do Not Disturb sign and stood by mumbling and yes-sirring to someone on his phone.

Rajput sir requested that the manager remain outside and led the way in, followed by Desai. Sita brought up the rear.

A fruity smell rose to meet them, and Sita wrinkled her nose before straightening her expression. She couldn't be a squeamish female officer.

"Search the washroom." Rajput sir handed out pairs of gloves to both of them, and pointed Desai to the glass pane that showed the huge white bathtub, the toilet bowl, and farther in, the sink and a separate glass shower. "Forensics will be here soon. Disturb nothing."

Desai was about to protest, but took the gloves as Rajput sir passed her a pair before wearing his own.

Just like *chawls*, rich people partitioned their toilets with curtains. Sita drew the blind across the large glass panel that separated the room from the bathroom.

"Examine the furniture and the window, Naik. I'm going to search the bed and the bedside tables."

On the table stood a dozen mannequin heads, on each a different wig.

"I've seen wigs like this before, sir."

Some wigs contained dark curly hair, others straight and blonde, red hair and blue, streaked hair and crimped. The mannequin heads faced the mirror, and Sita shivered a little at their blank gazes.

"Where?"

"The Remy Virgin Hair Factory. When I went to meet Tara and Pia on their visit."

"Check the desk for papers that might tell us more."

The remains of a meal lay covered on the desk, the dustbin filled with used tissues. Both stank, but not with that undercurrent of musty rot that filled the air.

Sita checked the drawers, flipped through the catalogs with samples of hair, and stopped when she saw the name on top. She pointed to them. "Papers from the Remy Virgin Hair Factory, sir."

"We need to pay Mr. Nimkar a visit, find out what leads men visiting his factory to die in gruesome ways."

A clatter from the bathroom interrupted them, and Rajput sir went in to check on Desai.

Sita went on with her search, going over the drawers with cutlery, the mini-fridge stocked with chocolates and cold drinks, and continued to the cupboard.

Two fancy suits on wide hangers. Crisp shirts in pale colors. Ironed trousers. Ties. This man took his appearance seriously. She opened the other cupboard door and reeled back from the fetid smell.

The suitcase. Navy blue and sturdy, one of those flashy pieces of luggage that cost more than what they carried. She knew she should let Forensics handle it, but she found herself dragging it out. Heavy. The object inside shifted when she laid the suitcase flat.

"Sir," she called out, "I think you should see this."

CHAPTER SIXTY-TWO

ARNAV

The stench hit him before he heard Naik call. He rushed out of the washroom, a few medicine bottles still in his hands.

"This might contain a dead body, sir," Naik said, her posture and expression taut.

"I've already called Tambe, left a message for him to be sent straight to this room," Arnav said. "Why don't you go through the bedside tables? Check for anything useful. Call in a few constables for backup, and ask them to come in plain clothes. I'll be back."

Arnav shoved his gloves into his pocket and strode out into the hallway to find the manager standing at the hotel phone. He cut the call when he spotted Arnav.

"I've spoken to the general manager," he said. "We'll continue to cooperate with the investigation."

"A murder might have occurred in the room."

The manager's eyes widened for a second before he collected himself. "Let us know what you need."

"The CCTV footage for this floor, for the exits any guests in this room may have taken, and the lobby. Our team will interview staff who interacted with the guest and seal off the room till Forensics releases it."

"The location of the body, sir?"

"We're not sure there is one yet, but it could be in a suitcase we've found. We'll know more once Forensics arrives."

"You have our full cooperation, sir. I'll take care of everything you asked for." The manager handed Arnav his business card. "This has my personal number, and I'll respond to your calls at all times. Given that the welfare of the other guests is our responsibility, could we request that the police presence be discreet?"

It was a reasonable request. No hotel wanted its name in the papers for the wrong reasons, and never the exact room in which a dead body was discovered. The hotel's public relations team would soon begin calling Arnav, so it was best to handle it now, with the manager.

"Yes. We'll move the body out via the hotel's rear exit. We won't put a crime scene tape outside the door as long as one of our plainclothes men can be present along with hotel security. You must ensure hotel personnel don't enter before Forensics releases the area. Can't have evidence contaminated."

The manager suggested a special gurney that could conceal the suitcase and prevent the reek from spreading. The body could be transported in an unmarked van.

Arnav had barely finished speaking to the manager when his phone beeped. A number he didn't recognize.

This is Ruchi. Ma says we can come stay with you. We will be at your place this evening. Thank you Uncle.

He smiled. So Bina had agreed, and the family would move to their place tonight instead of tomorrow. At least one thing had worked out well on this hellish day.

At a noise, Arnav turned to find the white-bearded Tambe stepping out of the elevator, his assistant in tow, and two constables behind him.

"Rajput, I thought we spoke about this."

Tambe hadn't wanted to come in. He'd received another call warning him to stay away from the cases. That call was also made from Bandra. The phone was a burner, and switched off immediately after. Arnav's team hadn't been able to locate the caller—but he'd noted that the call originated in Chitra Varli's neighborhood.

"We'll speak further, I promise. Thank you for coming, I appreciate it"—Arnav ushered the flamboyant man and his assistant into the hotel room—"this way"—and closed the door behind them.

Naik stood taking photographs of the room, while Desai sifted through the papers, holding a tissue to his nose. Both turned when Arnav and Tambe walked in; then went back to their work.

"The stench is the strongest here"—Arnav pointed at the navy suitcase—"but I wanted to show you these first." Arnav led Tambe into the large washroom.

He wore his gloves and picked up the bottles.

"What drugs are these?" Arnav said. "I found them hidden behind the counter."

"American brands," Tambe said. "High-dosage antipsychotics. These are prescription drugs for those with mental disorders like bipolar, but possibly others as well. We might find a prescription among his possessions, because he'd need those to bring the drugs into India."

Desai ambled over. "I might have found one. Let me check."

The man returned with uncharacteristic speed, and bumped into Arnav, who was typing a text. With Arnav's hand still in bandages beneath his gloves, the phone slipped, and landed inside the open toilet bowl. Arnav froze, then dived in with his gloved hand. The phone had switched off. Desai apologized and scurried off, leaving Arnav with a prescription in one hand and wet phone in another.

"Let it dry first," Tambe said, "and then we can disinfect it. Leave it with me."

Arnav nodded. A ruined office phone was the last thing he needed right now. No help for it, though.

"I keep saying this, but this time I mean it. This is absolutely the last time I work with you before I retire, Arnav."

"Agreed."

Tambe gestured to the suitcase visible through the glass partition that separated the toilet from the room. "You think there's a body inside that?"

"Well," Arnav said, "there's a decomposing object for sure. As a courtesy to the hotel we'll transport it to the morgue before opening it."

"That's a cabin-sized suitcase," Tambe said.

"Too small to hold a human body?"

"I told you I didn't want to be involved, Arnav. This could be a body chopped up into pieces." Tambe paused. "Or a child."

CHAPTER SIXTY-THREE

TARA

Tara stroked the cold heart-shaped locket. She couldn't open it. The tantric at the Kaali temple would do that, to place a strand of hair of her newborn. If only she could get him to say prayers for her family. All her life she hadn't believed in gods, and certainly not the goddess her mother worshipped, Ma Kaali.

But in the end, the goddess had saved what was important: Pia. Tara had rescued Pia two years ago, but she had help—like her mother would have said—divine help. She needed some of that now.

She shivered. The message on her phone. You will lose your friends and your family. Watch.

Someone must fetch the tantric for her. And that someone also must see that warning on her phone, and take action. Her husband. She could forward him the text, but she had to know he'd seen it and what he planned to do about it. Besides, she didn't want him to get it in the middle of work, and panic.

She dialed Arnav, but he didn't pick up. She wanted to toss this ancient phone that didn't do much other than send texts and make calls. She would've asked her daughter to call Arnav, but Pia was in her tuition classes and didn't have her phone with her.

Calling *Vaeeni*, she found the number switched off. Tara tried both numbers again, with the same result, then tossed the phone on the sofa near the window, resisting the temptation to smash it on the floor. Sita, then. Sita was at work with Arnav.

Sita—a woman who wasn't bloated with child, who held down a job, who could kick butt if needed. Not in a wheelchair. Someone Arnav spoke of with admiration and respect, who worked with him shoulder to shoulder.

When Tara had met Arnav the first time, he was single. Not so the next time fourteen years later. He had a girlfriend, a stunning, capable, caring woman. Arnav had broken off with her to marry Tara in a hospital bed, where she lay paralyzed, despite knowing she might never recover.

Arnav deserved someone like that girlfriend, or like Sita—who would be his equal, not someone lying in bed and trying her best to call him. Failing. Humiliating as it was, she had to call Sita to speak with her husband. She rang the nurse, got her to fetch the phone back for her, and raise the blinds so she could see the world outside. Once the nurse left, Tara dialed Sita's number. Sita picked up after a few rings.

"Tara?" Sita sounded guarded, anxious.

"Could you ask Arnav to call me?"

"Sure. Are you okay?"

"Yes, for now. Where is he?"

Tara had to ask that question, and hated herself and Arnav for it. Why would he not pick up her calls?

"At an investigation. ACP Bapat came down to check the crime scene. Rajput sir is with Bapat sir now. I'll ask him to call you the minute he can."

Sita's tone was gentle and kind, the sort Tara used with Pia when her teen was unwell. Tara's fury rose, so she thanked Sita and cut the call.

Breathing deep, she tried to calm herself. Her head ached, beginning to pound. Nausea. She sweated in the air-conditioned chill of the room. Outside the window, the monsoon tore down in sheets, coloring the world white. Occasional streaks of lightning broke through the gloom. Distant claps of thunder followed. The storm outside echoed the one within her body.

The nurse rushed in. "Mrs. Rajput? How are you feeling?"

"Not so good."

"I received an alert from your monitor. I need you to sit up"—the nurse helped her do that—"and I'm raising your legs now."

"Thank you." Tara gasped. "My head hurts. I feel like throwing up."

"I have paged Dr. Holkar. She should be here soon."

"What's wrong with me?"

"Your skin is cold to the touch." The woman touched Tara's thighs and shins, but as usual, Tara didn't feel it. "I'll take your blood pressure now. Breathe slowly. There's nothing to worry about."

A few minutes later, Tara's blood pressure stabilized. The nurse said her pressure had fluctuated, but she and the baby were both fine.

"What about Dr. Holkar?"

"I am not sure, Mrs. Rajput. She is not here, but her family says she left home. She might be stuck in traffic. Her phone is unreachable, but with the weather outside, I am not surprised. She will see you the moment she comes in. In the meanwhile, I will get another doctor on call. Try to relax."

"Are you sure the baby's okay?"

"So far as I can tell, yes. The fetal heart rate is stable. Dr. Holkar will confirm with a checkup when she's here."

An hour later, Arnav hadn't called back, and there was no sign of Dr. Holkar. Pia would be done with her tutions soon. Tara alternately fretted and soothed herself, wishing Arnav were next to her, or Zoya.

Zoya must have telepathy, because the phone rang and her name flashed on the tiny screen.

"Can't talk long," Zoya said. "Something went wrong. I don't know the details yet, but one of his men died. I'm going to work on him, but tell your husband to beef up security on you and Pia."

Zoya dropped the call before Tara could speak.

Tara's headache came back with a vengeance, and she began crooning to herself, crossing her fingers Dr. Holkar would arrive soon.

Tara checked the clock. Dr. Holkar had still not come in, but her phone buzzed with a call from an unknown number. While she struggled with her headache and debated with herself whether to pick it up, the line went dead.

CHAPTER SIXTY-FOUR

ARNAV

Arnav greeted his boss, Assistant Commissioner Atul Bapat, tamping down the shiver he felt in his damp clothes. Soon, the driest spots of Mumbai would drown—even these plush chairs in a small but private conference room provided by the hotel manager.

Bapat had insisted on a private chat in this room downstairs, while Tambe worked the crime scene with his assistant in the presence of Naik and Desai.

"Lay it out for me, then." Bapat looked like a whipped mastiff, beaten but not ready to retreat. "Why couldn't we take Iqbal Asif alive for interrogation?"

Arnav explained the circumstances, omitting his chat with Zoya. He'd kept his wife's connection with a mafia don's girlfriend a secret. He ended with another request to raid the hair factory: all of the victims so far had connections to the place.

"We'll see about that. Have you spoken to Nimkar again?"

"Yes, sir. He won't let us in without a warrant."

"What about the other lines of investigation? The tantric, what was his name . . . Ram Chandra, and Chitra Varli?"

"Ram Chandra has confessed to collaborating with her on porn movies—influencing girls to let themselves be filmed."

Bapat froze. He swallowed and found his voice a moment later.

"Can we trust Ram Chandra?"

"I'm not sure, sir. We'll have to conduct a raid on Chitra Varli's apartment to collect evidence, or send someone in undercover. I have a thumb drive from her apartment. We can't use it as evidence, but some of the scenes have been shot in her living room."

Bapat grabbed a glass of water from the table, and for a while far-away thunder and soft background music were the only sounds in the room.

"We can conduct raids till the cows come home, but none of it will work till you plug the leak at your station, Rajput."

"I'm working on it, sir."

"In the meanwhile, the suspects are free to roam the station."

"I'm having their movements tracked, sir."

Bapat knew better than to ask more. They both knew some of the methods would be outside standard protocol.

"Since you have Desai back on the team, do you need this Naik? Desai is an inspector and can use his team for the investigation, now that we have three similar cases."

"Sir, Desai is back, but Mr. Nimkar told me that Desai and he had come to an arrangement."

"What do you mean?" Bapat leaned forward.

"Desai was trying to get Vishal Nimkar's body cremated before the forensic examination was complete. He knew the victim's identity and tried to conceal it. And he's been seen exiting the factory even after he was suspended."

"Where's your report on this?"

"Sir, I'd sent him away on leave for obstructing the investigation. I wanted to hear from Desai before filing a report. I haven't had a chance to do that yet, sir."

Meaning, *You should have consulted me before reinstating an officer I'd sent away.* From Bapat's expression, he was either a good actor, or wasn't involved in a scheme of kickbacks involving Desai.

"I'll have a chat with him before I leave." Bapat cleared his throat. "Right, sir."

"Having an American murdered could develop into a diplomatic issue if the situation escalates," Bapat said, raising his hand in a gesture when he got a call. "I need to take this." He stood up.

Arnav breathed a sigh of relief. The briefing was over. He didn't want to speak to his boss about Raghav Naik unless he had to: that Raghav was friends with the tantric, and was Sita's husband. Bapat would insist on removing her from the investigation, and with valid reason.

With Naik the only reliable officer at his disposal, Arnav couldn't afford to lose her before he'd found and removed the mole. Besides, she'd already invested so much in the case, and his family owed so much to her.

And to *Vaeeni*. *Vaeeni* had agreed to stay with them, thank heaven— he must pass her and Tara his burner phone number.

On his phone, he downloaded the app that showed him coverage from the cameras and recorders he'd placed at the station. It showed no activity in his room, nor in the main room with the CCTV cameras that covered the lockup and exit areas.

Bapat returned. "That was the commissioner." Anxiety creased his forehead into a large frown, making him look older than his fifty-four years. "The news is breaking in the media now. We must make an arrest. Tell me what you need."

"Sir, like I've said before, we must raid two places. The hair factory and Chitra Varli's apartment."

"We can ask Nimkar if he can let in a few men in plain clothes to carry out investigations."

"I don't think he'll cooperate, sir."

"Nimkar has already suffered in the past week."

"Vishal Nimkar's death is not a secret any longer, sir, and Gary Scott Williams was their customer—his death will be on television screens soon."

"Let me check about the warrant. And I myself will speak with Chitra Varli."

Arnav weighed his options. Having Bapat chat with Chitra Varli about her porn business might get her to reveal more about the murders or her connection with the tantric.

"This is the thumb drive from Varli's apartment, sir." Arnav handed it over to his boss.

"Have you checked it?"

"I haven't, but my staff has, sir. This might get us a warrant for a raid. We can also interrogate Chitra Varli on all she knows about Ram Chandra."

"A raid on Varli will shift attention away from the temple murders. Let me see what I can do. At the least, it will buy us time."

"Right, sir."

"You'll either put this case to bed soon, or I'll find another lead investigator."

Arnav would have spoken up, but his burner phone pinged. He gave a nod of assent to Bapat, and hurried out.

The app had detected movement inside his office. He flicked it on, expecting a glitch. The camera showed the squat, unmistakable profile of Constable Mihir Kamble.

Arnav missed a step and leaned on a pillar in the hotel lobby as he watched the kindly constable's face scrunched in concentration. After pulling out his phone, the elderly man clicked pictures of a file one by one. Arnav had left the file at his desk—a fat report of the Kaali temple investigation with papers he'd asked the computer forensics technician to manufacture. He'd found the mole.

CHAPTER SIXTY-FIVE

I don't like the weather today. Too dark. Too stormy, too much like the day we lost our mother, when they came and broke down our door and carried her away and returned her to us over weeks, in pieces.

Who knows, though, maybe there's justice in this world. Maybe the same theater will welcome the show we've prepared.

Another party, and Bhai says he wants to take his time with this one.

CHAPTER SIXTY-SIX

TARA

One hour had flown by, and still no call from Arnav.

Long years ago, when Tara had first met Arnav, they were to go to a movie. Her boss had canceled her Sunday off at the last minute. Instead, he'd sent her on a private assignment. The naive fool she was, she'd accepted, and as instructed, left her phone behind. She'd returned to seventy-six calls from Arnav. He'd been worried out of his mind, because Zoya had told him she'd gone out.

"Where were you?" He'd picked up the minute she called him, way past 2:00 a.m. No trace of jealousy in his tone. Concern for her welfare. Anger at her not telling him before she left.

How would he react when he saw the many dozens of calls she'd left him in the past hour? Why had he not called back? His job leashed him with his phones.

She dialed him again. The number was switched off. On her previous phone, Tara had saved his spare numbers, and his office landline. Pia, while giving her this button-phone disaster, had keyed in only her father's official number.

Tara considered her options. She could call Sita again, and bother her about Arnav's whereabouts. Humiliating. Can't find your husband and call his colleague once, okay. Twice? She'd be called a nag.

She was about to dial again, when the nurse came in to announce a visitor. Tara liked this nurse, who had a soothing way about her. Nurse Kamble said it wasn't visiting hours yet, but someone had come to see her.

"It might do you good to chat, Mrs. Rajput. Help you relax a little. I can arrange for your friend to come up if you want."

Who could it be? Not Zoya. *Vaeeni* and Sita were her only other "friends." Both were at work.

"Who is it?"

"Sujata Shinde."

Vaeeni? It didn't make sense. Arnav was to go and see her. Why was she here instead of at work?

"Bring her up, please," Tara said. She waited, her hand on her locket.

Vaeeni gave a soft, anxious smile as she came in. "I'm so sorry, Tara. I didn't know."

"I missed you, *Vaeeni*. Arnav was trying to call you. We were worried when we couldn't get in touch. He was to visit you today."

"Oh, he stopped by. That's how I knew you're in hospital."

"Bina didn't tell you?"

"Our homes got trashed. She must have forgotten in all the chaos."

"Trashed?" Tara reached for *Vaeeni*'s hand, who caught it between hers.

"Goons smashed up our place, and hers. Arnav invited us to stay at yours, and Bina has accepted this time. I wanted to come and see you first, though."

"We've been asking you for so long. Both Neeti and Pia would be very pleased. But who would do such a thing? Has Arnav registered a report for you?"

Vaeeni frowned. "We do not want police involved."

"I know. I heard Neeti is being harassed."

"She told you?" *Vaeeni* raised her eyebrows.

"Pia told me. I hope it doesn't happen again."

"She talked about Paresh?" *Vaeeni* said. "And yet you did nothing?"

"Paresh Khare? What has he got to do with it? He's been missing."
Vaeeni straightened, eyes blazing. "What did Pia tell you?"

Strange. *Vaeeni's* anger made no sense—she should've asked Arnav
for help if her daughter's safety was at stake.

"That the local goons had harassed Neeti. I did ask you about it, if
you remember, but you said there was nothing to worry about."

Vaeeni simmered down. She stroked Tara's forearm. "I know. I said
nothing because you have enough going on. How are you feeling now?"

"Not well, *Vaeeni*. And your *laddoos* ran out."

Eating the power-packed sweets calmed Tara, and settled her
stomach.

"I brought some. You can have one now." *Vaeeni* reached into her
bag.

"Yes," Tara said. She'd asked Dr. Holkar, and the doctor saw no
harm in eating them—Tara had gotten her housekeeper to pick the
nuts, seeds, and *ghee* for *Vaeeni* to use. A dry-fruit *laddoo* was not a
cheap affair. She'd begun to crave them over the past months.

She accepted the *laddoo* and insisted *Vaeeni* take one, too. The
woman didn't eat enough. That would change when the family moved
to the Rajput home. When *Vaeeni* didn't take a *laddoo*, shy as ever, Tara
picked one up and put it to her mouth, and waited for her to take a bite.

Once *Vaeeni* had begun eating, Tara explained about calling Arnav,
who hadn't responded.

"He must be busy at work. I'm sure he will call you back soon,"
Vaeeni reassured her. "What is so urgent that it cannot wait?"

Tara spoke of the tantric. She needed him to do a small worship-
ping ceremony for the baby's safety and well-being.

"I'll get you your phone contacts when I go to your place," *Vaeeni*
said.

"Thank you. Would you mind calling Arnav on your phone? He might be upset with me for calling him so many times."

"My phone is broken," *Vaeeni* said. "I sent it for repairs."

Tara wanted to point out that she could see *Vaeeni's* phone in her half-open bag by the bedside sofa, but didn't. *Vaeeni* had her reasons for not lending her phone. Maybe she was embarrassed about its age and model.

Tara focused on talking to *Vaeeni*, telling her Dr. Holkar had still not come in. No one had heard from the doctor for hours now, at her home, or at the hospital.

Vaeeni excused herself and went to the toilet, half-eaten *laddoo* in hand, leaving her bag behind. Tara tried her husband's number another time, and when he didn't pick up once again, she reached out for *Vaeeni's* phone. *Vaeeni* wouldn't mind Tara borrowing it for a quick call—maybe she'd saved one of Arnav's other numbers.

Tara stretched to try to grab *Vaeeni's* bag, but it lay out of reach. She was about to give up, when a young woman in a cleaner's uniform ran into the room.

"Madam, take care"—the cleaner got her the bag—"you can't fall, not in your state."

Tara thanked her, and requested that she stand by as Tara snatched up the phone and tried to make a call. This was *Vaeeni's* own phone that Tara had seen before. Weird. Having seen *Vaeeni* unlock her phone many times, Tara ran her fingers over the number pad, only to freeze when she saw an open app with messages. The last message stopped her cold.

"Please return it where it was." She thanked the cleaner, who put the bag in its place, and left.

Tara switched off the device and shoved it under her inert thighs. Her stomach felt uneasy, but she ignored it. She had to remain calm until *Vaeeni* took her leave.

When *Vaeeni* came back to the room, she looked as ill as Tara felt, but Tara still retained her skills from those long-forgotten days as an aspiring Bollywood actress.

With an easy, relaxed smile, Tara told *Vaeeni* how pleased she was at *Vaeeni* and her family moving in. *Vaeeni* left, but Tara didn't dare take out *Vaeeni*'s phone. The woman might return, searching for it.

Tara's stomach cramps making themselves known, she dialed Sita from her own phone.

"Please call Arnav," she gasped, her breathing constricted.

"Tara? Are you okay? Rajput sir has left the hotel, but I'll call him."

"If you can't find him, please come here now. You must see this. It's an emergency."

Tara gave her room number and cut the call.

CHAPTER SIXTY-SEVEN

ARNAV

Had Arnav not seen it himself, he wouldn't have believed the cheerful, docile Kamble capable of such deceit. Who was he reporting to, and why? Heading out in his car, Arnav considered his next step. He could collar Kamble and ask him for an explanation, report him, and have him fired. That wouldn't help identify Kamble's shadowy boss.

At a traffic stop, Arnav called Ali. A funny thing, setting an informer on a policeman, but Arnav saw no other quick way to nail whoever Constable Kamble was working for.

"*Ji, saab,*" Ali said, "I can ask my friend to follow this man. He lives in the slum right across from your station."

"Sending you a picture. Give him ten minutes. And you stay on your toes."

Ali sounded worried. "I'm only picking up your calls. And talking to one or two people I trust."

Arnav then called Kamble, and instructed him to get to the Bandra Railway Station to assist another case in progress.

"Railway station? I have duty assigned here, sir. I need to photocopy some documents for the new sub-inspector."

He meant Naik. Naik had asked him to copy some papers. Those could be relevant to the case. He should've called Naik first and told her about Kamble.

"This is a new order. They're shorthanded at the railway station."

"Okay, sir. It is pouring, so this will take me time."

The station wasn't that far.

"Call me once you arrive."

"Yes, sir. Network coverage problem due to the heavy rains. I will go now."

Kamble didn't sound pleased, but he'd do as he was told.

Arnav dialed Naik, but she didn't pick up his call. He sent her a message.

DO NOT give work to Constable Kamble as per our earlier discussion.

She had the list of his suspects, which included Kamble, so she'd get what he meant. Was Kamble the lone mole? Who were his friends?

Arnav made a mental note of the policemen at his station—and for the next task picked a sub-inspector who didn't see eye to eye with Kamble. The tall, unpopular Raju Dinkar, who had earned his nickname, Dicky. Dicky knew what everyone thought of him, and didn't care.

"Find out where Mr. Nimkar of the Remy Virgin Hair Factory is right now. Do whatever you need."

"Yes, sir," Dicky said.

"Ask two constables to report to the office of the Ram Rajya Party." He gave the names, not men who had been seen with Kamble. "Plain clothes. And they should wait at the lobby."

"Right, sir."

Arnav cut the call as he drove through the rain. The drains by the road had overflowed, and on the radio, the DJ warned people to stay at home. The forecast spoke of heavy rainfall through the evening. They expected flash floods. After the dire warnings, the DJ followed up with romantic Bollywood songs, all set in the rainy season.

Arnav chuckled—Tara had once been obsessed with Raveena Tandon gyrating in rain-soaked movie scenes, and had wanted to learn those moves and expressions. He dialed his wife, but her phone was busy, so he called the cleaner at the hospital, the wife of an informer. It was her job to watch over Tara.

"Madam had a guest, *saab*."

"Outside of visiting hours? Who was it?"

"The nurse brought her upstairs, *saab*. Madam called her *Vaeeni*."

"Okay. Stay in touch with the others. Tell them if you need help, or see anything strange. Especially if you can't get me. This is my spare phone, and it's acting up."

"*Ji, saab*."

So *Vaeeni* had gone to visit Tara before moving into their house, even though it wasn't visiting hours yet. Such a *Vaeeni* thing to do—she was a stickler for tradition—tell the woman of the house first.

As he tried to make a turn on a flooded road, Arnav's car stalled. He should've gotten a driver and the office jeep today, but he'd wanted to stop by at *Vaeeni*'s. Using the work vehicle for personal business didn't sit right with him. He checked his burner phone—it didn't show network service. If the car didn't restart, he'd be in trouble, stranded in an area with no taxis or buses for miles.

With a gurgle and a cough, the car restarted, and Arnav huffed in relief. He'd nearly reached Raghav Naik's political office. According to Sita Naik, Raghav had started working with the grassroots organization of a local Dalit political party, its mission clear: bring power to the lower caste. From what Arnav remembered of Raghav Naik, he was the prickly sort, puffing into a ball of thorns at whatever he considered provocation.

Iqbal Asif was dead. Chitra Varli would be interviewed and her apartment raided. Ram Chandra's friend might provide the missing links. Given that Raghav Naik wasn't in jail, and had flown under the radar so far, he could be an accomplice to both the theft and the murders.

CHAPTER SIXTY-EIGHT

SITA

When Tambe had described to Rajput sir what the suitcase they'd spirited away might contain, Sita's mind had conjured nightmarish images. It had terrified her—the thought of never living it down if she lost her breakfast on the carpeted floor in the middle of a crime scene. Desai had stood by, his face like stone, and for once, Sita had wanted to copy him.

And now a frantic call from Tara. It was hard to tell if Tara's panic was based on a genuine threat, or pregnancy-related hormones. Sita dialed Rajput sir's burner phone again, but her own phone was low on network coverage. She dialed him from the hotel landline, but the voice mail told her Rajput sir was out of service range.

Tara had sounded frantic. In distress. *Please come here now. You need to see this.* The hospital wasn't far away. If Tara needed help, Sita would reach her much faster than wherever Rajput sir was at the moment. She called him again, with the same result.

Sita walked out to the hotel corridor and said to Desai, "I received an urgent call, sir. I'll need to leave."

He was the ranking officer. As per protocol, she needed his okay. They had wrapped up the crime scene—only a few interviews with the hotel service crew remained.

"On a case?"

"Not sure, sir. Mrs. Rajput called. Pregnant and hospitalized. The family has received death threats."

"Death threats?"

"Yes, sir. One of those threats led to her accident. Fell from her wheelchair."

"Are you sure she's in danger? She's in a good hospital, right?"

"I think it is to do with these temple murder cases, sir. I've received texts as well."

She scrolled down her messages and showed the text from a blocked number to Desai. Be careful what you wish for.

"Bapat sir put the temple case on top priority," Sita said, "and I can't contact Rajput sir."

Bapat's name changed Desai's mind. He'd had a long chat with the ACP downstairs at reception.

"All right. List what still needs doing here. Report to me when you arrive at the hospital, and if it is"—Desai paused, looking awkward—"a false alarm, head straight back here."

It wasn't as easy to reach the hospital as Sita had imagined. The wind roared, and the Arabian Sea, usually tame, had lost its patience. It hurled itself at the bund and splashed onto the road. The lashing rain that hadn't stopped in a week added to the deluge. It all looked increasingly like the great flood at the end of days.

Sita shivered as she sped as best she could in the police jeep. Cars stalled and struggled through inches of muddy water. Sita remembered the Mumbai floods of 2005, when she'd barely escaped with her life—entire slums had folded and cars got swept away. She sent up a prayer for the waters to recede. If the Arabian Sea invaded, this part of low-lying Mumbai would be done for.

Her phone beeped on her dashboard—finally some network coverage. Rajput sir had sent a message quite a while ago.

DO NOT give work to Constable Kamble as per our earlier discussion.

Kamble figured in the list of his suspects. The gentle Constable Kamble, who jumped to fulfill all her requests, was the mole. Close to retirement, how badly did he need money to betray his own police station?

She tried Rajput sir's number again, but his phone remained out of coverage area. Sita hoped he was fine, wherever he was, and recalled herself. She was going to meet his very pregnant, distressed wife. It wasn't her place to worry about him.

Her phone rang. Tambe. He would call Rajput sir, or Desai. She ignored it, but the call rang off and began anew.

"Naik here." She kept her tone brisk. "I'm driving."

"I can't get through to Rajput. I have an update on the suitcase."

Sita braced herself. "Tell me."

"A young adult. Bald—has alopecia—lost all his hair. Difficult to be sure with the decomposition, but I think he was"—Tambe's voice faded and then returned—"abused."

"Castration?" Sita made herself ask.

"No, but I noticed strangulation marks on the neck. Cause of death is likely asphyxiation, but I'll have to do a postmortem in daylight. I am headed home now."

Not a child then. Still, a teenager, with all his life ahead of him till he met a sudden end, possibly at Gary Scott Williams's hands.

Sita nodded, unable to speak, forgetting Tambe couldn't see her. She cleared her throat and gave her choked thanks before cutting the call.

Three men murdered in or around Kaali temples in what looked like ritualistic castrations. Now a young man found decomposing, stuffed in a cabin-sized baggage. She kept her eyes on the road, and focused on what lay ahead: a very distressed Tara and her call for help. Other things could wait.

CHAPTER SIXTY-NINE

Arnav

Arnav parked his car near the run-down, two-story building with peeling paint where Naik's informer had said Raghav had remained since morning.

Faded signage declared it as the Ram Rajya Party, a Mumbai Dalit front, and assorted spray-painted political messages, new and old, screamed from the outer walls. Arnav sprinted across, his waterproof windbreaker little protection against the thunderous downpour.

The entrance stood open, the collapsible iron gates pushed to both sides. Arnav marched in. Following the poster directions, he reached the reception area right next to the stairs going up. Raghav Naik hunched over a register, surrounded by posters on the walls, his table brimming with flyers. He looked up at the sound of Arnav's footsteps.

"Hello, Naik." Arnav didn't smile, feeling a hint of awkwardness at addressing Naik's husband with her surname. His surname, he corrected himself. This was the "original" Naik, his features unremarkable, like a curtain at a wedding hall. His artificial arm wasn't apparent at first glance, and Arnav ignored it, choosing to notice instead that Raghav didn't look startled.

"Hello, sir," Raghav said. "What took you so long?"

Of course. Raghav knew of the arrest of Ram Chandra Dome and the priest.

"Where can we talk?"

"Upstairs."

"Let's go." Arnav put a hint of command into his voice, and watched Raghav flinch but recover quickly.

He emerged and led the way upstairs. Arnav stayed alert—this was Naik's husband, but he'd also aided a suspect who was in custody.

The upstairs corridor opened into several rooms, where men and women sat bent at their tables working on old desktops and various files and folders, a low hum of conversation in the air. Arnav refused Raghav's offer of tea, though he could have used some—he needed to keep this brisk.

Raghav entered a small, windowless room to the left, and offered Arnav a chair.

"How do you know Ram Chandra Dome?"

"Before we speak about all of that, sir, I'd like to say thank you." Raghav raised his right hand a little, his gaze upon the stiff artificial limb. "This would have been harder without you stepping in."

"Sub-Inspector Sita Naik is a fine officer—we do what we can for our people in Mumbai Police."

"With due respect, sir, that's not been my experience. And now I see why my wife sings your praises." Here his tone took on a sour note.

"That's between you and Naik. I'm here about your connection with Ram Chandra Dome and the temple priest."

"I met them at the Kaali temple."

"That can't be why you helped Ram Chandra arrange that ritual he was performing when I arrested him."

"He called me, sir, not the other way around."

"With what phone? He was in custody, and his phone's with us."

"It was a private number, sir. I can show you my call records. He had a phone on him."

That was true. Naik had recovered a phone from the premises, but it had yielded no clues.

"You knew he'd escaped custody."

"He was on remand, sir, not in prison after a court sentence. Innocent, at least till proven guilty. He has been kind to me, seen me as a man, and given me respect. That is hard to come by when you have lost your limb."

Arnav's experience with Tara had taught him the truth of this. The disabled turned invisible.

"So, despite having been a police officer once, and with your family still working in the police, you gave aid to a man suspected of horrific murders. You must have seen the video that was all over social media. That was someone's son, a loved family member."

"Vishal Nimkar. If you ask me, he deserved it, sir. So does his father, the so-called pillar of society, the owner of factories, Mr. Nimkar. You should have heard the stories Ram Chandra told me."

"I'm all ears."

"Ram Chandra only found out recently, sir. Vishal was going out with prostitutes, and dipping into the company funds without explanation. Ram Chandra had noticed the discrepancies. Vishal was drunk and asked for more money."

"Ram Chandra refused," Arnav said, "and was fired. You're sticking to his story."

"That is only half of it, sir. Vishal was angry, so he laughed at Ram Chandra. He was only spending money on prostitutes, he said, but his father actually sent out little boys and girls to old men. To his interested foreign clients."

That suitcase. According to Tambe it could contain the body of a child. A child like his Pia. Maybe younger. Arnav gritted his teeth. Ram Chandra had not spilled the entire truth during the interrogations.

"Foreign clients?"

"He had American clients. British. More than one. All 'serviced' through that nonprofit that Nimkar and his clients support."

This was impossible. Why would a factory owner do this? Besides, Bina helped run the place.

"The nonprofit is run by Bina. Her sister is like my family."

"I'm only reporting what Ram Chandra said, sir."

"He didn't mention it during his questioning."

"Ram is a tantric, but he is not foolish. He knows what would happen to him if he opens his mouth."

"And yet you're telling me."

"You won't harm Sita's family. Sita has done enough and more to protect yours."

"She has, and we're grateful." Arnav leaned forward. "You know your wife's views."

"Which are?" Raghav remained seated.

"If it ever comes to a choice between herself and the right thing to do"—Arnav loomed over him—"she'll choose the latter. I'll get your statement verified, and if any of it turns out to be false, you'll be answerable to the law same as anyone else."

"All of it is true."

"Are you in touch with Constable Kamble at the Bandra station?"

"He used to work with me. He told me that Ram Chandra had been arrested again."

Raghav seemed confident, not trying to hide his connections.

"Write me the names of all Kamble's friends. Every single one."

"Yes, sir."

"Are you telling me all you know about Ram Chandra? Think before you speak, Raghav Naik."

Arnav used the man's full name, unable to overcome his unease at using Sub-Inspector Sita Naik's name for this man.

Raghav lowered his eyes. "I think so, sir."

The man knew more than he was letting on. If Ram Chandra had stolen the necklaces, he might have told Raghav about them. And about Chitra Varli's porn movie business. That information could be extracted in other ways, after taking Raghav into custody, if necessary. For now, Arnav needed Kamble's contacts, and a way to the killer.

Arnav tried to get a signal on his burner phone while he waited, but it kept flickering out. He was about to switch it off and back on when it pinged.

Mr. Nimkar is in his office at the factory.

Dicky had sent him a message.

Arnav had no solid evidence against Mr. Nimkar other than Raghav's unverified statement. Given his conversation with Bapat, he would have to wait for a search warrant on the factory.

If what Raghav had said was true, a killer had enough motive to murder Gary Scott Williams, and possibly Vishal Nimkar and Paresh Khare in case they were involved in the alleged child trafficking. And the killer could do away with Mr. Nimkar, too. The stormy night would provide excellent cover.

Who was the murderer, though?

Had it been Iqbal Asif, doing the killings at Rasool's bidding—was he biding his time at that *chawl* in order to target Mr. Nimkar next?

Someone who knew Chitra Varli and Ram Chandra? None of them fit the bill entirely.

He responded to Dicky.

Get a team together, and reach the factory in an hour.

The text didn't send. The phone signal had dropped.

"Do you have a landline?" he asked Raghav.

"Yes, sure. In the office room next door."

Arnav left Raghav scribbling in a notebook. Outside, he noted that Raghav could only go downstairs if he crossed the room Arnav was in. With an eye on the door, he dialed his station, and asked for Dicky.

Arnav gave him instructions to reach the hair factory with his team.

"Yes, sir, I can do that." Dicky sounded excited at an opportunity to take leadership. "The two constables you'd asked for earlier will be there soon, sir. Five minutes."

"Thanks. Ask them to wait at the lobby."

Arnav tried calling Sita and Tara next, but neither call went through. The storm outside had caused signals from all service providers to waver. He sent them texts instead. Their phones might receive messages if the signal returned for a while.

As he tried calling, his gaze searched the room. Raghav had helped Ram Chandra, and they'd both met Chitra Varli, as per Sita's report. Raghav wouldn't risk taking incriminating evidence to his tiny *kholi* he shared with his policewoman wife. He would stash it in his office.

Arnav touched the desks, the drawers, ran his hand along the table, even as he typed the texts. Raghav or anyone else might enter this office at any moment. Arnav's hand snagged against a protrusion on one of the desks, and he bent to check. He found a catch by the side of the desk. Tinkering with it, he was able to release the mechanism. A small drawer was inside, with a red velvet pouch. It was empty, but its golden tassels reminded him of the jewelry his mother stored in her locker. Most traditional jewelry came in pouches like these. He reached farther in, only to find another red pouch.

Raghav might have spotted him driving up to the office from the upstairs windows. There was a good chance these pouches came from the Kaali temple, and had once contained the two necklaces.

It wouldn't do to startle Raghav. It was his office, he could have a gun stowed away, and his supporters worked nearby.

"I'm sorry, but I'll have to place you under arrest." Arnav kept his tone bored and neutral as he entered Raghav's office.

"Sorry, sir," Raghav said, his lips trembling. "I haven't done a thing. You have to believe me. Ask Sita."

Raghav tried to sidestep Arnav and run, but Arnav tripped him and sat on the fallen man's back, handcuffing him in one smooth movement. The noise brought Raghav's colleagues, but once Arnav identified himself and yelled for his constables, they made way.

Raghav Naik struggled. Not wanting to hurt him, Arnav waited for the two constables to rush up the stairs and grab him.

Ten minutes later, with the room emptied out, Arnav stared down at Raghav, who was handcuffed to his chair.

"I have my rights, sir."

"I'm sure you do," Arnav said. "You used to be a police officer. I don't need to tell you how this goes: we can do it the easy way if you hand over the necklaces."

"Don't arrest me, sir."

"You'll let us search you, then."

"No, no, sir."

Arnav turned away. "Search him," he ordered the pair of constables.

"I have them, sir," Raghav said, his voice raised in alarm. "Let me take them out."

Arnav gestured for a constable to uncuff Raghav's left hand and watched the two constables hold back smirks as the man slipped the sacred gold jewelry out of his underwear. Tossing the velvet pouches to the constables to secure the necklaces, Arnav turned to Raghav.

"You have information."

"Yes, sir."

"I can't make any promises." Arnav would do his best for Naik's husband, but there could be no leniency for a thief, and a man possibly involved in a porn racket.

"Chitra, sir. Chitra Varli."

"What about her?"

"There are videos made at her premises, sir."

"We already know about her."

"She agreed to promote us in return for Ram Chandra helping her with the movies. She would launch the announcements for our party—become a partner."

"I don't see how all of this is useful."

"The whole thing was Ram's idea. With Chitra launching us on social media, we would need backup. His uncle would never report him, and the jewelry is insured, so he thought he could get away with it. We could sell it outside Mumbai, with no one the wiser, and help pay Chitra's fees."

"Do you have evidence to prove any of this? About Ram Chandra or Chitra?"

"Ram Chandra has some porn-video footage, sir. I'm not sure where it is, but it shows Chitra Varli's involvement."

"What do you mean?"

"I wouldn't be surprised if she were behind the Kaali temple murders also, sir. Ram Chandra being in jail keeps her business safe. She's wrapping up her porn business now that her social media and her videos have taken off."

Arnav considered it—could Chitra have framed the tantric? She certainly had the motive and opportunity.

The murders aside, though, given Raghav's testimony and any incriminating video footage, they could book Ram Chandra and Chitra for the porn racket and the stealing of the necklaces. The raid on her premises would no doubt yield more.

"If your information on Chitra Varli proves useful, we can discuss you turning a state witness."

"Thank you, sir. Give me some time with Ram Chandra, sir, and I'll get it all."

"Do you have the list I asked for? Kamble's known contacts?"

"There, sir." Raghav pointed to the table.

Arnav glanced through the list. Some of the names stood out. Vishal Nimkar, Mr. Nimkar, Chitra Varli, Ram Chandra Dome, Bina, Paresh Khare.

"Constable Kamble is connected to all these people?"

"His daughter used to go to the school run by the nonprofit. She died last year. Chitra Varli was a chief guest at the school's Annual Day ceremony. She handed the first prize for dance to his daughter."

CHAPTER SEVENTY

SITA

By the time Sita reached the hospital, it was already fifteen minutes after Tara's call. Tara's room was in an uproar. Two nurses struggled to get an uncooperative Tara onto a stretcher.

When Sita rushed in, the two paused for a moment.

"Tara?"

"You're here," Tara said, as if she'd been drinking tea in her living room and not wrestling two nurses. Turning to the women, she said, "Please give me two minutes with this lady, and then I'll come with you."

"Mrs. Rajput, there's no time to lose," the nurse said. "We still can't locate Dr. Holkar, and we only have junior doctors because of the storm. We need to take you to an operation theater."

"In that case, the sooner you give me the two minutes, the better. My husband's in the police, and she's his colleague."

The nurses looked at each other, and the one doing all the speaking said, "We will wait outside."

As soon as the door closed behind them, Tara said, "Look under my thighs."

"Tara?"

"Just do it," Tara said, her tone brisk, like she was the policewoman, not Sita. "You'll find a phone. Can't reach it anymore—it slid farther in with all my wriggling."

Sita burrowed her hand under Tara's thighs, and fished out the phone, still warm from her body.

"It is *Vaeeni*'s." Tara looked scared now, and in some discomfort.

"What?"

"Hear me out. Unlock it—make a Z with the dots on the screen. Check all the messages. You'll recognize some of them. Tell Arnav if you can. Keep him and Pia safe."

Sita did as Tara asked, and it was indeed *Vaeeni*'s phone. The screen-saver was a picture of her children, Neeti and Ashok.

"What do you mean?"

"She gave me something. In the *laddoo*."

"The *laddoo*? I've eaten those."

"This one wasn't right. It tasted a little funny, but I ate it to please her. I realized after I finished it. I think it made her sick, too. She didn't eat all of it, and threw up. That's why she was in the washroom for so long. Brought them for me, but didn't leave them behind."

Sita grew cold with each word from Tara. Poison Tara—why would the sedate, caring *Vaeeni* do that? She skimmed the texts on the phone and saw the line: Send her this: "Be careful what you wish for." Take usual precautions.

Vaeeni had asked someone to send her the message. Who? But she would think of that later. First, focus on Tara.

Tara's face was taut, but she continued, "*Vaeeni*'s not our friend. We can't have her family in our home." Tara gasped. "Have asked Pia to come here. Don't let her out of your sight. Promise me."

Before Sita could respond, the nurses returned.

"Mrs. Rajput," the lead nurse said, "should we go now?"

Tara said to them, "I have to throw up. Sorry."

Sita focused on *Vaeeni*'s phone, and scrolled the messages while the nurses helped Tara hurl into a bin.

Messages to other people as well—and most of them unsavory. Threats. Meetings and assignations. Sita pocketed the phone—she must deliver it to Forensics.

The nurses had begun to transfer Tara from the bed, when Sita spotted the name tags. KAMBLE, one of them said. Pure coincidence. Sita hesitated.

After one look at Tara's contorted face, she asked them to stop. She must ensure she wasn't sending Tara to further peril.

"What's your full name?" she asked the nurse named Kamble.

"Nishita Kamble."

"What's your husband's name?"

"Mihir Kamble." The nurse drew herself up. "He's a constable."

This was too close to be a coincidence, but Sita asked anyway.

"What station?"

"Bandra Police Station."

Sita took out her ID and flashed it. "I'm Sub-Inspector Sita Naik. I need to see a senior surgeon before she can be moved."

"She's our patient, our responsibility," the other nurse said.

"You're taking her for an operation—will either of you do it?"

"No, but—"

"No buts. Where's her doctor, the one who was treating her?"

"Dr. Holkar hasn't come in today," the nurse said. "She left home, but she's missing. Her family is calling the police."

This was getting increasingly dark. Where was Sita's doctor? Was that a coincidence, too?

"I'll help with that. Inform a surgeon."

"Only junior doctors are available in the department."

"Let me speak with someone in charge. Right now. If not, I can call my station for backup. Her husband is the senior inspector. You can explain to him why his wife is being put in danger at your hospital."

"No, madam!" The other nurse looked terrified. "I mean, yes, madam."

"And I don't want Mrs. Kamble treating this patient."

"You can't . . ."

"She brought her in." Tara pointed to Mrs. Kamble, gasping now.

Nurse Kamble with *Vaeeni*. Couldn't be trusted.

"I'll place her under arrest for endangering the life of the patient," Sita said. "She escorted a visitor here less than one hour ago, outside of visiting hours."

"I'll call the doctor." The other nurse scurried out.

"You"—Sita turned to Mrs. Kamble—"if you care about your husband, you'll sit on that sofa, and not move. Hand over your phone."

Nishita Kamble handed her phone over, tears streaking down her face.

The other nurse ran, and Tara grabbed Sita's hand. "Try calling Pia, please. She's coming with the driver."

Sita now understood why Rajput sir was smitten with his wife. Tara was in major discomfort, her life perhaps at risk, but her tone remained calm and forceful when she asked after her daughter.

Ten minutes later, having squared Tara away with a senior doctor, who'd assured her they were trying to get a specialized gynecologist to replace Dr. Holkar, Sita took the hospital manager aside. She told him of the possible poisoning.

He paled. "I'll do my best. Please call the next of kin. We need a sign-off on the operation to get the baby out of harm's way. I've taken note of your complaint about Nurse Kamble. She'll remain isolated until your men arrive."

Hoping it wasn't the worst mistake of her life, Sita scrawled out her signature on the consent form. "I'm from the police, and I take full responsibility."

She then turned her attention to her phone.

The first call, to Rajput sir, failed as before. The second, to Pia, kept ringing.

Up next, Desai.

"You mean that someone tried to poison Rajput sir's wife?" Desai said.

"Yes."

"Do you know who?"

Without concrete proof, Sita hesitated. "I have a suspect, sir. Which is why I'm requesting backup to the hospital."

"It will take them a while in this rain. I will send two constables."

They could keep Mrs. Kamble from mischief and protect Pia in case Sita herself had to leave in search of Rajput sir.

"I still can't find Rajput sir. The doctor wanted to speak with him."

"We can't reach him on his other phone, either. He asked Dicky to go to the Remy Virgin Hair Factory with backup, so he may be headed there. Keep me updated."

Desai cut the call.

That factory where Tara suffered her fall, where Pia was threatened one way or another, where *Vaeeni* worked.

Vaeeni.

Sita must check through *Vaeeni*'s messages. Figure out who she was talking to. Put a stop to that. But first, she must try to reach Pia again.

Before Sita could dial her, the girl herself burst into the room. "The doctor called. They want Papa." Pia's short hair was ruffled, her eyes wild.

"I'm here. We'll find your papa soon."

A clatter sounded from the corridor, and Neeti ran in.

"Neeti?" Sita asked Pia.

Tara hadn't said anything about Neeti. Given what she'd revealed about *Vaeeni*, this would complicate matters.

"Neeti and her family will be moving in with us tonight, so I brought her home with me from her school," Pia said.

"I didn't want to let her come alone," Neeti said. "How is Tara Aunty now?"

The concern in Neeti's eyes looked real, but Sita couldn't trust her. Why would *Vaeeni* want to poison a pregnant Tara? Everyone had gone mad. The Kambles, *Vaeeni*.

"Why don't you guys wait here and watch TV while I make a few calls?"

Out in the corridor, she checked her phone, and ignored the missed calls from her husband.

Her phone beeped. The *khabri* tracking Constable Kamble had sent in his report.

Instead of going to the railway station like he was supposed to, the mark is at the Remy Virgin Hair Factory.

The factory, again. Was *Vaeeni* there, too? *Vaeeni* didn't have her phone, but maybe she was with her sister? Sita could call Bina and check.

If she told *Vaeeni* that Neeti was at the hospital, and kept *Vaeeni* talking, she could get the call traced. Difficult in this storm, but she could try.

About to dial, she was startled by a whispered call of *"Naik madam."*

She turned. A woman in a cleaner's uniform waved at her from within a utility room. How did the cleaner know who she was?

"Message for Rajput sir," the woman whispered.

On alert, Sita approached her. A man stood behind the cleaner. "Good evening, madam," he said, "we work for Rajput sir. For Mrs. Rajput's security."

Naik nodded, still unsure.

"She has found a plastic box. The woman Mrs. Rajput called *Vaeeni* dropped it inside a dustbin."

Sita opened the box. The *laddoos*. She had to hand them over to the doctor—figure out what *Vaeeni* had fed Tara.

311

CHAPTER SEVENTY-ONE

ARNAV

Superman. Some days Arnav wanted to be the Man of Steel, who could detect ongoing robberies at the other side of the city, travel at the speed of sound, and smash through walls. He wouldn't mind wearing an unflattering blue suit and red underwear on top if all of that came with superhuman strength. He could use some of that right now. His car had stalled and his phone was out of juice, leaving his mind a hornet's nest of buzzing fears.

He'd tried calling Mr. Nimkar with no success. If he couldn't get the gates open, his trip in the pouring deluge would have been for nothing. Recalling that Tara had said the nonprofit and the factory shared a rear access, he'd called Bina with a sudden burst of life in his burner phone. When this was over, he would buy a reliable device as a burner.

Bina had passed the phone to *Vaeeni*, who'd said she could get him in if he wanted to meet Mr. Nimkar.

Bapat would be burst a blood vessel, but Arnav knew ways to deal with that. The flooding was as good an excuse as any. He could claim that the situation had escalated, with no way to contact the station. It was true.

Swearing at all the hiccups that had been his lot, Arnav pulled on his rain gear, scrabbled for a flashlight, and grabbed his gun, shoving it into his backpack. Though Mr. Nimkar posed no immediate danger, Arnav couldn't leave the gun in an unattended vehicle.

Guided by his flashlight, clothes soaked, he waded through knee-deep waters, hoping no uncovered manhole waited in his path. He checked his burner, but it remained dark. For once, he empathized with Pia, who suffered heart attacks without the internet or phone signal. If only he'd taken the police jeep instead of his own car, he would've had radio access.

Once he found *Vaeeni*, he could call his team using a landline, unless phone lines had gone down in this part of Mumbai. The factory would have a generator, or at least a working invertor. He must ring Naik and ask for updates. Ask Tambe what horrors the suitcase contained. And call Tara to check on her.

Full of plans and wary of making a false step, Arnav reached the unlit alleyway that led to the factory's rear entrance. A gushing stream of muddy water met him, more than ankle deep, but he didn't care. A few steps in, his flashlight spotted *Vaeeni* at a small gate, holding up a large black umbrella against the pelting rain. Lightning crackled above, showing up the gloomy buildings with spiky shadow and light, turning them into haunted castles.

"Sorry to keep you waiting, *Vaeeni*," Arnav said once he was near enough so she could hear him above the claps of thunder.

"No problem," *Vaeeni* said with her usual, gentle smile in the half light. "Your car?"

"It drank a bit of water and stalled, but I can still give you all a lift to our place later."

"That's good."

"Hope you have a landline. I haven't been able to call anyone. My phone's dead. No signal."

"Oh, dear. Yes, we have a phone. Come on in." She led him into a dark corridor. "Let us get out of the rain. We have made some tea."

"Bina is upstairs?"

"We both got stuck because of the rising waters. No bus service. Mr. Nimkar will stay back in his office if the storm does not let up."

"It's that bad?"

"Flood warnings. Things can get very dangerous."

Those were the last words Arnav heard before a large hand smothered him.

Strong chloroform.

Arnav threw a punch on instinct, hitting a muscled body, but it wasn't enough. A pinprick at his neck set off alarm bells.

The killer had drugged previous victims.

For a moment, Arnav savored the fact that he was right, that the culprit was at the factory. He kicked out and it landed on another body, but it only won him a muted humph.

Where was *Vaeeni*, though? He struggled, but more than one pair of hands held him down. Arnav lost the battle to keep his eyes open.

CHAPTER SEVENTY-TWO

SITA

This wasn't going to end well.

Sita had received a flurry of texts from Rajput sir, which came in all at once when the signal cleared.

He had gone to the factory. He'd asked Sita to reach the hair factory with reinforcements.

And the texts from his burner number didn't stop there.

Kamble was apparently a known entity at the nonprofit. Sita recalled running into him a few days ago while she watched the neighborhood. On the day she met Tara at the factory.

And according to Rajput sir's interrogation of Raghav, Mr.Nimkar might be trafficking children to clients like Gary Scott Williams.

When she called his number, the voice message declared it switched off. She dropped him a text about *Vaeeni*.

The thought of Rajput sir stranded made her want to drop everything and run to him, but his wife was in a medical emergency.

Sita headed to the tall senior doctor's office. He rose from his seat when he saw her.

"I've sent the *laddoos* you gave me to the lab for analysis, so we can figure out the right antidote. That might take time."

"You said she doesn't have time."

"We've stabilized her for now. We can't find Dr. Holkar and can't locate anyone specialized in pregnancies with spinal injury."

"But you can tell from her symptoms what the poison is?"

"She has labored breathing, high blood pressure and heart rate, abdominal pain, tremors, vomiting. We don't know how much of it is due to her pregnancy complications, and we can't tell the kind of poison from those."

"How long does she have?"

"I'm trying to contact someone who knows about poisons, and another obstetrician who can help the patient. But we need to know the poison in order to help her."

Sita swallowed the large lump in her throat that threatened to choke her. *Vaeeni* knew exactly what the poison was.

Sita peeked into Tara's room to find Neeti and Pia, their heads bent together over Pia's phone. Teenagers. No matter how upset they were, they found a way to distract themselves. Neeti looked up at Sita's approach.

"Where is your mother?" Sita said.

"At the factory. She said she will reach us at Pia's place."

"Stay here, both of you. Call me if the doctor says anything."

They nodded, their faces pale, eyes wide. She left them there, and having asked Rajput sir's security guy at the hospital to watch over them and contact her in case of developments from Tara, made for her car.

Inside her jeep, the radio crackled. Desai. The very man she didn't want to hear from, but she couldn't afford to alienate him, either. Rajput sir didn't have many friends. He didn't need more enemies.

"You were supposed to update me," Desai said.

"I was about to call you, sir."

Desai would decide whether she received any further backup to go to the hair factory, to find Rajput sir, and collar *Vaeeni*.

Sita didn't relish the prospect of showing up at that factory alone. A child trafficker inside. Or a murderer. Or both. Tall boundary walls, a huge gate. Rear access through the nonprofit was the only way in, but the alleyway might be flooded.

"Naik?" Desai's annoyed voice on the jeep radio jolted her into speech.

"Yes, sir. The suspect, the nurse I told you about earlier, her husband is a police constable at the Bandra station."

She told him about Kamble, his relationship to the nonprofit near the Remy Virgin Hair Factory, and the fact that he was the mole who could have helped the tantric escape.

Desai spluttered, "Are you sure? Kamble has been with us for many years."

As have you, Sita wanted to retort. *That didn't prevent you accepting a bribe to cremate Vishal Nimkar's body.*

"Yes, sir. Rajput sir sent me a message. I'm headed to the factory myself, sir. I'll need backup."

"Why? It is a factory. Bapat sir said Mr. Nimkar is cooperative. I know him, personally."

That was the issue. All these men protecting each other. Men, whether from the upper caste or lower, tended to stick together while women, well, some women seemed keen on poisoning their friends.

She needed the most strategic answer.

Desai and the assistant commissioner were both *savarna*, friends to Mr. Nimkar. Mr. Nimkar also had Desai on his payroll.

To sway Desai, she needed more, and if men could lie, so could a woman.

"Mr. Nimkar may be in danger, sir. Whoever targeted the men, including his son, could have him in their crosshairs next."

"What makes you think so?"

"Mr. Nimkar is at the factory, and all the victims have been related to that factory one way or another. It has to be someone he knows. If they killed his son, they can't wish him well."

"I will head there myself. I'll speak to your station, and bring men from there."

"Right, sir." This was excellent news.

"Bapat sir spoke to me. Rajput sir has done me a favor."

So Rajput sir hadn't pushed for Desai to be punished for accepting bribes. Sita digested that fact, and let the silence linger. Desai cleared his throat.

"I can't let him be stranded in a lower-caste area on his own," he said. "I told him the murderer was that low-caste tantric, but he wouldn't listen."

"Sir, he's a police officer first—evidence matters to him more than caste. And Ram Chandra Dome is still in custody."

"It is all these lower-caste people. Look at Kamble and his wife. They showed what they were made of."

"I'm also from the Scheduled Caste, sir. And this is my city as much as anyone else's."

Sita cut the call.

Damn the man. Damn all men. Yes, it was wrong to lump everyone together, but right now, she couldn't care less. Desai's will and efficiency didn't inspire faith.

She stalked to the back of the police jeep, checked she had enough ammunition, and brought her gear with her to the front seat. Thunder crackled and blinding streaks split the skies for a brief moment, mimicking her mood.

In her rearview mirror Sita thought she caught a blur of movement, but it was gone. Rage and concern warred within her. Rage at Desai and *Vaeeni*, worry for Rajput sir and his wife. Anger at herself. It wasn't her job to worry about Rajput sir. It was his family's.

After slamming closed the jeep door, she drove off into the pitch-black rain.

CHAPTER SEVENTY-THREE

ARNAV

Trussed up in a chair wasn't how Arnav had imagined finding himself ending his day when he woke up this morning. When he came to, long years of training curbed his instinct to open his eyes. His consciousness blurred, like a windshield wiped with a dirty rag. A stink of wet animal weighed the air—like rotting mushrooms, sulfur, and human waste.

The world beyond his closed eyelids seemed dark—no flashlight on his face. He would take that—if he was lucky, no one was watching him. The metal chair was cold—it came to him with a shock that he could sense no clothes. Someone had stripped him, leaving him naked as a babe.

He kept his breathing long and even, as if asleep, though strong restraints bit into his wrists and bandaged hands behind his back. Same with his feet. On his mouth he tasted a grassy cloth. The chloroform. His attackers had muzzled him with the same cloth they'd used to nab him.

They hadn't blocked his hearing, though.

"This was stupid," a harsh, yet high-pitched voice broke out in Hindi. Arnav had heard it before, but he couldn't place it.

"I'll decide if it was or not."

A ringing voice. A molten core of steel and fury, but Arnav recognized it all the same. It contained traces of the feminine lilt and softness he'd known so well. Over decades.

He resisted the urge to crack his eyes open to confirm what his ears told him. It couldn't be. Yet it was. The Shinde family. Hemant Shinde had stabbed him in the back, and now Shinde's wife. He bit his tongue to keep from making a noise. It was an appalling, dreadful day of death and betrayal.

"Today was meant only for Nimkar. *This*, this was not the plan," the harsh voice continued, undaunted.

"I decide, all right?" Sujata Shinde, the woman Arnav had called *Vaeeni* all his life, said. "I will tell you what we can and cannot manage. I wasn't married to my asshole police officer for so many years for nothing."

"All because of your phone? Because you left it in her room?"

Arnav listened with his entire attention. What phone? Whose room?

"Shut up. I took the risk. How was I to know she would make me eat one, too? Unless I dropped it elsewhere, we have to assume she took it when I was in the toilet."

"We have told you a thousand times to be careful. You should have gone back for it."

"She was not alone by the time I went back. This is the only way now. Besides, I did not call him—he called Bina. That phone is not registered in her name. It is easy for people to go missing on a night like this."

"Not a Mumbai police officer. His men will come here, sniffing," the guttural voice said.

"You will do the usual."

"*Na*, Sujata *Didi*!" The harsh voice sounded incredulous, mortified. "What are you saying? Those men—that was all right. The first two made life difficult for women in the *chawl*. The one after . . . disgusting."

Didi. Did *Vaeeni* have a brother or was this just a random accomplice? It wasn't strange in Mumbai for men to call women sisters. Besides, they spoke in Hindi, not *Vaeeni's* native Marathi.

"It *is* the same. Exactly like Nimkar upstairs. Destroying lives."

The vitriol in her voice jolted Arnav. She hated him, and had hidden it so well. How had he failed to notice it?

"Stop reasoning with her, *Bhai*." Another voice. He'd heard this one over the phone. The voice that had told him about Tara's accident. "She won't listen."

Bina, Sujata Shinde's sister. The one in charge of the nonprofit. And the man she called *Bhai*? Where had Arnav heard that voice?

"Sujata *Didi*, I said . . ."

"Shut up, Madhu," *Vaeeni* said.

Madhu. Madhu, the *kinnar* Tara liked so much. Madhu, the *kinnar* with the rough voice.

Sujata. Bina. Madhu.

These were blows to the head.

Madhu called Sujata Shinde, Sujata *Didi*. Elder sister.

Bina called Madhu *Bhai*, maybe a leftover from the days when Madhu was male.

Madhu was a sibling to Sujata and Bina.

Tara had tried to help them. He himself had invited Sujata and Bina to his house, only a few hours ago.

To share rooms with Pia.

Madhu had danced at Tara's baby shower. Blessed her.

"We are moving into his house tonight, are we not?" Sujata Shinde continued. "From your *chawl*? Have I not lived in your *chawl* these past two years? Have I led you astray?"

"Not so far, but we were supposed to go tomorrow."

"Has to be today. And we must hope the *laddoo* works, Bina. If she speaks to someone, there will be questions. That's why we need to shut him down."

Laddoo. Vaeeni made *laddoos* for Tara. Arnav twisted his hands slowly, checking whether he could loosen the binds. He'd asked for both Dicky and Naik to come with reinforcements, but the weather could delay them. It was up to him to escape.

"But how will we get out of this bind?" Bina's voice held a tinge of fear. "Why would anyone allow us into their house if he's gone?"

"Don't worry. Everyone knows how well I've taken care of them."

"And that phone?"

"Is not connected to me. There are no names leading back to us. No one knows."

"You never told us what you mean to do with him," Bina said. "And two men at the same time, in one evening. Impossible."

"This is for our children. For Ashok. Neeti. Ruchi. So that what happened to Madhu and you and me never happens to them."

"How will this help?" Madhu's gruff voice broke in. "You're not thinking straight. This"—the voice paused—"this isn't what we were doing. This looks like revenge."

"And what you did was not revenge?" *Vaeeni* laughed, a dry, hard sound. "I asked you to make their faces unrecognizable, but did you not go a step further? You said it was like a ritual, but didn't the cutting make you feel good? You threw their balls to stray dogs. Don't pretend like you're some activist, Madhu. You're not. I was there. I saw you smile."

CCTV had shown three people walking toward Paresh's murder scene, and a couple returning. Madhu, possibly in men's clothing, and *Vaeeni*. *Vaeeni* had watched the murder. Why did Paresh meet them at a temple at night? Arnav's mind raced even as his numb fingers tried to work the rope, sending his bandaged hands into spasms. The blisters from the burn wounds had opened.

"I've taken your shit for long enough," Madhu said. A chair scraped, and slammed against the wall.

"Sit down." *Vaeeni's* voice had taken on the tones of a mafia boss.

Who was this woman? How could she have looked so meek for years?

"I'm done." Madhu spoke in measured tones. "You want things done to this man, you do it. You two took off his clothes. Maybe you enjoyed it—much better looking than your husband, for sure. Do the rest. The knife is right there on the table. You can't make me."

Arnav opened his eyes a crack. At the far end of the hall, the three gathered around a table under a faint lamp. Their voices echoed, carrying to him.

"*Bhai.*" Bina's voice rose on a plea.

"Were you not the one who said you will make him pay, cry buckets?" *Vaeeni* hissed. "Pay for knifing my husband in the back? Pay for riffling through my house when my husband's corpse hadn't yet cooled? For tarnishing his reputation so I had to stay in a shithole the last two years? For making nice with my children while robbing them of their future? You are their aunt."

The *kinnar* identified as female, so Madhu was Neeti and Ashok's aunt. Yet neither child, Ashok or Neeti, had ever mentioned her. This was getting darker with each new word.

And *Vaeeni* had known everything, two years ago. Known that Arnav had searched their home for Shinde's papers. She'd reassured Arnav, said she understood him not attending Shinde's funeral—because Pia had been kidnapped. Not so. She'd hated him each moment.

"Yes, but this is not the way to do it. Those previous men were monsters." Madhu remained obstinate.

"And he isn't?"

"You've gone blind," Madhu said. "It is you who has kept your children in misery. He and his wife have always been kind."

Damyanti Biswas

"I didn't need their pity. They brought me low."

"Fine." Madhu gripped one of the chairs. "You're angry with him, but can you explain what you did to that poor pregnant woman? The both of you—you tell me how smart you are—and yes, I have blood on my hands. Don't you, too?"

Tara. Tara's accident. They caused it.

"Please, *Bhai*." Bina's voice grew softer, persuasive. "We can fight later. Let's figure a way out of this."

"A way out? Sooner or later they will catch me. A *kinnar*. I know what I have on my conscience. Nimkar deserves it, but this one . . . I'm not touching him."

"He deserves it, too."

"Even if I agreed, he's a police officer. They won't let it go."

"They think Rasool did it. We fed them enough evidence starting from that *shaadh* day when I first overheard him talk about it. Kamble gave them that CCTV footage of Iqbal Asif, and I heard there was a shoot-out this afternoon in a *chawl* nearby. Asif is dead. Rasool won't take it lying down."

"That's all very well, but police is police. We can't get away with this."

"A policeman is not a god," *Vaeeni* said. "Quite the opposite, I can tell you. We have one sitting guard on Nimkar upstairs."

"That's another foolishness"—Madhu paced the floor—"calling Kamble here. He's only helped with making the tantric the suspect. He hated all the others, and Nimkar. But he didn't know you'd bring his station boss here. He will squeal."

"Not everyone is the coward you are." *Vaeeni* wrapped the free end of her saree about her, and tucked it into her waist, as if readying herself for an unpleasant task.

A part of Arnav registered what they said; the other remained alert to dangers. He must use the time they left him alone in the dark. *Vaeeni* wouldn't stay talking for very long.

324

Nude mannequins stood about—ghostly sentinels, wigs of various shapes and sizes perched atop them. Hanks of hair hung from ropes strung across the hall, like black flags of doom—the source of the wet animal smell.

"Just because you know about police procedures, and can plant evidence, doesn't make you brave. I did the dirty work. You stood by." Madhu's harsh voice grew louder.

"Who lured them there?" *Vaeeni* stalked up to the tall *kinnar*. "Who supported you all these years? Who made sure you were fed and clothed on your bad days? Nimkar's father is responsible for what happened to you—from Madhukar, to Madhu—a man to a *kinnar*. You nearly died, you fool. And, what they did to Ma, to all of us. Have you forgotten?"

"I remember it all, and I've always listened to you," the *kinnar* said. "Not this time."

Keeping one eye on them, Arnav tried to take better stock of his surroundings. Without moving his head, he could see a few windows. Lightning flashed in through them from time to time. He sat in a hall, with balcony corridors all around, like a shopping mall. A lone stairway led the way down. The windows hung far above on the upper floor, flanking the corridors.

"You were fifteen when those *savarna* men chopped your balls off. We hung our heads and cried then, our family, everyone from our neighborhood. And all because our mother refused the lust of a *savarna* man. We're doing this for us. Our future."

Arnav flinched at *Vaeeni's* words. He'd known nothing about her, her family, and now that he did, it was too late. The rope rasped against his burned hand as he loosened the ties, but Arnav pushed past the pain. He had to keep moving, stop them from getting to his family.

"What future?" The *kinnar* wouldn't back down. "Ruchi sends those messages. She sent a threat to a pregnant woman in a wheelchair. What are we teaching her?"

As long as Madhu objected, Arnav could take advantage of their distraction, buy time till backup arrived. His clothes lay in a bundle on the table, not far from him. Next to the knife Madhu had mentioned.

"She's learning to cope in a world where *savarna* men hold all the power. Ruchi now knows about power. They turned her deaf when she was twelve. Or did you forget those slaps and punches on your niece? We didn't educate her for nothing. I cannot give you back your penis, nor Ruchi her hearing, but I'll do what needs to be done. So will you."

The next time lightning flashed through the windows, Arnav braced himself and moved the chair along with the rolling thunder while the three remained locked in their own struggle. Arnav repeated this. Another push or two, he might reach the knife.

"*Bhai* is right," Bina said. "This has gone too far too fast, Sujata. We were going to take this slow. We've involved Chitra Varli and that Ram Chandra. Planted evidence. This shit won't go down quietly. Chitra Varli won't keep her mouth shut."

"What's wrong with you?" *Vaeeni* said. "You forgot what she made your Ruchi do? Your daughter was in a porn film. I doubt we got to all the copies."

Having paced all this time from one end of the table to the other, walking between the sisters, the *kinnar* paused.

"We must think this through. I don't have much to lose—for me, inside the jail or death by hanging can't be worse than what I've already seen. You both have children."

"We can't back out now," *Vaeeni* said. "He might be a bastard, but he's not stupid. He'll connect this to us."

"Do what you want." Madhu's voice retreated as she walked up the stairs to a door. "Leave me out of it."

"Don't take another step."

"Or what?"

The hall echoed with the sound of a cocking gun, ready to fire. *Vaeeni* had either carried one, or had searched Arnav's backpack. Arnav had loosened his ties now, but he couldn't do much naked, with his feet tied up, against a crazed woman with a gun.

"I'm your sister, but my loser husband taught me how to fire this. I won't hesitate."

CHAPTER SEVENTY-FOUR

SITA

Driving through the pummeling rain and rising waters, Sita sent up a prayer to the goddess Kaali. She must reach the factory in Versova and find Rajput sir. In normal times it would've taken her less than half an hour. Today the spluttering jeep would take longer.

She laughed to herself. Rajput sir would never imagine her wanting to ride to his rescue. Her phone rang, and laughter remained in her voice as she picked it up.

"The girls are missing," a panicky voice said. Rajput sir's security hire.

"From the hospital? Where were you?"

"I am looking for them, madam. I checked the rooms, toilets, all the places where nonstaff can go."

"My men will be there soon. I'll ask them to check the CCTV. Keep looking."

Sita cut the call, connected her phone to the charger, and dialed Pia's phone. It was switched off.

Memories of the last time Pia had been kidnapped came flashing back. Rajput sir had asked for her help. The shoot-out at the farmhouse between the police and rival gangs. The search for Tara and Pia. How they had found a bleeding Tara, shot at the neck. Pia, unconscious. The

Rajput family's life had changed after that. Tara in a wheelchair. Pia, traumatized.

She radioed her team, but couldn't get through. Her phone signal had dropped—it came and went, depending on the area she was in. She sent them a text, telling them the details of Tara's poisoning, of Nurse Kamble being a possible suspect who aided in it. Long minutes later, the response came in. They were on their way to the hospital.

She stepped on the accelerator, uncaring of the water that splashed from the wheels and pitted the windshield, her vision restricted to a few feet ahead.

At the factory, Sita headed to the rear alley, but it resembled a river in spate. The alley wasn't wide enough to maneuver the jeep. The stream ran too swift and deep for her to risk wading in. The drains in the area must be blocked for the levels to rise this quick. Or the sea might be heading inland.

All kinds of rubbish came hurtling out of the alleyway, bits and pieces of broken slum households: bamboos, tarpaulin, asbestos sheets.

Rajput sir was around, though. She spotted his car parked across the street, the rising water covering its wheels. Any higher, it might carry the car away.

Sita backed out, and parked near the front entrance, where the water hadn't risen yet. She fitted her gun belt, securing the rounds of ammunition, and made sure her GLOCK was in working order. About to step out, she sensed a movement at the back of the jeep and cocked her gun, ready to fire.

"Sita Aunty," a small voice called to her. Pia's voice. Small and wavering.

"It is us, Aunty." Another voice joined her.

What the hell? Sita turned and gaped as Pia and Neeti emerged from under the rear seats of the jeep, the seats perpendicular, not parallel to the front seats, in order to accommodate more policemen.

"How the hell did you two get here?" she asked, too upset to care about her language.

"Aunty . . ."

"Shut up, Neeti. You girls have any idea how foolish you've been? What if I'd fired just now? What are you doing here? What if your mother needs you, Pia?"

"I won't be able to help, anyway. The doctors will only talk to adults. They asked me about Papa."

The truth of Pia's statement struck Sita. If Tara needed support, who would she turn to?

Sita called the hospital, but her phone signal flickered.

"I'll drive you back," Sita said to Pia.

"We must get Papa."

"Your mother might need you. Let me drop you back."

"You said Papa was at the factory. He's in danger."

"This isn't playtime, Pia. I can't leave you here, nor can I take you with me. We must turn back."

"Papa could be dead by then. You said that over the phone earlier. That's why we're here. We want you to see this." Pia eased forward, and placed a plastic circle in Sita's palm. It looked like a toy, a black button with a pink square at the center.

"These are remote trackers. Papa gave these to all of us, to have fun with. This is mine. Neeti has one, too."

Neeti showed another button, with a blue square.

"Papa left his remote at Neeti's place when he visited them today. He's got one of these buttons, too, same as Neeti's." She showed it to Sita.

"Yes," Neeti said. "He was showing it to Ashok today."

"If you click this"—Pia pointed the blue button on the remote—
"you'll hear his device beep. The range is one hundred and thirty feet.
At least that's what the manual says."

"It is loud, this beeping?" Sita said.

"Yes. It's a device for old people who forget their car keys or TV
remotes. It needs to beep loud and long for them to find it."

Sita held back her opinion on the phrase "old people." To a teen,
Sita herself was ancient. Using Pia's device might alert Rajput sir that
they were around, or even put him in further danger, but it would certainly help locate him, and fast.

The girls' welfare remained a problem.

She stared at their worried yet eager young faces, and cursed inside
her head.

Rajput sir's daughter. And the daughter of the woman who nearly
murdered his wife.

She couldn't leave them in the car, not with floodwater rising
around them. She had experienced the power of Mumbai's floods when
she wasn't much older than these two.

It was too late to turn back. The only way was into the factory.

She was sure she could climb the gates. Maybe Pia, with her martial
arts practice, could manage it. Neeti, not so much.

Besides, it was difficult to guess Neeti's intentions. She seemed worried, but she was her mother's daughter.

The choice was taken out of Sita's hands when a large sheet of
asbestos roofing slammed onto the jeep, shattering its windshield. Sita
looked up to see the maze of wires on the electricity poles sparking. The
girls shrieked and cowered.

Rising water. Broken electric cables in the vicinity.

Sita made up her mind. "We're going in."

CHAPTER SEVENTY-FIVE

SITA

Once inside, they quickly discovered surging rainwater filling in from the rear entrance of the factory. The iron gate they'd climbed over was unguarded. The small guardroom stood empty. The entrance sloped up, and the muddy waters from the back rushed down toward them.

In the darkness relieved by sporadic lightning flashes, the factory rose like a castle of doom. The girls crouched behind her, and Sita felt Pia shiver against her in the cold. The steady deluge had soaked them all, its drumming a terrifying background noise.

A strip of light startled Sita. She turned to find Neeti had switched on her phone light.

"No lights," Sita hissed. "Switch it off. We can't alert anyone we are here."

"It's so dark," Pia said.

"Give me your phones." Sita grabbed the phones before the girls could protest. "You two chose to sneak into my jeep, so listen to me as if your life depends on it, because it does. There is a killer inside."

Or two, she said to herself.

"Who is inside?" Pia's voice wavered. "Papa is here and he may be in danger? Do you think he's hurt?"

Sita tamped down regret at having scared this teen. Terror would teach her to be careful. She softened her tone.

"His main phone isn't working, and the burner wasn't a sturdy model. Maybe he's run out of battery," Sita said. She didn't believe a word.

"I can call my Ma," Neeti said. "She and Bina Aunty may be able to help us find him."

That was what Sita was afraid of. She bit back the curse at her lips and forced herself to speak in an even tone.

"We don't know what's going on inside. Calling her may warn someone we don't want to."

"Okay." Neeti sounded doubtful.

"I haven't seen the factory other than that one day I came with you, Pia," Sita said. "Neeti, do you know where Mr. Nimkar's office is? Rajput sir is here to speak with him."

"On the top floor." Neeti peered up at the building. "But I don't think he's here. There are no lights. When Mr. Nimkar is working late, the lights are on. They have an inverter for when the power goes out."

"The inverter may not be working," said Pia. "If Papa were stranded here, he would borrow someone's phone or a landline to call me."

"He hasn't, though," Sita said. "Which is why we've got to be wary."

"I know a side door that is left open for the night shift staff. I've gone in through there to call Ma," Neeti said. "We can check that out."

Vaeeni was involved, one way or another. This could be a trap. Or not. Sita hoped they wouldn't find out when it was too late. Unlike *Vaeeni*, she personally had qualms about killing people.

Sita could hit the beeper, but if it squealed too early, it could put Rajput sir in danger.

"Watch your step," she told the girls, cocking her gun. "Walk along the wall."

"Who are we afraid of?" Pia whispered.

"Not friends," Sita hissed back. "Quiet."

They crept beside a set of windows—Neeti in front, Pia behind her, and Sita bringing up the rear—in case someone caught them unaware.

They had to hurry—find Rajput sir, *Vaeeni*, and then get her to tell them what she'd fed Tara.

Sita peeked through one of the windows and, lit by a flash of lightning, spotted figures near a door, down below. Women in sarees. It was the hall she'd walked through to find Tara and escort her into the lift. Clotheslines with black masses hanging from them crisscrossed the hall, obscuring most of her view.

Women had no business inside the hall at 10:00 p.m. Most didn't work the night shift.

Pia's phone flickered in Sita's hand, and she glanced at it. A message from Z Aunty. Zoya, Rasool Mohsin's girlfriend. The one who'd given up her life to join the don, in exchange for help with Pia. She noticed the phone properly now. It wasn't Pia's usual phone. She flicked the message on.

> Doll, careful with your friend. Her mother has a gun. Our men are at factory now, to find your papa. He's tied up. Call me. Can't reach Tara.

Pia was in touch with Zoya? *Vaeeni* had a gun. There were gang members prowling the factory, trying to rescue Rajput sir? Sita's head spun. The phone in her hand now made sense. A satellite phone. It wouldn't lose signal. Rasool Mohsin was not the enemy.

She toyed with the idea of asking Pia to stay back outside while she tapped out a text.

> Ask them not to shoot. This is Sita. With Pia, at factory. More police here soon. Can't have shoot-out. Find Tara. She needs you. You'll be safe.

That message might cost her her job, but Sita pressed the send button, and within moments a response flashed back.

They will do as needed. Keep Pia safe. Going to Tara.

Relieved, Sita shot off a message to Desai. Don't use radio. Text on this number. Possible gunshots.

In that moment of distraction, Neeti sprinted forward before Sita could stop her. With no choice now, Sita clicked the button, hoping to locate Rajput sir. A distant, keening beep came from the door through which Neeti had just disappeared. She grabbed Pia as the teen made to follow her friend.

"Wait," she bit out. "Hold on. Me first."

CHAPTER SEVENTY-SIX

ARNAV

The wet dog smell from all that hair smothered Arnav like a clammy hand on his face. It didn't affect the three in the room.

From Arnav's vantage point, the towering Madhu seemed carved out of rock, her saree flying in the wind that came in from the door she'd opened. The light from outside outlined her. Rainwater gushed in around her feet.

"You want to shoot me now." Her voice was rough, but calm.

"Stop your foolishness, both of you." There was a note of dread in Bina's voice. "Put the gun down, Sujata."

Going by the crazed tilt of *Vaeeni's* chin, the gun could go off any moment. Arnav put all his strength in one heave, and the now-loosened bonds on his hands came apart.

"I'll do what I must," *Vaeeni* said.

"Go right ahead." Madhu looked down. "Use people, then kill them. You did that to Tara, why spare me?"

Madhu turned to the door, presenting her back to her gun-wielding sister in deliberate provocation.

Kill Tara? What did that mean?

Terror grabbed Arnav by the throat, making him want to cough so he could breathe. Tara. He struggled with the ties on his feet, ignoring the pain shooting up from his wrists. He had to get out.

A shrill wail rent through the taut strings of Arnav's fear. The beeper in the pocket of his jeans lying in a heap on the table. A blue light shone in the semidark. Neeti. The button was her color. *Vaeeni* had involved her daughter?

The noise froze all three siblings, and they turned, as one, toward him.

"That's the sound for Neeti," *Vaeeni* said. "That cannot be. She is with Pia, at their place."

"What do you mean?" Bina said as they ran toward Arnav. He remained inert as his mind scrambled for answers. He'd moved from where they'd left him. They would notice.

Vaeeni's voice rumbled with anger.

"I told her and Ashok to throw the cursed things away. This lout had given them one each to play with. To beep each other like some freakish hide-and-seek. How can that be Neeti's beeper? I remember it. It was blue."

"I don't understand," Madhu said.

"It means someone who has Neeti, or Neeti herself, is in the factory."

CHAPTER SEVENTY-SEVEN

ARNAV

Through hooded eyes, all Arnav saw was the gun in *Vaeeni*'s hand. He didn't want to lose sight of it for one moment even as the three of them rushed to him. He couldn't untie his feet now, not without risking being shot. No matter how still he sat in the chair, they would notice that he was no longer where they'd left him.

"What the hell . . . ," *Vaeeni* said before a cry from the door interrupted her.

"Ma? Is that you?"

Neeti's voice.

They all turned away, and covered by the thunder that rolled in from the flung-open door, Arnav dragged himself to the table and, snapping up the knife and his clothes in one swift motion, threw himself under it, along with the chair he was still tied to.

A gunshot split the air but missed him as he sawed through the ties that bound his feet, and slid on his underclothes. With no time for the pants, he slung them over his neck and, knife handle in his mouth, crawled under the table to get away from them.

"Ma!" Neeti's stunned voice rang through the hall.

"Get her, Bina," *Vaeeni* barked at her sister, who stood frozen. From behind the chairs, Arnav saw Neeti hurtle down the stairs and sprint toward them. He kept an eye on them as he wriggled into his pants.

"Was that a gun, Ma?"

"Take her away from here." *Vaeeni* spat the words.

Bina lunged at Neeti, who evaded her and barreled toward *Vaeeni*.
"No, Aunty. Ma, what's happening? Why are you all here in the dark?
What is Madhu here for?"

Neeti called him Madhu, not Aunty, like she did Bina. She didn't
know Madhu was her aunt.

"Don't stand there." *Vaeeni* shoved Madhu. "Go catch him. He has
your knife."

"Answer your daughter first." Madhu imitated Neeti's tone: "Is that
a gun, Ma?"

"You will hang if he gets away. He was awake. He heard us."

Neeti's rising tone had taken on a hysterical note. "Who is there,
Ma? What's going on? Why do you have a gun? Where's Arnav Uncle?"

Noticing that Madhu still made no move, Arnav slipped on his
soggy shirt and readied the knife. A knife was no match for a gun, and
his bandaged hands hurt like the devil, but Neeti hadn't come alone.

Along with the rushing water, a shadow crawled in unnoticed
through the open door.

CHAPTER SEVENTY-EIGHT

SITA

After the echoes of the gunshot died down, Sita hushed Pia as they crept in. They crouched next to a shelf in ankle-deep water that gushed in through the open door. Sita hoped the shadows in the hall would hide them because, other than the clothing lines from which masses of hair hung like angry witches, they had no cover. She glanced about and spotted a cupboard to the left. They needed to make their way behind it before taking stock of the situation.

"Sita Aunty," Pia whispered.

"Not now. Do exactly as I do."

They crawled on all fours, Sita hoping no one downstairs caught sight of them. Someone down there had a gun. Rajput sir was there, too, or at least the beeper was.

They'd almost reached the hiding spot when Pia said, "Zoya Aunty said she'll send people."

"She has. I saw your phone."

"They know me." Pia's face shone in the half light. "They're goons, but they're here to help Papa and me."

"I know."

They reached the cupboard, and Sita heaved a sigh. Pia's phone flashed again.

We're at the door through which you went in.

Zoya's men, with more satellite phones. Armed, well-kitted goons for backup. Shaking her head, Sita texted back a quick **ok** and focused on the events downstairs.

They could hear Neeti now, speaking with her mother in urgent tones.

"Go with Bina Aunty." *Vaeeni's* whiplash voice echoed across the hall. "You were supposed to be at Pia's place."

"Pia is here, too." Neeti's words came in gasps. "We came here to find Arnav Uncle. We could hear the beep. He's here. Have you seen him? Tara Aunty is very sick. Who are you looking for? And why the gun? Ma?"

"What do you mean Pia is here?" Neeti's mother said.

"She was right behind me."

"That's where you're mistaken. She's never right behind you. She's not your friend. I keep telling you, but you won't listen. Hide now. Let me finish this." *Vaeeni* looked up. "Pia," she called out as she headed toward the stairs, "where are you?"

"I can't tell you where Pia is," Sita called from behind the cupboard, "but the rest of my team are here, Sujata. Put your gun down, and we can talk."

"Ah, so *you* are here?" The madwoman they'd all known as *Vaeeni* immediately took cover behind a mannequin. "Why don't I hear your team? What, a one-woman police raid, Sita Naik?"

"You want to explain to your daughter why Tara is ill? Fighting for her life? That you fed poisoned *laddoos* to a pregnant woman?"

The satellite phone flashed.

We are five minutes out.

That was Desai.

Hunkered in the muddy water next to a now-sobbing Pia, Sita texted directions as a shot echoed in the large hall below.

"Madhu, take this flashlight. If you don't find him, one of these bullets will find you. Don't worry, I carried enough for reloads."

Madhu. So the *kinnar* was here. From her position, Sita couldn't see her, but the light flicked on, and lit up from below the bundles of hair hanging all over the hall like angry demons.

"Ma, what did Sita Aunty say?" Neeti wailed. "What are you doing? Who are you even? Ma!"

A hard slap, the raw sound of flesh hitting flesh. "Go. Now."

Sita peered from her hideout to see Neeti running in the other direction, away from them, followed by Bina, calling after her. Neeti stumbled and fell, and picked up what she'd stumbled on.

"Arnav," *Vaeeni* called out, "don't hide like the cur you are. Your daughter is here, I'm told. Let her see how brave you are."

"Your daughter is here, too, Ma." Neeti's voice wavered. "Maybe you don't want one. Or don't deserve one."

"Stop with your dialogues!" *Vaeeni* laughed, an ugly sound. "Can't study hard, won't do housework. Friends with that brat you can't stop talking about. What are you doing, Bina? Take her away, I said."

"Look at her, Sujata," Bina said, her low voice carrying in a lull amid the crashing storm outside. Water poured in from the open door, and flowed in steady streams from the high corridor onto the hall below.

Sita sneaked a glance, and her blood ran cold. Neeti stood on a table, her body lit up by Madhu's flashlight. She held a gun to her own head.

"So tell me, Ma? Did you try to kill Tara Aunty? And where is Arnav Uncle?"

CHAPTER SEVENTY-NINE
ARNAV

Arnav watched Neeti, transfixed.

If he spoke, he would be easier to track. Madhu knew the lay of the place and could reach him despite all the hair hanging about over tables, mannequins and chairs, and machines.

"Is it true, Ma?" Neeti trembled on the table, the gun shaking.

"Stop it with the drama," came *Vaeeni's* voice, loud and ringing against the noise of the storm raging outside. "Come down."

"I know how to shoot, Ma." The sound of a cocking gun.

Arnav saw Neeti's tiny head on his palm, still wet, her gaspy sobs. Arnav had made himself a promise to keep her safe. Pia came much later. It always was Neeti first. And here she was, trying to protect him. One person could not protect everyone. Maybe you needed everyone to protect each other. Neeti had saved his life by rushing in when she did. It was his turn.

"Neeti," Arnav said, low and calm.

"Arnav Uncle?"

"It's all right. Put that thing down." He wasn't far now. From the periphery, he could sense Madhu's approach, but there was no help for it.

"Ma should answer me first."

"That's okay. Take a breath, Neeti. Another. Just like we've done so many times, with you and Ashok and Pia."

"Arnav Uncle . . ."

"There's nothing to worry about." Arnav crept closer, maintaining cover. "Listen only to my voice."

His backpack lay under the table. The gun Neeti held, in her now-trembling right hand against her head, was his. She'd stumbled on his backpack, and found it.

When he reached close enough, he held her other hand. Gently, she lowered herself, holding on to his shoulders.

He took the gun from her. The knife slipped from his bandaged hands, and the clatter broke the spell.

"Get him," *Vaeeni* said, and Madhu lunged toward him. Arnav ducked, sending Madhu sprawling. He drew Neeti behind him and, taking cover, pointed the gun at Madhu.

"Let's get this over with, Mrs. Shinde," Arnav said. No longer *Vaeeni*. Never *Vaeeni* again. "You can't escape from here, you know that."

He didn't have time to argue. He had to get out of here with Neeti and Pia, and reach Tara as quickly as he could. Who was with Tara? How badly had she been affected?

Mrs. Shinde's response was to fire her gun as she retreated, taking her sister with her. She didn't go up the stairs, but ran toward the other corridor instead.

"Desai sir is here," Naik called down. "They're at the front entrance now. They've broken the lock, sir."

Naik ran down the stairs, and then waded through ankle-deep water, which was rising fast.

"Pia?" Arnav said.

"Zoya sent help. Pia recognizes the men. I left her upstairs. I'll take Neeti to her. Please get *Vaeeni*. We don't know what she gave Tara."

When you're panicked, slow down. Arnav's superiors had drilled those words into him long ago. Running blindly after Mrs. Shinde could lead to a trap. Arnav considered the *kinnar* whose hesitation and refusal had saved the night so far.

Madhu stood quiet, defeated, but she met Arnav's eyes.

"Tara was nice to me," Madhu said, voice soft. "I'm sorry my sister hurt her."

"What has she fed Tara?"

"I had no idea what they were up to. Only she knows. And Bina."

"What's she planning to do?"

"She's going to Nimkar. He's upstairs." Madhu pointed to a door. "That way. I tied him up. She'll try to take him down the lift and escape via the rear."

"Take her outside," Arnav said to Naik. "Let me go find Nimkar."

Ready to sprint in the direction Mrs. Shinde had gone, Arnav gave the sobbing Neeti a quick hug, telling her to be brave and find Pia. Naik handcuffed the *kinnar* and marched her up the stairs leading outside. Arnav had turned away when he heard the *kinnar* call out.

"Stop, *saab!*"

Arnav turned but kept walking, his bare feet cold in the rising water.

"I don't know how much you heard. She's locked up your wife's doctor. Mrs. Kamble may know where."

"Dr. Holkar?"

"Yes. Sujata locked her up. Your constable Kamble's wife helped her."

"I'll call my team in the hospital and tell them right away, sir," Sita said to Arnav, and dialed from her phone. She turned to the *kinnar*. "Why tell us now?"

Arnav didn't wait to hear, but the *kinnar*'s words floated up to him.

"All this while, and Neeti here doesn't even know who I am. Throughout my life people have told me what to do. Even my sisters. That stops now."

From the front entrance came the stamp of many boots. Desai and his team. Six men waded in through the door, calling Naik's name. The tall and worried-looking Dicky cut him a quick salute, while Naik hailed the constables, asking one of them to rush up the stairs for a better signal and radio her team at the hospital about Nurse Kamble and Dr. Holkar.

A constable took charge of Madhu, and Sita told them to find Pia, who waited on higher ground, near the reception area. Pia's dubious guards would melt away into the night as soon as they spotted the constables. Arnav couldn't shake off the irony as he snapped up the ammunition Naik and Dicky passed him.

His daughter was safe with goons, but not with the mother of her best friend. Rasool, a foe turned friend once again.

Fixing on the police radio Dicky handed him, Arnav sprinted toward the corridor leading indoors, sending water splashing beneath his feet.

"Wait here," he instructed Dicky when they reached the lift, "in case the suspect tries to escape this way. Don't be fooled by how gentle she looks in her saree and flowers. Maintain cover. Constable Kamble is helping them."

"Constable Kamble, sir?"

"Yes. He is working against us. Stay alert."

Desai hailed him on the radio. Arnav repeated the information about Mrs. Shinde and Constable Kamble to him.

"Senior Inspector Shinde's widow? Are you sure, sir?"

"Yes. She tried to shoot me. More than once. Cover all exits and send backup to the main office. She might have taken Mr. Nimkar hostage."

CHAPTER EIGHTY

ARNAV

Bounding up two steps at a time, Arnav darted upstairs in his clammy, muddied clothes as Naik gave him a quick bulletin on Pia's and Neeti's safety, Tambe's report on the teen's dead body in the suitcase, and all she'd learned about Sujata Shinde's misdeeds. A nightmare, all of it. One that must be so much more terrifying for his wife and their unborn child right now. He peppered Naik with questions about Tara, but Naik didn't meet his eyes.

"Not so well, sir. Madhu was right. They haven't found Dr. Holkar yet even after we called them. And they still don't know what poison was used."

"Mrs. Kamble didn't say where the doctor was?" Arnav came to a crashing halt. The blisters on his hands declared themselves, sending zings of burning and pain up his arm, but he ignored them.

"Mrs. Kamble doesn't know—Sujata did the last bit on her own. Somewhere on the upper floors of the hospital. Our men are combing the place."

"What about other doctors?"

Arnav wanted to kick himself. Once again, Tara suffered because of him. He wasn't by her side when she'd been pregnant with Pia, and he wasn't with her now. So much for him protecting her.

"I'm sorry, sir. No senior gynecology specialists due to the storm. They are trying to find another specialist who can treat patients with spinal injury. Tara's case"—Naik's face looked drawn in the glow of the flashlight—"is delicate."

All Arnav longed to do was rush to the hospital, but he had a job to do, for his wife and for his department.

"Well, one person knows where Dr. Holkar is and what poison it is," Arnav said. "We'll get that out of her."

"Yes, sir. Even if they find Dr. Holkar, unless she knows the poison . . ."

As he ran, his mind kept returning to his wife, who had asked Naik to investigate Neeti's harassment. Who made space for Neeti, Ashok, and their mother. Who had volunteered to help at the nonprofit and been threatened and hurt in return. Who'd eaten a sweet offered to her, in good faith, and might lose her life or their child as a result.

By the time they'd reached the top of the stairs and opened the door that led toward Mr. Nimkar's office, Arnav had managed to contain the ferocity of his rage. A blanket of numbness descended over him.

Naik switched off her flashlight, and both of them lowered the volume of their radios before opening the door a crack.

The two women paced inside Nimkar's glass office, its door ajar. Constable Kamble stood behind the slumped form of Mr. Nimkar. Had they already killed him?

"They'll find us here, Sujata," Bina said. "There is no getting out of this."

"Always the terrified one, you. Why are you such a coward?"

"If they are coming, we must run," Constable Kamble said. "Now."

"Without Nimkar as a shield, they'll shoot us down," Sujata said. "Let's carry him."

"Between the three of us, we can't haul him all the way out of the factory."

"I can't have them spot me with you both," Kamble said.

"Run, then. See how far that gets you."

Kamble subsided, sinking into a chair and holding his head between his hands. Kindly, affable Kamble working with Mrs. Shinde, the no-longer *Vaeeni*. Arnav had trusted and failed before, and not learned his lesson. He sank down on his haunches and waited for Desai and his team to take position. Inside the office, the argument continued.

"We can still save our children if we hurry," Bina said.

"With what money? Don't you realize I know where you get cash from? The hair you've been stealing from the women who donate to the nonprofit? Madhu might be stupid, not me. You stay in that *chawl* for appearances. And I know about Ruchi."

"Shut up," Bina said. "Ruchi works at an internet café. And don't call my *bhai* names."

Bina acted protective of Madhu, but Sujata Shinde was something else.

"Really"—Mrs. Shinde's words dripped with scorn—"that's what you want to talk about when these bastards are ganging up all around us? You trashed both our *kholis* to show that fool Arnav how goons had destroyed our homes—don't tell me you're such a truth speaker and paragon of virtue, all right? Now wake up this heel so we can get going."

Arnav had worried about them. About the attacks on their home. About Sujata Shinde, about Bina. He wanted to rush in and shake the woman he used to call *Vaeeni*.

"Can't help it if he won't wake up," Bina said. "I've tried it all."

"Try harder. And be quick. You gave him the drugs you got from Gary Scott—you know all the antidotes. We can't carry him downstairs. Without him, we won't make it very far."

"You won't make it far, anyway," Desai growled from the other side of the corridor. "Drop your gun. You're surrounded. There's no way down."

"What," Mrs. Shinde snapped, "you think I won't shoot because I'm a woman? You gave such a long rope to this heel." She shoved at Nimkar, whose head lolled on his plush office chair. "That's why we are where we are today, because you policemen won't do your damned jobs."

"I'm waiting for you to shoot," Desai said. "Go ahead, and see if I don't nail your *neechi jaat* heads."

"No one is shooting anyone," Arnav broke in from behind the door.

"Sorry, sir, but if we are fired at, we fire in defense," Desai called back. "That's the law."

The law used as a cover for "encounters"—where police shot unarmed suspects before they could be tried in court.

"In defense, yes," Arnav said. "We haven't been attacked yet."

"She fired at you," Desai said.

"Step aside," Mrs. Shinde said, "or I will shoot this miserable excuse of a human being."

In the half light of Mr. Nimkar's office, with rain pounding the windowpanes, she made a strange sight—her saree crumpled, tied to one side, her usually well-combed hair a mess, the flowers in it torn up, a smudge of ash on her forehead. Female mannequin heads sat on various tables and shelves, each with a wig, their features indistinct, like beheaded ghouls standing watch.

"It's flooded outside, Mrs. Shinde," Naik said. "None of us are going anywhere outside this building anytime soon."

"This man sure won't if you people don't let us go."

"You'll be charged along with Madhu," Sita said, "in the murders of all three victims, as well as your attempt on Tara. We're merely getting started. Make things easier on yourself."

"Easy?" Mrs. Shinde said. "Here you go—this is easy." She slapped the insensible Mr. Nimkar. He slumped forward. "His son raped women on the regular. Your Desai here never lifted a finger, didn't register a complaint, because Nimkar kept him well fed."

Another swing at Nimkar's face, and she continued, "Your Paresh Khare, Arnav, physiotherapist to your precious wife, tried to touch my Neeti. Your police station, they all laughed at us, Naik madam. Well, you're not laughing now."

"I'm looking into the complaints, Mrs. Shinde."

"Too little, too late. You're low caste, just like the rest of us. No one will listen to you. No one listens to women anyway. Why not take their manhood like they did to our poor Madhukar? He became Madhu. Neither here, nor there. Men hold all the cards, like that bastard *gora*, your Williams, who wanted boys, girls, he didn't care. This asshole here"—she slapped Nimkar again—"provided them. Williams killed the last one, didn't he? That's why he came to us, all groveling. We helped him, we did. You *policewalas*, you'll do nothing. We don't need to chop off your balls—you don't have them in the first place."

"Shut up," Desai said, "or I'll shut you up forever."

"And that"—Sujata Shinde addressed herself to her sister—"is how they treat us. Have always treated us. *Neechi jaat*, bloody Scheduled Caste. We can't enter their temples, can't drink from their wells, but they can rape our daughters, sell our children. They make us rub our noses on their shoes and slippers, and then they declare there's no casteism in India. Shut us up."

"Sujata, calm down now," Bina pleaded, trying to take Mrs. Shinde's gun away. "We have to think of the children."

Kamble tried to hold her other arm. "This has gone far enough."

"If we give in and walk out of here, we'll rot in jail, but Nimkar *saab* will use his money and his caste just as he has every time, and get away with it. Snatch his son's penis, his son's life, and he'll still sell children to predators. Like he sold your daughter, Mihir Kamble. Our children, Bina, will be better off without us. Certainly better off without him."

She raised her gun and fired once at Nimkar's head lolling on the office chair. Blood and bits of flesh and brains spattered the glass.

Kamble and Bina screamed.

Arnav stepped forward, but swerved as the next bullet shattered one of the glass walls and hit a mannequin in the corridor, sending the wig atop it flying.

"You poisoned Tara," Arnav said. He had to keep her talking so she wouldn't shoot. He needed the name of the poison.

"You killed my husband. Fair's fair."

"He threw himself in the path of a bullet. I didn't even know he was there."

"Same difference. He considered you more important than his wife and children. And you felt your career was more important than his family."

"What has Tara done to you? And that unborn child? Why would you do this? What poison did you use?"

"Why should I tell you? I cooked for you, I sent you gifts each Holi-Diwali, I trusted you with my children, and what did you do? You searched my home when I wasn't there, after my husband had died. You found papers that blackened his name."

"Ashok and Neeti are like my own. I was doing my job. If you need to punish someone, that's me. Let Tara live. Drop that gun."

Mrs. Shinde stared at him, a crazed gleam in her eyes.

"Enough with your whining about your wife, Arnav. It was Bina who gave me the liquid, so ask her."

"Drop the gun, Mrs. Shinde," Sita said, but Sujata Shinde didn't look at her.

"You'll get the last laugh. You men always do. Explain this to my children, then." She put the gun to her own head, and the entire room was blood and a keen, ringing silence that Arnav would hear for years to come.

CHAPTER EIGHTY-ONE

In the end she didn't listen. Just like always. I'd told Bhai *we must be careful. Had it been only the two of us, we would have made it, but Sujata had to go and screw it all up.*

I've given them the name. Nicotine. I gave her nicotine to put into those damn laddoos. *Vaping liquid is already scented, easy to disguise behind the cardamom in the sweets.*

And its poisoning symptoms—dizziness, throwing up, raised heartbeat are the same as a distressed pregnant woman with spinal injury would normally have. Impossible for them to diagnose. My daughter had helped me research it all on the internet.

That tea seller boy got enough of it that we could make the girl in the wheelchair fall ill, very slowly. It was to be our backup plan to send her to the hospital, but the poor woman fell from her wheelchair and made our job easy.

How was I to know our sister, the dear fearless leader, would spike a small batch, intending to kill? I'll never understand what made her do that. Didn't she care a whit about her children?

Up to me now, like it's always been, picking up her shit. Her daughter won't look at me anymore, but I have my daughter who understands, who will come and visit me tomorrow, before they take us in for our hearing.

I'll see Bhai, *and we'll chat again, and I'll get to hold his large hands and tell him it will be all right—it will all be all right.*

CHAPTER EIGHTY-TWO

ARNAV

Arnav wouldn't forget that night: the shooting, the frantic calls to the hospital to find out how Tara was doing. The flood had stranded them in the building—forcing them to detain the accused in different rooms of the factory.

One person had made a run for it, and fallen into the torrent running through the street outside: Constable Kamble.

The floodwater had reached epic speeds in the narrow alley, and carried him away. His bloated body would be found two days later. Arnav had forbidden the staff from trying to exit the building at night as the sea entered land via the Versova beach and drowned out the entire neighborhood already struggling with choked drains.

It was Zoya who'd held Tara's hand again through her labor, just as she'd done during Pia's birth. Arnav had only been able to wear out the carpet in the reception room of the Remy Virgin Hair Factory. The mannequins' heads had stood vigil as he paced nonstop, his hands burning, his mind afire with anxiety and betrayal.

He'd watched Madhu, a stone statue, brooding in one of the rooms as Bina spoke to her. The *kinnar* didn't speak a word all night. The murder and castration scenes flashed before Arnav's eyes, and torn between this, and his desperate anxiety for Tara, he tried to reassure himself by checking on Neeti and Pia from time to time. They clung to each other on a sofa, sobbed, and never fell asleep, but the sight of them, safe and warm, gave him hope. Tara would be fine, she had to be. Zoya was with her, but had been asked to leave her phone outside.

Arnav continued his ceaseless pacing as the constables raided the pantry in order to prepare tea for Desai and the indefatigable Sita Naik, who wrote her case notes by flashlight.

After a while he'd let silence take him, the kind of silence that was dark rain with its volume turned down, and let the montage of the years wash over him—the laughter, the tears, the longing, the fear—till it swallowed his terror for Tara and their unborn child, allowing him to sink into a cushioned numbness and surrender. He couldn't be by Tara's side as she fought for their family: he was not the only protector. Tara was one, too.

Morning brought two pieces of news.

A death and a birth.

The housekeeper in the Rajput household had found a package at their doorstep, and had shrieked and fainted after she opened it. He'd identified the head of the victim from the picture she sent him afterward.

Ali.

Rasool had sent a note.

This is the last time my family saves yours. You took one of mine, so here's one of yours.

The news of a head being delivered to his door had slammed Arnav into immobility. Ali. He'd met the man a handful of times, but Ali had been Arnav's lieutenant of sorts. Rasool had dug him out even on a night when all of Mumbai was swept in a flood.

Arnav would take care of Ali's family, and Tej's children—keeping his promise to the two criminals who helped him do his job as a police officer.

With Rasool, there would come a day of reckoning.

A few minutes later, Dr. Holkar had called.

"Congratulations, Senior Inspector Rajput. Your wife has given birth to a daughter."

Relief had coursed through Arnav's veins like water released into canals left bare by drought, cool and life giving. He'd sunk down into a chair at the factory reception, thanked the doctor, and asked about their welfare: his wife and daughter.

"They are safe, for now. We'll talk more when you're here."

When he first held his new daughter two days later, Arnav wept. Dr. Holkar made him sit, wearing scrubs and a mask, in a reclining chair with his feet up. The kindly, whispering nurses brought the tiny form out of the glass case that would be her home for the next two months, swaddled within their confident palms like a gently squirming blind puppy, connected to so many fine tubes it terrified him to hold her. Chuckling, they laid her on his chest, where she curled back to sleep, and covered her in a pink blanket. The nurses held up his inert, bandaged palm, and placed it over the blanket, cradling her.

He'd held Neeti sixteen years ago, but Neeti was a full-throated baby, not like this fragile little creature who fitted under his right palm. He didn't make a promise to protect her. He knew this now—Superman existed only in comic books. Normal, everyday people protected each other. Tara, Sita, Neeti, and Pia had come together to save the family. It was his job to protect them, but they protected him, too.

Dr. Holkar stood over the two of them, beaming, having worked a miracle. She'd gotten other doctors to flush the nicotine out of Tara's system.

On that fateful night of Tara's labor, his men had found the good doctor trussed up, gagged, and dehydrated in her hospital attic, and like any self-respecting superhero without a cape, she'd chugged electrolytes and rushed to Tara's aid. They had barely made it in time to save this impossibly small creature snoozing on his chest. He hadn't dared touch her, but laughing through his tears, he'd called her by her name. Dwidha.

Dwidha, from *Duvidha*. Both of them shaking with exhaustion and relief, Tara and Arnav had named their daughter after an enduring moment of complete uncertainty, of devastation, of guilt—but also of unity, of seeing both sides to the story: *Dwi-dhara*, of living in two worlds, straddling two paths, bringing them harmony despite their disparity—the Rajput family, and the Shinde children, Ashok and Neeti.

CHAPTER EIGHTY-THREE

SITA

Two days after that grisly evening at the factory, Sita sat at her Bandra Police Station desk, trying to make sense of both her case notes and her thoughts. Neither seemed possible.

Begin at the beginning, Rajput sir often said. Dig for it. It all begins somewhere. Then follow the trail of evidence to the end.

Where had it begun for her husband? How had Raghav decided that partnering with a porn racket was a good idea to support his Ram Rajya Party? Why would he, an ex-officer of Mumbai Police and a staunch Hindu, keep stolen gold necklaces from the Kaali temple? An investigation revealed he'd even tried to sell them. Was this enough for her colleagues and her family to let her consider separating from the man?

Sita shook her head—she must wrap up the case before she started thinking about her personal life.

Rajput sir had taken a leave of absence for three weeks in order to be there for his family. ACP Bapat had okayed it, and put Sita in charge of digging out further evidence and preparing documentation for the case.

Bapat himself was busy basking in the limelight. He'd interrogated Chitra Varli. Using the video evidence recovered with the help of Raghav from Ram Chandra Dome as well as a raid on her premises, he had arrested her on charges of exploiting unsuspecting young women. Ram Chandra Dome and the priest remained in custody, awaiting trial for their roles in aiding and abetting crimes.

Predictably, the case had exploded on social media, where Chitra Varli fans and decriers were fighting digital battles. Bapat claimed credit for solving the case, with a brief footnote for "his team."

Sita scrolled through Rajput sir's case notes, hoping to reconcile them with her own.

When she came to the bit about Rasool Mohsin and Iqbal Asif, she moved them to a different folder—both evil men, but with no relevance to the actual culprits. The investigation into the shoot-out involving Iqbal Asif would begin soon. Before going on leave, Rajput sir had overseen the filing of cases by the families of the informers Ali and Tej. She had a feeling he wouldn't let those cases languish for very long.

At a knock on the door, Sita looked up from her work.

A constable poked his head in the door. "The interrogation room is ready, madam."

She'd interrogated Mrs. Kamble already, and terrified of losing her husband's pension, she had spewed enough details that the next one, with Bina, should go easier.

The room Sita entered was sparse, but clean. No hard interrogation in this room, none of the methods adopted for the likes of Ram Chandra, or his uncle, the priest. She had a different sort of leverage on Bina.

Bina sat hunched in her chair, not looking up when Sita entered. The woman had aged years in two days, and despite the nature of her crimes, Sita felt a measure of pity for the woman, who'd watched her sister murder a man, and then shoot herself.

Bina gave routine answers to the questions Sita asked, in a soft monotone, her head lowered, until it came to her role in the murders.

"I was in the background, always. Sujata was younger than me but ever the smarter one. She got out of our neighborhood when she married, all Marathi-speaking, holier-than-thou, and hated it when she had to return. She was the one with the plan—she persuaded Madhu, recruited Kamble, and Govind, the tea stall owner."

"Govind?"

"He's Ruchi's fiancé. Same caste as us, and Kamble was very fond of him. Sujata got him to do all the odd jobs. He helped Kamble steal papers from the Bandra Police Station when he went there to deliver tea. He put the bloodied boot prints at the Kaali temple. Delivered the CCTV footage of Iqbal Asif. Hid the boots in the tantric's place. Took the tantric from the jail to the warehouse. Followed Arnav and his family. Made the calls with Ruchi's guidance, all from places near Chitra Varli's home, which wasn't far from his tea shop."

"Why frame Ram Chandra?"

"He was friends with Chitra Varli, and they worked together for those horrible videos. My Ruchi got trapped—she used to work as Chitra's digital assistant, and the tantric assaulted her. They made a video. Sujata said we could get both Chitra and Ram Chandra at the same go."

"How?"

"I can tell you, but you must agree not to press charges against Ruchi."

"If her information leads to the sentencing of those we've arrested, then she'll be given juvenile detention, not jail."

"Are you sure?"

"It depends. Tell me about Chitra and Ram Chandra."

"We decided to film the first murder and put the video on social media, but through Chitra's account. Ruchi had the old passwords and emails, so she could access it. She's very good with computers."

So Chitra's account had been hacked, and Ruchi had done it.

"Did Ruchi send those threats? To my phone and Tara's?" Sita burned to punch someone when she remembered the notes. To think that a young girl had sent them, with advice from her mother and aunt.

"Yes, Sujata said you needed to spread fear in order to get people to make mistakes."

"You caused Tara's accident with the wheelchair?"

"No, but we did send the note. Ruchi wrote it, and her fiancé gave it to the girl to pass it to Tara."

It was Bina's word on this—they had no way to determine whether she'd planned and executed it. Sita moved on to a chargeable offense.

"And you sent the children to Gary Scott Williams?"

"Not me, madam, that was Mr. Nimkar. I'm a mother. I didn't know how he sent them. We wanted to put an end to it, especially after Kamble's daughter fell victim."

"So Madhu killed Gary?"

"She's confessed to all of it anyway, madam, so yes, she did."

"How did you get Gary there? Why did all the victims go to the Kaali temples?"

"Sujata. Whatever else you say about Sujata, she was very clever. She had learned so many police tricks from listening to her husband. Knew all about CCTV, fingerprints, DNA. How to make Rasool Mohsin and Ram Chandra Dome look guilty. She made my *bhai* wear a raincoat, so no one saw the splashed blood once he took it off. She lured Vishal Nimkar to the temple, saying she would bring Ruchi there. To Paresh Khare, Sujata said she needed money and would get him Neeti. She promised Gary help with the dead body in his room. He had killed the teenager in anger when he realized the boy wasn't that young, only underfed. They met to arrange it. All those men deserved it, madam."

"You attacked Rajput sir." *He certainly didn't deserve it,* Sita wanted to add, but held back.

"We hadn't planned on it. Sujata initially said we were to get him into trouble with the unsolved cases at the Kaali temples, make Tara unwell, and move into their home. She changed her mind after she left her phone in Tara's room. I think she went a little mad at the end—trying to kill Tara instead of only making her sick."

"The Rajputs had already invited Sujata to stay with them. They had asked so many times over two years—why would she wait that long?"

"She wanted us all to go. Me and Ruchi, too. And she wanted to ruin the Rajputs from the inside, she said. Ruin Arnav's career. She earned Tara's confidence over time."

"So all three of you siblings conspired against a man who was trying to help Sujata and her family?"

"It was Sujata all along. She wanted revenge. Madhu was in it to punish those who deserved it, including Mr. Nimkar. I wanted justice for Ruchi. The Kambles wanted Mr. Nimkar and his American client dead: the two men had harmed their daughter."

Bina paused, and raised her eyes, meeting Sita's gaze. "But I don't blame Sujata. She was angry, you know? Absolutely pissed about us being trampled upon. We didn't get them all, but I'd say she did a pretty good job, don't you?"

A part of Sita, the part born into a low-caste family, orphaned early due to poverty and discrimination, wanted to agree, but she was a police officer first and foremost. She would let justice take its course. She asked the one question that had puzzled her, because she didn't want to upset Pia by asking it.

"What happened that afternoon on the rooftop? It was one of you, right?"

"It was Govind. He protested, but Sujata gave him no choice. She told him he could only marry Ruchi if he obeyed her without question."

Whatever he'd done would be hard to prove. Sita made a mental note to give Govind the Mumbai Police "special treatment" during interrogation.

"What did he do?"

"Sujata asked him to frighten the girl, and get hold of your phone, so we could plant a bug. We did, but it didn't last long because Tara fell off the wheelchair and broke the phone. He molested her in order to make her afraid. Twisted her arm, groped her breast, and told her he would rape her and her mother and kill them both. That it was only a matter of time."

And Bina had watched him do this to a fifteen-year-old. All thoughts of calmness and the course of justice vanished from Sita's mind, and the room resounded with the slap that sent Bina flying from her chair.

Sita stalked out, seething, upset as much at her own loss of control as at the world that contained women like Bina and Sujata and the men who drove them to the brink. She stepped out of the station and onto the pavement. Sunshine dazzled her, reflecting off the glass windows of the buildings opposite, the puddles on the road where she stood. After weeks of storms, light.

She got into her jeep and drove off into the brilliant afternoon—her mind a blank other than the determination to find her own path. As a woman, and a police officer.

The Sita of myth had jumped into a pyre to prove her purity and loyalty to her husband. That was not this Sita.

Her husband was certainly not a godly paragon of all virtues. She would make sure Raghav received a sentence, and served time.

Sita was a disciple of Ma Kaali now, the dark goddess whose tongue dripped with the blood of sinners, who wore a garland strung with demon skulls, her long dark mane of hair unbound, her heart equal parts fury and compassion.

CHAPTER EIGHTY-FOUR

TARA

Ten months later

Mayhem at the dining table, just the way Tara liked it, even though she complained to Arnav once in a while.

Neeti and Pia had turned quiet, clinging to each other ever since that night at the factory, but Ashok and Dwidha made up for it.

Dwidha blew raspberries while Ashok fed her a mashed banana, cooing to her as she smeared herself and her baby-table with banana paste. *Bhai*, she babbled, the first word she'd spoken. Brother. She had decided that her *bhai* was her favorite person in the whole wide world, followed by Neeti and Pia. Ashok had recovered, and was now a strapping boy of ten.

He called his tiny sister Dia. *Dia*, a lamp that brought light.

And they needed plenty of light—Tara would go for her operation to remove scar tissue from her spinal cord, and her doctor said it could lead to movement in her lower limbs. There was hope, he said. Her physiotherapy had helped, as had her sense of purpose now that she handled the nonprofit Bina had founded, trying to set to right all the wrongs committed over years.

Arnav, Neeti, and Pia rushed about, readying her bags for the hospital. They'd timed the operation for the holidays, so Arnav and the girls could take care of little Dia and the household while Tara was away.

Zoya would have liked to be part of it all, but there were whispers of marriage, at least from Rasool. Zoya had yet to say yes. Their daughter would turn six months old soon, and had already reduced the don into a mushy father. During the sporadic phone calls from Dubai, this was a major topic of conversation, besides Arnav. Though the killer of Arnav's dead informer, Ali, was sentenced, Arnav had gone brooding and silent.

Tara watched her husband's gaunt face—he'd lost weight, and his nightmares had returned. He wanted to make Rasool pay, but their family connections tied his hands. In his dreams he called *Vaeeni's* name, and Shinde, his erstwhile best friend, *Vaeeni's* husband. Tara had heard all about that horrific night at Nimkar's office, the brains, blood, bits of scalp and hair on the glass walls. Sometimes Arnav hollered for Tej or Ali in his sleep, which startled Dia into crying.

The hospital had fired Nurse Kamble, but she'd stayed out of prison by turning state witness. Madhu and Bina languished in prison, their trial ongoing, Ruchi and her fiancé in a halfway house for young delinquents. Sita kept tabs and updated Tara, because Arnav refused to speak about them. Tara would need Bina's and Madhu's approval for what she and Arnav had in mind. Adopt Neeti and Ashok for their own.

Once they were all done, Dia bathed and dressed, they gathered in the living room with Tara's suitcase, and Ashok ran to Arnav, begging for his phone. He wasn't allowed much access to mobile devices, but this time, Arnav relented.

Ashok set up the camera, his fingers nimble on the screen, while he yelled instructions to them on how to pose. Dia on Tara's lap, Arnav beside her, Pia and Neeti behind them. Ashok ran back and kneeled on the floor, just as Dia reached out with a chortle and grabbed a hank of his hair. *Bhai*, she cooed. Everyone laughed, and as they left for the hospital, that was the picture Tara carried with her. Her family.

ACKNOWLEDGMENTS

The Blue Monsoon is my first attempt at writing a sequel. Sequels are tricky beasts: they give you the setting and the characters, but they also hem you in with so many limitations.

If you've read *The Blue Bar* and remember how it ended, you'll know I didn't make it easy for myself. I may never have written this novel without my fabulous agent, Lucienne Diver, who helped me brainstorm various outlines and shape the narrative, and read the draft twice to assure me I was on the right track.

Jessica Tribble, my very insightful editor at Thomas & Mercer, honed it further and taught me valuable lessons on structure and pacing. Charlotte Herscher was a wonderfully understanding editorial partner as I struggled with many rewrites, and her suggestions helped make the novel so much better. Huge thank you to the dream team at Thomas & Mercer: Sarah Shaw, Tamara Arellano, Robin O'Dell, James Gallagher, Sarah Vostok, and Miranda Gardner.

This is a book that has truly scared me: it refused to become anything I wanted it to, stubbornly going to places I had no intention of visiting and that I knew little about. Jess Everlee, Dr. Mary Gatter, and Dr. Tammy Euliano assisted me with my very complex OB-GYN queries about pregnant women with spinal injuries, and many other technical aspects besides. I'll not go into details lest I give spoilers in case you're looking at this section without finishing the book. Dr. J. L. Delozier spoke of important medical aspects and gave me wonderful insights on other parts of the novel during her very insightful reading. Huge thanks to the sensitivity reader Shuja Khan, who made extremely helpful comments on caste and religion. I owe so much to the authors who have written various books on casteism and religion in India, and their research has informed this book.

Vaishali Ghorpade assisted with information on Mumbai police and their methods of inquiry. I received helpful advice on the anatomical descriptions of castration and resultant bleeding from Justin Cottle, marketing and lab director, Institute of Human Anatomy. Thanks to my friend Samantha Bailey for the connect with Justin. Sarika Joshi and Soniya Kulkarni advised on the geography and nuances of Mumbai. Roshni D'Souza's inputs were invaluable in polishing the narrative, making the lifestyle depictions of Mumbai more plausible, and making the characters more authentic.

The 2023 Debut slack has been the source of much support and succor. Publishing is a true roller coaster, and without them I might have given up during the lows.

Huge thanks to my #bookstagram family, who supported me with their shares on social media, the giveaways on which they collaborated, and signing up in advance for the review copies. You make me feel like my words matter.

Readers keep books alive, and keeping the feedback for *The Blue Bar* in mind, the publisher and I have worked together on a cast of characters and a glossary—so many reviews of *The Blue Bar* asked for them.

My yoga teacher Sunny Kumar has been indispensable in his support—being an author means taking care of your health and your back. I stay sane thanks to my yoga lessons.

No acknowledgment would be complete without a mention of Swarup Biswas, my husband and best friend, who has kept me together in the past year of health challenges and mental trauma, and helped me stand tall for what I believe in: in life and in writing.

GLOSSARY OF TERMS

Aarti: Aarti is a Hindu ritual in which a light, usually a wicker flame or similar, is offered to the deities being worshipped. It is usually accompanied by songs of praise, incense, flowers, and offerings of fruit or sweets.

Achoot: The untouchables, who are outside the fourfold Hindu caste hierarchy. Though untouchability is illegal according to the Indian Constitution, it exists in many forms in urban and rural areas. *Achoot* is a derogatory term. They are also called *Avarna*, because they are outside the castes or varnas. Some sections of their community have also adopted the term *Dalit*. See author's note for more details.

Aum: Aum or Om is a sacred sound, a primal syllable in Hinduism. It is believed to represent the essence of the divine. In the context of this novel, it is a syllable used at the beginning of a written or spoken spiritual incantation.

Bhai: A term that means brother, but in Mumbai can also mean a mafia don, especially a Muslim don.

Brahmin / Kshatriya / Vaishya / Shudra: The four main categories of the caste system. See author's note for more details.

Bun muska: A teatime snack served at Iranian cafes in Mumbai. The bun is a soft, sweetened, fluffy round bread, sliced in half, slathered on the inside with muska—a homemade mixture of butter and cream.

Chawl: A large tenement house, especially in the factory cities of India, which offered cheap accommodation to laborers in textile mills. Each floor of these buildings contains rooms (called *kholi*) in a single row with a common corridor and toilets. In modern times, people from various professions find basic housing in chawls.

Chikna: Mumbai street slang for a good-looking or attractive young man.

Dholak: A dholak is most often used in Indian folk song. It is a two-headed hand drum, with two different-sized drumheads.

Dhoti: A traditional lower garment worn by Hindu men in the Indian subcontinent. It is a large rectangular piece of unstitched cloth wrapped around the legs and knotted at the waist to resemble draped trousers.

Dojo: A dojo is a place or hall for immersive learning, especially for the martial arts. It hails from Japanese, where it means "Place of the Way."

Dome: Usually spelled as *dom*, but spelled in the novel as "dome" to prevent any borrowed implications from BDSM. In various parts of India, the tantric scriptures defined those who lived by song and dance as "dome." Over centuries they began to bury dead cows (considered sacred by Hindus), lived in segregations outside the villages, and in certain parts of India helped in the cremation of dead bodies. They were considered casteless, and untouchables, attracting considerable discrimination and stigma under the caste system.

Dupatta: A dupatta is a North Indian word that means an unstitched shawl or a scarf. It is usually worn as part of a traditional getup, versatile in its use. It can be wrapped around the neck, the shoulders, or the head. It has been a symbol of "women's modesty" in India, but is increasingly worn as a fashion accessory.

Ghaat: Ghaat can have other meanings, but in the context of this novel it is used for a series of steps constructed along a river or pond. A cremation ghaat is built near an area where dead bodies are ritually cremated at the pyre.

Ghee: Clarified butter that is used in various forms of Indian cooking.

Gotra: Gotra indicates patrilineal lineage, claiming descent from the same mythical forefather.

Hafta: This is a slang term in Mumbai for illegal protection money paid to thugs or corrupt police on a weekly basis so the business can proceed without issues. The Hindi word *hafta* simply means "a week."

Harmonium: An organ that creates music with hand-pumped bellows.

Hijra / Kinnar: A community of eunuchs and transgender or intersex individuals, with or without male external genitalia, who identify with the female gender identity. See author's note for more details.

Kadhi-chawal: A popular meal in South Asia, the recipe of which differs from one region to another. The Kadhi consists mainly of a yogurt and gram flour sauce, tempered with spices, and often contains onion fritters, called pakora. Chawal is steamed rice—so kadhi-chawal is the kadhi eaten with rice.

Kathak: A classical dance from North India.

Khabri: An informant. Especially someone who gives information to the police.

Kholi: A room in a *chawl* (definition above).

Kurta: A versatile garment: a loose, often collarless shirt worn in India by men or women, depending on the styling.

Lakh: A unit of Indian currency: 100000 Rupees.

Laddoo: is a spherical Indian sweet, which can be of varied types, depending on ingredients. In the context of the novel, the *laddoo* is a nutritious snack for a pregnant woman, made with nuts, seeds, dates, raisins, and ghee.

Mandapa: This is a part of Hindu temples, a pillared hall or pavilion for public rituals and prayer, usually situated between the gate and the home of the deity, the sanctum.

Mangalsutra: *Mangal-sutra* literally means "sacred thread." It used to be a traditional social practice where a groom tied a sacred thread around the bride's neck for her protection from evil eyes. Today it has evolved into a necklace of varied design that works as a visual marker of married status, predominantly for Hindu women.

Nakabandi: A system of patrolling the streets by sealing off certain areas with checkpoints and roadblocks.

Namaste: *Namaste* is a Hindu greeting, the word often accompanied by folded hands, palms touching with fingers pointing upward, and thumbs touching the chest. The word loosely translates to "bowing to the divine within you."

Neechi-jaat: Literally means "lower caste." It is a derogatory term used in North India to those who are casteless. See author's note for more details.

Panditji: An honorific used to address a wise or learned Hindu man in India, in the context of religion or the arts.

Peepal: The peepal tree is a variation of the sacred fig tree, with heart-shaped leaves. It is considered sacred in both Hinduism and Buddhism and is often found planted near temples. It can gain immense height, canopy, and spread of roots, as well as a life span of hundreds of years.

Poha: Literally means "flattened rice." In the context of the novel, it is a light, nutritious vegetarian dish made with flattened rice, herbs, and spices. It is a traditional breakfast preparation in the state of Maharashtra, of which Mumbai is the capital city.

Policewala: This is a colloquial Hindi term that means "police officer."

Poori-bhaji: A traditional breakfast dish in North India, consisting of poori (puffed, pan-fried golden bread) and bhaji (spiced potato dish, with or without gravy).

Prasad: A food item usually first offered to a deity or a revered individual during a ceremony like aarti or other forms of worship, and then distributed to devotees or followers as a token of blessing.

Puja: Ceremonial worship, which could occur in a domestic or communal setting. The venue could be a common gathering place or a temple, or a place of deep sacred significance. It involves the offering of flowers, incense, fruits, and other holy items in adoration of a deity.

Saab: A term of respect used, especially during the colonial era, when addressing a European. It is now mostly used in North India to mean "sir."

Savarna: Literally, "those with a varna." Or the dominant or higher castes. Not to be confused with Savarna Brahmins, which is a particular group of Brahmins. See author's note for more details.

Shaadh: A traditional ritual held for pregnant Hindu women in West Bengal in their third trimester that involves giving the woman her favorite foods, along with the blessings of elders. It is usually organized by the woman's mother.

Shanti-pooja: Literally, "peace-prayer." It is a Hindu ritual of worship that seeks to remove all obstacles and ensure peace, happiness, and prosperity.

Shendi: A long tuft of hair on the back of the head worn by upper-caste Brahmins. Various meanings are attributed to it, depending on the tradition the Brahmin follows, but the usual significance involves a one-pointed devotion to God, cleanliness, and sacrifice.

Sindoor: Vermilion powder, worn by Hindu women in the parting of their hair to signify their marital status, and also in the worship of female goddesses.

Tabla: A pair of hand drums used in Indian music, one of which is slightly larger than the other.

Teej: A generic name for certain festivals celebrated by women in India involving fasting, dressing up in traditional clothing, sharing of fables, and dancing. The most popular are the monsoon festivals like Hartalika Teej, which celebrates the bounty of nature.

Teetar: A ground-dwelling bird, also called gray partridge or francolin, found in the dry regions of India.

Vaeeni: A Marathi word, from the Indian state of Maharashtra. It's a respectful term for sister-in-law. In India, even people unrelated by blood call each other by terms of respect—a person close to the age of one's parents is called Uncle or Aunty, for instance. The wife of a male friend would be called *Vaeeni*.

Yoni: The word *Yoni* in Sanskrit means "the womb" or the female sexual organs. It has a special place in tantra, especially for those who follow female deities or engage in Shakti worship. It is part of the duality of Yoni (feminine world) and Linga (masculine self). See author's note for more details on tantric worship.

NOTES ABOUT *THE BLUE MONSOON*

The Blue Monsoon began life as a few scribbled notes after the basic story of *The Blue Bar* was finalized.

At the end of *The Blue Bar*:

(Below are spoilers. If you haven't read that book—skip the next paragraph.)

We see Arnav discovering he has a daughter he knew nothing about. We see Tara getting shot and being left in quadriplegia. And we have the happy-for-now family: where Tara's disability weighs on her as a reduction of independence and on Arnav as guilt.

The story of *The Blue Monsoon* came from Arnav and Tara, and their journeys. The seeds for the crimes in this novel were planted in the last one. Essentially, though, it is a story that chose me and grew organically the way fungi do, or flowers, so a few aspects of Indian history and systems have seeped into what is otherwise a straight-up police procedural / thriller. India is a country that lives in several centuries at once, be it in its habits, its conflicts, or its beliefs—and Mumbai, as a melting pot, witnesses many of them, taking both the ancient and the modern in its stride. Some of that is briefly explained in the notes below. These are deep, and often fraught subjects, impossible to encapsulate in a few paragraphs. For further information, I would urge you to check out the list of books cited below the notes.

CASTE SYSTEM

This thriller builds on a plot that features the caste system. Caste is an extremely divisive topic, and probably has been since its inception in 1500 BC. It was part of the religious, social, and cultural fabric of ancient India, and it was adapted and concretized by those who invaded or colonized the subcontinent: the Mughals and, later, the British. Both of them used it as an administrative device and structure to manage the local populace.

Depending on where your birth landed you in the caste system, you received social privileges or disadvantages. The caste system consisted of four main divisions (*varnas*): *Brahmins* (priests and teachers), *Kshatriyas* (rulers or warriors), *Vaishyas* (landowners and merchants), and *Sudras* (ironsmiths, weavers, and similar). Outside of this system were the fifth group—those without caste—untouchables, the *avarnas*, called Dalits and officially termed the Scheduled Caste.

In 1950, the Constitution of India prohibited the practice of untouchability and the government established special quotas or a system of positive discrimination in schools, colleges, and government institutions to aid those underprivileged within the caste system, in order to afford them equal opportunities.

The traditional discrimination against the Scheduled Caste ranged from segregation to persecution and murder, and while the practice is illegal, opinions differ on whether casteism has been wiped out or is now entrenched even deeper in all public and private sectors in India. Reports of caste-based violence, especially against women and children, abound in news reports. Caste-based political parties are a reality, and political fortunes can be made or destroyed based on their support. The sanitation and cleaning departments employ five million people, of which 90 percent belong to the Dalit communities.

In urban and rural sectors, within India and the Indian diaspora, caste has different connotations and impact, depending on the individuals and the community.

If you'd like to read more, I've listed a few texts at the end of this note that can help provide further insight.

TANTRA AND TANTRIC PRACTICES

Tantra is an ancient yogic tradition that developed in both Hinduism and Buddhism. The word *tantra* means "weave, or warp," but its meanings have changed over millennia to mean texts, theory, system, instrument, and practice. The West sees *tantra* as a kind of ritualized sex, which ignores the nebulous, complex, and nuanced accumulation of techniques, chants, texts, and meditations that comprise the ancient tantric tradition.

For the purposes of this crime novel, the details derive from a very specific Hindu, *Shakta* tradition, following the *Shakti tantras*, which hail from around the ninth century, and a specific strand that worships the belligerent goddess Kaali, the first of the ten *Mahavidyas* in the Hindu tantric tradition. The tantric rituals in the novel are very basic. They aren't detailed representations but reflect the image of tantrics in Indian popular culture in the past few decades. The impressions and inspiration of Shakti worship come from my own family background, which subscribes to the Sri Ramakrishna order and holds the goddess Kaali as a sacred goddess: a fierce Feminine.

KINNAR OR HIJRA

The estimated six million *hijras* or *kinnar* in India are seen as a monolith, but in fact they consist of eunuchs and transgendered or intersex individuals, with or without male external genitalia, who identify with the female gender identity.

They've been part of the sociocultural makeup of the subcontinent since ancient times: the Kama Sutra, the Hindu text on sexual behavior, mentions them as early as some time between 400 BCE and 200 CE. The *kinnar* play a part in the Mahabharata and the Ramayana, the two major traditional Hindu epics. One of the pillars of the Hindu trinity of Vishnu, Brahma, and Shiva, the Lord Shiva is also worshipped as Ardhanarishwar. *Ardha-nari-ishwar* literally means "half-woman-lord," and it refers to his androgynous form when he merges with his consort Parvati and is worshipped as neither male nor female, but both. It symbolizes the coexistence of the male and female principles in the Universe, and the *kinnar* or *hijras* are respected as such a symbol.

The Mughals employed the *hijras* as protectors of the harem, important messengers, and influential officeholders privy to the secrets of the imperial household. The British colonizers criminalized them in the 1800s, and ever since then there's been a stigma attached to the community, who live in segregated ghettos. Depending on which part of India or the community they're from, they call themselves *kinnar* or *hijras*. Since the novel is set in Mumbai, and the community all over India is diverse, some wishing to be called the *kinnar* and others claiming the term *hijra*, I've employed the Mumbai street usage below: the *hijras*.

The community earns a living dancing during births and marriages and begging on the streets. Many are involved in sex work. They live in tightly knit, hierarchical, secretive groups, led by a *hijra* leader, a guru. The guru who initiates novices in the *hijra* way of life could be be a don, a spiritual mentor, or a pimp, and often fulfils all three roles. Many from poor families choose this lifestyle after being shunned by their families for being born intersex, or with gender dysphoria, and find support in their adopted *hijra* families.

Though the Indian government now recognizes transgender as the third gender after a Supreme Court ruling in 2018, and some states offer gender confirmation surgery at government hospitals, a large number of *hijras* go through brutal, crude, and dangerous surgeries in the form of castration. They call this ceremony the *nirvaan*, and this formally makes them part of the *hijra* community. There have been recorded instances of kidnapped preteens and teens forcibly castrated in order to force them into the *hijra* lifestyle, which gives this community a dark aura in news and media.

The *hijra* community rejects this image and has begun to fight for the rights the law gives them. With equal work opportunities, they seek to break the vicious circle of poverty, crime, and sex work, and take up space in politics, local government, and the arts.

As a crime novelist, my job is to tell a story, and do it as well as I can: to present individuals and their decisions, and the crimes that occur as a result.

All human stories, to one extent or another, are about a power struggle between individuals or communities. Those who have it. Those who don't. Those who want to wrench it for themselves. My attempt is to tell the story of this eternal conflict: the ones who win, others who lose, and the rare few who surpass both.

BOOKS I READ WHILE WRITING
THE BLUE MONSOON

Here are a few books that I read during the year I wrote *The Blue Monsoon*, which might help provide additional context to my notes above:

- *With Respect to Sex: Negotiating Hijra Identity in South India* by Gayatri Reddy
- *Entanglement: The Secret Lives of Hair* by Emma Tarlo
- *Why I Am Not a Hindu* by Kancha Illiah Shephard
- *Annihilation of Caste* by Dr. B.R. Ambedkar
- *Writing Caste / Writing Gender* by Sharmila Rege
- *Jhoothan* by Om Prakash Valmiki
- *Caste: The Origins of Our Discontents* by Isabel Wilkerson
- *Coming Out as Dalit* by Yashica Dutt
- *Ants among Elephants* by Sujatha Gidla
- *The Persistence of Caste* by Anand Teltumbde

ABOUT THE AUTHOR

Photo © 2021 Swarup Biswas

Damyanti Biswas is the author of *The Blue Bar*, the first novel in the Blue Mumbai Thriller series, and *You Beneath Your Skin*, as well as numerous short stories that have been published in magazines and anthologies in the US, the UK, and Asia. She has been short-listed for Best Small Fictions and Bath Novel Awards and is coeditor of the *Forge Literary Magazine*. Damyanti is also a supporter of Project WHY, a program that provides quality education to underprivileged children in New Delhi. Apart from being a novelist, Damyanti is an avid reader of true crime, a blogger, and an animal lover. Her ambition has always been to live in a home with more books than any other item, and she continues to work toward that. For more information, visit www.damyantiwrites.com.